A war-torn country.
A deadly new front in the fight against terrorism.
A battle for freedom America must win . . .

CI: MISSION LIBERTY

Hoolie Vasquez tapped DeLuca on the shoulder and handed him his GPS-linked handheld. On the screen, DeLuca saw a map of the area, with Camp Seven at the bottom of the screen. Above the camp, to the north, was a field of red dots representing troops marching south, perhaps five kilometers away. Estimated strength: two thousand men.

DeLuca looked at the sun, setting in the west. In another hour or so, it would be dark. "We'll have to work with what we have," he said.

"Spoken like Davy Crockett at the Alamo. Remember the Alamo?"

"Who could forget?" DeLuca said. "With one difference."

"Which is?"

"They had a fort."

Paul Asabo looked at the two Americans with a puzzled expression on his face.

"Famous American battle," DeLuca told him. "Nothing to worry about."

ALSO BY DAVID DEBATTO AND PETE NELSON

CI: Team Red

CI: Dark Target

CI:Mission
Liberty

DAVID DeBATTO
and PETE NELSON

WARNER BOOKS

NEW YORK   BOSTON

Copyright © 2006 by David DeBatto and Pete Nelson
Excerpt from *CI: Homeland Threat* copyright © 2006 by David De-
Batto and Pete Nelson. All rights reserved. No part of this book
may be reproduced in any form or by any electronic or mechanical
means, including information storage and retrieval systems, without permission in writing from the publisher, except by a reviewer
who may quote brief passages in a review.

Cover design by Jerry Pfeifer
Book design by Stratford Publishing Services

Warner Books and the Warner Books logo are trademarks of Time
Warner Inc. or an affiliated company. Used under license by Hachette
Book Group, which is not affiliated with Timer Warner Inc.

Warner Books
Hachette Book Group USA
1271 Avenue of the Americas
New York, NY 10020
Visit our Web site at www.HachetteBookGroupUSA.com

Printed in the United States of America

First Printing: October 2006

10 9 8 7 6 5 4 3 2 1

To Cathy and Ray—for keeping the home fires burning while I was off saving the world. My humble and sincere thanks. Thank you to SGM Jeffrey Galland (Ret), Department of the Army (G-2) and MSG Michael Marciello (Ret), senior counterintelligence special agent.

—*David DeBatto*

Thanks to Greg Ford for his technical expertise. Thanks to Mari Omland for bringing me to Africa years ago. Many thanks to Laurent Chaline for helping me with my French translations and to my nephew Benjamin Mackenzie, whose recent semester in Ghana supplied me with many details. Thanks to Dr. Ben Osborne for his medical advice, and to Peter Haas for explaining global oil economics to me, and finally to my wife Jen for helping me along the way.

—*Pete Nelson*

CI:Mission
Liberty

US forces poised off coast of Liger

Deadline for cease-fire, rebel withdrawal nears

By Roddy Hamilton
ASSOCIATED PRESS

BAKU DA'AL, Liger—Over five thousand United States Marines from the 3rd Marine Division, out of Ft. Bragg, North Carolina, are waiting 10 miles off the coast of Liger aboard the landing ships USS *Cowper* and *Glover* for final word from the White House to begin Operation Liberty. In addition, 10,000 reservists from the 27th Mountain Infantry Division at Ft. Drum, New York, are on standby.

The White House has said General Thomas Mfutho, leader of the Ligerian People's Liberation Front, has until midnight Saturday to pull his troops out of the capital city of Port Ivory to positions held as of the first of the month, and to honor the cease-fire agreement currently in place, or the president will give the order for U.S. troops to come to the assistance of beleaguered President Daniel Bo's government.

"We want General Mfutho and the others to understand that the president's resolve in these matters is as strong as it was in Afghanistan and in Iraq," said White House spokesman Daryl Firth. "We will not sit by and watch while another Rwanda transpires."

Civil war in the West African country of Liger began six months ago in the famine-plagued northern region of Kum when rebel faction leader John Dari accused Bo of using food as a weapon.

The Pentagon fears that an alliance between rebel forces and the group IPAB or Islamic Pan-African Brotherhood may lead to wider-spread violence in neighboring countries. IPAB may be associated with Al Qaeda, says Marine commander four-star General John Kissick.

"We're here both to provide air and logistic support and to put boots on the ground, wherever they need to go. We've shown, in Afghanistan and again in Iraq, that quick decisive U.S. military action is the best way to avoid unnecessary loss of lives."

The war escalated a month ago when President Bo sought to nationalize the Ligerian oil industry. Liger is the United States' fourth-largest supplier of oil, pumping at a prewar rate of over 1,200,000 barrels a day. Production has dropped to under half a million barrels per day since the fighting began.

Liger was a British colony from 1674 until 1962, when a bloodless revolution left King Mufesi Asabo in power. Asabo was dethroned and placed under house arrest in 1972 by General Sesi Mutombo, who was

(continued on next page)

displaced in 1980 in a bloody coup by President Daniel Bo, Sr., father of the current president. Strife in Liger has generally been between the president's mainly Christian Fasori tribe, in the south, and the traditionally Muslim Kum people in the north, with the Animist-Christian-Muslim Da people of central Liger caught in the middle. Fears of religious genocides are ever present (see story p. B1).

"In order for democracy to flourish and take root in West Africa or elsewhere on the African continent," said U.S. Ligerian Ambassador Arthur Ellis, "the people on both sides of the issue need to realize that without dialogue, there can be no freedom."

"Despite its oil wealth, Liger is one of the poorest, most corrupt coun-tries on earth," says People Against Yet Another War president Carol Kennedy. "There's never going to be democracy in Liger until Ligerian resources are more equitably divided among its people."

Aggravating Liger's political dif-ficulties are five consecutive years of drought and a plague of locusts that have left the northern regions of the country devastated by famine and dis-ease. Nearly two million people have been forced from their homes and into refugee camps, where they're preyed upon by bandits or recruited by IPAB. Accusations of atrocities in the region perpetrated by both sides, including mass executions, rape camps, and mu-tilations, are unconfirmed, according to a State Department spokesman. ∎

U.S. Ambassador Ellis, staff evacuate embassy

Takes refuge in former slave castle

By Kurt Hess
REUTERS

PORT IVORY, Liger—In advance of the arrival of rebel troops from the Ligerian People's Liberation Front, under the command of General Thomas Mfutho, the decision was made late last night to move American Ambassador Arthur Ellis, his staff, and his contingent of Marine guards from the U.S. embassy to the Castle of St. James, a former slave-trading stronghold.

"We decided rather than take unnecessary chances on the safety of our people, we could relocate to a more defensible position," says State Department spokesman Dennis Abney. "No people, papers, or documents were left behind."

The embassy came under threat when angry mobs began to surround it a month ago. Before that, it was the site of frequent protests against United States involvement and international oil interests.

Government troops under the command of General Kwesi Emil-Ngwema are believed to be positioned just west of town, ten miles from the castle. Also in Liger are 300 African Union troops, commanded by General Ismael Osman, and 500 United Nations peacekeepers led by Belgian General Rene LeClerc.

"Our plan is for the safe and orderly withdrawal of embassy personnel in the next few days, depending on developments in the city," said a representative of Marine General John Kissick. "Captain Allen, of the embassy's Marine contingent, assures me that his people are fully in control of the situation on the ground."

"It's tempting to draw parallels between this event and the fall of the U.S. embassy in Teheran, or even the evacuation of the U.S. embassy in Saigon at the end of the Vietnam War," says Assistant Secretary of State for African Affairs Tai Rutledge, "but the circumstances are entirely different. We still have a friendly government in power, not to mention 5,000 Marines offshore. When order is restored, and we expect it will be soon, we'll know more about what's going on, but we don't think the ambassador or his staff are in any danger. We are in communication." ■

President's spiritual "guru" still missing

Last seen in Liger central region

By Madeleine Stern
HOUSTON CHRONICLE

HUMBOLDT, Texas—"He'll be back," says Alice Dunn of First Baptist Church in this dusty east Texas town of 6,000. "If you're a person of faith, you have to believe that the Lord is watching over him."

Dunn's pastor at First Baptist on Plain Street, the Reverend Andrew Rowen, disappeared two weeks ago while touring the central part of war-torn West African nation Liger. Having once served as a missionary in Liger for the Baptist church, Rowen, a friend of the president and frequent White House guest, returned to the country in hopes of fostering peace. He was last seen leaving a refugee camp in a white Land Rover, accompanied by soldiers from the African Union.

"We're still awaiting word," says State Department representative Sabina Lake. "Unfortunately, communications in Liger right now are so poor that it's possible Reverend Rowen doesn't even know we're looking for him."

Rowen received the nickname of the President's Guru after converting the former Texas governor to born-again Christianity in 1995. Rowen gave the prayer at the president's first and second inaugurals.

Critics have said they're afraid that the president has made this both a holy war and a personal mission to rescue his close friend and advisor.

"That is patently ridiculous," says Lake. "First of all, the president needs the approval of Congress before he can declare war on a sovereign nation. There are no personal wars.

"Second of all, we don't even know that Rowen is missing."

"It's a matter of great concern," said Minority Whip Senator Lester Solomon (D., IL), "that we should even give the appearance of waging a holy crusade of any kind."

Solomon is making reference to a statement by the president yesterday, when he said, "This is not a holy war, but our cause is holy. Freedom is sacred. Liberty is holy."

"I think if we have to send troops and our boys have to die to protect Christians, then we have to do it," says First Baptist parishioner Leon Spivy. "Look at it the other way—would we turn our backs on people, simply because of their religion? I don't think so."

"I went to high school with Andy Rowen," says Humboldt mayor Ray Lamont. "I know that if anybody could survive something like this, he could. He's a strong man."

Rowen was born in neighboring Ghana, where both his parents were missionaries from 1951 to 1962. He attended Harvard from 1968 to 1971, where he and the president were roommates. ∎

Chapter One

THE CAR BOMB HEADING FOR THE U.S. EM-
bassy, a fifteen-year-old Isuzu passenger van carrying two
sixty-four-gallon drums marked "ammonium nitrate,"
enough to sink an aircraft carrier, was driven by a young
man wearing a vest that appeared to be packed with C4
explosives. He was joined on his mission by four men in
ski masks carrying AK-47s and glancing nervously at the
mobs that were throwing stones and looting stores and
burning everything that had the taint of "foreigners." A
fifth man rode on the roof, grabbing the roof rack for support whenever the vehicle hit a pothole or crossed one of
the open sewers.

Down an alley, they saw a group of men with machetes
chasing three boys who slipped through a hole in a fence.
At the next corner, they were slowed in their progress
when four women with babies strapped to their backs
crossed in front of them, carrying portable stereos still in
their boxes. The palm-lined avenue called Presidential
Way was strewn with debris, the smoking shells of burned
and overturned cars, the blackened armor from what used
to be a military half-track with two burned bodies falling
from the back, one corpse with its head intact and one

without. Groups of children dressed in cast-off clothing
donated by American charities, wearing T-shirts bearing
logos for Georgetown University or faded images of Brit-
ney Spears, huddled in doorways, aiming toy rifles and
broomsticks at the passing vehicles and laughing. Mixed
with smoke and cordite and the pungent aroma of raw
sewage flowing in the gutters was the faint smell of tear
gas in the air, lingering in the areas where government
troops had beaten a retreat in the face of the onslaught.
Uncontrollable mobs now surged through the streets of
Port Ivory, driven forward by rebel troops in green forest
camo uniforms and red berets. Many of the regular rebel
forces hadn't been paid in weeks and now took their com-
pensation in the traditional way of conflict, seizing whatever they could load into their Jeeps and trucks or carry in
their arms, and in whatever pleasures could be gained
along the way.

The driver of the Isuzu, an Arab man in his early twenties, slowed as they passed the British embassy, where
thick black clouds of smoke poured from the former colonial governor's mansion beyond the cast iron fence, the
fire not enough to deter the gangs of looters darting in
and out of the building, braving the flames in search of
treasure.

The Isuzu slowed again as it approached the American
embassy, on the opposite side of Presidential Way from
the British embassy. Their target was Ambassador Arthur
Ellis, but they feared they were too late, the grounds of
the American compound overrun by Ligerians and rebel
troops, the top corner of the building blown away where a
shell from a seized Ligerian tank had detonated, the windows all broken, pieces of roof tile scattered across the

yard. A thick black plume of smoke poured from inside the embassy, the image captured by a film crew with Belgian flags taped to their shirts. There was a large U.S.-made M-113 military transport parked in front of the gates, where six men in green uniforms and red berets fired their rifles in the air in celebration, a response that was returned by the man on the roof of the van, raising his AK-47 in the air in a gesture of victory.

A man whose uniform bore the insignia of a captain approached the van, smiling, his eyes hidden behind his wraparound sunglasses, his machine gun hanging casually from a strap over his shoulder.

"Where is the ambassador?" the driver of the van asked the captain in accented English. "We come for the ambassador."

"They moved him," the captain said. "I don't know when."

"Where did they move him?" the driver asked, at which point the captain pointed down the road with his gun.

"To the castle," he said. "They could not defend this place. We were too many. Too strong! They have their Marines, but not so many. We have them up a tree, man."

"I will see," the terrorist leader said. He made a brief inspection of the embassy. In the ambassador's office, he found shredded papers, a wastebasket in which documents had been used to light a fire, and atop the fire, burned and melted CDs and videotapes. All had been destroyed. He returned to the van. The massive Castle of St. James loomed at the far end of Presidential Way, at the opposite end of the esplanade from the presidential palace, which was also under siege.

"Can you take us there?" he asked the captain. "To the castle?" The captain nodded, glancing inside the van at the drums of explosives in the back. He ran to the transport and ordered his men to take their guns and get in. The troops moved slowly, too drunk to move any faster. The leader of the car bombers saw a man dump a half dozen empty beer cans out the rear of the truck in front of them.

"We have an escort," the man in the front seat said.

"Praise Allah," a voice from the backseat added. "God is great."

They heard machine-gun fire from inside the soccer stadium, an open-roofed ring of concentric concrete risers where the banks of lights already blazed white as the twilight approached. There was no telling who was being killed inside the stadium or how many, though the men in the van saw a half dozen orange school buses parked just inside the gates, as well as another dozen military transports. Throngs of barefoot onlookers pressed up against the fence that enclosed the parking lot to see if they could get a glimpse of what was going on inside, with mothers crying out for their sons and wives crying out for their husbands.

The Castle of St. James loomed immense above the town, originally a trading outpost built in 1534 by the Portuguese and later captured by the Dutch and then by the British, both powers adding to its original fortifications, though in each case, the main defenses were focused inland, to protect the occupants of the castle from attack by Africans, and not toward the sea where an attack could come from rival colonial powers. It stood on a natural mount, its outer bastions and casements forming a wall that girded the fortress on three sides, its fourth side backed against the sea atop a natural rock precipice where the wild surf from the Bight of Benin pounded on the foundation and the rocks below. A barbican village had grown up around the castle, where Fasori traders did their business with the Europeans, first in ivory, then in gold, then in human beings, and now it formed the oldest part of the city. Cannons from inside the fortress had destroyed the town of Port Ivory, or parts of it, on three separate occasions over the centuries, but the city was always rebuilt, brown and gray houses of wattle and daub and cinder block with red tile and corrugated tin roofs, open stalls, street vendors, shops, and merchants, the air hazy and stinking of kerosene cook fires and curry, car exhausts and the open sewers that ran down both sides of the streets in shallow gutters, and everywhere, chickens, goats, sheep, donkeys, and mangy short-haired dogs with curly tails. And rats. Several shops near the castle were on fire, filling the air with black smoke and an acrid stench.

The M-113 parted the crowds, the soldiers in it occasionally firing their rifles in the air in warning. Some who saw the Isuzu van behind the transport, filled with men in masks, seemed bewildered, while others cheered and blew kisses. The truck stopped at the base of a long curving stone ramp leading uphill for fifty yards to the castle's main portcullis. The gatehouse forming an outwork at the base of the ramp had been seized, with loudspeakers set up atop one of the turrets, from which Radio Liger blared, inciting the crowd, a voice saying, "Kill them, kill them all, you have much work to do . . ."

The captain walked from the transport back to the van. He was smoking a cigar. When he offered one to the man in the van's passenger seat, the man refused.

"We have machine guns and RPGs on the roofs surrounding the castle," the captain said, "and many SAM-7s hidden. SAM-9s. We think they will send their helicopters, and when they do, we will shoot them all down."

"Where are your SAMs?" the Arab in the passenger seat said in Arabic. The captain looked confused, so the man repeated the question in accented English.

"We have one in the church steeple, there," the captain said, pointing with his cigar, "and one is in the mayor's office, right there. And we have another in the red truck over there. That one. Yes. I chose the locations myself."

"And the men firing them, they've been trained? They're not your children warriors—they're actual soldiers?"

"Oh, yes," the captain said. "They are my finest. Hand-picked."

"You've done well," the Arab said. "Keep them there. Now move your truck, please."

"What will you do?" the captain asked.

"We came for the ambassador," the Arab said. "We have his family. He has said if we release them, he will take their place. Move the truck now."

The captain gave orders, and the M-113 was moved. The man atop the van attached a large white flag to the barrel of his rifle, and then the Isuzu began to inch forward up the ramp. The curtain wall forming the outer bailey was lower than the bulwark inside, allowing the American soldiers visible at the rampart's embrasures to shoot over it, if they chose to, but they held their fire. The crowd below watched in anticipation. Many backed away, expecting a massive explosion as word spread that a car bomb had penetrated the American defenses. The Arab in the passenger seat saw a pair of fifty-millimeter guns mounted atop the parapet guarding the main gate and told the driver to slow down. When the gates opened, the van drove slowly through, and then the gates closed behind it.

The driver parked in the inner ward, just in front of the castle keep, and then the men got out of the van. They were met by a pair of Marines, who escorted them into the historical museum's main exhibit room. Ambassador Ellis, wearing a helmet and a flak jacket, accompanied by a half dozen Marine bodyguards, stood in front of a large glass exhibit case, inside which was displayed a long flowing garment called, according to the brass plaque at the top, the Royal Sun Robe, worn, historically, by a succession of Fasori kings. The man who'd been riding in the passenger seat took off his ski mask, saluted, and extended his hand to the ambassador.

"Special Agent David DeLuca, U.S. Army counter-intelligence, Team Red," he said. Some of the soldiers looking on were surprised to notice that one of the "men" in the ski masks was in fact a woman. "Thanks for not shooting us. I wasn't sure you got our message. My driver is Agent Zoulalian. This is Agent Sykes, Agent Vasquez, and Agent MacKenzie. Sorry we weren't able to visit you under happier circumstances. Your wife and kids are fine, by the way, but the cover story is that we're swapping them for you, so they've been kept out of sight on the carrier."

"This is Captain Allen, in charge of my security detail," Ambassador Ellis said. "Sorry we had to leave the embassy. What's the plan? They've been jamming my goddamn SATphone."

"Who do you have here for staff?" DeLuca asked, scanning the massive stone walls. It was the kind of place where a few Marines with machine guns could hold off an entire army, for a while, anyway. He could hear the staccato stutter of gunfire beyond the castle walls, the voice from the loudspeakers at the gatehouse muffled, as if coming from a pair of headphones left on a pillow.

"Just my secretary," Ellis said. "Everybody else got out. What's the situation at the embassy?"

DeLuca shook his head.

"How about the British embassy?"

Again DeLuca shook his head.

"The British pulled out yesterday and lost seven men trying."

"I'm blind here, DeLuca—fill me in. Why can't I use my phone?"

"We believe they're using U.S. jamming equipment we sold the government," DeLuca said. "Where do you want me to start?"

"Where's General Ngwema? What's Osman doing? Where's LeClerc?"

"LeClerc can't move until the Security Council says he can," DeLuca said. "Osman's AU forces are waiting to hear from Addis Ababa, but I don't think they have what they need, even if they get clearance. Most of the city's Christians have fled. Ngwema's holding the ground west of town. We think the majority of the refugees are behind him."

"Why isn't he moving?" Ambassador Ellis said. "What's he waiting for?"

DeLuca shrugged.

"He might not be waiting for anything. He might be protecting the oil fields and letting the city fall. We're not sure just what his mind is."

"Bo?"

"President Bo is in the presidential compound, which, from the looks of it, is more strongly fortified than this place," DeLuca said. "We can debrief on the carrier if you want, sir, but I'm not sure I'm the person to do it, and I'm quite sure this isn't the best time or place."

"Why did they send you?" the ambassador said. "No offense, but there are only four of you."

"Five," DeLuca said. "We couldn't do anything until we had more intel." He turned to the Marine captain. "We want to fly in a couple of jollies for you and your men with CAS and AI but we weren't sure what your ADOCS were," DeLuca told Captain Allen.

"We lost prepositioning along with our APS grids when the embassy fell," Captain Allen said. "I have a lieutenant who served with a COLT in Kabul as the 'lino' and a sergeant who spent a week with a FIST team, but we could use an artillery intelligence officer for the DISE. We took a G/VLDD (he pronounced it "gee-vlad") off a Hummer and mounted it at the top of the turret but it's not going to be much use without the pulse codes."

"Agent Zoulalian has the codes," DeLuca said, turning to his driver. "Run upstairs and program the laser. Number one is the church steeple, two is the mayor's office, and three is the red truck parked across from the gate-house."

Zoulalian took off on the double. Captain Allen looked at DeLuca quizzically.

"We found a rebel captain who was only too eager to brag about where he put his SAMs," DeLuca explained. "I think the intel is good, but my worry is that he wasn't telling me everything. That and the RPGs—what's your sense there?"

"We haven't seen much, but I'm sure they have 'em," Allen said. "The question's what we can suppress."

"Shock and awe," DeLuca said. "Works for me."

"Plain English, gentlemen," the ambassador said. "I know I'm a civilian, but I'm still in charge here."

DeLuca's orders had been to take charge if he had to, but for now he could let Ellis continue under the illusion that he was in control.

"I was asking Captain Allen if he had any deep ops co-ordination system," DeLuca said. "He told me he has a man who served as a liaison officer with a combat ops laser team and another man who served with a fire support team. A gee-vlad is a ground/vehicular laser locator designator—that's the laser we use to paint targets for the smart bombs. He took one off a Humvee and mounted it on a tripod on the tower. The rebels have three Soviet shoulder-fired antiaircraft missiles, in the steeple, the mayor's office, and the red truck parked by the gates. The lasers emit a pulsed code to tell the bombs where to go. My sergeant is upstairs programming the codes into the laser. What we're going to do is blow those three things up and then fly in a couple of helicopters . . ."

"Jollies?"

"Yes, sir," DeLuca continued, "under close air support and air interdiction. Noise and smoke. With minimal collateral, if we're lucky. They're going to get the Marines out, but what we don't know about are rocket-propelled grenades, which can still down a helicopter."

"It sounds risky," Ambassador Ellis said.

"It is risky," DeLuca said. "That's why we're going to take you out a safer way."

"Which is?"

"The same way we came in," DeLuca said. "You look like you're about a forty-four regular, am I right?"

Deluca pulled the *abaya* he was wearing over his head. Beneath it, he wore his "second chance" ballistic body armor, but beneath that he wore dress pants and shoes and a white shirt (soaked with sweat) with a red bowtie of the sort that Ambassador Ellis was famous for wearing, his identifiable trademark. Back home, the only time DeLuca ever wore suits was when he had to testify in court in the trial of somebody he'd arrested. He asked the ambassador if he could borrow his sport coat. The ambassador complied. Over the sport coat, DeLuca donned the bomber's vest that Zoulalian had rigged from a Kevlar flak jacket, a spare set of distributor wires, and six cans of black Play-Doh, but it looked real. DeLuca bade Ambassador Ellis to don the flak jacket, the *abaya*, and a ski mask and then handed him an AK-47.

"Is it loaded?" the ambassador asked.

"It is," DeLuca replied patiently to an incredibly stupid question. "But if we do this right, nobody's going to fire a shot. In fact, they're going to cheer you as you leave. I'll bet you weren't expecting that."

"We're done setting up the Mark-10s," MacKenzie reported, referring to the oil-drum-sized smoke bombs that had been disguised as explosives in the back of the phony car bomb, one in the near corner of the inner bailey and the second in a bartizan upwind from the keep. "Dan's setting the delays."

"We've got a J-STAR zeroed with a Hellfire on the jamming gear they're operating, in a building about a block from here," DeLuca told Allen as he climbed onto the roof of the van. "Once that goes, your coms should work. You'll hear it when it does. Fire support will call you at that point. It's going to happen fast." DeLuca saw Zoulalian returning at a quick jog. "You all done upstairs?"

"Roger that—locked and loaded," Zoulalian said, turning to Vasquez, who'd resumed his position atop the van. "You wanna drive?"

"I'm good here," Hoolie replied, raising his AK-47 and setting the safety, testing the trigger to make sure the safety had engaged. "How often do I get the chance to take my team leader hostage?"

DeLuca turned his back to Hoolie and placed his hands together. Hoolie used a pair of flex cuffs to bind DeLuca's hands behind his back, but with the plastic teeth filed off so that the cuffs were only on tight as long as DeLuca pulled on them. Hoolie threw a knit ski mask over DeLuca's head with the eyes in back, though the fabric was of a wide enough mesh that DeLuca could see through it.

"Make sure the bowtie is visible," DeLuca said. "Mr. Ambassador, if you'll take a seat in the back next to Agent MacKenzie, we'll be on our way. We have a SEAL team with a fastboat waiting about a mile down the beach and a pair of Predators watching our every move, but we're still going to need a bit of deception until we get there, so just keep your mask on and wave your rifle and look angry and we'll do the rest. Do you know any Arabic?"

"*Allah akbar,*" the ambassador said.

"That'll do," DeLuca said. "We armored the sides and the doors but not the windows, obviously, so if somebody starts shooting, stay low. Dennis, let's not give anybody too much time to think. Captain Allen, the jollies will be here in ten minutes, so get your men ready. See you on the *Johnson*."

Zoulalian started the car, with Sykes now in the passenger seat and MacKenzie and the ambassador in the back. DeLuca knelt on the roof with a black mask over his head while Hoolie held a gun to his neck, lifting the loose folds of the mask with his rifle to make sure the red bowtie was visible. The image was going to be a compelling one when it was shown on Al Jazeera later that night, a U.S. ambassador with bombs strapped to his chest being led from his stronghold at gunpoint by a brave band of terrorists.

They breached the portcullis and were halfway down the ramp when Zoulalian was forced to step on the brakes. At the base of the ramp, the M-113 was parked across the drive to block the way. The rebel troops had dismounted and had their guns pointed at the van. The captain, his cigar still in his hand, shook it in the air and gestured for the van to come forward.

"What the fuck?" Vasquez said under his breath.

"Easy, everybody," DeLuca said into his transmitter. "Remember Mog. Dennis—commence ranting and gesticulating."

Zoulalian got out of the car and screamed at the rebel captain, gesturing with both arms to get out of the way and let them through. When the captain waved him forward, Sykes got out of the car and walked down the ramp to speak with the man in the red beret and the wraparound sunglasses.

"You have to move your truck," Zoulalian said in accented English. "We have to get through. Now!"

"Give the prisoner to us and we will take him," the captain said. "We can provide security for him."

"We don't need security," Zoulalian screamed. "We have more than enough of that. We have to get to the soccer stadium."

"Inducements, Mr. Dan," DeLuca transmitted.

"Perhaps you could lead the way," Sykes said to the captain, reaching into his pocket beneath his *abaya* and pulling out ten hundred-dollar bills, American. DeLuca always found it charming, the way people who hated America still liked its money. "Of course, we would want to pay you for the overtime. One hundred for each of your men and three hundred for you. Does that sound fair?"

The captain saw the money and moved his body so that his troops couldn't see the cash while he considered his options.

"Give the money to me, and I will pay the men," the captain said. Sykes handed him the cash, which the captain pocketed surreptitiously. "You will follow me, then."

He turned and ordered his men to get back in the truck.

Zoulalian followed in the van, inching through the crowd. Hoolie did his best to block the things the people in the crowd were throwing at "the ambassador" to express their dislike for U.S. foreign policies, mostly fruit, vegetables, cassavas, one man picking up and flinging a piece of dog shit that struck DeLuca in the arm.

"Tell that guy he's going to hear from my cleaner," DeLuca said.

"What do you care? It's not your suit," Hoolie said.

"Sorry for the delay, *Johnson,*" DeLuca told the mission controllers on the aircraft carrier, who he knew were watching them, both from an INMARSAT view and from a UAV-borne camera closer in. "What are you seeing?"

"It's going all to hell between you and the extraction point," the voice in DeLuca's earpiece came back. "But we expected that. Make time if you can."

"I don't think our escort is going to let us pass him," DeLuca said. "We'll do our best. Meet you on the sands of Iwo Jima."

They were three blocks from the castle when they heard the first explosion behind them, a JDAM-5 destroying the building where the rebels' communication-jamming equipment was operating. The decision had been made to use laser-guided ordnance first, because of the greater accuracy, but DeLuca understood that the destroyer USS *Minneapolis* was cruising eight miles offshore, ready to deploy six- and eight-inch guns that were nearly as accurate, should the first round of smart bombs fail to do the job. Within seconds, they heard another explosion as a missile struck the mayor's office. Hoolie took the hood from DeLuca's head in time for DeLuca to see the church steeple disintegrate in a ball of flames, and then a fourth missile hit the red truck, flipping it and lifting it thirty feet in the air. The crowd dispersed and chaos quickly followed, men firing their rifles into the air or toward the castle, where a pair of CH-47 Chinook helicopters coming in low over the water climbed the seawall and descended on the courtyard, supported by a half dozen Apaches, swarming over the city like very angry bees. A pair of F14 Tomcats screamed over the area, a mere fifty feet above the rooftops.

"Hit it!" DeLuca shouted to Zoulalian. He lay down atop the van and braced himself against the roof rack. Zoulalian floored the accelerator and turned right down a side street. DeLuca saw, briefly, the look of surprise on the face of the rebel captain from the back of the truck.

"*LBJ*—can you cut enemy radio traffic?" DeLuca asked, aware that the E-6 Prowler in the air high overhead carried communication-jamming equipment.

"Not without doing yours, too," the answer came back. "They're using our stuff. It's your call."

"You getting SIGINT?" DeLuca asked.

"Negative," mission control came back. "Our Ligerian friend here says they're not speaking Fasori. It's some northern tribal dialect he doesn't know."

"Might as well keep the channels open, then," DeLuca said, dismayed that the mission had already crept beyond what had been intended, but then, he'd long considered "military planning" something of an oxymoron. "Loose the dogs of war" wasn't even the right metaphor, because loose dogs at least run in the same direction. "Shit hitting the fan" failed for the same reason—war was Brownian motion, chaos and anarchy, and it changed every five seconds. "We'll just have to outsmart them."

"You being ironic?"

"Nothing personal," DeLuca said.

As the van sped toward the sea, DeLuca turned and saw that the troop transport had backed up and was following them. He opened fire, as did Vasquez beside him, but the Isuzu was veering and careening around or across potholes at a speed that prevented firing with any accuracy.

"Any time, Pred One," DeLuca said into his radio. "Let's lose the tail."

The AGM-114B Hellfire was a laser-guided solid pro-
pellant missile, five feet four inches long, seven in diameter, with a weight of about one hundred pounds and a
warhead capable of defeating any tank made. The M-113
following the van was no match for it, the subsonic rocket
penetrating the front windshield on the passenger side,
where the captain in the red beret was sitting, before
blasting the vehicle into a million flaming particles.

"I'll bet that lit his cigar," Hoolie said.

Zoulalian, taking directions via his headset, turned left
when the falcon view from INMARSAT told him the
street connecting to the beach road was blocked up ahead
by an overturned vehicle that was burning. He was instructed to turn right at the next intersection, but when
he did, he stopped when a pair of "technicals" came into
view, two Toyota pickup trucks, one green, one white,
with .50-caliber machine guns mounted in the back. A
rebel in the green truck opened fire as Zoulalian hit the
brakes, backing up to speed forward again on the street
he'd tried to turn from. The green truck followed while
the white truck raced parallel to them, firing at them
whenever there was a gap between the houses, doubtless
causing serious collateral damage with rounds that didn't
make it through the gaps. DeLuca shot at the truck behind
them, though the road was so uneven with potholes, exposed cobblestones, and eroded excavations that it was
impossible to steady his aim, and he knew he was firing
more for demonstration than effect. The rebel soldier
manning the machine gun looked to be no more than fifteen or sixteen years old, but for all DeLuca knew, he'd
been fighting half his life.

"What do we have?" he called to support. "Taking fire."

"Stay your course," command and control came back. "*Minneapolis* has it."

He estimated their speed to be fifty or sixty miles an hour. As the next intersection loomed, he turned toward the sea. With the green truck bearing down on them from behind, slowing down was not an option. At the intersection, beyond the corner house, he looked down the street, his weapon ready. He saw the sea, and then he saw the white truck appear, and then he saw it launched into the sky when a shell from one of the destroyer's six-inch guns struck it. The van was through the intersection before DeLuca had a chance to see the truck land.

"Nice shot, *Minneapolis*," he said.

"We'll give the computer an assist on that one," a voice in his headset said. "Apache Three at your back door." He turned in time to see the AH-64D Longbow attack helicopter descending on the green truck, closing the distance rapidly. A burst from the Apache's M230 chain gun, mounted beneath the fuselage, sent a stream of 30mm rounds down the center of the green Toyota, which veered suddenly into a wall before flipping and barrel-rolling on its side a half dozen rotations before coming to rest on its collapsed roof.

The Apache climbed quickly, at low altitudes an easy target for shoulder-fireds and RPGs.

"You're three blocks beyond the take-out point," DeLuca heard in his headset. "Come back, come back three!"

Zoulalian turned right, then right again onto the street that paralleled the beach, racing past a row of fish vendors and an open-air bar, speeding another block before turning left at a marine repair shop when the way ahead was

barricaded by a pair of overturned cars. He threaded his
way between overturned brightly colored fishing boats
and turned right again once he hit the beach, the van fish-
tailing and slowing as the sand grabbed at the tires. The
way ahead was clear, until DeLuca saw a man rise from
the sand and wave his arms at them to stop.

"Navy SEAL, Navy SEAL!" he heard in his earpiece
as Zoulalian hit the brakes. "Claymores directly in front
of you—do not proceed!"

Team Red spilled from the van, MacKenzie staying by
the ambassador's side, while DeLuca gazed seaward,
where he saw the destroyer USS *Minneapolis,* and closer
in, the LST from which the helicopters had launched. The
USS *Lyndon Johnson,* the aircraft carrier that was their
final destination, cruised beyond the horizon.

The SEAL stood in the sand, pointing to a spot at his
feet and gesturing with his arm for the team to approach.

DeLuca turned the binoculars up the beach, in the direction of the soccer stadium and presidential palace. He
saw, perhaps a thousand yards off, several hundred rebel
troops running as fast as they could in his direction. When
he turned 180 degrees and looked toward the castle, he
saw another group of rebel soldiers, larger than the first,
headed their way.

"Det cord, right here," the SEAL said, clearing away
the sand to show DeLuca and the others where he'd
buried a line of explosive detonating cord, capable of
killing anyone who stepped on it or tripped over it. The
drab green cord, about the thickness of a cotton clothes-
line, was rigged to a half dozen Claymore mines, stuck
into the sand on tripods with the curved side facing the
approaching rebels, capable, when detonated, of killing

anybody within one hundred feet in a ninety-degree arc. DeLuca assumed the SEAL team that had prepared the take-out point had mined the beach in the opposite direction as well.

"Lieutenant John Riley," the SEAL said. "Step over the cord and follow me. Do you have wounded?"

"We're good," DeLuca said, as a rocket-propelled grenade fired by one of the rebel soldiers destroyed the Isuzu behind them. Pieces of shrapnel rained down around them, a rear wheel rolling down the beach and curving into the sea. Then a machine gun opened fire from the rooftop of a four-story beachfront apartment building. DeLuca fired on the machine-gun position, joined by the SEAL with his M-5, chromed against corrosion from seawater and vented to drain.

To the west, DeLuca saw palm tree after palm tree splinter and fall, mowed down like blades of grass by the incoming rounds as the *Minneapolis* opened up with all its guns, six-inch and eight-inch shells raining down with incredible precision. A pair of F14 Tomcats crisscrossed in the sky above them, strafing the beach in either direction as the Apache they'd seen before returned to send a fire-and-forget wave-seeking Hellfire at the automatic weapon on the apartment building roof, taking it out with the first shot.

Down the beach, a pair of SEALs rose from the surf, gesturing for DeLuca and his party to join them.

"It's too dangerous to land a craft but once you're in the water, your target profile is minimal," Riley explained. "Mr. Ambassador, are you a strong swimmer?"

The ambassador shook his head.

Riley handed him a float vest from his pack and told him to put it on, while the others jettisoned their gear, dropping it in the surf that crashed all around them. DeLuca was happy to lose the tie.

"SEAL four, five, six, and seven, need your help," Riley barked into his radio, and in an instant, four other SEALs in scuba gear rose from the water where they'd hidden, submerged.

"Sorry we're late," DeLuca said as the Apache circled back to strafe the beach in the direction of the presidential palace. "Traffic was bad."

"That's all right," Riley said. "Any chance I get to work on my tan is always appreciated. We're not used to doing this in daylight." The second and third SEALs held remote detonators, one looking west, the other east. Riley regarded the screen on his handheld, which showed infrared satellite images of the approaching rebels.

"We should go," he said, extending his arm and pointing into the sea.

The water was warm, rising in broad swells beyond the breakers. Each member of the team had a Navy swimmer as a partner, Lieutenant Riley taking the ambassador by the back of his vest and pulling him forward. DeLuca turned briefly when he heard an explosion on the beach where a rebel soldier had tried to cross the hinter line, which the SEALs had also mined. Three rebels streaked in through the beach, firing on them with AK-47s.

"Don't worry about it," his SEAL swim partner said. "Hitting a person this far out is like shooting at a coconut."

Then the *Minneapolis* put a round on the beach, directly in front of the shooting rebels, and when the smoke cleared, DeLuca saw only body parts.

One hundred fifty yards from shore, the SEALs directed them to form a line and hold their right arms in the air. A PBR fastboat appeared, its .60-caliber deck gun blazing toward shore. A SEAL in a Zodiac tethered to the starboard side dropped rings attached to lines over their arms, at which point they closed their arms over the rings, and then the PBR yanked them out of the water one by one, never slowing to less than five knots. Two SEALs with arms the size of buffalo haunches hauled them into the Zodiac and helped them roll into the fastboat. When the last man was out of the water, the PBR throttled up, hydroplaning at fifty knots as it sped toward the waiting LST, bouncing across the waves.

DeLuca gazed astern. He saw plumes of black smoke rising above the city, several buildings on fire in the neighborhood beyond where the Castle of St. James sat atop its mount. A single CH-47 Chinook flew toward the carrier.

Over the radio, DeLuca learned that the Marines holding the castle had lost a "jolly" on liftoff to a rocket-propelled grenade, taking three casualties in the process before the flight crew and passengers could be transferred to the remaining helicopter. He passed the news on to the ambassador, who'd said very little since leaving the castle.

"Believe it or not," DeLuca said, "it looks like we took the easy way out."

"Agent DeLuca, I'm recommending you for the Congressional Medal of Honor," the ambassador said. "I believe your conduct today has been absolutely outstanding."

"Thanks, but no thanks," DeLuca said. Evidently the ambassador had no idea what the Medal of Honor was for.

"I'm not being humble. The more attention I get, the harder it is for me to do my job."

"Then I'll buy you a beer," the ambassador said.

"Thanks, but I don't drink," DeLuca said. The fact was, DeLuca drank as much as the next guy, but if the next guy was going to be Ambassador Ellis, he'd pass. They were paying him to rescue the guy, but they couldn't pay him enough to like him.

Chapter Two

DELUCA AND HIS TEAM CHANGED INTO DRY clothes aboard the LST, the USS *Cowper,* then choppered to the USS *Lyndon Johnson,* to debrief and await transport to a British base in Ghana, where they would, if everything went according to plan, catch a flight home.

DeLuca knew, when he saw his friend, General Phillip LeDoux, waiting for him in the briefing room aboard the *Johnson,* that the plan was about to change. They were joined by a dozen others, including the captains of the *Johnson,* the *Cowper,* and its sister ship the *Glover,* two admirals, a Marine four-star, an Army two-star, Ambassador Ellis, and a handful of civilians DeLuca knew he'd be introduced to soon enough. He saluted his friend. At the time that they'd both been accepted to OCS, DeLuca's ratings were higher than LeDoux's, but DeLuca had chosen to go in another direction. LeDoux's career vector had been the proverbial skyrocket, distinguishing himself in Panama, Gulf One, Kosovo, and Iraqi Freedom. Sometimes DeLuca wondered if somebody was trying to slow LeDoux down, putting him in charge of counterintelligence. "Why do they have you watching over guys like me?" he'd asked his friend, who'd replied, "Because it's the toughest job in the Army and I'm the only bastard up to the task." In mixed company, DeLuca saluted, but between the two of them, they were as equal as a three-star general and a chief warrant officer could be.

Night had fallen. Given that DeLuca had been up for nearly twenty-four hours, planning the day's mission, which they'd launched before getting official approval, he accepted LeDoux's offer of coffee with gratitude.

"Navy coffee any better than Army coffee?" he asked.

"Light-years," LeDoux said. "This is Starbucks. The *LBJ* is subcontracting with 'em on a trial basis. Army still has KBR."

"I didn't expect so many important people to show up, just to hear me describe my day," DeLuca said.

"They didn't," LeDoux said, stating the obvious. "This isn't about you."

"You sound like my wife."

"I'm afraid you're not going home just yet."

"I was afraid of that, too," DeLuca said.

At the last minute, a half dozen civilians entered the room. DeLuca recognized two, one a senator from California, the other a representative from Florida. The others were either congressmen he didn't recognize or their aides—it was, no doubt, a fact-finding commission of some sort. DeLuca wondered what part he was going to play in the dog and pony show.

"Gentlemen," the *LBJ*'s captain said, a man named McKinley who DeLuca had been told was a distant relation to the former President McKinley. "If we could all be seated, we'll get started. As your host, please let me know if there's anything I can get you. There are drinks and light snacks in the captain's mess afterward for anybody who's still hungry, and I apologize for the late hour, but we wanted to wait until Ambassador Ellis could attend. Mr. Ambassador, welcome aboard."

"Captain," the ambassador said.

The table was large, oval, made of teak, with a glass of water, a black three-ring binder containing a report, and a notepad and pen at each position. The carrier's captain stood in front of a seventy-two-inch plasma screen, mounted on the wall behind him, and on it, a map of Liger, divided into three sections. He also had a laptop on the table in front of him.

"We've got some special visitors who I'd like to introduce first, and then I'll let General Kissick introduce the others. We have with us tonight, just flown in from Washington, Senators Todd and Morelli, Representatives Lacey, Stephens, and Hokum, and their aides."

Each member of the delegation nodded when Captain McKinley said his or her name. DeLuca shot LeDoux a look, but LeDoux didn't respond.

"They're here to find out the latest intel regarding Operation Liberty and to get a sense of our preparedness," McKinley said. "We welcome you, ladies and gentlemen. Welcome aboard. Please let me know personally if there's anything I can do to make you comfortable. Now I'll turn the floor over to General Kissick. He'll get you up to speed."

The Marine general, wearing his DCUs, was a slender man with close-cropped hair and a voice that sounded more like a high school math teacher than a more typical boo-ya Semper Fi jarhead—he sounded more like an accountant than what DeLuca expected a Marine general to sound like.

"I know some of you have already been fully briefed but some haven't," Kissick said, "so those who have been, bear with me, and the rest of you are going to have to drink from the fire hose on this. Most of the names and facts I'm going to give you are in the report in front of you. Those of you freshly arrived from Washington have no doubt been reading the newspapers as well as the official briefings. My name is General John Kissick, United States Marines. Why don't we go around the table and introduce ourselves."

"Admiral Donovan Webster, Sixth Carrier Group, Task Force 32," the man to Kissick's immediate right said. He was about fifty, with fair hair and a default facial expression that stopped just short of a smirk. "We're here to provide close air and missile support."

"Rear Admiral Stanley Pulaski, Task Group 32.5," the next man said. He was smaller in stature than Webster and a few years older, balding, with round wire-rimmed glasses and bushy eyebrows that made him look a bit like a troll. "We're here to put the Marines on the beach, or wherever they need to go. I believe we have a number of Army Rangers who are going to need taxis, too."

"Captain Henry Long, with the *Cowper,*" the next man said. He looked as if he was barely out of his twenties, clean-shaven to the point that DeLuca wondered if he could grow a beard if he tried.

"Captain Alan Gates, with the *Glover,*" said the man next to him, early forties, handsome, good posture, hair beginning to gray above the ears.

"Wes Chandler, CIA station chief for Liger," the next man said. Chandler was corpulent and pasty, like a hairless rat on an unlimited cheese budget. DeLuca's first thought was that for a station chief in Africa, Chandler didn't appear to get out and about much. "I'll be the general travel advisor."

"General Phil LeDoux," DeLuca's friend said. "Commander G-2, DOD Ops Intel."

It was DeLuca's turn.

"Special Agent David DeLuca, U.S. Army counter-intelligence," he said, "and as far as I can tell, I'm just here in case you need to send somebody out for pizza."

"A bit more than that," Kissick said, after the laughter died down, "but all in good time."

The man next to DeLuca introduced himself as Hanson Sedu-Sashah, assistant to United Nations general secretary Kofi Annan and the UN's liaison with General Rene LeClerc, commander of the UN peacekeeping forces in Liger. "I am Ghanaian," he said, "but I know a bit about Liger, if you have questions."

The man next to him introduced himself as Hans Berger, with WAOC, the acronym for the West African Oil Consortium. "My group includes Dutch Shell, Exxon-Mobil, Chevron-Texaco, and Agip. I am here only to listen, but I can also answer any questions you might have about the oil industry in Liger."

"Lionel Ayles-Kensey," the next man said, his British-ness given away by both his accent and his bad teeth. "British foreign service. My family had a farm outside Baku Da'al until the locals had enough of the Brits and threw us out in '62. I could give you a bit of historical background, I suppose, but I'd better not speak for the prime minister—I believe General Denby was going to be here for that . . ."

"General Denby was unable to attend," Kissick said.

An African man of about forty, in combat fatigues with three stars on his collar and with a face showing the markings of ritual scarification, introduced himself as General Adala Bukari, representing the African Union, another peacekeeping force, as DeLuca understood it, unable to keep the peace anywhere it went but probably still a good idea, an alliance of military personnel from across Africa tasked to observe elections and cease-fires but not interfere.

"I have been working, for some time," he said, his voice barely rising above a whisper, "with Ambassador Ellis and with President Bo, to oversee the camps. And food shipments. General Ismael Osman is our contact in Liger."

The last man at the table was a full bird colonel named Suarez, representing the 27th Infantry Division out of Ft. Drum, New York, where ten thousand reservists were getting ready for deployment. The division commander, General Gaines, had stayed behind to oversee the preparations.

"Liger," General Kissick began, a map of the country appearing on the plasma screen. "Mr. Kensey has written a more complete history for you in your printouts, but let me thumbnail it for you so we're all on the same page. You can bridge the oversimplifications yourselves. British colony since 1674. Dutch before that, Portuguese before the Dutch. Three main tribal regions, with the Fasori in the south, along the coast . . ." He pointed to a line on the map. "The Da in the middle and the Kum people in the sub-Saharan north. The Sahel. The European traders built a string of fortresses and castles along the coast but never ventured more than a few miles inland, which was considered 'The White Man's Graveyard.' The whites traded with the Fasori. Most of the slaves who passed through the castles were Da, captured either by Fasori slave traders or by Kum warriors bringing their slave caravans south to market. Because of their contact with Europeans, most of the Fasori today are Christian, maybe half Catholic and half Protestant-Pentecostal. It used to be 85 percent Catholic, but the Pentecostals have been making inroads and doing heavy missionary work throughout the country. The Kum have traditionally been Muslim, moderately so until 1990 or thereabouts, when radical extremists began preaching a more Wahhabist point of view, U.S. as Great Satan supporting the evil Zionists and that whole tune. If you were to ask an average Da what his religious affiliation was, he'd probably tell you that he was an animist, a Christian, and a Muslim. They don't seem to understand that you have to pick one, nor do the Christians or the Muslims understand that, actually, you don't."

He clicked on the laptop to add an overlay of red dots to the map, half of them concentrated in the south along the coast and the rest scattered along the country's eastern and northeastern border.

"This might sound like ancient history to some of you, but none of this is irrelevant to the current conflict. I'll say this, for the lay people among us. The struggle in Liger has always been between the Fasori and the Kum, and the Da have always been caught in the middle. Religious fundamentalism on both sides in recent years has only accelerated and amplified what was already there.

"Liger became independent in 1962. As revolutions go, this one was as soft as you get. The Fasori have traditionally been the ruling class in Liger, the most highly educated, controlling about 90 percent of the economy.

Prior to 1962, the British governor worked with the monarchy, in the person of Fasori king Mufesi Asabo, who asked for and negotiated the British departure. Asabo, who was very popular, was overthrown in 1972 in a bloodless coup by General Sesi Mutombo and assigned a more symbolic role, something like the British monarchy. Mutombo was overthrown by President Daniel Bo, the father of the current president Bo, in 1980. The king was placed under house arrest. Mutombo was captured, tried, and beheaded, all in the same day, and then his body was literally hacked into a thousand pieces by the crowd that had gathered to witness the execution. Last year someone tried to sell one of the pieces on eBay, so they're still around, kept as souvenirs.

"The red dots you see are oil deposits. Those along the coast and offshore were developed by British Petroleum and by Shell. The deposits in the east and north represent more recent discoveries, being developed by Exxon-Mobil and Chevron-Texaco and the Italian Agip group."

Kissick clicked four more times, each click adding in overlay a shaded area that began in the north, labeled 1990, and extended south in multiyear intervals. By 2005, the shaded area covered the northern half of the country.

"These overlays represent drought, and with it, famine. Conditions of near-drought and near-famine extend south from these lines for about one hundred kilometers at each interval. Theories as to the reasons for the drought vary, including global warming, deforestation, and so on. We're concerned more with the effect, which has been to cause tremendous social and political upheaval. For years, the Kum and the Fasori held to a kind of truce where it was possible for one group to keep to the north and the other to the south, with the Da region as a buffer zone. With the drought, famine, disease, cholera, starting in the north, the Kum reached the point where they depended on assistance from the government, which was and is, as I indicated, Fasori and Christian. President Bo, who I have to stress has long been an ally and staunch supporter of the United States, began to realize he could use that dependence for leverage when he needed concessions, mainly to develop northern oil assets. Liger is, today, the United States' fourth-largest supplier of oil, ordinarily at about 1,200,000 barrels a day. Instability in the north has cut production to four hundred thousand barrels a day, and you all know what's happened to gas prices back home as a result."

Kissick clicked on a new map, showing the northern half of the African continent, strewn now with blue dots against a tan field.

"Enter IPAB," Kissick said. "Islamic Pan-African Brotherhood. The blue dots are training facilities, all in the Sahel region, sub-Saharan, which, as far as we can tell, no country has ever figured out how to govern or police. It's mostly training for military or terrorist activities, but some are more like schools for Islamic study. IPAB was initially an offshoot of the Muslim Brotherhood, which began in Egypt in the fifties. Bin Laden's number two man, Abdullah al-Wahiri, was one of the founders of the Muslim Brotherhood. Beginning around 1995, various small, not terribly well-organized rebel elements in Liger began attacking oil facilities in the north, provoking various reactions by the government and by the oil companies, which found it necessary to hire and train their own security forces, with the blessing and cooperation of the government. Such attacks were sporadic and poorly planned, at first, but with the help of IPAB, rebel factions became better organized and better armed. Al Qaeda certainly had a hand in the training and in the funding, but we think it goes beyond Al Qaeda."

Kissick clicked again to show the satellite image of an African village.

"So here's what's going on today," he said, clicking again to zoom in one level of magnification. "After 9/11, rebel forces inspired and emboldened by the attack on the World Trade Center declared full-out civil war against President Bo's government with the intention of overthrowing him and establishing an Islamic government. If you count the number of Muslims in Liger, and include the number of Da who add Islam to the list of religions they embrace, then Muslims represent the majority by about 65 percent or so. If you count Christian Fasoris and add in Christian Da, you get about 50 percent. Bo suspended planned elections after the declaration of civil war, but he'd promised and suspended them for several years prior to that, seeking to avoid the same fate as Sesi Mutombo, I gather. The war smoldered until six months ago, when civil unrest in the north escalated. That unrest flared up again a month ago when President Bo said he was going to nationalize the oil industry, in order to better defend it. The main body of the rebel forces is calling itself LPLF or Ligerian People's Liberation Front, led by General Thomas Mfutho. Mfutho was at one time thought to be third in command in Liger, behind Bo and General Emil-Ngwema, Bo's right-hand man, but apparently some years ago he decided he could do better on his own. We estimate he has between seventy-five hundred and eight thousand troops, poorly trained, most of them, moderately equipped. Minimal air support, a handful of helicopters and triple A. However, in the last month, a large amount of arms and equipment supplied by the U.S. to the Bo government has fallen into enemy hands. We also believe he's been supplying himself from weapons cached in Iraq that we, unfortunately, failed to prevent from leaving the country."

He clicked again to zoom to a lower level of magnification. DeLuca saw a collection of circular structures that he took to be the thatched roofs of a number of huts or houses in the village.

"Let me show you what's going on in this country. There are currently about two million displaced people in northern Liger. That includes Da, Kum, Ashanti, Twi, Fur peoples driven out of Sudan by the Janjaweed, who still occasionally make raids on horseback into Liger. The joke going around the Pentagon is that we're going to have to dust off some of our old cavalry uniforms from the 1800s and dig up John Wayne to lead the troops."

The Republicans on the congressional fact-finding delegation laughed. The Democrats didn't.

"Most of the time, however, the Pentagon is not in a joking mood."

He clicked to a lower level, at the same time adding a pair of insets, photographs of two men, one of whom DeLuca recognized, the other not.

"On the right, this is Samuel Adu. You may have read about him in the paper. It looked like he was going to overthrow the government of Sierra Leone until the Sierra Leonese government brought in white South African mercenaries to kick him out. He took exile in the northern

Ligerian capital of Kumari, not because Bo invited him in but because Bo lacks the power right now to kick him out. As dangerous as Adu was in Sierra Leone, he accomplished most of what he accomplished there with nothing more than machetes and a few hundred AK-47s. Now that he's hooked up with IPAB, he'll be much better armed, particularly after IPAB forces overran the government armory in Baku Da'al last week and seized a significant amount of equipment. We're trying to get an inventory but right now that's not possible. We suspect the rebels are still reading the manuals, but we'd like to hit 'em before they finish. And we know that some of the IPAB training camps teach recruits how to arm and fire captured U.S. weapons. Again, some of the weapons in country were also from looted armories in Iraq.

"The man on the left is Kum warlord Mujhid John Jusef-Dari, popularly known as 'Brother John' Dari. This is a high school picture, but it's the most recent one we have, and we suspect he's altered his appearance. Educated in Massachusetts at Mill River Academy, after he was brought over and sponsored by a Baptist church in Oklahoma whose missionaries discovered him when he was orphaned after his parents disappeared, possibly at the hands of the government. Originally a member of the Da tribe. Converted to Islam in prep school and returned to Africa after he was expelled for having sex with an underage girl. They call him 'Brother John' because he's seen as something of a Robin Hood figure, robbing from the rich and yada yada yada. Some call him the Ace of Spades. A reference to the deck of card designations we used in Iraq. So let me show you what this so-called 'Robin Hood' and his people are up to."

He clicked again. DeLuca saw the village in greater detail, an array of broad plank tables on one edge of the village where the locals dried their cocoa beans, and in the middle, a central common. Another click revealed a large crowd of people gathered in the common. A subsequent click showed that some of the people gathered were holding guns on the others, including a group that seemed to have been taken prisoner. In the center of the common was the communal cooking area, Kissick said, and then he clicked without saying anything. He zoomed in, until they saw, as clearly as if the picture were taken from atop a tall ladder, two large cast-iron cook pots, in one, human heads, and in the other, hands.

"These pictures were taken above a village called Yamagor, about halfway between Kumari and Baku Da'al. This is one of the cannibal gangs operating in the country. The come into a village, round up the leaders, and then they mutilate them while they're still alive and eat the parts. I apologize, but there really isn't a more delicate way to say this. They especially like the hands. They make everyone else in the village watch. Sometimes they force the onlookers to partake. This is terrorism at its most undiluted level."

He clicked again, showing only a map of Liger. The sense of relief that swept over the room was palpable.

"Believe it or not," Kissick said somberly, "I've spared you some of the worst pictures. Those involve women and girls. We believe this behavior is organized and intentional. There is also much behavior going on that is neither, but rather acts of random violence, instigated by radio exhortations or simply as the result of mob behavior, but equally horrible. Ambassador Ellis's embassy issued a directive two weeks ago that all American citizens were to evacuate. As you know, the president has vowed that he will not sit idly by and allow another catastrophe to occur similar to what happened in Rwanda, 1994. And unfortunately, a number of Americans decided to ignore the directive to evacuate—Ambassador, about how many, do you think?"

"Too many," Ellis said. "Maybe a thousand."

"And Mr. Berger, how many of your oil workers would you say have remained in country?" Kissick asked.

"About five hundred," Berger said. "We've hired protective services, but the danger is still great."

"Officially, the main rebel faction is the LPLF. We're actually much more concerned with Adu and Dari, and through them, IPAB. The White House has given General Mfutho until Saturday, seven days from now, to pull his troops back above the line you saw on the map dividing traditional Kum and Da territories, and to turn over to UN troops anyone suspected of being connected to IPAB or Al Qaeda. And to respect the cease-fire. We do not anticipate compliance. Failing that, we have twenty-five hundred Marines on the *Cowper* and another twenty-five hundred on the *Glover* who I'm told are so eager to deploy that they've started to chew holes in the bulkheads. And we have the 27th Infantry ready to fly in once the Rangers have secured the airfields. We don't expect any significant resistance. People are going to say we're trying to fight three wars at once. We're not. It's the same war, on three fronts. The president's well of human compassion is anything but dry. Prompted in part by the capture of this man."

He clicked again. DeLuca saw the picture of a white man, perhaps forty, standing in the white light of the sun with his wife and two children.

"This is Reverend Andrew Rowen. You may have read about him. Rowen disappeared ten days ago. The CIA believes he was taken in an effort to forestall the invasion, and as close as the president is to Andy Rowen, he's made it clear that his concern for his personal friend will not have any effect on matters of national security. He would, if possible, like to at the very least know where Rowen is before we start the air campaign. Just to make it clear in everybody's mind, this is a matter of national security. Letting our friends in Africa know they can count on us to protect their liberty is absolutely essential. Stopping the spread of IPAB is as important as stopping Al Qaeda. IPAB was Al Qaeda's sister organization when they blew up the embassies in Kenya. Stopping IPAB here stops a pan-African jihad."

"It's also believed that if the oil supply of Liger falls into the hands of John Dari or IPAB, within a year, the price of oil in America will rise to over four dollars a gallon, at which point our global economic dominance, and therefore our security, will be severely compromised. I emphasize that we'd like to circle-slash the idea that we see this as a war of blacks against whites and Muslims against Christians, because that's not going to pass anybody's smell test, but that is effectively at least part of what it is, a race war and a holy crusade. We didn't make it that way. We're not even there yet. That's the rule for IPAB in Liger. And for the LPLF. Kill the whites and kill the Christians. The report in front of you lists some of the atrocities perpetrated so far against whites and Christians.

For all these reasons, the delicacy of this matter cannot be overstressed. Mr. DeLuca, do you have any questions yet?"

"Pepperoni or sausage?" he replied, surprised to have been called upon. In fact, a great many questions were forming in his head, but this was not the place to speak before they were fully formed.

"What we want you to do," Kissick said, "is find Dari. We've had a task force on Adu for a while now, but Dari is going to require your more specialized skill sets and core competencies, vis-à-vis leveraging linguistics, under-cover work, and that sort of thing. Plus we don't know where he is. I'm told this is the sort of thing you were doing in Iraq, and that you were better at it than anybody. I understand you like to prep your missions yourself, but with this following so close on the job you did today ex-tracting Ambassador Ellis, we couldn't overtask you by asking you to plan two missions at once, so we've done as much of the groundwork for you as we could to get you started. That said, on such short notice, it's quite likely that you're going to have to do a certain amount of ad-libbing, but again, General LeDoux has assured me that one of your finer qualities is going off script. CIA intel on Dari is in your report. Mr. Chandler, is there anything you have to update it?"

"I have a man in Baku Da'al who'll be able to give you more than what I've put in the report, but we don't have a com link with him at this time," Chandler said. "My own data stream stopped when I left the embassy three days ago."

"Did you leave anything behind that could find its way into rebel hands?" DeLuca asked. "I understand that the embassy fell rather suddenly."

"Just my Callaways," Chandler said. "But I promised them I'd come back for them."

"I wouldn't worry about it," Hans Berger, the oil consortium representative, said. "I don't think they'll be able to hit them any better than you could."

Again, the men gathered round the table laughed. DeLuca smiled, though his instinct told him the best thing he could do, at this point, would be to pick up Hans Berger and Wes Chandler and throw them over the side of the ship. The waters were shark infested, he'd been warned, but the sharks could take care of themselves.

"General LeDoux will brief you further after we're done here," Kissick said. "Does anybody have any questions or comments? Now's the time to brain-dump."

"General Denby will be CCed as to all of this?" Lionel Ayles-Kensey asked. Kissick nodded.

"What is the situation on the ground, as we speak?" Hanson Sedu-Sashah asked.

"Better than it was six hours ago," Kissick said. "General Emil-Ngwema's forces re-entered the city shortly after today's raid by Agent DeLuca and his team. As I understand it, the rebel forces have pulled back, with heavy fighting still at the soccer stadium and at the airport. I gather the Ligerian air force finally figured out where they'd hidden their airplanes and managed to get a few of them in the air. President Bo has already gone on national television to declare victory and urge everyone to stay calm, so one may surmise from that that the Presidential Guard managed to hold the palace."

"Slippery fellow," Ayles-Kensey said. "Like father like son."

"Anything else?"

"Just one," DeLuca said. "What do you want me to do, once I find Dari?" He was tempted to say *if* I find Dari, but he didn't dare express a lack of confidence, not when everything was going so swimmingly well.

"Report in," Kissick said. "The course of action will be determined at that time."

At that time, DeLuca had no doubt, there would be, at the very least, a UAV armed with a Hellfire missile already overhead or a pair of Super Hornets scrambling into the air from the deck of the *Lyndon Johnson* to take Dari out.

"If there are no further questions, then I'll leave you to your individual preparations. CENTCOM will be here, with myself and Admiral Webster, until such time as we can establish something on the ground. We're calling this Operation Liberty, by the way. Please refer to it as that, should any of you become authorized to speak to the press. Seven days, gentlemen. My aides will be happy to help you with any questions you might have once you've read the briefing report."

"Wanna take a walk?" LeDoux asked DeLuca.

"Yeah," DeLuca said. "Cocktails on the poop deck."

"Not here," LeDoux whispered. "Let's take it offline, as General Kissick might say."

Chapter Three

DELUCA FOLLOWED LEDOUX OUT ONTO THE
flight deck, where they found a seat on a blast deflector.
LeDoux handed DeLuca a cigar.

"We're not allowed to smoke," he said, "but I thought
you might want something to chew on, other than my ass."

It was a moonless night, but there were so many stars
in the African sky that it felt almost bright enough to read
by. DeLuca gazed toward shore, watching a faint orange
glow on the horizon, where an unknown number of buildings burned in the city of Port Ivory.

"If you're standing on the beach," LeDoux said, "the
surf here glows a bright blue from microbial aquatic or-
ganisms that turn phosphorescent when they come in contact with the air. Bright blue. It's one of the most beautiful
things I've ever seen."

"On a positive note," DeLuca said.

"On a positive note," LeDoux agreed.

"Permission to speak freely?" DeLuca asked.

"You need permission?" LeDoux replied.

DeLuca unwrapped his cigar and bit down on it,
breathing through his nose for a moment before looking
his friend in the eye.

"I know you're coming up with the best possible response," DeLuca said, "and I suppose I should feel honored. But this is one solid hundred-ton brick of horseshit. And you know it is, so I know you wouldn't be part of it unless there was no alternative."

"Fuck it," LeDoux said, glancing around to make sure there were no munitions or spilled pools of jet fuel nearby before pulling out his lighter and lighting his cigar. LeDoux clicked the lighter shut. "I'm a general. I can smoke where I want to."

"Damn straight," DeLuca agreed, lighting his from LeDoux's lighter.

"I figure we have about three minutes until some irate ensign comes out to tell us to extinguish, and then another five until he goes away and gets someone of a high enough rank to come back with the same request."

"About that," DeLuca said.

"It'll have to do," the general said. "Remember those old *Mission: Impossible* shows, at the beginning, where the voice on the tape recording always said, 'Your mission, Mr. Phelps, should you choose to accept it . . .'? Just once, I wanted to see him throw his envelope full of photographs in the fireplace and say, 'The hell with it—I'm going fishing.' Too bad it doesn't work that way."

"Too bad."

"If it makes it any better, I only found out myself this afternoon while I was watching the Dave DeLuca show on satellite television."

"But they knew before they brought us here," DeLuca said.

"They probably did."

"Probably?" DeLuca said.

"Tell me what you think," LeDoux said.

"Here's what I think," DeLuca said. "I think the White House is trying to cover its ass after the whole WMD intelligence fiasco in Iraq. I think they want to say they had boots on the ground in Liger, so with a week to go, they send in the boots and they don't really care who's wearing them or what happens to the people who lace 'em up. They just want to say they tried. Why else would they give me my assignment in front of a goddamn congressional delegation? What kind of bullshit little performance was that?"

"You kids these days," LeDoux said. "You're so cynical."

"They don't really give a shit about the mission—they just want to say they sent the most elite team they had," DeLuca said. "Am I wrong?"

LeDoux didn't correct him.

"This is horseshit. You and I both know how much can go wrong, even with months of planning. We were lucky today. Everything went to shit in no time, and the next thing we know, we're careening down the alley on two wheels with people firing rockets at us. I don't think it's possible to be so lucky, twice in a row."

"It probably isn't," LeDoux said.

"Here's what else I think. I think Kissick is angling to be the first Marine to chair the JCS, and this is his ticket, so he's covering his ass. He sounds like a fucking CEO, not a Marine. No wonder he's the Sec-Def's favorite little leg-humper. The mission is lame. We'd need at least three days to work up our covers, for chrissakes," DeLuca said.

"They're actually not half bad," LeDoux said. "I had a chance to look at 'em. DIA is doing much better work in that department since we increased their budget. The bottom line is, this came from the White House. End of the day, we have to send someone. CI's always been who they send when they don't have a plan yet. You know that. I'm sure we can both see the dangers that present themselves. It's ad-lib as hell. I'm not going to pretend it isn't."

"Ad-lib is another word for half-assed," DeLuca said. "I signed on for added risk. What I mind is chaos and stupidity. I'll take my people into harm's way in a heartbeat, you know that, but I also consider part of my job is to keep them from the kind of harm perpetrated every day by goddamn Pentagon planners and PlayStation generals and standard Army-issue Remfro rear-echelon mother-fuckers and shit-for-brain congressional armed forces committee pissants and all the other flaming dickwad ass-holes who don't have the slightest idea what it means to walk across a road while somebody is aiming his rifle at you."

DeLuca drew on his cigar until the ember glowed, holding the smoke in before letting it out slowly.

"You done, or do you need more time?" LeDoux said.

"I'm just getting started," DeLuca said. "But go on. I guess I needed to vent."

"I know," LeDoux said. "Why do you think I asked them to leave the blast deflectors up?"

"Just tell me why I'm really going back in," DeLuca said. "I don't want to hear about the president's guru or whites or Christians or for that matter oil. Been there, done that. I don't want to hear about terrorists or making the African continent safe for democracy because I've been there and done that, too. Why am I going?"

"You're going," LeDoux said, "on the very real chance that you can make a difference. The fact of the matter is, we don't have any good intelligence on John Dari. CIA makes him a warlord. I think that's too easy a label, and I think this administration prefers labels to complexities, so that's what the CIA gives them. You, on the other hand, don't. This guy could well be the African Osama bin Laden. If he is, then it's best we're rid of him. And if he isn't, we need to know that, too. It could mean millions of lives, and I'm not talking about suitcase nukes or dirty bombs or nerve agents. I'm talking about good old-fashioned hunger. This country is a fucking mess, and it's going to stay that way until somebody straightens things out. In the meantime, the food can't reach the camps, and every day, thousands of people die. Saddam put people in mass graves and tortured them once in a while for kicks, so we stepped in. Here, they just walk off into the sand and fall down, or go to bed and don't wake up. We've got more food and medicine waiting to ship from our bases in Cape Verde and Diego Garcia than this country could use in a year, tons and tons, and we can't get it on the ground or in the hands of the people who need it. Everybody says we didn't plan on how to win the peace once we occupied Iraq. That's the mistake they're trying to correct this time. It's going to be like the Oprah Winfrey show—we're going to give everybody a new car and groceries for a year."

"Well *that* ought to make 'em happy," DeLuca said. "I have a good idea—why don't we just skip the war and go straight to the peace?"

"Gee," LeDoux said. "Why didn't *we* think of that?"

"I just hope nobody makes soup out of my head," DeLuca said.

"It would be so bitter I don't think anybody could swallow it," LeDoux said. "Come on. I have somebody I want you to meet. Plus I think the hall monitor finally caught us."

"Stand to!" a young member of the Shore Patrol said, approaching at a brisk pace. "No smoking on the flight deck, goddamn you . . ." He stopped in his tracks when he saw who he was talking to. "Oh. Excuse me, General. I didn't . . . I mean . . ."

"At ease, sailor," LeDoux said, handing him his cigar as DeLuca did the same. "Just testing your battle-readiness. Did you see me or did the bridge send you?"

"I saw you, sir," the young sailor said.

"Excellent. I was afraid they might be sleeping up there," LeDoux said. "What's your name, sailor?"

"Ortega, Luis, sir," he said. "Seaman first class."

"Good work, Ortega," LeDoux said. "I'll put a commendation for you in my report. Please toss these overboard, if you will."

LeDoux led DeLuca to the guest officers' quarters and knocked on one of the doors. A soft voice said, "Come in." DeLuca saw a black man lying on the bed, reading a book, a pair of wire-rimmed glasses on the end of his nose. He was dressed in a white shirt and black pants, barefoot. He got to his feet and offered his hand when Phillip LeDoux introduced him. DeLuca put him at six foot two and two hundred pounds and handsome, a bit like a young Muhammad Ali, back when he was known as Cassius Clay, but without the brashness.

"Paul Asabo," LeDoux said, "this is Agent DeLuca, U.S. Army counterintelligence."

"Call me David," DeLuca said.

"Please, sit down," Asabo said. There was, however, only a single chair in the room, which was ample for naval quarters but less than half the size of a small motel room. LeDoux gestured for DeLuca to take the chair. Asabo sat on the edge of the bed. LeDoux closed the door behind him, then leaned against it.

"Paul is going to be going with you," LeDoux said. "He was helping us today with our translations. Last I checked, David, none of your people speak Fasori, right?"

"You're a translator, then?" DeLuca said.

Asabo looked up at LeDoux.

"Paul is the son of Kwame Mufesi Asabo."

"The king?" DeLuca said, remembering Kissick's briefing. "Deposed 1972. See, I was listening. I just looked like I wasn't."

"Paul also went to school with John Dari. He might be the only one on our side who can identify him. Paul?"

"John was my roommate at Mill River. I was sent there by my father when it became unsafe for me to stay in Liger. We had little in common, but they decided because we were both African, we would get along."

"Dari is Da. Is that right?"

Asabo shook his head.

"John is Somalian. He was born in Mogadishu but he lost his parents in the war. He was a 'Lost Boy,' as they called them. He was found by a doctor in Sudan and went to a missionary family in Baku Da'al, and they sent him, their church did, to Mill River because he scored so high on the tests he'd been given."

Asabo spoke English without an accent. Most people who learned a language without an accent did so only if they began to study it before they reached puberty.

"We were both headed for Bennington when he was expelled," Asabo continued, "so I went and he came back here."

"And you've spoken to him in the interim?"

Asabo shook his head.

"We exchanged letters."

"E-mail?"

Asabo shook his head again.

"He wrote me about becoming a Muslim. Returning to the religion of his father, of his early childhood, after temporarily adopting the religion of his sponsors. He did not consider it a conversion. But in one of his last letters, he said he could not do e-mail because he'd decided not to own a computer. He felt that the Internet and the pornographic images that Islamic youths were downloading across the Arab world has meant the death of Islam as anybody has understood it historically."

"I'd have to agree with him there," DeLuca said. "And you think you'd recognize him? We were told he'd altered his appearance."

"He underwent scarification," Asabo said. "On his face. Most African men who do it have it done when they're young, as a rite of passage and progressively of manhood, but John had missed the opportunity."

"But you don't have it," DeLuca said.

"It's not a Fasori custom," Asabo said. "But it's quite widespread throughout West Africa. It shows a sense of piety. And ethnic unity. I think John wanted to be accepted among his people."

"And who does he consider his people?" LeDoux asked.

"Black African Muslims," Asabo said. "He's traveled too much and lived too many places to narrow how he identifies himself. So he is Somalian, he's Da, he's Kum, he's Muslim. I think he might even say part of him is American, but I don't know. He was bitter about how he left."

"And he's charismatic?" DeLuca said. "People follow him?"

"People always followed him." Asabo smiled. "He was the star on the soccer team. Quite popular among all the boys. And the girls, too."

"He was expelled because of a girl," DeLuca said. "Do I understand that correctly?"

Asabo shook his head again.

"Are you keeping score?" DeLuca said to LeDoux. "Is this three major things the CIA report got wrong, or four?" He turned again to Asabo. "What exactly did happen, then? You can speak freely—we were all teenage idiots at one point ourselves."

"And everybody is," Asabo said. "I know. I don't know how they did not understand that. There was a girl who perhaps lacked self-esteem. I don't know. I think her name was Karen. Or Kari. What I know is that one night at a party, she performed oral sex on three boys."

"On Dari?"

"Not that time. But a few days later, she was asked to do it again and she agreed, this time with five boys, in the locker room, after soccer practice. Again, it was consensual, but this time they were caught, and because the girl was only fifteen, it became a legal matter."

"Where were you?" DeLuca said.

"I was studying," Asabo said. "In the library. I was not athletic."

"So they expelled him?" DeLuca asked.

"No," Asabo said. "John and the other boys were suspended for a week but not expelled. John left school because the church that was sponsoring him financially decided they could not support such behavior. They were a conservative Baptist church from Oklahoma and they said John had betrayed their moral values. I told him he was the one who was betrayed. I think for all he knew, he was just being an American. When he followed the others, that was why. To fit in. I'm not sure he even knew that this sort of behavior was even unusual. He was just finding his way. As we all were."

"And you got along, personally?" DeLuca asked.

"Yes. Though we were quite different in our upbringings. He used to tell me how I came from privilege and wealth. I told him it wasn't like that but he could not believe me. When I was quite young, perhaps, but my father was overthrown well before I was born. He was only a figurehead after that. It became a kind of house arrest. And then when I was a senior, President Bo considered him a threat, because my father was speaking out against the things the government was doing, and put him in prison. And killed my brothers, Thomas and Daniel, because he was afraid of them, too. That they might overthrow him. But by then, John Dari and I were no longer in touch. I was in college. I don't know what he was doing."

"And you haven't been back?" DeLuca asked. "To Liger?"

Asabo shook his head again.

"It would not have been safe, I think. I work in Washington, for Conservation International," Asabo said. "They tell me when we go in, you will be posing as my colleague."

"I haven't got that far yet," DeLuca said.

"We've given Paul a passport with a different last name," LeDoux said, "but the rest of his backstory will be more or less true."

"How do you feel about going back?" DeLuca asked. He couldn't imagine.

"I think I might be able to help," Asabo said.

"We're going to have a briefing with the team in the morning," DeLuca said. "I'm not quite up to speed on all of this myself, yet. Get some rest and I'll talk to you after breakfast. Try the coffee—it's delicious."

"I know," Asabo said. "The beans come from Liger."

DeLuca made his way to his own quarters and turned the light on, enjoying the luxury of having the cabin all to himself. When he tried to lift his duffel onto the top bunk to make more room below, his ribs hurt so much that he gave up, setting the bag on the desk instead. His neck ached as well, from an old injury suffered in Iraq, when he'd been thrown through the windshield of a Humvee. It was always something. He stripped to his skivvies and lifted his shirt to look in the mirror where something had left a large bruise on his right side. He felt like he'd been clubbed in the ribs by a baseball bat, but other than that, he was undamaged.

He lay down on the lower bunk and opened the documents he'd been given to read, setting aside the packets meant for his team, one for Dan Sykes, one for Hoolie

Vasquez, one for Dennis Zoulalian, and one for Colleen MacKenzie. Thousands of people had been looking for Osama bin Laden for years now, without any luck. He would be one of five people, given a week to find Mujhid John Jusef-Dari, the "African Osama."

That made sense.

He opened the briefing file and began to read.

Hours later, he awoke in exactly the same position, having failed to read a single word before falling asleep, exhausted.

He shut the light off. He would deal with it in the morning.

CI, he reminded himself. It's just a state of mind.

Chapter Four

"YOU GOTTA BE SHITTING ME," DAN SYKES said. "I've been training hard for six months. My sensei says I'm as good as he's ever seen me."

"If you just really need to kick somebody's ass, you could kick mine," Vasquez offered. Sykes had been planning on entering the Intra-Services Full Contact Karate Championship, being held this year at Eglin AFB in Ft. Walton Beach, Florida. First prize was an all-night lapdance pass at the Gold Club in Panama City. Second prize was getting mooned by all the other competitors.

"Thanks, Hoolie," Sykes said. "I appreciate that, but I could kick your ass any time I wanted to."

"In your dreams, *cabrón*," Hoolie said.

"Everybody read your packets," DeLuca said as he distributed them. "I've skimmed each of them but I want everybody to study your own and then we'll brief each other. I'm sure we can find Dan an ass to kick. Think of what questions you have or any special needs that might arise. The mission is to gather intel on Mujhid John Jusef-Dari, popularly known as 'Brother John,' northern warlord, leading an army with a strength estimated at between one and two thousand men, according to CIA estimates. For what it's worth—I'm not big on what the CIA is telling us about Liger. We are to determine his whereabouts and his viability, prior to and as of one week from today, 2300 Zulu, at which point in time, unless certain conditions are met, Operation Liberty commences, as per the president's announcement. My sense is that, as in Baghdad with various parties, were we to locate Mr. Dari early, in a way that locks in his GPS with confidence, he might be visited by a JSOW or some such ordnance in advance of Liberty. TF-21 is in country to paint targets, so that's not our problem. Should you meet someone from either TF-21 or the CIA, he will identify himself with the phrase, 'David Letterman went to my high school.' The CIA report on Dari is at the back of your packet, but read it with a grain of salt. No, read it with a ten-pound bag of salt, because we find it flawed. When you're done reading, Mr. Asabo here will answer your questions about Dari, or about Liger."

They'd occupied a smaller conference room below the flight deck. There was a hot tray full of scrambled eggs, limp bacon, and pancakes that seemed to get larger and larger in DeLuca's mouth, the longer he chewed them, but there was fresh fruit as well, and the coffee was good.

"My name is Mary Dorsey," MacKenzie said at last, still reading. "I'm Irish. I sound like a washerwoman."

"I wanted to be Irish," Vasquez said, affecting an exaggerated brogue. "Saints be praised, sweet Mary mother of mercy, I'll be havin' another Guinness down at the local . . ."

"You sound like the leprechaun in *Darby O'Gill and the Little People*," MacKenzie said.

"I know," Vasquez said defensively. "That's what I was trying to sound like."

"I'm with the United Nations Women's Health Initiative," Mack continued. "Does the United Nations know that?"

"It's against international law and the United Nations charter for military personnel to pose as UN troops," DeLuca said, "but the charter doesn't say anything about posing as a UN relief worker. They don't like it and you'll hear about it if your cover is blown, but technically, we're okay. DIA set up a fake phone number in New York with an automated phone menu that's so confusing that whoever tries to check up on you will give up."

"I *knew* those things were DIA," Zoulalian said.

"CENTCOM thinks Dari is using the refugee camps for cover," DeLuca said. "The question has been, how do you hide two thousand men? That's how. He's also recruiting from the camps. You're going to have to get over on UN personnel for transport and security."

"I can travel alone if I want?"

"If you feel you have to." DeLuca nodded, aware of how MacKenzie bristled, justifiably, whenever he created the appearance of making special considerations or allowances due to her sex. "Just remember how men treated you in Iraq. I'll say this to everybody—this is a place where there is going to be strength in numbers. There is also some strength in media attention. I'm not saying bring reporters with you or pretend to be one, but if they're around, be aware of the effect. There are some things these guys are going to want to draw world attention to, and some things they're not. This is a tool we might want to apply."

"Dari shuns attention, right?" Hoolie interjected.

"He does," DeLuca said, "but the number-two guy who wants to succeed him might not. Whoever that may be."

"Mary Dorsey," MacKenzie read. "Ph.D. anthropology, University of Dublin. Nursing degree, Bardesley College, Liverpool. Hey, I get to use my EMT training. She worked for six years with the World Health Organization. Divorced. Damn, that's sad. Two kids, Liam, six, and Molly, nine. I love the name Liam. My ex is a doctor. I'm guessing our work was so important to both of us that we drifted apart and never had time for each other. I felt neglected. He felt misunderstood." She put on an Irish accent. "And of course, there was the drinkin'. He was a man just like me Da. Bastard used to take me lunch money and spend it at the pub. Me sainted mother kicked him out of the house when I was nine, but that was just the first time—she always took him back . . ." She dropped the accent. "Something like that? Without the clichés."

"Maybe there was something about her health that made you dedicate your life to women's health issues?" Vasquez suggested. "Breast cancer?"

"From living too close to a toxic waste site," Mack finished. "I like it."

"Dennis," DeLuca said. "What do you get?"

"Surprise surprise," he said, throwing his folder down on the table in front of him. "Khalil Penjwin, act two. I guess I won't have to study too hard for that one." It was the name of the identity he'd used when he'd gone undercover in Kurdish Iraq, almost two years before Iraqi Freedom began, posing as an entrepreneurial kid who'd grown up smuggling cigarettes and alcohol across the Iraq/Iran border for his uncle, a tribal leader and a U.S. ally during the time after Gulf One when U.S. planes were enforcing the northern no-fly zone. Zoulalian had cross-trained out of Air Force para-rescue and into counterintelligence largely because of his language skills, but the attraction to danger was what had drawn him to both. He'd allied himself, in Kurdistan, with a group called Ansar Al-Islam, a small band of extremists led by a man named Abu Waid that hoped to overthrow Saddam, and later the Great Satan–led coalition. Working as a double agent, "Khalil" had helped DeLuca and his team track down Mohammed Al-Tariq, the former head of Saddam's Mukhaberat, his primary secret intelligence agency. Al-Tariq had been funding an operation to ship to the United States weaponized smallpox, until DeLuca and his team tracked Al-Tariq to his headquarters deep underground at a place called the Ar Rutbah Salt Works, in the desert near the border with Syria. A combination of carrier-launched cruise missiles and "bunker-buster" smart bombs had turned the salt works into a giant smoking crater in the earth.

"According to TF-21," Zoulalian said, "Rahjid Waid, Abu Waid's oldest son, is running an IPAB training camp in northern Liger. My story is, I survived the bombing at Ar Rutbah and I've been hiding out in Syria ever since, but now that things are getting dicey in Syria, I need a new place to go. Other than that, everything is the same as before. I know who we can ask in Iraq to tell Rahjid I'm coming. I'm going to need to get to Syria to catch a commercial flight so that Rahjid can send somebody to meet my plane."

"I'm sure Captain McKinley can find one of his pilots willing to give you a lift," DeLuca said. "There's no in-flight movies, but on the other hand, you'll be flying at Mach 2. Hoolie?"

"Luis Avila," Hoolie said, holding up his new fake passport. "You know what they say—if you look anything like your passport photo, you're probably not well enough to travel. From Arecibo, Puerto Rico. I work with the National Oceanographic and Atmospheric Administration, manning a weather station at the top of El Yunque. Holy Jesus—I have to *read* all this? 'A Multi-Study Overview on the Combined Effects of Sub-Saharan Desertification and the North Atlantic Vortex on Caribbean Particulate Deposits and Childhood Asthma.'"

"You'd better read it," DeLuca said. "After all, you wrote it."

"So I did," Vasquez said, noting the authors of the paper. "'By Dr. Luis Avila, and Dr. Helen Kossman.' I have a Ph.D. from the University of Mayaguez. That's an outrage—I did all the work and she gets half the credit? Who does she think she is?"

"She's with NOAA and she actually wrote the paper," DeLuca said. "She'll back up your credentials if anybody asks or checks, but nobody will. I'm Donald Brown, with the World Bank. I'm here to determine how much money we're going to need to loan Conservation International to help stop the deforestation of West Africa. Paul, you've been working on a grant proposal for exactly that for the last two years, am I correct?"

"You are," Asabo said.

"Can you tell us, in a nutshell, what your work has been about?"

"A nutshell is not big enough," Asabo said. "A thousand years ago, a band of rain forest extended from the

Congo region of central Africa across the coastal regions all the way to Senegal and north for several hundred kilometers, and there it became savannah, before giving way to the desert. As populations increased, the pressure has grown to take sustenance from the rain forest, as people have done for thousands of years, by harvesting the bush meat but also by harvesting the trees for cook fires or for the timber industry, as well as to clear the land for agriculture, even though the soil for farming is poor. The reduction of the forests has decreased the land's ability to hold water, so instead of recycling here, it blows away, and the desert creeps southward. We lose 20 million hectares, maybe 50 million acres, of rain forest each year, globally. In Africa, the Sahara grows by 60 million hectares a year, 150 million acres, since 1990. About 235,000 square miles, or an area the size of Montana and Wyoming combined. As Dr. Kossman's report will tell you, the dust from the desert is blowing across the Atlantic and coming to earth in the Caribbean, and in North America. It is in part a result of the greenhouse effect on global warming, and it is in part the cause of it. So at Conservation International, we are working to keep the forests, but that means giving the people who live there a way to live that won't deplete the forests. You can't just kick people out without giving them something else to eat or to do. And of course, with the drought and the famine that comes with it, the pressure to eat bush meat is greater than ever. And because of political conditions, these things become ignored, at best. At worst, we have seen soldiers using elephants for target practice with their RPGs. This is what we're trying to stop."

"CI," DeLuca said, "and by that I mean Conservation International and not counterintelligence, has had a standing invitation from President Bo to visit Liger for the last two years. So we're taking him up on it."

"In the middle of a war?"

"It's always the middle of a war, in Liger," Asabo said. "We discussed this at Conservation International in Washington. Our mission is peaceful, but if we only work where there is peace, then the cause is lost. I have had some training with guns."

"If we do this right, you're not going to need it," DeLuca said, turning to the others. "We've all got brand-new SATphones, but spend some time memorizing each other's numbers because these are programmed to not store call or contact lists, in case one falls into enemy hands. They do have internal caller ID."

"What about suborals?" MacKenzie asked, referring to the nanotransmitters DARPA had developed, mouth-held radios small enough to swallow if you had to.

"Not this trip," DeLuca said. "Get caught with one of those and you might as well be wearing a U.S. Army uniform."

"What are you smiling about?" Mack asked Dan Sykes, who so far had remained silent, reading his portfolio.

"I'm a bodyguard, apparently," Sykes said.

"See?" Hoolie said. "I told you you'd get a chance to kick some ass. Who for?"

"Gabrielle Duquette," Sykes said.

"No seriously, man—who are you a bodyguard for?"

"Gabrielle Duquette," Sykes said.

There was a long silence.

"The actress dude," Hoolie said. "Gabrielle Duquette makes Halle Berry look like the mom on *The Jeffersons*. Are you shitting me?"

"She's here on a fact-finding mission," DeLuca said. "She's a special good will ambassador for the UN. Whatever that means. Two years ago, she adopted a kid from Liger, and when she was here, she met with John Dari, so at the very least, she'll be able to recognize him. She said in a press conference that she hopes to meet with him again—she might even be our best bet. Plus she's going to have access to places we otherwise wouldn't be able to go. I think both sides want to use her to get publicity."

"My ID's the same," Sykes said, reading from his cover file, "but I'm retired from CI. Now I work for Blackwood Security, out of North Carolina."

"Much as we all hate contractors," DeLuca said, "the cover is good. With the exception of Dennis, we'll operate out of the Hotel Liger in Baku Da'al. That's where all the white people have stayed in central Liger since colonial days. Right now, I don't think we'll have much problem getting a room. We'll arrive separately and meet in the bar, but don't order the monkey brains. In Liger, that's not the name of a drink they serve at frat parties. Paul, what do we need to know about John Dari, that's not in the report?"

"Just that he is very smart," Asabo said. "At school, I had to work very hard with my studies, but he didn't. He got better grades than I did, and it came very easy for him. I don't know why he changed so much, but I think maybe there is something he feels that the reports you have don't mention."

"What's that?"

"Well," Paul Asabo said. "I think he is lonely. I was his best friend, but I knew in school that that was not enough. He had a longing. He came from a big family and they were all killed. I know he always wondered why he was the one who was not. He thought there had to be a reason why he was spared. Something big that he was meant to do. So perhaps leading these forces, perhaps that's the thing he believes he was meant to do. And perhaps his troops are his family. And his country. Like an LA street gang. Perhaps."

"You make being a warlord sound like a domestic situation," Hoolie said.

"I don't believe he is a warlord," Asabo said.

"Is that what your gut says?" DeLuca asked. "Don't get me wrong—I make my living listening to people's guts."

"I knew him in high school," Asabo said. "And junior high. Prep school. That is the time, and I think the place, where people are going to be cruel, if they have cruelty within them. John had plenty of reasons to have cruelty within him, given the things he saw as a young boy. But he was not cruel."

"People change," DeLuca said.

"Have you changed?" Asabo asked him. "How long have you been studying war?"

"A long time," DeLuca admitted.

"And yet although you are wiser," Asabo said, "have you lost your humanity? Have you changed, apart from simply growing older? People are who they are, I think. John Dari was my friend. I think he still is. But perhaps I will be disappointed."

"As far as I can tell," DeLuca said to end the briefing, "the White House doesn't particularly care if we succeed, as long as they can say they tried, and the Pentagon only cares insofar as we can supply command and control with targeting data. The temptation would be to phone it in and play it safe. You will, at all times, take whatever precautions you can to remain safe, but if anybody here thinks they're going to phone it in, tell me now and I'll find you a mop you can use to swab the decks until we get back. The only thing more dangerous than a dangerous mission is a dangerous mission that you don't take seriously. We deploy in two hours. Dennis, I'll talk to the captain about your ride. You may want to leave sooner than that. Any questions?"

"How are we armed?" MacKenzie said.

"Everybody in Liger is armed," DeLuca said. "You'll probably attract more attention if you're not. Just don't be conspicuous. Dan, take a MAC-10 in addition to your sidearm. It's what all the Blackwood guys are wearing these days. DARPA has also given us new handhelds to field test, called CIMs or Critical Information Minimodules—the army is also calling them FBCB2s or 'Fee-bee-cee-bees,' for Force Battle Command Brigade and Below systems. It's a pocket PC that they hope will turn every soldier into an intelligence-gathering unit. Read the manuals. They look like civilian PDAs, or at least the version they gave us does, with built-in GPS for maps and data uplinks in real time to MILSATs and what have you, so spend some time getting to know how to use them. You can wi-fi to SIPERNET or the Internet, but if I catch anybody playing Grand Theft Auto on his, I'm taking it away. Paul, can I offer you anything?"

"Guns?" Asabo said. "I don't think so. If they discover who I am, it would be best if I were unarmed. Plus I don't like guns."

"I don't like cars," DeLuca said, "but it beats walking."

After the briefing, DeLuca used his new handheld PC to collect his e-mail. The first thing he'd done, upon awakening, was e-mail his friend Walter Ford back in Boston and ask him to get on the Web and look for any information that the briefing report might have omitted, sending the report as an attached file. He didn't expect a reply so soon, but then he remembered that Ford, a retired cop and a professor in the Criminal Justice program at Northeastern, was one of the most diligent people he'd ever known. He'd stay up to finish a task, no matter how late it got.

Dear David,

Hope all remains well with you. Martha suggests I remind you to dress warmly. I told her you were in tropical Africa, but you know Martha. She would still be trying to get you to wear a sweater.

As to your questions, I'm supplying links to a number of Ligerian expatriate Web sites, but to give you the gist of it, the bottom line is, President Bo's popularity ratings rank significantly lower than Bill Clinton's. Ligerian expats hate him (Bo, not Clinton), as do many of his citizens, though he has the support of the Fasori elite, who he favors in return with tax breaks, import tariffs, bribes, etc. He had the full support of big oil and their hired mercenaries until he started talking about nationalizing the oil industry a few months ago, largely a populist gesture, but WAOC was not amused.

Bo has two rivals for power, both of whom he keeps on a short leash. One is General Kwesi Emil-Ngwema, vice president and head of the army. Ngwema was, for years, Bo's go-to guy when he needed somebody thrown out of a helicopter. Lake Liger was his favorite drop zone, mostly because it's full of cichlids that can make a corpse impossible to identify in about three seconds. I had some in my aquarium and they ate all my other fish, my bad, not theirs, but they're worse than piranhas, IMHO. Lately Ngwema has stayed away from Bo. One Web site says he's planning a coup, with WAOC funding. Another says he's waiting for LPLF to do his dirty work for him. Either way, he's playing his cards pretty tight right now.

The other rival is Bishop Duvallier. The majority of the nation's Christians are Catholic, incl. lower-class Fasoris and most of the Da Christians, who mainly supply the workforce for the oil industry. Pentecostals making inroads, however. Question: Would Duvallier let Muslims kill Pentecostals? One Web site says yes. Both Bo and WAOC have been greasing Duvallier for years. One Web site says Duvallier is a cannibal who eats young boys. The Vatican loves him for his firm stand against birth control/abortion/same-sex marriage. Duvallier's emissaries personally intercepted and destroyed a shipment of condoms sent by the WHO. FYI, AIDS in Liger is about 28 percent among women and 24 percent among men, second only to Uganda, but thanks to Duvallier, at least unmarried people

*aren't having sex, because they're all dying in
hospitals.*

*And by the way, the ambassador you rescued was
investigated for taking a seat on the Ligerian gravy
train, accepting gifts, safaris, etc. from Bo, from
whose Presidential Guard Ellis selected his house-
hold staff, whom he doesn't pay. One site alleges that
the U.S. ambassador keeps slaves. Lots of cocktail
parties at the mansion, champagne, feasts with roast
pigs, etc. The investigation said Ellis may have crossed
the line at times but that his actions were in accord-
ance with traditional diplomacy. Sumptuous feasts
when up north, two thousand plus people a day die
of starvation. I wonder why so many people hate
America?*

Let me know what else I can do.

Best, Walter

Chapter Five

DELUCA, VASQUEZ, AND ASABO, BEARING false papers identifying them as Don Brown, from the World Bank, Luis Avila, from the National Oceanographic and Atmospheric Administration, and James Hawkins, with Conservation International, were flown to Ghana, where they caught a commercial flight to Port Ivory. Sykes and MacKenzie were to enter in a similar fashion via Lagos, transferring first at an offshore oil rig. Asabo spoke English without an accent and could therefore pass as an American, though he'd never actually taken his American citizenship, but was allowed to stay in the United States indefinitely with the immigration status of a political refugee.

"Don't forget," DeLuca reminded Asabo, "from here on, you don't speak Fasori, or anything local."

"Fa-shizzle," Asabo said dryly.

It was the first time DeLuca had seen Asabo smile. If the younger man felt any emotion, returning to his home country after so many years in exile, he didn't show it. An official examined their passports, then stamped them without further ado. Asabo smiled to see crowds of children surrounding them as they passed through customs, kids trying to sell them clear plastic bags of potable water, bars of soap, loaves of bread, Pez dispensers, packs of chewing gum, brass napkin holders, polished gourds, anything they could get their hands on that they thought wealthy foreigners might want to buy. Other children simply held out their hands and begged, pleading with their eyes, some licking their lips or touching their lips with their fingers to indicate they were hungry. Soon Asabo stopped smiling.

"Look at their teeth," he said to DeLuca, who noted that most were missing teeth or were in need of orthodontia. "When I left, there were no candy bars in Liger, and none of the children had cavities. Now they all do, apparently."

Grown men held out thick stacks of Zudas, the local currency, offering to change their American dollars, though the exchange rate was fluctuating wildly on virtually an hourly basis, depending on how the war was going. DeLuca held on to his cash. Dispersed throughout the mob were soldiers carrying machine guns, unsmiling men in maroon berets and wraparound sunglasses, their pants tucked into matching maroon gaiters.

"If we can get to the cab rank without getting shot," DeLuca said sotto voce, "I think we're in the clear."

He asked the cab driver, a man named Jumee, to take them, first, on a tour of the city. The driver complied as best he could, although the central part of the city along the coast, between the presidential palace and the Castle of St. James, was cordoned off by soldiers manning roadblocks, black smoke still rising above the skyline, an acrid stench of burning rubber leaking in through the taxi's windows. When DeLuca asked the cab driver if he had any idea what the situation was at the soccer stadium, he just shrugged as if he didn't and hadn't heard anything. DeLuca noticed a spot on the dashboard where Jumee kept his small statuette of the Virgin Mary, which now rested on the seat beside him, out of view. The radio played nonstop music, innocuous Afro-pop and smooth-grooved crap by Sting and Phil Collins, without commentary or commercial interruptions. He saw men carting away rubble in wheelbarrows and hand-drawn carts from broken buildings, funeral processions of mourners clad in decorous local textiles, children wandering alone, little short-haired dogs with skin conditions, a church where a line of young men in white shirts and baggy dress pants but no shoes waited to enter, holding Bibles in their hands. He saw broken shop windows, dumped garbage, looted stores, empty boxes in the streets, broken televisions and DVD players smashed against the pavement, walls mottled with bullet pockings, bloodstains, raw sewage, people crouched around cook fires, and whenever they slowed, children begging at the taxi's windows with their hands out, adults, too, asking for anything, anything at all. He saw overturned and burned cars, the shell of an armored troop carrier, a van on its side with the words "One Lord—Jah Love" painted on the side that was showing, two of its wheels missing. He saw church steeples damaged by tank rounds, streets cratered by bombs and artillery shells, houses with the roofs blown off, or the fronts, the sides, the backs, and in the exposed rooms, kids playing or simply gazing out. He saw crowds of men gathered on street corners, taking security in numbers, men glancing nervously through slits in doors and gates, lone men ducking into doorways or running away in advance of their approach, and government soldiers in maroon berets stopping people to look at their travel documents or identification papers, government soldiers loading men with their shirts pulled over their heads into trucks, government soldiers in a circle, down one alley, kicking someone who'd fallen while a woman nearby screamed, "Please don't take my son." DeLuca didn't see any bodies lying dead in the streets. He wondered how many there'd been, and where they'd gone. He saw the Muslim neighborhood, now a wasteland of rubble and debris, where two weeks earlier, President Bo had sent in a fleet of bulldozers to destroy all the Muslim homes and shops in what he'd dubbed "Operation Trash Removal."

"It was very bad," the driver, Jumee, said. "Many people are now without homes."

The driver took them, finally, to the headquarters for the African Union peacekeeping mission, a one-story tin-roofed pale yellow building centered in a dusty courtyard filled with date and fan palms, a half dozen chickens, a pig chained to a stake. There were two white Jeeps and a white Humvee parked in the dust, guarded by six soldiers in khaki uniforms with blue berets and green kerchiefs around their necks to identify them as neutral observers and not combatants. The Humvee had been modified by someone with a welding torch who'd added rough-cut iron plates to the doors and fender panels, until the vehicle resembled something out of a Mad Max movie, pure Road Warrior. U.S. soldiers had done the same thing to their un-armored Humvees in Iraq. The vehicles had the letters AU painted on the doors, and a white flag flew above the building featuring the same African Union logo.

An aide asked them to wait a moment, then showed them into a dusty office.

General Osman was a large barrel-chested no-necked hulk of a man, hairless save for the bloom of white chest hairs sprouting from his open shirt collar. When DeLuca told him, after introducing himself and his companions, that he had an appointment, Osman looked suspicious, eyeing his lieutenant, who appeared to be doing his best to become invisible.

"What appointment did we have?" Osman asked. "This is the first that I have heard of this."

"You didn't get the call from my office?" DeLuca said. "We spoke with General Bukari. I'm not sure who my secretary spoke with, exactly, but she informed me that you would be expecting me." He was bluffing, but it was a reasonable assumption that in the chaos of the civil war that surrounded them, Osman's staff was likely to have lost track of an appointment or two. Osman had no way of knowing that this wasn't one of them, and DeLuca didn't have time to wait for an actual appointment.

"My aide," Osman said, "has not informed me. We've been without communications as well. Please forgive me—please be seated—how is it that I can help you, Mr. Brown?"

"I appreciate your making time for me, General," DeLuca said. "My colleagues and I do understand how busy you must be. I trust that your men are all right. I know that yesterday was not a good day for Liger."

"The days seem quite the same, from where I sit," General Osman said.

"I won't take up any more of your time than I have to," DeLuca said. "We're looking for John Dari. We have a business matter we would like to discuss with him. I'm not free to disclose what that matter is, but we were hoping that you might be able to tell us either where John Dari is or who might know where he is, if you don't."

Osman seemed taken aback.

"And how is it that you think I would know this?" he asked. "Dari is in the north. I am in Port Ivory. Do you think if he were in Port Ivory, he would call me and we'd have tea?"

"No, I don't," DeLuca said, "but I know that you have men with eyes and ears in various parts of the country. Men who are Christian and men who are Muslim. Men who might have heard something in their role as observers, either during the cease-fire or during the recent conflict."

Osman threw up his hands.

"I have three hundred men," he said. "I don't dare send them anywhere in numbers smaller than a platoon. And if we meet with resistance, we must back down because we have nothing in the rules of engagement that allows us to fight. And, sir, we could not fight if we wanted to, I will tell you that, because President Obasanjo and his friends in Addis Ababa have decided the AU may not carry more than a single clip of ammunition for each soldier, or we would be seen as a threat. So tell me, how can I learn what I need to know in Liger? How can I tell you what I need to know myself?"

"Perhaps you can't help," DeLuca said. "But you could help me, I think, spread the word that I would like to speak to Dari. I'm not with the United States, General. I'm not with the UN, and I'm not with ECOMAS either. Despite what you may have heard, the World Bank is an independent organization. We have an opportunity to bring considerable funds to bear on whatever needs Liger might have toward rebuilding its infrastructure. The time to establish a no-fire zone, negotiated between all interested parties, is now, not when it's too late. And you see, General, I can't travel, even with assurances from the government, because there are large areas of Liger right now where the government itself can't go. But your men, as neutral observers, can. I understand that you're understaffed, and I sympathize. I'm only asking that you do the best that you can. I might add that the World Bank has also been studying ways to assist the African Union, as I'm sure you know."

DeLuca waited. If Osman was going to ask for a bribe, now was his chance. DeLuca had been warned by a cynical friend in the State Department's Africa program that "African Union" was an oxymoron—"like 'scented deodorant,'" the friend had said. DeLuca was betting that Osman's relationship with AU headquarters in Addis Ababa was less than satisfactory. It was also his own personal experience that in third world countries with ethically challenged leadership, men in positions of power rarely sought the high road and could be bribed, and nine out of ten times, the ones who wanted bribes came right out and asked for them. Osman wasn't part of the Ligerian government, but he was in Liger—perhaps he was playing by the house rules.

Osman didn't take the bait, and in fact seemed oblivious to it.

"You would deal with this criminal, then?" Osman said. "This person who kills children? Who puts tires filled with gasoline around the necks of his enemies and lights them on fire? This is the person you will do business with?"

"No," DeLuca said. "I wouldn't. But as a soldier, you

understand that throughout history, whenever the end of a war is negotiated rather than imposed, men who've killed have to learn how to talk to men who've killed, in order to stop the killing. It's not an easy thing to sit down across the table from your enemy, I know. What the World Bank wants to do is make such a thing attractive and economically appealing to both sides."

"Well," Osman said. "I will be honest with you. I don't know where Dari is, Mr. Brown. I have a report that he might be in the hills west of Kumari, but I have another that he is moving on the oil fields three hundred kilometers to the east of that. I don't really believe either report. I think he could be anywhere."

"Do you know in what numbers?" DeLuca asked.

"Five thousand men," Osman said with a shrug. "I have also heard twice that."

"I was told one thousand," DeLuca said.

"Possibly two," Vasquez added.

Osman shook his head.

"Maybe a month ago," he said. "But not now." He eyed them a moment longer. "So yes, Mr. Brown, I will pass along your message to my men and ask them to make inquiries for you. But I don't expect to have success, and I should tell you, I don't believe John Dari will meet with you even if he gets the message, only because you are white. He has said this himself. But perhaps on behalf of the people he is leading, he will. In my opinion, whoever comes within ten feet of him should shoot him through the eyes and ask questions later. But of course, we are not allowed to shoot. We can only observe. Do you know what we observe, Mr. Brown? This morning, my men went to the village of Dsang, a small Da village, where the boys had formed a militia to protect their mothers. With sticks. We found twenty-six bodies of boys with their penises cut off and shoved into their mouths. Because John Dari is afraid of boys with sticks. So when you meet him at the peace table, please ask him about the boys of Dsang. And ask him about their mothers, because we could not find them."

After the meeting, they instructed Jumee to take them to Lions' Park, a casino and golf resort that President Bo had built on the northern end of the city. The driver told them Lions' Park was closed. DeLuca said he knew, but that that was where President Bo's office had instructed them to meet the convoy that would take them north to Baku Da'al, unless, DeLuca said, the cab driver was interested in making a longer trip, an offer Jumee immediately declined.

The casino, built by the government in an attempt to emulate South Africa's Sun City, had squandered millions of dollars that might have been better spent on food or schools or roads, Paul Asabo explained, but Bo needed a playground to entertain his fellow despots and dictator friends. Bishop Duvallier had pulled the lever on the first slot machine at the opening ceremonies and, to everyone's surprise, he won nearly a million Zudas, which he remitted to the church, of course. In its opening year, the casino had hosted concerts by Elton John and Sting, but as it began to decline, it was booking people like Gallagher and Robert Goulet, and then Gallagher and Robert Goulet impersonators. The decline hastened when a report said 90 percent of the prostitutes working the bars of Lions' Park had AIDS.

"If you hired a team of the best architects," Asabo said,

shaking his head, "you couldn't build a better monument to stupidity and greed."

Many of the windows in the thirty-story-high hotel had been shot out, as had the massive neon sign out front, the gray concrete walls pocked with bullet holes and stained the color of dried blood where the oxidized iron rebars had rusted through. The jungle had begun to reclaim the golf course, all but the eighteenth hole, where goats grazed on the fairway and the bunkers had been converted into machine-gun nests.

DeLuca showed his transit papers to the captain in charge, who examined their passports and a letter from President Bo himself (forged), and then pointed to a white bus, tapping his wristwatch with his finger to indicate they'd be leaving shortly. A dozen young soldiers in maroon berets rode on top of the bus, their weapons slung casually over their shoulders, the convoy comprising perhaps forty vehicles, including Jeeps, Humvees, M-113 troop transports, and some sort of armored carrier DeLuca didn't recognize, two at the head and two at the tail, German, he thought, though he'd need a closer look to be certain. He thought briefly of the book *Heart of Darkness,* the journey into the savage interior that Joseph Conrad described so well. DeLuca had read it first in college, and again before deploying to Liger, hoping it would yield new insights. It had: Don't go.

On the bus, he let Hoolie and Asabo take the first open seat and moved toward the middle, where he saw a familiar face, one of only a few white faces in a crowd of Africans. The man in the black shirt and priest's collar moved to the window as DeLuca sat down beside him.

"Of all the gin joints," DeLuca began. "Don't tell me—David Letterman went to your high school?"

"Used to beat his ass and take his lunch money every day," the priest said with a thick southern accent. "Never thought he'd amount to much."

"Don Brown," DeLuca said, offering his hand to the man he knew from the time they'd worked together in Iraq as Preacher Johnson with Task Force 21. "World Bank."

"They told me you'd be on this bus. Father O'Connell," Johnson said, shaking DeLuca's hand. "Or O'Connor. O'Connor?" He checked his passport. "O'Connell. Father O'Connell."

"You might want to memorize that," DeLuca said. "Just in case it comes up again." It didn't appear that anyone seated near them could speak English, and once the bus began to move, the engine noise drowned his words anyway, but it was still wise to be cautious. "I didn't know you were working in Liger."

"Oh, yeah," Johnson said. "Special emissary from the pope. Who's a close personal friend."

"You met the new pope?" DeLuca said. "What'd you think?"

"Him, I liked. Her, I didn't," Johnson said as the bus rocked after hitting a massive pothole. "Damn. I think I just lost a filling."

He explained that there were only two paved highways in Liger, one running along the coast and the other connecting Port Ivory with Baku Da'al and extending north to Kumari. The rebels had held this road until today, retreating only when planes from the Ligerian air force were able to take command of the skies.

"The government had a sat-cam looking for ambushes,

but then the kite string broke and it crashed," Johnson said. "I spoke in prayer with some of our angels this morning and they thought the way was clear, but I'm still thinking it's a good idea to sit in the middle of the bus. That way if they shoot us from in front or behind, there's plenty of bodies to take the rounds."

"You want me to take the window seat?" DeLuca offered.

"That's all right," Johnson said. "It's fifty-fifty they shoot from your side anyways, and if they do, I'm bailing. How was your flight? I hope this time you took an airplane."

Johnson was referring to the last time he and DeLuca had met, during a raid into the Sinjar Jebel mountains, 160 kilometers west of Mosul, Iraq, near the border with Syria. Preacher Johnson was somewhere in his late fifties, tough as depleted uranium, the leader of Task Force 21, an elite squad of special ops troops culled from among the best of the Rangers, SEALs, Delta, and other special forces, the cream of the crop, working deep undercover in Baghdad and elsewhere in Iraq before, during, and after Iraqi Freedom, disguised behind long beards and native *abayas*. They'd been the brawn to the CI brains. The raid had been on an Ansar Al-Islam hideout in a monastery where Saladin had once turned back the crusaders in the twelfth century. DeLuca and Sykes, along with TF-21, had executed a High Altitude Low Opening or HALO jump from thirty-nine thousand feet in the dead of night, in head-to-toe puffy suits to protect them against the minus-one-hundred-degree wind chill, to reach the LZ in a field above the monastery, a mission that had by and large, but not entirely, cured DeLuca of his fear of flying.

The mission had ended with DeLuca being thrown through the bulletproof windshield of a Humvee during a high-speed chase down a winding mountain road and hurting his neck, but other than that, traveling with Preacher Johnson had been a pleasure.

"How about you?" he asked. "You flying Delta?"

"Attached to," Johnson said. "Working with most of the same people as before. We lost one man. Not here. But otherwise we're mostly intact."

"I'm sorry," DeLuca said.

The countryside rolled by, empty country marked by an occasional cocoa or rubber plantation, bare clay fields, scrub brush with tall trees rising singly and well spaced, villages of wattle and daub with thatched roofs or cinder-block houses with tin roofs and glassless window openings, shade-tree mechanics working on cars flipped on their sides in lieu of hydraulic hoists, boys tending goat herds or sheep flocks, women walking down the side of the road with large tin pans or straw baskets loaded with food or dry goods or laundry balanced on their heads.

"You're looking for John Dari?" Johnson asked. "Let me know how I can help, but it's been damn hard. These guys have people so scared they're not giving up much. Though I'm not so sure about Dari. Most of his people are Da. I put him more toward the center than some people think."

"Samuel Adu?"

"Real piece of work," Johnson said. "As a man of the cloth, of course, I must pray for his redemption, but as a purely practical matter, I've given orders that if anybody working for me sees him, he's free to send Adu on to meet his maker and let him deal with matters of the mortal soul, though I'm not sure Adu ever had one."

"You hear about Dsang?" DeLuca asked.

Johnson nodded.

"Confirmed?"

Johnson nodded again.

"We're mostly far north, in the Vacant Zone, they call it. Sahel, accent on the 'Hell.' You think Iraq was all dust and camel shit, try the VZ. Delta's been there for months training what they're calling the 'Sub-Saharan Peace-keeping Battalion.' Men from Niger, Mali, Chad, Mauri-tania, pretty soon Algeria, Tunisia, Morocco, and Senegal. Two hundred men and a bunch of Toyotas to patrol a chunk of desert four times the size of Alaska, looking for IPAB hadjis and LPLF lowlifes who outnumber, outgun, outsmart, and outrun us on a daily basis. SIGINT is use-less because nobody has coms and infrared only works at night because of the heat during the day. We call it the BS Battalion, but be that as it fucking may, somebody in a very oddly shaped building which shall remain nameless thinks they're going to hold the northern frontier for us when the shit hits the fan. Hold their dicks is more like it."

"What brings you south?" DeLuca asked.

"Little of this, little of that," Preacher Johnson said. "Mostly just sitting on a wall, eating shit and drinking piss. Isaiah thirty-six, verse twelve, my son. We cached some material to prep an LZ for CC on a farm outside the next village, actually, which is where I'll be getting off to have a look-see. Some indications that it's been disturbed, but I'll believe it when I see it. I think maybe the gnus have been digging around some with their hooves."

DeLuca waited.

"Go ahead," he said at last. "You know you want to."

"So no gnus is good gnus," Johnson said.

DeLuca nodded.

"Gnus travels fast," Johnson added.

"One's enough," DeLuca said.

"Where y'all stayin'?" Johnson asked.

"Hotel Liger," DeLuca said. "Baku Da'al."

"Aha," Johnson said. "Otherwise known as the Worst Western. Ask for a nonsmoking room. Those would be the ones that aren't currently on fire."

"I'll try to remember," DeLuca promised.

"Actually, when you're there, talk to a man named Robert Mohl. M-o-h-l. He'll be on the stool at the end of the bar closest to the lobby. He's the CIA field agent, but he never leaves his stool. He's like Norm in *Cheers*. Actually, that's not fair. Sometimes he ventures as far as the table by the door. Ask him about Imam Isfahan Dadullahjid. He's the Non-Commissioned Ayatollah in Charge for the Kum. He might know where Dari is, and Mohl might know where Dadullahjid is. After the last few days, you'll recognize Mohl by the pee stains running down his pants."

Johnson leaned his head toward the window. Ahead, DeLuca saw smoke rising into the sky from something burning.

"This is my stop," Johnson said, stooping to grab his bag from beneath the seat. "You're the one who got the ambassador out, right?"

DeLuca nodded.

"Just as well," Johnson said. "We were plan B. Blow the shit out of everything, with our customary panache. You hear the rumors about Ambassador Ellis?"

"Which ones?" DeLuca said. "That he's a shit?"

"No," Johnson said. "That he owned slaves."

"I heard that one," DeLuca said. "Does President Lincoln know about this?"

"It's not all that uncommon in Liger, actually," Johnson said. "Especially in the rural villages. Some family pisses off the tribal chief, so to make amends, they give him their daughter for ten years. Bo has them in his palace. People think he gave some to Ellis as a gift. A party gift, if you catch my drift. I heard Ellis liked to videotape himself. It's probably not true, but that's what people say."

"People say the darndest things," DeLuca said. He moved aside as Johnson crossed to the aisle, stepping over a goat that someone had brought on board.

"You take care of yourself, Don Brown," Johnson said. "Ethnic tension–wise, this place makes Iraq look like a board meeting at the American Library Association."

"You have a number I can reach you at?" DeLuca asked. "Just in case I get lonely?"

"Already told you," Johnson said. "Isaiah thirty-six, v. twelve. Twenty-third book, thirty-six, 'v' Roman numeral for five, and then twelve. Two-three-three-six-five-one-two, same prelims and country codes as yours, which I have. But don't worry, you won't get lonely. And if you ever get in trouble, remember, just say, *'Kwa maana jinsi hii Mungu aliupenda ulimwnegu, hata akamtoa Mwanawe pekee, ili kila mtu amwaminiye asipotee; bali awe na uzima wa milele.'* That's John three-sixteen in Swahili. Nobody here speaks Swahili, but it sounds good, don't it? Take care. Don't let the bedbugs bite. That's not just a figure of speech in Liger. They vo-racious sons-of-bitches in this neighborhood."

Chapter Six

MACKENZIE'S PALE BLUE UNITED NATIONS helicopter set her down outside a place known only as Camp Seven. She'd been the lone passenger, the remaining available space in the Russian-made chopper filled floor to ceiling with cases of baby formula and diapers. As the helicopter landed, it was possible, even in the dimming light, to gauge the misery below, centered in a sea of makeshift shelters, plastic tarps, and blankets held up by sticks, the landing zone a circle in the dirt formed by a cordon of African Union soldiers in blue berets and green kerchiefs keeping back a throng of displaced people surging to meet the aircraft and obtain a portion of its cargo.

As she ducked her head into the backwash from the rotors, she was met by a young man who took her by the elbow and led her to a lean-to made from a large piece of corrugated tin roofing, a transport parked next to it that had to be forty years old.

"My name is Stephen Ackroyd," the young man said above the din. "What's yours? We didn't know anybody was coming."

"Mary Dorsey," MacKenzie said. "United Nations

Women's Health Initiative. I hitched a ride. I would have called ahead, but . . ."

"Welcome, Mary Dorsey," Ackroyd said, still shouting above the sound of the rotors, which had slowed but apparently weren't stopping. She watched as soldiers off-loaded the helicopter, moving the crates and boxes onto hand-drawn carts. To one side, she saw a group of people, waiting on stretchers, she guessed to be medevaced.

"Would you like me to take you to Dr. Chaline?" the young man asked her. "I think he's in the infirmary. It's a bit hard to find unless you know where to go, particularly after dark. Can I carry your bag?"

"I've got it. Thank you," MacKenzie said, following him.

"Watch your step," he said. "I left my flashlight in my tent because we're low on batteries. We'll get there sooner if we take the path instead of the road."

She'd seen the sun set a deep blood red as she flew. The sky was now dark, the Milky Way streaming like a vivid river of light across the heavens. There were few lights in the camp, a candle here and there but no electricity save for a floodlight up ahead where, she assumed, they were going. The smell was overwhelming, a stench of human waste and vomit, and yet as she walked she heard children laughing and mothers singing lullabies to their babies. She saw huts made of sticks with corrugated tin or fiberglass roofs, shelters made of plastic sheeting, huts made of woven grass mats, World War I–era canvas wall tents and nylon tents and Mongolian yurt-style tents, solar-powered cookers, a windmill, and women carrying water cans and cook pots, blankets, hoes, children in flip-flop sandals several sizes too big for their feet, young boys in hand-me-down T-shirts with the logos of American sports teams on them, men examining ration cards to make sure people had eaten, or that nobody had eaten twice, people living in doorless, engineless cars, and monkeys picking through trash heaps.

"Believe it or not, this is one of the nicer camps—in Gula, Zaire, in 1994 after the massacre in Rwanda, we had 1.2 million people cross the border into Zaire in forty-eight hours. What exactly does the Women's Health Initiative do?" Ackroyd asked, once they were away from the helicopter and no longer had to shout and could speak in normal voices. He was a good-looking man, Mack thought, a bit on the thin side and more soft-spoken than most of the men she met, but that wasn't a bad thing, gentle-featured, with thin lips and long sandy brown hair that hadn't been washed in weeks, judging from how it shone, and it kept falling in front of his eyes even though he kept pushing it back under his Red Sox cap. He had a patchy stubble of beard on his face that made him look even more boyish for its lack of thickness. He was wearing jeans, hiking boots, and a plaid long-sleeved shirt, untucked and unbuttoned, the end of his belt hanging down below his shirt.

"I'm here on a fact-finding mission," she told him, keeping to the story that had been prepared for her. "I'll be making a report to the UN when I'm done on the status of women and how they're being treated in the conflict. How about you—what brings you here?"

"I'm a writer," he told her. "I'm doing a story for *Men's Journal,* but I think it's going to be a book too. My agent thinks she can sell it. Where are you from?"

"Dublin," Mack said. "How about you?"

"I'm from the States," he told her, as if she hadn't surmised that. "Near Chicago. Evanston. Near where Al Capone was from."

"I know where Chicago is," she told him. "I come from Coldwater Road. Bono, from U2, went to my high school. The nuns and the priests didn't know what to make of him."

"Oh," Ackroyd said. Now was his chance to mention David Letterman. He didn't. "Do you know Evelyn Warner? Do you get the BBC in Ireland?"

If she'd had the time to prepare her own identity, or study the one that had been prepared for her, she might have known the answer to that question.

"I've seen her reports," MacKenzie replied evasively. "We do have cable TV in Ireland, Stephen. I know who Larry King is, too, though some of the more remote villages in Ireland don't get HBO. Why do you ask?"

"Sorry," he said. He seemed embarrassed, flustered. She'd only meant a gentle tease. "I was just asking because she's working here, on a story. She's at the health center. I'll introduce you."

MacKenzie knew her Irish accent was good enough to fool an American, or an African, but whether she could get across on a Brit remained in doubt. She had other concerns—Warner had worked with DeLuca in Iraq, the Englishwoman one of those globe-trotting journalists who seemed to find the hot spots before they got hot, always squinting into the sun in her khaki safari vest or trying not to flinch in front of the camera as the bombs burst in the background and missiles lit the sky, casting fiery orange highlights onto her wind-tossed yet somehow ever-perfect hair. Mack doubted Warner had any way of connecting her with Team Red or DeLuca (they'd never met in Iraq, though they'd passed each other in the hallway of a combat area support hospital), but if she somehow slipped up, her cover could be blown.

The path dipped down by a river, filled recently by heavy rains to the north, where a hand-drawn sign indicated in pictures that defecating or urinating at that place was forbidden. Across the river, the landscape was dark. The path rose from the river up a sandy bank and wound through another population of refugees, the candles and kerosene lamps glittering beneath the African sky giving the feel of a kind of vigil. Ackroyd explained that they were moving from an area where people were generally healthy, hungry or starving but otherwise without major infections or illnesses, to an area where the sick were located. They'd had an outbreak of cholera due to sanitation problems and *V. cholerae* bacteria in the river.

"We can give you Mutacol or Dukerol if you want," Ackroyd said. "Neither are available in the States, yet, anyway. We have about seven hundred people here, all women and children, and maybe half are ill. It's one of the smallest IDPs in Liger, but that doesn't necessarily make things any easier. We're a little worried because we don't have water purification equipment, and the last convoy of water trucks was hit by the rebels. Only one made it through with potable water. Two were captured and two were destroyed. The water just poured out onto the ground. We're boiling what we can, but we're running out of kerosene to boil, too, and gas to power the generators. You could save almost everybody if you could just rehydrate them, but that's proving to be more difficult than we thought it would be. I'm sure you know this already, but don't drink any water unless it's bottled or boiled, don't eat anything that hasn't been well cooked and isn't still warm, don't eat any fruit you didn't peel yourself, and don't, it goes without saying, go in the river. I mean, don't go swimming."

"Why is this camp all women and children?" Mack asked. "Where are the men?"

"There are camps with men, too," Ackroyd said. "The feeling was that the Muslims didn't want men and women housed in the same camp. Evelyn Warner thinks they just want to put the women where they know they can find them. It's not safe here and all we've got is about thirty AU troops, led by a young corporal named Okempo who's never actually fired a weapon in his life. We took a mortar round last night that killed a dozen people. It came in from across the river. For no reason, just to kill people and make them afraid."

"From who?" Mack said. "IPAB or LPLF or someone else?"

"What difference does it make?" Ackroyd said. "That's the infirmary. The staff compound is behind it—that's where you'll be staying."

She saw lights ahead, a GP-large tent illuminated from inside with electricity, glowing orange beneath the African stars, oversized human figures projected in silhouettes against the canvas. She heard generators starting and cutting out. She felt, as she followed her guide, utterly conspicuous, the eyes of the sufferers who surrounded her watching her, mothers and children, but unlike the crowds she'd seen on the streets of Port Ivory, where kids begged for handouts and adults clamored for assistance, here everyone was for the most part silent, save for the occasional low voice of someone singing a lullaby to help her baby sleep.

At the tent, Ackroyd left her alone while he made inquiries. He returned to say that Dr. Chaline was out having a walkabout in the camp, and that his assistant, Dr. Leger, was attending a birth, even though the mother was so underweight and malnourished that the survival of either mother or newborn seemed doubtful.

A white woman, mid-thirties, Mack guessed, sat at a folding table outside the staff tent, smoking a cigarette beneath a broad acacia tree, a Styrofoam cup of coffee on the table in front of her. A young black woman was seated across from her. The white woman was wearing a pair of short-sleeved loose-fitting navy blue coveralls, the zipper drawn down to reveal a white tank top beneath it. The black woman wore green fatigues and a white short-sleeved shirt.

"This is Evelyn Warner, who I was telling you about," Ackroyd said, "and this is Cela, our translator and a relief worker. Evelyn, Cela, this is Mary Dorsey from the United Nations Women's Health Initiative."

"Have you eaten, Stephen?" Warner said, nodding to MacKenzie.

"I will," Ackroyd said. "I wanted to go check on section ten to see if Udal brought them the lime they needed."

"Why don't you eat now and check on that later?" Warner said.

"I'll just be a minute," Stephen said, making his exit. "Mary, it was nice meeting you. I'm sure I'll see you around."

"Mary Dorsey, welcome to Camp Seven," Warner said. "We heard a rumor that a new *Obroni* was on her way—

you wouldn't happen to have come with a load of diapers and infant formula, would you?"

"I did," MacKenzie said. "They were unloading the helicopter when I left." Warner closed her eyes and sighed with relief, then opened them, smiling.

"I didn't mean, 'Did you have any on you?'" Warner said. She turned to Cela. "That must be where Claude went. Now if we just had something to mix the formula with, we'd be all set, wouldn't we?"

She turned her attention again to the visitor.

"So do tell, Mary Dorsey, what exactly is the United Nations Women's Health Initiative? And forgive me for being blunt, because I was going to say, 'What can we do for you?' but frankly, I'm much more interested in what you can do for us."

"I'm here to learn," MacKenzie said. "Just to see for myself, I suppose. I can't make any promises, but what I *can* do, when I get back, is make recommendations."

Warner didn't say anything. Mack wondered if her accent had given her away somehow. There had been times, during her career with counterintelligence, when MacKenzie had taken a certain amount of pleasure, even pride, in the role-playing her job required her to do, and in fooling people. This was not such a time. This was one of those times when she hated—hated—having to lie to people.

"I suppose that must sound terribly inadequate to you," she continued, "and for that, I apologize. The bottom line is that we can't commit relief funds without verification. That's why I'm here. That probably seems hard to believe, for you, when the proof is all around you, but in New York, they can't rely on word of mouth or satellite photographs, so they sent me. I was hoping to take with me a list of what your needs are."

"What our *needs* are?" Warner said. She exchanged glances with Cela, and then the two women laughed, a prolonged chuckle despite the Englishwoman's best efforts to suppress her mirth. "Oh dear, that's rich," she said. "I'm so sorry," she said at last, "we're not laughing at you, really we aren't, but I think the first thing we'd need would be a very long roll of paper upon which to write you a list of the things we need. Maybe it would save time if we told you what we don't need. We don't need dirt. Or fresh air. Everything other than that, we need."

"We're also worried about security," MacKenzie said, sticking to her agenda. "My superiors are worried about relief supplies falling into the wrong hands."

"And whose hands would those be, exactly?" Warner said.

"Maybe you could tell me," Mack said. "The Council on Relief is concerned that anything we bring in will be seized by IPAB forces led by John Dari—that sort of thing."

Again, Warner exchanged glances with Cela.

"Well, first of all," she said, "you should tell your bosses to get it straight, because John Dari doesn't lead IPAB forces. The people he leads don't call themselves anything, though I've heard them referred to as the SJD or the 'Sons of John Dari.' And second of all, this oh-so-delicious corn-soy porridge that Cela and I have just supped on, of which you will also surely partake if you stay with us, may have been originally shipped by Oxfam or President Bo or the U.S. or whoever wants to take credit for it, but it was delivered into our hands by John Dari's men after it sat in a warehouse on a government air force base in Baku for God only knows how long, so you should tell your 'superiors,' if I may use that word, that John Dari is not your problem."

Mack felt like she was being scolded by a kindergarten teacher.

"Forgive me, Mary, I don't mean to snap at you," Warner said, "because I know it's not your fault, but you should know that while people elsewhere spend time arguing about who to give aid to or how to get it here or who should transport it or who gets credit for where it comes from and all that sod-off crap, the people here who are waiting for it are dying, in great numbers, every day, in this camp and in others. So when we see people on 'fact-finding' missions, we tend to think, my God, if they could just send one shipment of food for every observer and famine-tourist they think they need to send, real people would be alive."

MacKenzie stood still while Cela gave Evelyn Warner a look.

"Now I must ask you, with all the humility I can summon, Mary Dorsey, to forgive me," Warner said. "That was completely out of line. You've just arrived, you mean good entirely, and I've gone and made you feel like you're to blame. You know, the thing is, we've actually noticed this—Stephen and I were talking about it. You live here and you get very angry, and it builds and builds inside you, but we all feel the same thing, so what's the point in talking about it? And then someone new comes along, and we dump on them, just because we have somebody new to dump on. Can you forgive me?"

"Of course I can," MacKenzie said. "Of course. You wouldn't be human if you didn't feel that way."

"Human? Speak for yourself, but I won't be 100 percent human again until I can get a nice dry martini and a big red steak," Warner said, getting to her feet. "If you'll forgive me, I really need to find Dr. Chaline, but maybe Cela could show you the nursery. Cela? Would you mind? Take Corporal Okempo with you. I think that would be a good place to start. We can show you the rest in the morning. Give you more *facts* than I imagine you really want to find, but it is why you're here, isn't it?"

Mack followed the black woman, who said she was Kenyan by birth but had lived in Liger since she was a teenager. Corporal George Okempo looked younger than advertised, a lanky man with a broad smile and big ears that stuck out from the edge of his blue beret. He carried his weapon awkwardly, as if he were trying to not carry it, or to hide it. The nursery was another GP-large, about fifty feet from the staff area, lit inside by a single kerosene lantern in the middle, propped up on a wooden crate. In the tent, Mack saw the faces of perhaps thirty or forty children, ranging in age from newborns to five-year-olds, some held by older girls but many who were alone. A large woman in the middle of the room sat on a short stool, surrounded by children gathered at her feet.

"These children," Cela said softly, so as not to disturb the proceedings, her accent thick, "have no mothers or fathers. This is the orphanage, yes? Some came here with them and their parents died, but some were alone when we found them. A few have AIDS, but mostly no. The queen mother, the woman there, is telling them a story."

The large woman in the center of the circle took a small stick, stuck the tip of it into the flame of the kerosene lamp, and then used it to light two dozen candles on a large unfrosted birthday cake. The children's faces lit up as the woman lit the candles.

"The government said they were sending us a million candles," Cela explained. "And we were glad until we learned that they were only birthday candles. So we have parties, whenever a new child enters, we say it is his or her birthday."

The old woman asked the children a question, and the children responded with a loud cheer.

"She asks them if they would like to hear a monster story," Cela said, translating as the woman spoke, leaning forward conspiratorially, gesturing broadly with her expressive hands. "Once upon a time, a monster lived in a jungle near a volcano. He is picked up in a truck accidentally and goes to the city, and when the sun comes up, he runs and hides in a bakery."

MacKenzie leaned in, even though she didn't understand a word. The queen mother had an animated, dramatic speaking style.

"So when the baker comes," Cela translated as the woman spoke, "the monster hides in a flour bin. He is only so big, like a bush baby, but with long scary teeth. So the baker scoops it up accidentally, because she does not see it, and then she puts the monster in a cake mix, and then in the oven, but the monster is from the volcano, yes? So it likes the heat in the oven and falls asleep and wakes up inside the cake."

The children giggled.

"Do they have birthdays and cakes in Liger?" Mack asked. Cela shook her head.

"We tell them about what the children in America do," she said. "Some of them hope to go to America. So the monster wakes up and hears children singing the birthday song, and then he hears the little girl tell her mother, 'Mother, give me the knife and let me cut the cake, because I'm old enough now, I think. Nothing will go wrong.' She pokes the cake with the knife and the monster giggles because it tickles."

The children tittered again.

"And then a child at the party dips his finger in the frosting and the cake giggles again. Oh, no—what will happen next? So all the children at the party lean in, and then the birthday girl puts the knife in the cake . . . and then . . . the monster jumps out of the cake and shouts, 'Hey now, what is it that you're trying to do to me?' And the children run away!"

The camp orphans screamed with delight, laughing and hugging each other in mock fear.

"But then they come back, the children, and they are angry, and they say, 'You bad monster, you ate all our cake—give it back!' And the monster says, 'I will get you another one,' so he goes back to the bakery and returns with a great big cake and he says, 'Now children, here it is, but I cannot guarantee that there isn't a monster in this one, too.' And the children, no matter how much they want to, they cannot eat it because they are afraid, and so they leave, and do you know what? The monster eats the second cake too!"

Again the children howled. The storyteller waited until they had quieted down.

"And do you know what the moral of the story is?" the narrator asked them. They shook their heads. "Well," Cela translated, "there are two. First, just because there is a monster in the first cake doesn't mean there's a monster in the second one. That is the first moral. And the second lesson is, never listen to a monster, because they do not tell the truth."

She brought out the cake, which was made out of mud, and then the child who was being honored blew out the candles, and the others clapped.

It was all MacKenzie could do to keep from crying.

DeLuca was in his room at the Hotel Liger in Baku Da'al, standing on the balcony that overlooked the central market, when his SATphone chirtled. The central market was closed for the night, a handful of colorful canopies and umbrellas lit from below by dim light bulbs or the glow of television sets powered by gas generators where the merchants lived in their stalls. As he answered his phone, the lights of the city extinguished themselves in unison, save those powered by generators, Baku having power only for two hours of electricity in the evening and two in the afternoon. On the phone, Zoulalian explained that all was well, and that an agent of Rahjid Waid had met his plane to take him to the IPAB training camp. He wasn't sure when he'd get a chance to report in next.

"My driver doesn't think much of the recruits they're getting," Zoulalian said. "He used an Arabic word that translates more or less as 'hillbillies.' Personally, I always thought the concept of 'Islamic brotherhood' was a contradiction in terms. They don't get along any better than anybody else. Anyway, if you're a veteran from Iraq, you're pretty much golden around here. Thanks for getting Khalil on the blacklist—it can only help. By the way, I don't know if it means anything, but my driver's never heard of John Dari. Maybe the guy's keeping his head down even inside the brotherhood, but I found that odd. Gotta go."

The next call came from MacKenzie. DeLuca wasn't surprised to hear that Evelyn Warner was in country—she was the sort of person who went wherever she damned well wanted to go, one of those people the Pentagon hated, always insisting on showing, in her television news reports for the BBC, the cost of war in human terms, the collateral damage, "all that kid-crying-with-no-pants-on shit," as DeLuca's former commander in Iraq had called it, adding, "Why don't they ever talk about the good that we do?" That commander had resigned when an investigation indicated that he'd given his men an order to fire on a group of Iraqis who were trying to surrender, including an eight-year-old boy; now the guy was showing up on Fox News, talking about "the good that we do."

DeLuca found Evelyn Warner a bit more credible. Perhaps it was because he'd spent twelve hours being held hostage with her, and another twenty-four crossing the Iranian border with her, but he knew her to be brilliant and resourceful and good company, even with her hands flex-cuffed behind her back and a bag over her head. There'd been an attraction, but that was all. Mack told him what Warner had said about John Dari.

"Could you run the name 'Stephen Ackroyd' for me?" Mack said. "He's a journalist I met here. It's not a lead, I think. I'm just curious."

DeLuca used his CIM to Google the name, but nothing turned up. He sent Walter Ford a quick e-mail, asking him to run a more thorough search, then went down to the bar, taking the stairs when he remembered that the elevators weren't working.

The hotel bar was in the corner of the ground floor, open-aired on two sides, filled with wing-back rattan chairs and leather sofas polished from use, potted palms, rattan footstools, a terra-cotta-tiled floor, woven grass rugs and African masks on the walls, the walls painted a lovely periwinkle blue, offset by trim painted a high-gloss white. There was a monkey cage the size of an elevator car by the door to the lobby, empty, and a wall of bookshelves where travelers were free to take a paperback they hadn't read yet on the condition that they leave one they had. A second large cage containing two huge blue parrots sat by the front door, where the parrots served as greeters, though neither seemed particularly hospitable today.

The hotel front opened onto a large veranda with broad low eaves to protect against the tropical rains, the view blocked by a bank of sandbags six feet high, and a concierge's desk manned by four soldiers carrying machine guns, but other than that, the lounge retained its colonial charm, accented by the candle globes on the tables and bar. There were bamboo groves and fragrant flowering plants, the yard in front of the hotel landscaped with date palms and fan palms and bird-of-paradise and hypernic plants within its walls, the palms shading small circles of Adirondack-style chairs, unoccupied.

There were two bartenders, both young men in white shirts. When DeLuca asked if the kitchen was still open, he was assured that it was, so he asked for a menu. He ordered chicken, only to be told that they were out of chicken. He tried the rock lobster, but they were out of that, too.

"What's the special of the day?" he asked.

"Beefsteak," the bartender said softly.

"I'll have that, then," he said.

"I am sorry, but we don't have it," the bartender apologized.

"Do you have any food at all?" DeLuca asked.

"No," the man said.

"All right, then," DeLuca said. "I'll just have a Guinness. That's a meal in a glass anyway."

The bartender smiled.

DeLuca moved to a poker game in the corner of the room where six middle-aged men were playing Texas Hold 'Em, a large loose stack of paper Zudas in the middle of the table, next to a kerosene lantern, its wick turned up just to the point where it was starting to smoke. He stood behind an empty chair for a few minutes, watching. Finally a white-haired man in a black short-sleeved shirt spoke with a South African accent.

"If you're waiting for an invitation, you're not going to get one," he said. "If you want to lose all your money to us, you must do so of your own free will—otherwise you're going to think we're taking advantage of you."

"What's the buy-in?" he asked.

"One million Zudas," a second man said. "Which, I believe, is about one dollar and thirty-eight cents, American."

"Pretty steep," DeLuca said, sitting down. The man in the black shirt threw in his cards and offered DeLuca his hand to shake.

"Tom Kruger, Fox News," the man said.

"Don Brown, World Bank," DeLuca said, shaking his hand and giving him a dollar to change. Rather than count, the man simply grabbed a handful of bills and handed it to DeLuca.

"World Bank," Kruger said, as if he were impressed. "That means you have deep pockets, Mr. Brown, because I happen to personally know that the World Bank has well over a jillion Zudas in its reserves, and I intend to win them."

"Roddy Hamilton," the dealer next to him said, offering DeLuca his hand. He had a British accent, in his early thirties, thin, with a long neck, big ears, close-cropped hair, and a prominent forehead. "*London Times*/Associated Press. And this is Robert, but don't tell him anything because he's a spy."

The man he called Robert said nothing. He was slightly paunchy, slightly slouched, and listing to the left, dressed in a blue striped oxford shirt with the sleeves rolled up to his elbows and a navy vest, unbuttoned, the tie around his neck loosened and askew, his eyes watching the cards behind horn-rimmed glasses, in his late forties, but he seemed older, wearier, with good hair and more of it than he deserved, in DeLuca's opinion.

"And don't talk about women," the man next to the CIA agent said with a German accent. He was about forty, with blond hair, and he wore wraparound black sunglasses. "He just got a 'Dear Robert' letter from his wife saying she was leaving him. And now the poor fellow is alone and overweight and he drinks too much and he's stuck here in Baku Da'al in a career that is going nowhere. And he's ugly."

"Spoken with the depth of compassion you Germans are so justly known for," Robert said. "Does Reuters actually pay you a salary, Kurt, or do they just expect you to loot and pillage to support yourself?"

The fifth player was the oldest, perhaps sixty, wearing purple plaid pants, a maroon and yellow rugby shirt, and a blue seersucker sport coat, his reading glasses dangling from a chain around his neck, large bushy eyebrows and gray hair swept back from his face. He was drinking sweet vermouth and lime from a large pilsner glass and appeared to be completely sloshed, his eyes glazed over but twinkling all the same.

"Elliot is with *Connoisseur* magazine," Roddy Hamilton said. "Your fellow American. Doing a story on the wine industry of Liger, of which there will be nothing left by the time he's polished off the national inventory."

"*Connoisseur*?" DeLuca said. "Really?"

"Something of a mix-up," Elliot said. "Some press junkets are better planned than others. You now know the five remaining white men in Baku. Our Arab friend here is Hassan bin-Adel, but don't bother him—he has a hard time concentrating when he's about to bluff."

The sixth man looked up from his cards but didn't say anything.

"He's with Al Jazeera," Elliot said. "Didn't smoke or drink until he met us, but look at him now—one of the boys. We're so proud of him."

"You are the son of Satan and will die a thousand horrible deaths at the hands of the jihadi martyrs," Hassan spat. "And by the way, Arabs never bluff. Are you going to deal the cards, Roddy, or are we going to simply *chat* the night away?"

Hamilton dealt. DeLuca folded a six-ten off-suited. The flop turned red queens and the seven of clubs.

"Any of you guys know a guy named Stephen Ackroyd?" he asked. "I met him in Port Ivory."

A chuckle spread around the table.

"You met Grasshopper?" Hamilton said, betting one hundred thousand Zudas.

"Thank God he's all right," Kruger said, calling the bet. "I was afraid somebody would have made him into a casserole by now."

"He'd be very tender, wouldn't he?" Kurt said, licking his lips in a mocking fashion. He tossed his cards violently into the pot. "What do you say, Elliot—does your magazine have any good recipes for pretentious young writers?"

"Sucker tartare," Elliot said, looking at his cards again before betting. "You really don't want to overcook them, because they're already half-baked."

"Oh, good one," Kruger said sarcastically. "Mr. Brown, we tease because we love. Mr. Ackroyd has the unfortunate habit of telling people they're not doing their jobs, without ever having done one himself. I think he grew up with too much money."

The turn was a ten of clubs, the river an ace. Hamilton won the pot with a full house, queens over aces.

"If you see him, tell him we miss him," the German said. "Tell him we need him to give us more of his advice. Tell him this time we promise to fold our hands when he's bluffing instead of calling him because we knew every time what he was doing. If you play cards with him, Mr. Brown, watch when he starts blinking his eyes rapidly. It means he's lying."

When DeLuca sat out a hand to get another beer from the bar, the man he knew only as Robert joined him, signaling to the bartender that he would pay for DeLuca's beer and wanted one for himself.

"I hope you're not staying long," he said to DeLuca. "Not to sound unfriendly, but this place is a hellhole—I wouldn't wish anybody to stay long. Bob Mohl." He offered his hand. DeLuca shook it.

"A week at best," he said. "I'll be in and out, but we're headquartering here. My associates are arranging for a car right now."

"You have security?"

"We have travel papers," DeLuca said.

"I hope they have pictures of Benjamin Franklin on the front," Mohl said. "What sort of work will you be doing?"

"Land conservancy research," DeLuca said. "Deforestation. With Conservation International."

"Who've you got, handling your payouts inside the government?"

DeLuca shrugged.

"I'm sure the World Bank has people, but I might be able to recommend somebody if you'd like. I know a man who'll know who to grease and won't take anything off the top beyond what you pay him. That's about all you can really hope for."

"Are you really a spy?" DeLuca asked him. He wasn't sure yet whether to tell Mohl that David Letterman went to his high school.

Mohl straightened up and gave a mock salute.

"Serving your espionage needs since the National Security Act of 1947." He slouched again, leaning heavily against the bar. "Don't listen to them. I'm just a lowly

Boeing executive trying to sell a few planes. I sold Burkina Faso the only two airplanes they owned, and then they hit each other. Just remember—in Liger, there's no such thing as an NGO—nothing is nongovernment. Bo has a hand, or at least a finger, in everything. No banky, no panky."

Mohl sipped his beer, staring thoughtfully for a moment at the candle burning on the bar.

"Too bad about the power shortage," he said. "The air-conditioning doesn't do a damn thing, but I miss the ceiling fans."

"Were they teasing about your wife?" DeLuca asked.

"No, no they weren't," Mohl said with a weak smile. "But don't worry—that's been over for years. Are you married, Mr. Brown?"

DeLuca nodded.

"Happily?"

DeLuca nodded.

"You know what the secret to a happy marriage is?"

DeLuca shook his head. Robert Mohl leaned in, lowering his voice conspiratorially to a near-whisper.

"Don't get drunk every night and don't have affairs. And if she hits you, don't hit her back. You follow those rules and you'll be just fine."

Chapter Seven

"NEW DEVELOPMENT," THE VOICE ON DELUCA'S SATphone said. "Sorry to wake you. You're not busy, are you?"

"How could I be busy at 5:00 A.M.?" DeLuca said. "I was having a helluva dream, though."

"Mefloquine?" Phil LeDoux said.

"No doubt," DeLuca said. "Sometimes I think I'd rather have the malaria."

"No, you don't," LeDoux said, and DeLuca knew his friend was speaking from experience. "Anyway, back to real-life nightmares. Last night a chartered C-130J landed at Liger International containing seventy-two mercenaries, all of them white, about half South African and a quarter Russian and the rest a mix. The leadership is British. The top guy is Major Simon Bell, ex-SAS."

"Is this Artemis Corp. or something different?"

"Something different," LeDoux said.

"Okay," DeLuca said. "What's it to me?"

"It's this," LeDoux said. "Bo knew. He had his Presidential Guard meet the plane. The mercenaries are sitting in a hangar at the airfield, under heavy guard. Bell is being interrogated, but he's not going to give anything up.

I suspect he's the only one who really knows what the mission was. Him and us."

"We know?" DeLuca said.

"MI-6 surveillance," LeDoux said.

"They briefed us?"

"Not exactly," LeDoux said. "The mission was to take out Dari. Not that we're necessarily opposed. The sponsor is WAOC. The broker is a guy named Hugh Lloyd. He chartered the Hercules. MI-6 has their panties in a twist. Guess why?"

"I'll take a stab and say Hugh Lloyd is related to somebody," DeLuca said.

"Good instincts," LeDoux said. "His father is Alistair Lloyd, former MP and the current PM's chief advisor."

"Again, what's it to me?" DeLuca said. "Or to us, I should say."

"Nothing, a week from now," LeDoux said. "Until then, everything. Liberty barely has the appearance of a coalition. We have the British, the Poles, and Spain, for now, and only the British are sending ground troops. Hugh Lloyd apparently hasn't spoken to his father in twenty years, but the blood connection still pairs English interests with big oil, since the old man is so close to Blair. If this breaks in the media, we could lose British support. We don't want that, any more than we want MI-6 to know we've been hacking their SIGINT. The problem is, we don't have a lot of assets in country right now to keep their ears open. We don't expect you to be able to keep this down, but we'd like to know it's going to explode, a few minutes before it explodes, if that's possible."

DeLuca considered a moment.

"Maybe I'm being completely dense," he said, "but

I'm still not quite sure why you're telling me. Why not tell CIA? Wait a minute. I get it. MI-6 is hacking Langley."

"We could go there," LeDoux said, "but we have better things to do, don't we? If we're lucky, our seventy-two mercenary friends sit in their hangar playing Twister, Simon Bell is released, or somebody pays Daniel Bo a few million pounds to let them go, they get back on the plane, and nobody's ever the wiser. If we're not lucky, it blows up, the Brits pull out, and John Dari and his friends have even more reasons to kill white people. I've got a meeting with Hans Berger in twenty minutes and I'm going to ask him what's going on. He may or may not tell me."

"You could always dangle him from a helicopter," DeLuca suggested.

"It didn't stop you, did it?" LeDoux said. "There's one other reason to let you know. You knew that Evelyn Warner, your old friend, is working in Liger?"

"I'd heard that," DeLuca said. "I wasn't making any plans to see her."

"Well, if you do, you should know that Hugh Lloyd, Lord Lloyd, was her first husband. First and only. That might be something you could use. Obviously, she's media, so if she has any contact with her ex—did they have children, do you know?"

"She never mentioned any. I doubt it. Thanks for the heads-up," DeLuca said. "Now if you'll excuse me, if I'm lucky, I still have enough mefloquine in my system for one last bad dream before my real day starts."

He closed his eyes, but when sleep wouldn't come, he turned on his CIM and used his satellite uplink to log onto the Internet, where he found an e-mail from Walter Ford waiting for him.

David,

Greetings and salutations. The boys at Doyles were asking about you. Sami says hello as well and to call him when you get back, but not before then.

A couple things. I Googled "Stephen Ackroyd" (also "Steven Ackroyd") and got nothing. There's a guy by that name in Alaska studying waterfowl, but I don't think that's who you mean. If this guy's a writer, I can't find anything he's published, but maybe he means literary quarterlies and that sort of thing. Not everything is online. Sorry.

Also, see attached or go to www.transparency.org (or www.globalsecurity.org) for the latest on corruption in Liger. I know you don't have time to download, so in brief (forgive repetitions from previous e-mail), it started before the current President Bo and before his father (British colonial), but kicked into high gear in the late sixties when oil was discovered—the linkage between WAOC members and various ministries is profound/historical. WAOC was basically founded to coordinate the bribes the oil companies had to pay to everybody from the oil minister to Education to Transportation to commissioner of national parks fees/ licenses/inspectors/special taxes, etc. Liger, Norway, and UK were the only countries that stood by U.S. during the first oil crisis in the early seventies and Liger essentially helped break OPEC's back. In return, *gratitude, etc., we sold them weapons—nothing new about that, long history there of countries trading guns for whatever Africa has to offer. Estimates say $3–4 per barrel goes into Bo's pockets or trickles down from there, and maybe 100,000 barrels a day goes missing entirely. Transparency International estimates Bo has a personal fortune of maybe $65 billion in Swiss accounts. That's not a typo—billion with a "B."*

Some thought he was cooking the goose that laid the golden eggs before they hatched, so to speak, when he talked about nationalizing the oil industry. Two schools of thought on that—one, he's bluffing to extort higher kickbacks, after a huge new find of oil in the northeast, Kum territory (estimated 12 mil. bpd × 50 yr. once exploited or 219 billion barrels). The find is officially just a rumor, but the people at TI say it's for real. The bluff is that Liger doesn't have the infrastructure or the human knowhow to run their own oil industry, and the U.S. can't afford the dip in production that would occur while they got up to speed, were they to attempt it. The second thought, however, and the big fear, is that Liger might not have the know-how but IPAB does—Arabs know plenty about oil. Would Bo bring in IPAB? Right now, they're coming whether he wants them or not, and he's a survivor who is likely to cut a deal. Either way, it's something up with which WAOC cannot put.

Thought you'd be interested. Let me know if there's anything else I can do.

Walter

When Dan Sykes knocked on the door to the penthouse suite at the Port Ivory Hilton, he expected to be met by a large entourage. A contingent of soldiers had been waiting downstairs and in the lobby, and he'd assumed they were there to escort the actress, but he'd supposed there would be others, stylists and hairdressers and such. He was surprised when she answered the door herself.

"Who are you?" she asked him.

"Dan Sykes," he said. "Blackwood Security. I think you've been expecting me."

She stared at him. She was easily the most beautiful person he'd ever seen in his life.

"I'm with Blackwood Security," he repeated, reaching for his ID. "They sent me."

She scrutinized his identification.

"Who's 'they'?" she asked.

"The people insuring your next picture, I believe," he said. "Apparently they're going to feel better if I'm here."

"No one told me anything," she said. "I have thirty government soldiers traveling with me. Why do I need more security?"

"Because thirty-one is better than thirty," Sykes said. "Plus I speak English."

"I would prefer to have a black head of security," she said. "Don't misunderstand me, Mr. Sykes. My father was white. I'm thinking only of the political climate in this country. I'm simply trying to do everything possible to make certain that I accomplish what I came here for."

"I understand," he said. "And I am here to help you. You're free, of course, to hire somebody else, but I don't know who you're going to get, given, as you put it, the political climate. I have a sixth-degree black belt in karate and I'm certified on anything from a pocketknife to an M-4."

He was still standing in the hallway. The actress was dressed in khaki shorts and a white shirt with the sleeves rolled up, a tan bandana around her neck, white socks, and hiking boots.

She remained suspicious.

"Just tell me one thing," she said. "What do you think of me?"

"As an actress?" he said.

"No," she said. "What do you think of me being here?"

"You're a special UN ambassador," he said. "That's good."

"I want you to tell me what you really think," she said. "I read a story before I left comparing me to Jane Fonda, visiting North Vietnam."

"You came anyway," Sykes said. "That means you believe in what you're doing."

"Do you think I should be here?" she asked.

"I think this country is a very dark place," Sykes said. "Dark places need light. And bright lights follow you wherever you go."

"Good answer," she said. "Come in, please. I'm almost ready." She began sorting through stacks of documents spread out on her bedspread. "Don't get me wrong, Mr. Sykes—for reasons that still sometimes baffle me, I do understand that I have a hugely disproportionate amount of attention on me. I don't claim to deserve it, but since I have it anyway, I goddamn well intend to use it properly. I'm here to make sure that for as many nights as possible, the nightly news and the *New York Post* and *Inside Edition* and whoever else runs pictures of what's going on here, even though I'm sure to get hammered in the press by writers who'll say I'm just some idiot actress, in over her head, talking about things she doesn't understand."

"You know that President Bo isn't going to let you see anything he doesn't want you to see, don't you?" Sykes said. He saw a framed photograph of a smiling black child on the bedstand. "It that your son?"

"Jonathan," she nodded. "So you're ex-military—is that correct, Mr. Sykes?"

"Call me Dan," Sykes said. "And yes, I am. Counter-intelligence."

"Call me Gabby. And what is that?" she asked, taking an orange juice from the minibar and offering him one. He declined. She shook her drink. "That sounds like the opposite of intelligence, which would be stupidity."

"That's only true of the leadership positions," Sykes said. "Counterintelligence is to the military police what the FBI or the CIA is to your local police. That's the best way to describe it."

"Have you ever killed anybody, Dan?" she asked.

"Yes," he told her. "In combat, I have. That's what soldiers do."

She looked at him again, hesitating.

"I suppose it means you understand something that I don't. Okay, you can stay," she said.

"What would you like me to do?"

She glanced about the room, her eyes falling on a metal suitcase with formidable-looking clasps on it, the case the size of a large overhead bag, and then on her purse, which she picked up and opened.

"You can do two things," she told him. "The silver Zero case is your responsibility. If I said, 'Guard it with your life,' would you take that literally?"

"I guard people with my life," Sykes said. "Suitcases, I need a little more information. What's in it?"

She hesitated.

"I suppose I have to trust you, don't I?" she said, biting her lip. "The case contains the scripts for *Star Wars VII, VIII,* and *IX.* The cover pages are bogus, but the scripts are real."

"I thought there weren't going to be any more," Sykes said.

"That's what you're supposed to think," Gabby said. "I play Han Solo and Princess Leia's daughter. If those scripts get stolen and/or leaked onto the Internet, the whole thing falls apart. I also want you to make arrangements for me to meet this man."

She handed him a piece of paper with the name *Hubert Nketia* written on it, along with an address.

"This is in Kumari," Sykes said. "The last I heard, you're going to need more than thirty troops to get to Kumari. LPLF roadblocks start just north of Baku."

"Hubert helped me when I adopted Jonathan," she said. "He knows everybody in Kumari. He's told me he'll arrange for rebel troops to meet us halfway and escort us. You just get us there. Have you heard of a man named John Dari?"

"I have," Sykes said.

"I'm going to be meeting with him after I meet Hubert," Duquette said.

"Why are you meeting with Nketia?" Sykes asked.

"That would be my business, wouldn't it?" the woman said.

MacKenzie awoke to the sound of men shouting. When she stuck her head out of her tent, she saw three girls running in the opposite direction, their bare feet pounding the dust. At the same time, a girl in a green jumper, resembling something like a Girl Scout, approached her out of breath and said something in a language Mack didn't understand.

"I speak English," MacKenzie said.

"Dr. Chaline," the girl said. "I have to find Dr. Chaline."

"I don't know where he is," MacKenzie said. "I just woke up."

The girl ran off.

Mack quickly dressed and ran to the scene of the shouting. Nine men carrying machetes had entered the camp and were having a violent discussion with Evelyn Warner and an older African male who was trying to translate for her. Corporal Okempo, holding his rifle at an angle across his chest, stood at her side. Mack thought he looked frightened out of his mind. The leader of the men with machetes was wearing a bright green shirt. He was bald, about forty, and spoke with his machete raised in the air to accent his speech. He shouted, pointing toward the refugees, and at his compatriots, who seemed equally angry and equally dangerous.

Mack found Cela hanging back from the center of the dispute.

"What's going on?" she asked Cela. "What do they want?"

"I'm trying to understand," Cela said. "They are looking for a girl named Sara Ochora. They think she is here."

"Is she?" Mack asked.

Cela nodded.

"What do they want with her?"

"The man in the green shirt is explaining," Cela says. "Sara Ochora was promised to his brother, but now he is dead. The brother is dead, who she was betrothed to. So the man in the green shirt is claiming her as his right."

"What did Sara have to say about the betrothal?"

"This happened before she was born," Cela said. "The man in the green shirt is saying she has shed blood in an unclean way and now his ancestors have taken high offense, and the gods have, too. This is why these calamities have been happening to him and to his family and his village."

"I don't understand," Mack said.

"Shh," Cela said, listening a moment longer. "He says she had sex with four men before her nubility rites. She was not purified and so she has committed *kyiribra*. This is a moral depravity. Her cousin reported her to these men and told them where they could find her. The cousin was obligated to do this. And so misery will come and befall them until she has been taken back and removed from her abominable state."

Evelyn Warner spoke with an equal vehemence, the man at her side doing his best to keep up with the translations.

"Tell him she was raped," Warner said. "Tell him it's the men who did this to her who have upset his ancestors and not Sara."

The man in the green shirt screamed again.

"He says that it was voluntary," Cela said.

"No!" Warner shouted. "No, not with four men! They

told her if she didn't go with them, that they would kill her family."

"They kill them anyway!" the man in the green shirt shouted in English before returning to his native tongue. His grip on his machete appeared to tighten.

"He says she should have let them kill her rather than submit to them," Cela translated. "He says they will take her with them—oh, my God!"

The man in the green shirt knocked the old man down, then pushed Evelyn Warner aside as she tried to stand her ground. A second man grabbed Warner, holding her by the arm. When Corporal Okempo tried to intercede, three men knocked him down. Mack stepped forward.

"Stop!" MacKenzie ordered, standing in front of him and holding her hand up. "Let her go. United Nations—if you have a complaint, you can bring it to me."

The would-be husband regarded her for a split second, scowled, knocked her hand aside, and brushed past her.

Mack drew her service Beretta and pointed it at the man, ordering him to stop.

Green Shirt froze.

She moved in front of them, holding the sidearm with both hands, then pointed it at the man who was restraining Evelyn Warner.

"Let her go!" Mack commanded. "Everyone lay down your weapons. Now!" The raiding party paused but kept their weapons. She raised the pistol, aiming it squarely between Green Shirt's eyes. He tipped his head back, smirking, defiant, so she stepped closer, lowering the weapon until it was pointed at his balls.

He dropped the weapon. His clan members dropped theirs as well.

"Everyone lie down," she commanded. "On your stomachs. Corporal, bring those two over here. Everybody down, now! Cela—help me out here. Tell them what I want."

Corporal Okempo regained his authority and came to her assistance, covering the men with a fierce expression on his face, shouting at them in a tongue Mack couldn't identify. She'd grabbed a handful of flex cuffs from her bag and used them, quickly moving from prisoner to prisoner until she'd bound each man's hands behind his back, looping the cuff through their belts whenever possible. She looped a heavy orange extension cord through their arms and around a mango tree before tying it off with a reef knot to deter them from fleeing, and when she was done, she told Okempo to come back with enough men to control the situation. She finally commanded Cela to take some girls with strong arms and throw the machetes into the river, as far out as they could throw them.

Evelyn Warner had been tending to the old man, picking him up and dusting him off. He seemed to be all right. She sent him away, then approached MacKenzie.

"Are you all right?" Mack asked her.

"Thank you, Mary, I'm all right," Warner said. "You?"

"I'm well," MacKenzie said. "What'll we do with these fellows, though?"

"I've sent for the queen mother," Evelyn said. "The matriarch of their clan. She happens to be here, too." Warner leaned in and whispered. "I don't know who you are, or what your real name is, but you're not with the United Nations Women's Health Initiative—that much is certain."

"I don't know what you mean," MacKenzie said. "I grew up with six brothers, that's all. A girl learns quickly how to handle herself under such circumstances."

Warner held her arms out in front if her, her forearms touching hand to elbow, made horns with her top hand and waggled the fingers on her bottom hand, which MacKenzie recognized as American Sign Language slang for "bullshit."

When the queen mother arrived, an older woman who walked with a cane, accompanied by two attendants, Warner and Cela explained to her what had happened. The old woman listened, then went to the man in the green shirt. She spoke scoldingly at first, then listened to him for fifteen minutes as he pled his case to her. When he was done, the old woman stood and walked around in contemplation for a few minutes before returning to him to explain her decision to him. Cela translated for Warner and MacKenzie.

"She says to him she will perform *anoka* to reverse the *kyiribra*," Cela explained. "And pour libations to *Onyankopen, Aasse Yaa, nananom abosompem* and *nananom nsamamfoe*. To God, the earth, the thousand gods of the ancestors, and to the spirits of the dead. She will cover Sara Ochora's genitals with the blood of a sheep and break an egg over her head. Then Sara must agree to never return to her village. This will lift the curse and bring peace to his tribe."

"Why didn't I think of that?" MacKenzie said.

Mack was in her tent, going over what had happened in her head and wondering if there might have been a better way to handle the situation, when Warner entered and sat on the cot opposite hers. Mack smiled weakly. Warner took a tape recorder out of her pocket, took the microcassette out of the recorder, and laid the two pieces on the cot.

"This is off the record," Warner said. "I'm going to need to know who you are. I can't force you to tell me, but what I can do is tell Dr. Chaline my suspicions, and he'll have you removed. I suspect you have good reasons to be here, but I'm not going to let you stay here and jeopardize the lives of all these women—don't interrupt me."

Mack opened her mouth, then closed it.

"It's just too fragile here to have to factor in an unknown element," Warner said. "You may not have noticed it, but we're having our little tea party here on the top of the proverbial powder keg. We're about three minutes away from utter chaos at all times, so if you don't talk to me, I'm going to have to take you out of the equation. I like you and I'm grateful to you for what you did, and I dare say a little impressed, but enough."

Warner waited.

Mack considered her options. She had none.

"Agent Colleen MacKenzie," she said at last. "United States Army counterintelligence. I'd show you my badge and credentials but we were advised to leave them behind. My boss, David DeLuca, told me not to blow my cover, but if I did, to give you his regards."

"David's here?" Warner said, a smile spreading slowly across her face, warm and forgiving. MacKenzie nodded. "How is he? Last I saw him, he was in hospital with a rather ghastly-looking halo of metal around his head with screws holding it in place."

"Screwy as ever, but all right," Mack said. "He told me I could trust you. I guess I don't have any choice."

"You don't," Warner said, "but you can. Why are you here?"

MacKenzie explained that their assignment was to gather intelligence on John Dari and his followers. She told Warner that Stephen Ackroyd was currently arranging for her to meet with Imam Isfahan Dadullahjid, to see if he might be willing to help. She said her government was concerned with curtailing the influence of the Islamic Pan-African Brotherhood in West Africa.

"And what are you going to do, exactly, with the intelligence you gather on John Dari?" Warner asked.

"We want to gather the facts," Mack said softly. "The truth. What happens to the truth after it leaves our hands is out of our control. I don't personally think we know enough about him to make the call, right now, but I know people are worried that he's either a warlord like the ones we've been dealing with in Afghanistan, or he's the African Osama bin Laden. We just don't know. We have satellite photographs of cannibal gangs doing things, committing atrocities—I've seen them with my own eyes. He calls himself the 'Ace of Spades' like he can't wait for us to make up our Ligerian deck of the fifty-two most wanted. The satellite photographs I saw showed ace of spades playing cards. It's our government's position that what happened in Rwanda in 1994 is not going to happen in Liger."

Warner rolled her eyes.

"What?" Mack said.

"I'm sorry," Warner said. "It just starts to sound a bit disingenuous after a while. I can say that—I'm English. We were the world's moral policemen for a hundred years, and look where it got us." She dropped her voice to a whisper. "And just between us girls, I'm going to take a wild stab and say it has something to do with oil, too."

She winked conspiratorially.

"I think if there'd been a drop of oil in Rwanda, Bill Clinton would have zipped up his pants and been on the job before anybody could say, 'Bob's your uncle.' And unless you have pictures of John Dari himself stirring the pot, don't assume Dari's involved, just because somebody leaves a few aces of spades playing cards around a campsite. I'd be willing to bet the cards are a reference to *Apocalypse Now* and not to Iraq. This place is steeped in American pop culture. That's part of why the Muslims hate you, by the way. Your pop culture is much stronger than theirs."

"Maybe," Mack said. "As our president might say, those who don't repeat history are doomed to study it. I'm trying to stay focused on John Dari."

"Well, you can't really separate him from African history," Warner said. "He's a product of it. I don't think Dadullahjid is going to help you. I have some rather hideous advice, but if you go, let Stephen do the talking. Dadullahjid hates women. Veil and head scarf at the very least. You could ask me about Dari, if you don't think I'm part of the elite liberal media that can't be trusted."

"I'll ask anybody," Mack said. "We know people who knew Dari, but that trail goes cold when he returned to Africa."

"Maybe I can pick it up for you," Warner said. "He worked here. I'm not sure when he started. Hmm. Father Boateng would be able to tell you when exactly."

"Worked here doing what?"

"In the IDPs," Warner said. "When you work in an internally displaced persons camp, you do just about everything from driving a truck to performing surgery. Dr. L'Heureux, who worked at Camp Five and then here briefly before Dr. Chaline, was trying to convince John to go to medical school because he was so good at helping out in the infirmary. I did a story on the famine, long before the war started, in 1999. John Dari was my interpreter. The interpreter the Ligerian Press Office assigned me wasn't telling me what people were actually saying. I found that out when I interviewed Dari. When we were done, John looked at me and said, in perfect English, 'Miss Warner, I think you're being taken advantage of.'"

"You didn't know he spoke English?"

"He didn't want anybody to know," Warner said. "He told me about the famine relief work he'd been doing with the Red Crescent, and how Bo was withholding food from the Kum to starve them intentionally, to get them to move into the IDPs or to other countries. There was an outbreak of plague in one of the camps. The medicine was sitting in a warehouse in Baku Da'al, but the government wouldn't release it, because they claimed the LPLF wouldn't guarantee safe passage for the troops he needed to deliver it. So John Dari got a hundred men and went to the warehouse and took it. He did the same thing when he heard the government was hoarding food supplies. He took his men all the way to Port Ivory to seize a shipment of relief supplies right off the ship. I don't know how much food they finally managed to bring north, but it was the Ligerian equivalent of your Jimmy Doolittle's raid on Japan during World War II—little actual damage done, perhaps, but an enormous psychological effect. After that, people started to seek him out, to join him. I'm not sure at first that he had anything for them to join—he was just trying to keep people from starving to death and using force to do it. I think when General Mfutho declared war against the government in Port Ivory, John Dari probably wanted nothing to do with it."

"But now?"

"But now, I think you know what the 'but now' is. But now is chaos. My ex-husband's family was involved in Liger for years, and my ex-father-in-law used to say, 'If you want to understand Liger, Evy, don't go to Liger—you'll only become hopelessly confused.' I thought he was just being patronizing, the way he was about every-thing else, but once I got here, I understood what he meant."

"What about IPAB?" MacKenzie asked.

"IPAB," Warner said, "right now, is mainly an arms dealer for the locals, with a few tech support people to show them how to plug things in and where to point them. That's not a minor thing—Sammy Adu wreaked havoc in Sierra Leone for years without half the arms IPAB is pouring into the Sahel. In a piss-poor country, it doesn't take much. IPAB is Janjaweed, it's Al Qaeda, it's Ansar Al-Islam, it's whatever sort of displaced terrorist you want to name, but it's not a significant force in Liger, apart from a handful of advisors. Maybe they're waiting in the wings in greater numbers. I don't know. If the United States wants to look for a unifying force in Africa, I'd suggest looking in the mirror. Nothing unites these people more than a common enemy, and that's you, darling."

"And the Ligerian People's Liberation Front?"

"LPLF is Mfutho and the Muslim half of the Ligerian

army. It's also men, and boys, whom he's recruited or co-
erced. He gives them guns and he pays them," Warner
said. "I don't know where he's getting the money to pay
them, but as I understand it, he's made it attractive to join
him. I say he has the Muslim half, but he can't do anything without Dadullahjid's approval. Bo has the Christian half of the army, but if you ask me, General Ngwema
is taking that away from him. There are commanders
under Ngwema who back him, some who back Bo, and
some who're trying to carve out their own little piece of
the pie. There's so much misunderstanding—I've read
that the Ligerian People's Front, the LPF, not to be confused with the LPLF, is an armed force. God, the LPF is a
group of entirely unarmed pacifist missionaries preaching
nonviolence à la Mahatma Gandhi, but they're listed as
aggressors. Factor in Adu's merry band of random psy-
chopaths and twisted teenage murderers, and five or six
independent mercenary militias contracted by WAOC or
the diamond companies or the coffee growers or the
cocoa growers, all acting occasionally in concert but in-
variably in their own self-interest, and the SJD starts to
look pretty good. I don't think the Sons of John Dari are
your biggest problem. Though I'd love to know why
somebody thinks so."

"He's an unknown," Mack said. "Why do you think?"

"He has charisma," Warner said. "That threatens people
who don't have charisma. I would include both your president and my prime minister in that category. Have you
heard of the LRA?"

"Lord's Republican Army," MacKenzie said. "I
thought they were in Uganda."

"They were, and are," Warner said. "Last week, two thousand people fled into southern Sudan because the LRA had stepped up their activities. You know you're in deepest shite when you're fleeing *into* southern bloody Sudan because it's safer than where you've just come from. They're led by Joseph Kony, who, I am not making this up, believes he's possessed by the spirit of an Italian soldier named Lakwena. Lakwena apparently commanded the woman he first possessed, this was two possessions before Kony, to rid Uganda of witchcraft. The LRA supports the Ten Commandments and even added a few of their own, though apparently 'Thou Shalt Not Make Parents Eat Their Own Children or Children Their Parents' wasn't one of them. What Kony does is kidnap boys as young as four and force them to be his soldiers—the initiation ceremony usually involves killing someone else. Once he's indoctrinated them, he gives them weapons and tells them if they smear themselves with shea butter, enemy bullets will bounce off of them. Or pass through them harmlessly, I forget now exactly which it is. I could go on, but here's my point. John Dari was with the LRA for a month, before he managed to escape. He doesn't talk about what happened, but you can imagine. If people naturally follow John Dari, it's because he's one of the most self-invented self-possessed people I've ever met."

"His followers believe he has magical powers," MacKenzie said.

"Americans believe George Washington threw a silver dollar across the Potomac and chopped down a cherry tree and couldn't lie about it," Warner said. "Maybe Africans tend to mythologize a bit more than we Westerners do. Africans do believe in juju. And witchcraft. I doubt John

Dari can control what people believe about him. Why aren't you looking for Samuel Adu? He kills people with his bare hands, on videotape, and then he makes copies and sends them to his friends. He used to be a heavy-weight boxer so he likes to keep in shape by beating people to death and mutilating their bodies. The atrocities his men committed in Sierra Leone are beyond descrip-tion. Why aren't you looking for him?"

"We were assigned Dari," Mack said. "Somebody else has Samuel Adu. We heard he's north of Kumari."

"I heard he's on the other side of that river," Warner said, pointing. "I also heard he's in Port Ivory drinking Long Island iced teas on the beach. You can't trust what you hear in Liger. Which I suppose is precisely why you're here. I'm doing my best to limit my concerns to what's going on right here at IDP-7. Sara Ochora's hardly an isolated case. Do you know what the age of consent is in Liger? Thirteen. In many of the villages, older men of wealth shower young girls, or their families, with gifts and then have sex with them because they think it's the only way to avoid AIDS, but of course, many of the sugar daddies already have it, so the girls become infected."

"I'd read about that in my briefing material," Mack said.

"That said," Warner continued, "we have six women who have death sentences waiting for them in their home villages simply for having sex out of wedlock or before their *anoka* ceremonies. You might think having the queen mother promise that Sara won't come back to her village is something Sara might actually want, but I assure you, she does not. Some of these women don't know anything but their villages, and their extended families—the idea of going home is all that's getting some of these poor girls through. I don't know if you've noticed how this camp is segregated. We have one section for rape victims. One for Muslim girls. One for married women, one for single women, one for Da, one for Kum, one for AIDS victims, one for otherwise sick women, subdivided into those we can save and those we can't. One section where women who are menstruating have to go, not because we say they have to go but because it's their custom to 'go behind the house.' Last month we had a woman doing female circumcisions until we talked her out of it, but we didn't force her to stop. The idea is to make this place feel as much like home as possible. Which isn't possible. Sara Ochora owes you her life, but living it out in exile, away from her home village, is hardly a happy ending. By the way, if you see our friend in the green shirt again, be careful. He thinks you're a witch. It's the red hair. In this part of Africa, witches are identified by light emanating from the body."

"I told the woman at the salon to go easy on the highlights," Mack said.

"He's told his friends the reason he was powerless to fight you was that you cast a spell on him," Warner said. "Fear of getting his balls shot off played no part. Unfortunately, now, if he dies, he won't be able to join his ancestors and he'll have to live as a ghost. His only recourse is to kill the witch who cast the spell on him."

"Terrific," Mack said. "I'll be careful."

They were interrupted by a man of about fifty, handsome, wearing a soiled white shirt with the sleeves rolled up, a stethoscope dangling from his neck. He seemed in a hurry. MacKenzie understood the man to be Dr. Claude

Chaline, the head of the team from Docteurs Sans Frontières. Her fate was in Evelyn Warner's hands—she could blow Mack's cover or not. Chaline would send MacKenzie away simply because her presence in the camp increased the danger to everyone, despite how she'd handled the Sara Ochora situation, merely because she was U.S. Army.

"Claude," Warner said. "This is Mary Dorsey. United Nations Women's Health Initiative. We've been showing her around a bit."

"The one from earlier?" Dr. Chaline said.

Mack nodded.

"Why do you have a weapon?" he asked, suspicious. "Who taught you how to use it?"

"I was trained at the UN," Mack said. "We're authorized to arm ourselves. Since Rwanda."

Chaline accepted her explanation at face value.

"Do you have medical training, Mary Dorsey?" he asked.

"I'm a certified EMT," she said. "But it's been a while since I've done any work as one."

"Wash your hands and meet me in the OR in fifteen minutes," he told her. "I have a C-section to perform. The fetus is underweight but I believe we can help the mother. Evelyn, I noticed Stephen didn't eat his dinner again. Perhaps you could speak with him."

Dr. Chaline left. Warner waited until he was out of earshot.

"Where is David?" she asked. "I'd love to see him again."

"He's working out of the Hotel Liger in Baku," MacKenzie told her. "But I'm not sure where he's going from there. Can I ask you a question?"

"Sure," Evelyn said.

"How's my accent?"

"It's good," she said. "Though I knew you weren't Irish before you interceded with our merry little wedding party today."

"How?"

"Stephen told me you said you were from Coldwater Road and that Bono went to your high school. I knew Paul Hewson before he started calling himself Bono Vox. He went to a nondenominational arts high school. There weren't any nuns or priests."

"Are you going to tell Stephen?" Mack asked.

Warner shook her head.

"Your secret's safe with me," she said. "But you might want to tell him yourself at some point. He's enormously trusting but a bit naive. I think somebody hurt him once by lying to him. He might take it personally."

DeLuca was on the veranda when his SATphone chirped. He'd been talking to an ex-employee of Dutch Shell who'd been holed up at the hotel after they'd fired him for refusing to travel to a testing station that had briefly been overrun and occupied by LPLF forces near a village called Sagoa, fearful that the soldiers might return and find him there unprotected. He'd been drunk for the last two weeks, Mohl warned DeLuca, but he might have some useful information. "I'll tell you what they don't want you to know," the man slurred to DeLuca. "There's more goddamn oil in Liger than in Kuwait, Alaska, and Venezuela combined, but the IMF won't loan them the money to get it out unless they make the oil itself collateral and repay from revenues. They did that in Lagos to stop government officials from pocketing the money. Bo is shitting in his pants. You know what I think? I think WAOC and Ngwema made a deal. WAOC is sick of dealing with Bo. Ngwema is so deep into WAOC's pocket their balls are hitting him on the head."

"Excuse me," DeLuca said, holding up a finger to say he'd be a minute and flipping his phone open. "Don Brown, who's this?"

"Herr Totenbrau," General LeDoux said, referencing the brand of home-brewed beer they'd made while stationed together in Germany, several years, wars, and worlds ago. "Can you talk?"

"I can listen," DeLuca said. He doubted the oil man was sober enough to remember anything he'd overhear, but why take chances?

"It's all falling apart," LeDoux said. "IMINT shows major troop movements in the north, IPAB or LPLF, trying to be in place and knock Bo out before we launch. So much for ultimatums. I'll send you the details on your CIM. Three basic columns driving south hard, one to your west, one to your east through Camp Seven and Sagoa, and one's coming right down the pike, your way, I'm afraid. You should be seeing retreating Ligerian forces any minute."

"That's interesting," DeLuca said, glancing down the street in front of the hotel.

"We also have pictures of a village called Mbusi. About fifty klicks northeast of you. It's not good."

"How many?"

"Can't say," LeDoux said. "The bodies aren't intact. We're counting limbs and dividing by four. Plus we can't tell how deep the piles are. Eight hundred people, give or take a few. Mostly Da Christians. TF-21's going in to eye-ball it."

"Do we know who?"

"The government is saying it's Dari," LeDoux said. "For what it's worth."

"They wouldn't lie to us, would they?" DeLuca said. "How does this change our timetable?"

"Not ours, but yours, maybe," LeDoux said. "We'd prefer it if we could send one H-60 to one LZ to get the bunch of you. Any chance you could circle the wagons for us?"

"You're ordering us to evacuate?" DeLuca asked.

"Advising," LeDoux said. "It's up to you. The call from here is that the window is closing. Right now we can fly, but the longer we wait, the more likely it is we get lit up."

"How long do we have?"

"Depends on where you are," LeDoux said. "If we wait till it's hot, we're going to need support."

"Negative on extraction," DeLuca said, making a deci-sion. He wasn't willing to risk the lives of flight crews on the chance that something might happen, at some vague time in the future. If it happened then, they'd deal with it then. He was fine, Hoolie was fine, Mack was okay, Dan was all right, and he hadn't heard from Zoulalian, but he probably had his reasons for going dark. The idea wasn't to run away at the first sign that they were in harm's way. "Somebody here delivered a letter to the front desk today. Unsigned. It said Dari will be at the Park Motel tomorrow, outside Tsotho National Park, at noon."

"From?" LeDoux asked.

"Don't know who it's from," DeLuca said.

"Trap?" LeDoux said.

"Possibly," DeLuca said. "Or he wants to meet. I think we need to go and find out."

There was a long silence. LeDoux could order them out, if he wanted to.

"Keep me posted," LeDoux said. "We'll send whatever we have to send. You understand our position."

"I do," DeLuca said. "And you understand mine. We can still do the mission. I'll give you a call if we need a limo."

Chapter Eight

ZOULALIAN WAITED IN THE COURTYARD OUT-side the mosque at Kumari, told that he was in charge of the second vehicle, a two-year-old white Mitsubishi Mighty-Max 4×4 pickup with the spare tire mounted on the front grille. The mosque was modest, at least by Middle Eastern standards, and felt more like a community center than a religious edifice. Rahjid Waid had gone inside to speak with Imam Dadullahjid. Zoulalian had not yet been told what they were doing there, but he knew it had to be important because Rahjid had come along in person rather than waiting back at the camp. Zoulalian had six men under him, including four seasoned Algerians who looked like they'd cut your heart out with a butter knife, and two black African teenagers who were trying not to show how scared they were. When Rahjid introduced "Khalil Penjwin" to the camp upon his arrival, he'd exaggerated Khalil's credentials a bit, saying he'd killed over a hundred Americans with roadside bombs and IEDs, and that he'd been the number-two most wanted man on the Americans' blacklist, just behind Ibrahim Al Durri, when he left Iraq to come help the cause in Africa.

A group of kids played soccer beyond the outer walls

of the mosque. Zoulalian could tell that his black soldiers wanted to put down their guns and join the soccer players.

"Some day, the World Cup will be played in Africa," he told the boys in Arabic. They smiled.

"African football is too beautiful," one said. *"We are too good. They don't want to be embarrassed."*

Rahjid had told them to keep their weapons hidden beneath a tarp in the back of the truck, five AK-47s and a pair of shoulder-fired grenade launchers. The Algerians were chewing on some sort of weed that made Zoulalian's lips tingle when he tried it. They were high. He couldn't tell how high, but their eyes were glassy and wild.

Rahjid reappeared and crossed to where Zoulalian was standing. He was a short stumpy man, with a close-cropped black beard and wire-rimmed glasses, dressed in desert camo except for the white *kaffiyeh* on his head. Khalil was dressed similarly.

"We will wait here," Rahjid said. He eyed the two younger soldiers.

"They are nervous," Zoulalian said, keeping his voice down. *"I think they want to know why we're here."*

"They'll find out soon enough," Rahjid said.

"I think it would be better if they had time to think about it," Zoulalian said. *"If they're to become martyrs, I think they want to begin their prayers. It would help them fight the urge to panic."*

"They will not become martyrs today," Rahjid said. He paused, appearing to reconsider. *"Three people are coming. A Frenchman, an American reporter, and a woman from the UN. The imam wants to talk to them, and when he's done, we'll take them to our camp. He wants to keep them to use to negotiate, when the American troops come.*

Not here though—we will follow them a ways and then take them, away from the mosque."

"Okay," Zoulalian said. He needed to get away from the others so that he could use his SATphone to warn MacKenzie. *"I need to use the bathroom. Could you tell me where it is?"*

"I'll do better than that—I'll go with you. I have to go, too," Rahjid said. *"Come on."*

MacKenzie wore a scarf over her head but raised the veil only when they approached a roadblock, or when the dust was too great. Dr. Claude Chaline drove, with Stephen Ackroyd in the backseat. The Doctors Without Borders logo on the side of the Land Rover got them through the variety of checkpoints marking the seventy-kilometer distance between Camp Seven and the mosque outside Kumari, the landscape changing from forested savannah to desert. Evelyn Warner had gone to Baku Da'al. Streams of displaced refugees walked in the opposite direction, women with baskets on their heads and children in tow, old men pushing two-wheeled hand carts, boys driving livestock, undernourished goats with their ribs showing, occasionally a truck or tro-tro so packed with people they reminded MacKenzie of the little cars full of clowns she'd seen at the circus as a child. The sun beat down relentlessly, the temperature well over a hundred degrees, and yet Chaline chose to save on fuel by driving with the air-conditioning off and the windows open. Instead of refreshing, the wind made it almost harder to breathe.

Chaline grilled her most of the way, his French accent making him hard to understand at times above the noise. What was the reason she'd come to Liger? What could the

Women's Health Initiative do for the women in IDP-7, or the women in camps elsewhere across northern and central Liger? When he started listing the supplies and medicines they needed, she entered what he said into her CIM, feeling both appalled at how much they lacked and horrible that she was lying to him, and that all her promises were empty, and that she'd be unable to deliver on any of it. They needed surgical supplies, water purification equipment, all kinds of medicines down to the most basic antibiotics and pain relievers, penicillin, aspirin, and the more sophisticated AIDS medications—they needed everything. Chaline pointed to a collection of tin-roofed houses at the top of a hill when they came to an intersection.

"What does that look like to you?" he asked, not slowing down.

"I don't know," she said. "What is it?"

"That's a 'boom-boom,'" Chaline said. "It's a whorehouse. President Bo built new roads up here to move the oil equipment and the tankers and service vehicles, so the boom-booms sprang up at the intersections so that the prostitutes could service the truck drivers. The imams, including Dadullahjid, were morally outraged and blamed Bo, but a lot of the truckers themselves were Muslims. In five years, AIDS in this country went from 2 percent to almost 25 percent, and it's almost two-thirds among the sex workers. We had people in the boom-booms handing out condoms but Bo stopped us. The church is against contraception, so Bishop Duvallier told him what we were doing was against God."

"So President Bo did him one better," Ackroyd chimed in from the back, "and said all relief shipments had to be inspected by the government first to make sure no contraband was getting through to assist the rebels. He made a big public show of it when they found a supply of birth control pills and dumped it into the harbor."

"How he thought the rebels could use birth control pills to their advantage, I don't know," Chaline said. "We've treated people who've been tortured in his prisons. Cigarettes in their ears and eyeballs. I have a colleague who believes Bo introduced Ebola into a village of Da that had been friendly to the LPLF. We can't prove it. My colleague is afraid Bo is going to bring Ebola to one of the camps. In ancient times, when a hemorrhagic fever came to a village, they'd block all the trails in or out and put the sick people in a quarantine hut, where they would stay until they either recovered or died. Today, with roads and cars, such viruses cannot be isolated or contained anymore. I'm going to speak to Dadullahjid because I have a plane in Burkina Faso full of medicine with a pilot who's willing to fly to Camp Seven, but I need Dadullahjid to tell his men not to shoot it down."

MacKenzie also saw troop convoys, armored transports and half-tracks, artillery and heavy equipment, moving south in long columns, soldiers who looked suspiciously into the Land Rover as they passed. She kept the veil up and rolled her sleeves down to cover her white skin. Chaline had told her to leave her sidearm behind because they were certain to be searched. She'd considered hiding it somewhere in the vehicle, just in case, but in the end she complied with his request. She pasted the list of medical supplies onto an e-mail that she sent to General LeDoux, just in case there was anything he could do about it. She added a note to the e-mail:

Rebel forces moving south in large numbers. Appear well armed and organized. Singing.

Mack

When she was finished sending, she deleted the e-mail and the list in case her CIM was seized. They approached a checkpoint, Dr. Chaline waiting in line behind a man on a motor scooter and an ancient Volkswagen microbus with a red cross painted on the side.

"What are you going to say to Dadullahjid?" Stephen asked her.

"I want him to protect the safety of women," Mack said. "And other noncombatants. I want a guarantee. I want him to give me a letter with his signature and his seal on it, or whatever he has, so that if troops come, I can show them the letter. I have a favor. Evelyn told me it would be better if you spoke to him. I wouldn't ask you if it wasn't important."

He hesitated.

"Okay," he said. He seemed flustered, his eyes blinking nervously.

"But what? Be honest with me."

"Well," he said, "I was worried that if I got involved, as a journalist, that it could put the other journalists in Liger in danger. But I'm already involved. And it's not like they'd look out for me."

The soldiers ahead of them pulled the man off his motor scooter roughly and dragged him away, while two other soldiers moved his scooter to the side. Ackroyd's hand reflexively reached out for Mack's.

"Hopefully, all they want is his scooter," Dr. Chaline said.

When it was their turn, the soldier took a long time reading the papers that Stephen Ackroyd handed him before handing them back.

"*National Geographic*?" he asked. Stephen nodded. The soldier held up Ackroyd's passport and looked at it, then at Stephen. He repeated the process, then handed Stephen his passport. Mack caught a glimpse. The man in the passport photograph looked about thirty or forty pounds heavier than the man sitting beside her in the Land Rover.

"You didn't tell me you were working for *National Geographic*," she said.

"I'm not," he said. "I'm freelance. I just needed a letterhead."

Men's Journal, he'd in fact said. She recalled quite clearly. She made a mental note of the discrepancy, though it seemed of little import.

They drove another half hour, passing, along the way, another thousand refugees and a second convoy that appeared to be more a support column than combat units (she counted trucks, to report later), before turning onto a main thoroughfare and finally into the mosque compound. Two guards at the gate examined their papers, then directed them through. A group of armed men waiting in the courtyard told them where to park, pointing with their guns. Stephen was directed to leave his camera in the vehicle, and then they were taken to a room off the courtyard where they were searched, forced to lean with their hands against the wall and their legs spread. When the man searching MacKenzie appeared to be spending too much

time feeling her breasts, Ackroyd said, "That's enough!"
A man raised his rifle butt, as if to strike Stephen, but
paused. Stephen didn't flinch. The man frisking MacKenzie backed away with a scowl.

Dadullahjid sat behind a desk in the prayer hall. Three
men stood behind him. One, MacKenzie didn't know. The
second was Rahjid Waid, who she recognized from the
briefing file she'd read. The third was Dennis. She tried
not to give any sign that she knew him or was surprised to
see him. She was, for the first time, glad she had the veil
to hide behind. Claude Chaline approached the desk and
spoke to the imam in French.

"Je m'appelle Dr. Claude Chaline. J'ai un avion
chargé de medicaments pour le Burkina Faso. Je voudrais
le piloter au Camp Sept, mais j'ai besoin de votre aide,"
he said. He'd explained earlier that Dadullahjid had lived
for three years in Paris, and hoped that that connection
might mean something. He had a plane full of medicine,
he was saying. He needed assurances.

Dadullahjid listened without responding, his arms
folded across his chest.

MacKenzie made eye contact with Zoulalian. His face
was hidden half in shadow, but even so, MacKenzie read
the message Zoulalian was sending with his eyes, coming
across in a way that couldn't be clearer. "This is a trap,"
they were saying. "You're in trouble. You are not safe."

She touched her nose to ask for confirmation.

He sniffed. Sniffs meant yes. Touching the ear meant no.

Chaline spoke for a moment longer, gesturing softly
with his hands. Mack took in the room, noting the windows and exits. An instinct told her nothing was going
to happen inside the mosque, a space that was sacred, or

should have been, to those who would harm her. If something happened here, Dennis would take out one of the men next to him and she would move on the other. Was Dadullahjid armed? She doubted it.

"These are innocent people," Chaline said, finishing in English. "They are sick and need medicine. They are women and children. They are no threat to anyone. They are victims of displacement and violence and war. I know that the Koran teaches mercy and compassion for the innocent. Letting my plane through would be an act of compassion."

Dadullahjid thought for a moment longer. Mack thought she saw a figure move furtively, concealed behind a pair of louvered doors.

"I think you overestimate what I can do," the imam said at last. "I am one man. I don't have some fancy communications center. If you want to fly your plane, fly your plane and I will ask those I know to tell the others, but I can guarantee nothing. I can guarantee your own safety only within these walls. I myself have been the target of President Bo's assassins three times. I cannot give you what you want. It's not within my power. I can ask, but beyond these walls, there is only so much I can do. *Si les femmes et les enfants sont des Musulmans, alors Allah prendra soin d'eux. S'ils ne le sont pas, alors je ne sais pas qui tendra à leurs besoins.*"

Mack's French was several levels below conversational, but she understood the gist of what Dadullahjid had said. "If the women and children are Muslims, Allah will look after them. If they are not, I don't know who will."

"*Merci,*" Claude Chaline said. "*J'ai la foi dans la puissance de vos mots.*"

When Chaline was finished, Stephen stepped forward. MacKenzie took a step toward the desk with him, her head bowed.

"My name is Stephen Ackroyd," the writer said. "This is Mary Dorsey. We speak on behalf of the United Nations Women's Health Initiative. We've come in the hope—"

"Enough," Iman Dadullahjid said, rising suddenly and walking out the rear door without saying another word.

Stephen looked stunned. He took two steps back and turned, his head down.

"It's not your fault," Mack whispered. "I don't think our friend was in a mood to listen."

"This reminds me of a date I went on in college," he said.

She stepped forward, rushing toward Zoulalian, who raised his AK-47 in front of him to block her approach.

"Tell the imam he has to protect the women and children in Camp Seven," she said, getting in Dennis's face. "You can tell him. Grown men have nothing to fear from women and children."

Zoulalian grabbed her roughly by the arm, putting his mouth next to her ear in the struggle and whispering menacingly, *"Deux camions. J'essayerai d'arrêter les autres,"* before throwing her roughly back and causing her to stumble. Rahjid Waid laughed, as did the third man. "Two trucks," he'd said. "I'll try to stop the others."

"You have to tell him," Mack again implored. "In the name of God."

They were led to their vehicle. Mack noticed that the two white trucks previously in the courtyard were missing, a white 4×4 pickup and a white Montero, if her memory was correct. Two men guarded them as they walked.

"Dr. Chaline," she said, "would you mind if I drove?"

"I will drive," Chaline said.

"Dr. Chaline," she said, taking his arm and squeezing it firmly. *"Il est très important que vous me laissiez conduire. J'expliquerai plus tard."*

He looked at her and then, reluctantly, surrendered the keys. She saw the scornful looks on the faces of the men at the sight of a man surrendering his car keys to a woman.

She started the car.

"Seatbelts, please," she said. She scanned the walls of the compound for gunmen but saw none. The gas tank was half full, not enough fuel to get back to Camp Seven. They had two ten-gallon steel jerry cans filled with gasoline attached to the back of the Land Rover. Either was certain to explode into a spectacular ball of fire if struck by a bullet. There wasn't much she could do about it. Removing the gas cans, at that point, would have raised suspicion.

She put the vehicle in gear and moved toward the gate. The Rover had seven forward gears, three of them in the low range for off-road traction or towing. The exit was protected by a gate, which swung open once the guard nodded to them, as well as by a zigzagged sequence of concrete barriers, forcing her to leave at a walking pace. At the last barrier, she stopped to adjust her rearview mirror and to drop her veil. The Montero was parked on her left, the white pickup on her right, with Dennis behind the wheel. There were four soldiers in the back of the pickup. She couldn't tell how many men were in the Montero because the windows were tinted.

"Everybody grab hold of something and stay down," she said.

She put the car in first with the clutch in, stepped on the gas until the engine reached 3,000 rpms, then popped the clutch, the vehicle lurching forward, spraying gravel, but holding a true line with all four wheels turning.

"What are you doing?" Chaline shouted, but Mack kept the gas pedal to the floor as she worked through the gears. She heard a burst of machine-gun fire and then two bullets shattered the rear passenger window, broken glass flying across the passenger compartment.

"Stay down!" she commanded. "Is everyone all right?"

"What's going on?" Stephen shouted.

"I don't know, but I don't want to find out," she told him, her speedometer reaching sixty miles an hour on a road so rough that nothing above forty was advisable. Goats and sheep scurried out of her way as she honked the horn to let the people ahead of her know she was coming. She wove past a man on a bicycle, forced a boy to dive out of the way, and veered around a parked truck until it felt like she was riding on two wheels. In the rearview mirror, she saw the Montero, gaining ground.

Zoulalian had tried to get in front of the Montero but didn't have enough horsepower from the starting line to do it. He saw a man leaning out the window of the Montero, aiming a rifle at the Land Rover they were chasing. They'd gone perhaps a mile before he saw his chance, riding on the tail of the Montero and then passing it when it braked for a cart, which he struck as he passed before taking the lead in the chase. Two of the Algerians were firing from the back of the truck, so he tried to jerk the wheel every few seconds to throw off their aim.

Mack saw in her rearview mirror that Dennis had passed the lead chase vehicle and was now behind her. She hoped that was a good thing.

Zoulalian saw his opportunity ahead where the road narrowed to a constriction between two buildings, and narrowed further by a telephone pole at the corner of one building. He double-checked to make sure his seatbelt was fastened, glanced briefly to note that there was no passenger-side airbag, tapped the console at the center of the steering wheel (as if that might somehow ensure that his own airbag was going to successfully deploy—all he could really do was hope), then slowed to about thirty miles an hour before steering the pickup into the telephone pole, to strike it head on squarely with his right front bumper. Either his demolished vehicle would block the road, or the Montero would crash into it or stop of its own accord, or maybe they'd swerve around him and continue their pursuit, but it was the best he could do under the circumstances—DeLuca had warned them that they would have to improvise. He only hoped he'd know whether he'd been successful, once he regained consciousness. Perhaps one of the soldiers in the back would slam through the cab's rear window and kill him from behind.

There was no time to change his mind now.

When DeLuca logged onto his CIM to check his e-mail, he found a message from his son, who had been working in Image Analysis with the 23rd Air Expeditionary Force out of Kirkuk since the beginning of Iraqi Freedom. He also found an offer for Viagra from an online pharmacy and three offers for home equity loans.

"Unbelievable," he muttered under his breath. "How did they find me?"

Scottie's e-mail read:

Hey Pops,

I know you're busy. Greetings from Washington, first of all. Also I've been made captain, with a new assignment you may be interested in. I told "Uncle Phil" I wanted to break the news to you myself. I trust he hasn't told you anything. After the last mission, his office decided Team Red needed its own JIOC officer. The idea of Joint Intel Op Centers is to "coordinate systems and flatten echelons." We'll see. Anyway, when he asked me who I could recommend, I might possibly have mentioned something about being open to a change of assignment. He thought I was right for the job despite the obvious conflicts of interest. The designation was by committee after blind review, and I was one of five candidates, so you don't have to worry about the appearance of nepotism. I wasn't going to tell you if I didn't make it, but there's no way to hide it now. The only thing keeping this from being permanent is your approval. I will, of course, miss Kirkuk . . . I think I found a house I want to buy in Silver Spring, but I need to talk to you about how to go about it. I tasked SIGINT to go over what the mortgage/loan officer was telling me but they couldn't understand it either. On to business.

ACTION: Attached find photographs General Kwesi Emil-Ngwema, taken yesterday 1640 hours at the Port Ivory airport. The man with him is Col. Jumar

Inshal-Mukebo, former commander gov forces, Kum region with Ligerian Second Army. Caucasian number one is Simon Bell, head mercenary forces arrested/ confined two days ago, and number two is Hugh Lloyd, the money man. At 1730 hours, a British Hercules took off bearing 48 degrees northeast, destination Benghazi, Libya. Zero off-load, refueled, still there. Why fly an empty plane to Libya? The aircraft was briefly towed into the hangar at the PI airfield where mercenaries were being held under guard. One cell-phone call from hangar to South Africa, nothing hard (Boer): "Things are changing rapidly, I'll be in touch," etc. The suspicion is that the C-130J picked up and airdropped mercs, somewhere on flight vector. Un-fortunately, our bird went off-range at 1748 hours, so we have no IMINT past that time. No current sign of guards at hangar. Possible destination—WAOC has directed employees to relocate to El Amin oil facility for safety (40K NE you—see GPA attached).

ANALYSIS: *Ngwema will act in WAOC's best interests, allied with Mukebo/northern forces.*

ACTION: *SIGINT/IMINT indicates Ngwema adopting defensive positions only to direct/divert rebel forces against loyalist troops, similar to analysis his actions re Port Ivory—you were there, you know. Appears to be allowing deep incursions southward, where only Presidential Guard/Port Ivory area will/can mount significant resistance.*

ANALYSIS: *Ngwema wants rebels to defeat Bo, then his forces can encircle/defeat rebels (IMINT confirms—*

*see map). Expect heavy casualties/collateral damage.
Also expect no support—you are in the middle.*

*ACTION: LPLF/IPAB in three columns (see map/
falcon views). Leadership unclear at this time.
Massacres in Mbusi, Angasa, Bok, Dasai, Pomogoso.
Ligerian version of "shock and awe," largely along
eastern flank/west central. Will spare you the imagery
unless requested. Enemy troop identification not
possible at this time.*

ANALYSIS: The shit has seriously hit the fan.

*I will alert you to movements on your position,
20K radius. You may want to set your alarm to silent.
Have advised others of same. Currently Mack has
departed Kumari (high speed/ground). Sykes is flying
into same, private helicopter. Zoulalian signal lost,
cause unknown.*

*Went to 9/11 Memorial site with Mom and left flowers
for Aunt Eileen. Mom is worried. She knows not to ask
but she knows I can't lie to her either. We chitchat.
Carolyn is staying with her. FYI.*

Scott.

DeLuca smiled.

"Good news?" Hoolie asked him as he drove. Paul
Asabo was in the passenger seat, staring out the window,
the foliage getting thicker and thicker as they traveled
toward Tsotho National Park, a section of the Ligerian rain
forest that had, so far, survived the pressures that had leveled so much of Liger's southern jungle, isolated kakum

and kapok and mahogany trees rising from the lesser growth to stand three and four hundred feet above the ground. They'd passed coffee and cocoa plantations with gates guarded by armed men. The Park Motel was down the road from the park's northern entrance.

"Not entirely," DeLuca said. "My son made captain."

"Congratulations," Hoolie said. "What's it like to have a kid who outranks you?"

"It's not that much different from having a teenager," DeLuca said. "I can still kick his ass at eight-ball. That's what matters."

"My father and I played chess," Asabo said. "I used to beat him, but it has occurred to me since then that I never would have beaten him if he hadn't let me."

"I let Scottie beat me at tennis once," DeLuca said. "I learned my lesson. He was furious at me for letting him win."

"My father beats me at accordion playing," Hoolie said. "He used to study with Fred Zimmerle. When we play and he says, 'Take it,' I say, 'Keep it.'"

"Bocce," DeLuca said. "Long Island Bocce Ball Association. My old man played every Friday and Saturday. I couldn't come close to beating him. When he died, we put a bocce ball in his coffin. I used to tell Scottie that when it thundered, it was his grandpa, playing bocce ball in heaven."

"I would like to visit my father's grave," Asabo said, still staring out the window.

"Maybe if there's time, we could arrange that," DeLuca offered. Asabo turned around and looked at him in the backseat.

"First, we would have to find out where it is," Asabo said. "Can you tell your satellites to search all of Liger for him?"

DeLuca couldn't quite tell whether Asabo was being sarcastic or sincere. There was more sadness in his voice than bitterness. DeLuca had wondered what it was like for Asabo, coming home after all these years. He'd lingered at the stalls when they'd taken a short tour of the open-air market across from the hotel, running his fingers along the various fruits and vegetables, sparse though the selection was, smelling them, feeling the handwoven textiles and bragging that Ligerian weavers made the finest cloth in all of Africa. They'd gone to get a feel for how the public felt about the rebels in general and about John Dari in particular, but for Asabo, it was a full immersion in lost memories. He'd told DeLuca and Vasquez about a delicacy called *jashi*, which was barbecued bush meat in a spicy peanut sauce, and he was shocked to learn it was no longer available and hadn't been for years. He was surprised to see booth after booth selling bootleg American movies on DVD. The market had once sold strictly African products, but now half of what was for sale was made in America or Japan, plastic dinosaurs and surplus McDonald's Happy Meal toys, Las Vegas key chains, knockoff Atlanta Braves and Los Angeles Lakers jerseys. Occasionally he would see portraits of his father, old postcards for sale, commemorative plates marking his royal enstoolment, pictures of the king resplendent in the Royal Sun Robe of golden feathers, his staff in hand, smiling. "They haven't forgotten," Asabo had said in the marketplace. "I thought that maybe by now they would have."

"I'm sorry," DeLuca said in the car, a beat-up Toyota Cressida they'd rented at the hotel. "America should have done something."

"That is the popular conception in Africa, you know," Asabo said. "That during the civil war in Rwanda, the Americans were watching the whole thing on television from their satellites. And knew what the *interahamwe* was doing, from the beginning. I've heard some say it was shown every night on popular American television. I have told people that was not true, that only the government had access to the pictures. It was an intelligence failure."

"I think 'intelligence failure' is my favorite new euphemism," DeLuca said. "Half the things that go wrong aren't 'intelligence failures'—they're stupidity successes. Often spectacular stupidity successes, like Rwanda."

"How would you explain it?" Asabo said.

"I'm not sure I can," DeLuca said. "I was a Boston police officer in 1994. But I will tell you one thing. The military has always placed too much value on satellite intelligence and not enough on human intel. Look at Gulf One, goddamn Norman Schwarzkopf with his goddamn slide shows every night, showing nose-cone footage from smart bomb cameras of cars scurrying across a bridge and laughing and saying, 'There goes the luckiest man in Iraq.' He was so proud of the technology that he made the war look like a big video game. Anyone with any brains knew the footage of bombs dropping on actual people got left on the editing room floor. The people without any brains, who number more than a few, unfortunately, got the idea that we're omnipotent and we can see where we want to see and go where we want to go, any time we want, without consequences. I swear to God, 9/11 wouldn't have happened if Al Qaeda didn't think we were taunting them, saying, 'We can hit you but you can't hit us.' As you may have noticed from Iraqi Freedom, we don't do that anymore. We don't run our intel in PowerPoint shows on national television."

"Did you have pictures?" Asabo said. "Of Rwanda?"

"I'm not sure," DeLuca said. "Some, I think. I don't know. I wouldn't say we were blind. Just confused. And maybe numb. I met Iraqis who thought America watches the whole world, 24/7. And that we know what's going on."

Hoolie laughed at the thought.

"Half of North Korea's military establishment works deep underground," DeLuca continued, "because they think we're watching them. After Gulf One, if you lived near Canaveral or Vandenberg or Greely, you would have seen launch platform after launch platform throwing up milsats. You wouldn't have known what it was, but you would have seen a lot of rocket plumes. Before Gulf Two, I think it was four or five launches a month, just getting ready to invade Iraq with all our birds up and running. We still couldn't find anybody. That's why I was there. And for that matter, that's why I'm here—that's what you're part of. Team Red was formed to put a new emphasis on gathering human intelligence."

"The whole WMD thing in Iraq was an intelligence failure," Hoolie said. "Maybe I should say a stupidity success. We didn't have enough human intelligence. We were too reliant on satellite imagery."

"Satellites are fine," DeLuca said, "if you know where to point them, and when, and what to look for, and how to follow up. If you don't, all they do is make you over-confident."

As he spoke, he downloaded and examined the falcon view of the Park Motel, which was now three kilometers ahead of them. He saw a large pond and a set of buildings, but zooming in and out, he saw no sign of military vehicles or unusual activities. He looked at his watch. They weren't early. Was the letter he'd received a hoax? Or was he driving into a trap? If so, where was the trap?

A large sign marked the entrance, reading, WELCOME TO THE PARK MOTEL, LIGER'S FINEST RESORT SPA. EASY ACCESS TO TSOTHO NATIONAL PARK. AIR-CONDITIONING. IN ROOM TELEVISION. HBO.

"Good thing the TVs are in the rooms," Hoolie said. "I hate it when you have to look out the window to watch TV."

The proprietor greeted their arrival personally. The only other car in the circular drive beneath the palm trees was a blue Honda Civic with the motel's name painted on the door. His name, he said, was Mohammed Ali, and he was smiling from ear to ear, shaking hands, searching with his eyes to see if there was any luggage to carry.

"I'm very pleased to meet you," he said, "do come inside. I'm afraid I'm a bit short-staffed today because business has been slow, so I've sent some people home, but I can show you to your rooms myself . . ."

"Thank you," DeLuca said, "but we don't need rooms— we're just here for a meeting. Is there somewhere we could wait?"

"Yes yes yes," Mohammed said, "please follow me, you can wait in the bar."

The hotel was one large central building and a line of smaller cottages following the shoreline of a five-acre pond, DeLuca estimated, the buildings all painted a bright pink with blue trim. The shore was lined with trees festooned with the nests of bowerbirds, woven grass globes about the size of small cantaloupes, dangling from the trees like Christmas ornaments. Bright yellow and orange birds flitted about, as did blue kingfishers and green hummingbirds, darting amidst the flowering bushes that Ali had used to landscape the property. The bar was a large open-air thatch-roofed structure built on pylons about thirty yards from shore, connected to land by a wooden bridge that reached out and then ran parallel to the shore before connecting to the bar. There was a large monkey cage in one corner of the bar, where four colobus monkeys cavorted, chattering loudly and grimacing and reaching through the bars for handouts.

"Don't get too close," Ali said. "They will settle down in a minute. My sons named them John, Paul, George, and Ringo. I will go start the generator. If you would like tea or limone or whatever you will have, please help yourself. There is beer, too, and I would bring it to you myself but as a Muslim, I do not touch alcohol, and my barman is not here, so help yourself and you will pay me later. Please."

He crossed the bridge and disappeared into the main building. The late afternoon sun moved westward across an azure sky. DeLuca heard birds chirping and warbling, insects buzzing, the wind activating a set of gentle chimes that hung beside the monkeys' cage, and from the kitchen, the faint pulse of a radio playing reggae music. With a little imagination, it was almost possible to pretend they weren't in the middle of a civil war.

Hoolie read the note printed on the back of the menu.

"It says here this place started as a fish farm. The pond is stocked with tilapia. When the birds came and made nests, the guy figured it would make a nice place for a motel. The bread on the table is for us to feed the fish. Toss a piece in and see what happens."

DeLuca picked up a dried roll that was probably a few days old and cast it onto the water. Within seconds, the roll was being pecked apart by a swarming school of small reddish gray fish, roiling the water and churning the surface white.

"Well that's pretty cool," he said. "Jesus Christ!"

He nearly jumped from his chair as a pair of massive jaws emerged from the water and snapped loudly down with a splash into the middle of the school of swarming fish. Hoolie laughed as the first crocodile was joined by a second, then a third, all feeding on the tilapia. DeLuca counted four more pairs of eyes gliding silently across the surface of the water toward the commotion. He'd drawn his weapon without thinking, alert to the possibility of an ambush.

DeLuca put his Beretta back in his concealed nylon holster and sat down.

"Excuse me while I go change my underwear," he said.

Hoolie continued to read from the back of the menu.

"'Why did I decide to stock the pond with crocodiles also?' it says. 'This is a question that is asked frequently. I tell those who ask, I did not decide to stock the pond— this is Africa. The crocodiles just come. You are advised to avoid swimming in the pond, but be certain otherwise that they will not hurt you. Remember, hate attracts hate. Love attracts love.'"

There were no fences or barriers of any kind at the edge of the pond.

"I wonder what keeps them from walking into the rooms?" DeLuca wondered.

"Fear of spiders," Asabo said.

They waited for nearly three hours before DeLuca suggested perhaps they should head back to Baku Da'al. Asabo said Liger was a place where if you showed up on the same day as your appointment, you were considered punctual. DeLuca kept checking the falcon view on his CIM, but even at maximum zoom, they appeared to be alone. He'd asked for a Predator to be posted overhead, armed with a Hellfire missile, but he was beyond the reach of rescue teams and past bingo-fuel for Blackhawks—the Hellfire offered a one-shot option, and after that, they were down to the sidearms they had on them.

Then a figure appeared in the twilight between two of the guest cottages. The man stood, quite still, and DeLuca watched him. A second figure appeared, a third, and then he saw perhaps a hundred soldiers, armed mainly with Kalashnikovs, but here and there, men carrying rocket-propelled grenade launchers. More soldiers appeared by the kitchen, the motel office, and on the road. DeLuca realized they were effectively surrounded, but then it didn't matter, because they hadn't come to put up a fight. The Sons of John Dari appeared to be disciplined and well-equipped, DeLuca noted, without the ragtag aspects of Africa's other boy armies and militias.

"Everybody stay cool," DeLuca said softly. "We knew we couldn't beat the numbers anyway, so let's all take it easy."

Three men separated themselves from the others and approached the bridge to the bar. Asabo recognized John Dari at the center. He looked, of course, older than his high school photograph, but he retained a basic youthfulness, the main difference being the crescent-shaped scars carved into each cheek, bisected by a line extending down half an inch. The two men with him were enormous, each approaching six foot six and three hundred pounds by DeLuca's estimation, presenting the image of a quarterback with a pair of NFL linemen forming a pocket on either side of him, though unlike NFL linemen, Dari's protectors also carried M-10 machine pistols.

Dari and Asabo's eyes met, though neither man said anything. Then Dari spoke softly to his guards, in a language DeLuca couldn't identify, and the two men withdrew to the bridge.

"Hello, John," Asabo said at last.

"Hello, Paul," Dari said softly, looking at DeLuca and Vasquez. "Why don't you introduce me to your friends?"

"This is Don Brown, from the World Bank," Asabo began.

"That's all right, Paul," DeLuca interrupted. He extended his hand to Dari. "Special Agent David DeLuca, United States Army counterintelligence. This is Agent Vasquez." He held his hand out a moment longer, and when Dari didn't take it, he pulled it back.

"Delta Force?" Dari asked. DeLuca shook his head.

"Different group," he said.

Dari turned his attention to Asabo.

"Why have you come?" he asked.

"I've come with these men," Asabo said. "To talk to you."

"To talk to me," Dari said. "And what will we talk about? I read that the Red Sox won the World Series. Shall we talk about that?"

"I think Paul and Hoolie and I have come to listen," DeLuca said. "The people who sent me wanted me to learn everything I could about you."

"You want to learn about me?" Dari said. "Why don't you just go to my Web site?"

"We didn't know you had one," DeLuca said.

"I don't," Dari said. "I'm joking. Why would you want to know about me?"

"Because we feel like we have a responsibility to Liger," DeLuca said. "We know that you've become an important person in Liger. But we don't know what that means."

"What were you told?" Dari said. "Just because I'm curious."

"We were told you're leading a rebel militia," DeLuca said. "That you're linked to Arab terrorists, and possibly supported by them or aligned with them. We don't know what your allegiances are exactly, or your goals. To be honest, we're afraid of you."

"So you don't know if you should kill me or buy me, is that it?" Dari said, smiling. "Shoot first and ask questions later, isn't that the American way? I saw those John Wayne movies, you know. I grew up in America, like Paul here. I know America. The only difference is that he said he would come back, but didn't. I said I wouldn't, but I did. The prince and the pauper."

"We're here to open a channel of communication," DeLuca said. "With the idea that we could both benefit from it. If you really knew America as well as you think you do, you'd know that we don't send people to kill any-body anymore. We send bombs and missiles first, and then we send people. I didn't come here to harm you."

"Oh, yes," Dari said. "I forgot—you have a responsibility to Liger. It's not that you want all of our oil and you want it for free, if you can get it. You have sixty thousand men waiting on ships because you want to come ashore, out of the goodness of your hearts, because you saw pictures on television of doe-eyed African children with big bellies and now you want to help us. You give President Do $30 million in military aid and now you want to get rid of him for us. You have a born-again fundamentalist president who has talked about the new crusade and how God has told him he cannot stand by and watch the slaughter of innocent Christians in Liger, while his armies and his bombs kill one hundred thousand innocent Muslims in Iraq. Or can only a Christian be innocent?"

"We could talk politics, or we could talk religion," DeLuca said. "I was hoping we could talk about things that are more practical. We can talk about oil. I'm not going to bullshit you and say we're not concerned about the world oil supply, because I have a Ford Expedition sitting at home in my driveway, and I'd just as soon not pay forty dollars to fill my tank when I get home, just like everybody else. We also have over a thousand aid workers in this country and hundreds of thousands of American aid workers around the world, vaccinating kids and driving trucks full of food and rebuilding towns where a tsunami killed a quarter of a million nonwhite non-Christian non-American people. When the earthquake hit San Francisco in 1989, I don't remember seeing a whole lot of Ligerian aid workers flooding into California to hand out blankets in the shelters. Maybe we should talk about Mbusi, or Angasa, or Bok, or Dasai, or Pomogoso. I mean, gosh, things are going so well in Liger—maybe we should just step aside and let it all play out. You think?"

Dari was silent.

"We don't really have time to bullshit each other. Only idiots see things in black and white," DeLuca said at length. "You're not an idiot, and neither am I, Mr. Dari. If you tell me what you want, I'll tell you what I can do, personally, and what my country can do. I can only guarantee what I can do personally, but I keep my promises. If I didn't, in my line of work, I would have been dead a long time ago. I am your access to the United States government. That's not a small thing, and you know it."

"You ask me to tell you what I want," Dari said. "Did you know my grandfather was a scout for the United States Army during World War II? He helped them fight Rommel. My mother was Acholi but my father was Somalian Arab. He provided intelligence to the United States Army when they went into Mogadishu. The Army told him they would protect him. After the U.S. pulled out, my father was killed, and my mother after that. The U.S. Army said they would take care of them. Do you really think I will believe that you keep your promises?"

"I can understand how you wouldn't," DeLuca said.

"This man," Paul Asabo said, "is not like the others, John. This man doesn't want war. I came back for my own reasons, but I also came back to help you. And to help the country where I've lived. I am Ligerian and I am American. I am both. I respect the choices you've made, but you can respect mine as well."

"So this is how you pay me back?" Dari said. "Is this your atonement? Did he tell you about Mill River, Mr. DeLuca?"

DeLuca looked at Asabo, who lowered his eyes.

"I was briefed about the incident," DeLuca said.

"Oh, you were briefed then," Dari said. "And what did they tell you?"

"That the people who sponsored you, the church, turned their backs on you. And that you had reason to be bitter toward Christians."

"Bitter toward Christians?" Dari said. "Well now. That would be thinking in black and white again, wouldn't it? And in case you're wondering about my language skills, yes, Mr. DeLuca, I intend the pun. I am not bitter about Christians. Or whites, even though I was the only one they wanted to try for rape, because they thought I was older than sixteen. They only dropped the case because I had no birth certificate, so there was no proof of my age. I am bitter about the First Unification Pentecostal Baptist Church of Enid, Oklahoma, but even there, there were people who sympathized with me. Why don't you tell him, Paul? Tell him what happened at Mill River? I'd like to hear how you explain it. Tell him about Roxanne."

DeLuca looked at Asabo. Vasquez shifted in his chair. Somewhere in the distance, a bird cried out.

"Who was Roxanne, Paul?" DeLuca asked. "Was that the girl?"

Asabo nodded.

"We had heard that she did things, at parties. To boys. That she liked to do things. Nobody made her do them. I mean, the boys used their persuasive powers, but nobody forced her. She'd done it twice before, with groups of boys. So we heard there was going to be another party . . ."

"You were there?" DeLuca asked. Asabo nodded. "You weren't in the library studying, like you said?"

Asabo shook his head.

"So we went and we waited our turns. I was still new in America. I didn't know what was customary or expected of me, but I wanted to fit in," he said.

"Is that the royal 'we' you're using, Paul?" Dari asked.

"I waited my turn. John did not. He left. But afterward, when we were caught, I was ashamed, for myself and for my father. I was the heir to the Fasori stool. I thought that I could not have it come out that I had participated in such a thing."

DeLuca added it all up.

"How much did he pay you to take the blame?" he asked Dari.

"A thousand dollars," Dari said. "I thought that was a lot of money. So I said it was me, and what did Roxanne know, one black dick from another? I thought, what of it— I was innocent, so why should I feel shame? But I felt shame, not that I touched the girl, but that I took the money."

The two Africans looked at each other. DeLuca wondered what exactly passed between them in the glance.

"When I was fifteen," DeLuca said, "I went to a party where there was a girl who let boys put their hands up her shirt. I was one of them. We never got caught. It didn't even occur to me that what I'd done was wrong until years later. I thought it was one of those moronic things kids do to experiment. That doesn't make it right, but when all is said and done, there's nothing anywhere near as stupid as a fourteen-year-old boy with a boner. Expecting them to act like adults is like expecting chickens to dance the tarantella."

Dari was expressionless. Asabo spun his beer bottle between his fingers.

"It's the biggest mistakes that we learn the most from," DeLuca said. "I suspect it factored significantly into the reasons why you returned to Islam."

Dari looked at him.

"What happened in Mbusi?" he asked softly. In an instant, DeLuca knew by the look on Dari's face that the question was genuine. Dari didn't know. He wasn't involved. "How many people?"

"Maybe eight hundred," DeLuca said. "We're not sure."

"And Angasa, and Dasai? Pomogoso?"

"Same story," DeLuca said. "They're finding playing cards in the villages, the ace of spades."

"That is Samuel Adu," Dari said.

"That's what I thought," DeLuca said. "He's trying to make it look like you."

"He will go to trial," Dari said. "In The Hague. Sooner or later, for what he did in Sierra Leone. And here. So now he thinks he's become clever."

"We're looking for him, too," Vasquez added.

"I agree with what you say about black and white," Dari said, "but when I think of Samuel Adu, I see only a black so dark and impenetrable it kills the light that touches it. Will you kill him?"

"Do you want me to?" DeLuca asked.

"I would kill him myself, if I could find him," Dari said. His face was grim, but then he smiled, turning to his old friend. "I am glad to see you, Paul. I had thought that one day I would, but I didn't know you'd come home to this. It was always a sad country, but now there aren't enough tears."

"Tell me what you want," DeLuca said. "I can promise that I'll pass it along and fight to make sure you're heard. It probably goes without saying that my government is concerned about the influence of IPAB."

Dari shook his head in mock disbelief.

"Somebody should write a book about the relationship between monotheism and monolithism," he said. "Your president thinks a Muslim from Mauritania and a Muslim from Egypt and a Muslim from Iraq and a Muslim from Malaysia are all the same person. Do you see these boys? They are mostly Da. That big man, he is Muslim, Christian, Hindu, Ashanti, Da, and maybe something else. He is a polytheist, and he is polylithic in his religious philosophy. If you put him in one category, you miss the other five. Yes, IPAB gives us guns, because we need guns to do our work, and who else will give them to us? IPAB gives medicine because people are sick and the medicine makes them well again. Yes, I deal with IPAB. But some of the Islamic brothers I've met are as evil as anybody else. Some have taken the most beautiful religion in the world and corrupted it utterly and twisted it into something I can't recognize. What do I want? What do you think I want? I want food for the people who are starving to death in the camps. President Bo has starved more people to death than Saddam Hussein ever killed in his prisons or torture chambers, but now your soldiers and airplanes and missiles are waiting offshore to defend Bo, because he serves your interests. I want President Bo to leave. I want a government that feeds its people. I would like an autonomous Islamic government in the north, with control over its own resources, including oil. But that won't happen, so I want to see Liger become a true democracy, and that won't happen either, because the U.S. says it wants democracy and freedom and majority rule, but since the beginning of the Cold War, you would never allow democracy in a country where the majority would vote for communism, or for *sharia,* so you don't *really* want democracy now, do you? You said we should talk of practical matters. So I'll just say we want food. We want food and a safe place to eat it. We want medicine. And we want peace, so that people can go home."

DeLuca could see now. Dari was not the killer or the terrorist DIA was making him out to be. His instincts told him, now that he'd met the man face to face, that Dari was sincere, intelligent, honest, and somebody who could not be bought but who could be negotiated with, in short, the sort of person a wise administration would include and support. He wasn't sure the current administration fit the definition, but he was paid to make his recommendations and to use his own judgment. It was why he said, to his team and when he was a counterintelligence instructor at Ft. Huachuca, that counterintelligence was a state of mind. That intuitive sense, the first impression, the innate ability to read a man's character by his mien and body language and deportment, the tone of his voice, his posture, the space within his silences—it was all something they'd never be able to program a computer to do. It wasn't something image or signal intelligence could ever reveal. Human intelligence was not quantifiable, not digitizable, not given to easy explication, and anathematic to the usual military mind, which was why the Pentagon bureaucratic shitheels and the rear echelon motherfuckers had such a hard time trusting it, but in the end, it was what produced the best results. Dari's charisma was palpable, but DeLuca wasn't factoring it in—Hitler had charisma, if the history books were correct. Dari was, for lack of a better word, spiritual. DeLuca knew he'd have to find another way to put it when he made out his report.

"If you want peace," he said, "would you sit at a table and negotiate for it?" He knew this was a loaded question. In Iraq, hundreds of people had been killed as the various elements within the country vied for positions at the peace tables and within the provisional government. It wasn't anywhere as simple as saying, "Come here, sit down, let's discuss how to govern in peace." Dari had developed a constituency and a following. Only he knew what he wanted to do with it.

"With whom?" he asked.

"Who would you want to sit with?" DeLuca asked. "Negotiation begins with speaking truth to power. You've made your opinions about the people in power clear. Would you sit down with President Bo? Or General Ngwema? Would IPAB sit down with them, or the LPLF?"

Dari considered.

"Under the supervision of ECOMAS and the AU, I would sit," Dari said. "With the United States at my side, I would not."

"I understand," DeLuca said. "United Nations?"

Dari nodded.

"How will we contact you?"

"I'll contact you," Dari said. "If the Marines don't come. If they do, then I won't."

"It's not up to me to make that decision," DeLuca said, writing down the number to his SATphone and handing it to Dari.

"I understand," Dari said, taking the number. "And you understand my position."

He turned to Asabo and spoke to him in their native dialect for another minute, then stood and crossed to the bar, where he shook the hand of the motel's proprietor, who was waiting there, conversing with him pleasantly.

"What did you say?" DeLuca asked.

"He asked me if you'd drink *zuzu*," Asabo said. "Truth tea. *Zuzu* is a native plant. When there's a dispute in a village, where one man claims a cow is his, for instance, and another man says he stole it, they'll go to the shaman and he'll make a tea from the *zuzu* plant, from the roots. The tea will kill you if you drink it and you are lying, but it won't harm you if you drink it and you're telling the truth. So he asked me if you would drink it. I said I thought you would."

Dari returned to the table and spoke to DeLuca.

"Do you know where Samuel Adu is right now?" he asked.

"If you could wait a moment, I can try to find out," DeLuca said. He turned on his CIM and sent Scottie an e-mail asking for the information. Within seconds, a map of Liger appeared on the illuminated screen, with an icon indicating Adu's estimated position, fifty kilometers north of a point halfway between Camp Seven and the village of Sagoa.

"This is what we believe. There is a margin for error," DeLuca added.

Dari looked at the screen before leaving, then tapped it with a finger in both locations.

"These places," Dari said softly, referring to Sagoa and to Camp Seven. "They are in grave danger. Good-bye Agent DeLuca. Good-bye Paul."

He joined his men at the bridge.

They'd just set foot on land when the night was split by a horrendous explosion that rocked the bar and took out a large section of the bridge where Dari and his men had stood, moments before.

DeLuca was thrown to the floor.

A hail of gunfire rained down on them as dozens of automatic weapons opened up from a hillside opposite the road on the north end of the pond. Dari's men took positions behind the cottages and returned the fire, catching DeLuca and the others in the middle and pinning them down.

Men shouted.

Men screamed.

"Hoolie! Paul," DeLuca called out, drawing his weapon. "Are you hurt?"

"Paul's been hit," Hoolie said

"I'm okay," Asabo said. "It's nothing."

They scrambled across the floor until their backs were against the bar itself.

"Can you move?" he asked Asabo. "Where are you hit?"

"My arm," Asabo said. "I'm fine. It's nothing."

"Hoolie, what's your guess?" DeLuca asked, dialing his SATphone.

"Twenty or thirty men on the hill," he said. "I doubt that's the whole picture."

"We gotta get out of here," DeLuca said. "Predator, can you target the hill at the northern end of the pond?" he asked, once Scottie answered. "Taking heavy fire."

"We gotcha," Scott said. "Coming around now—hang on."

Hoolie had moved to the entrance. DeLuca joined him, a round shattering one of the bottles behind the bar, another splintering the wood. Another grenade exploded in front of one of the cottages, then a third. The monkey cage had blown open as well, George, Paul, John, and Ringo scrambling about and shrieking.

"Did you see if Dari was hit?" DeLuca asked.

"I didn't see," Vasquez said, ducking again as a tracer round passed overhead.

"Let's go," DeLuca said.

"Hold on a second," Vasquez said, grabbing him by the arm. "We have a problem. The bridge is gone."

DeLuca saw that the bridge extended for perhaps ten feet from the bar, and beyond that, a gap of about twenty feet, too far to jump to shore.

"We swim then," DeLuca said.

"What?" Vasquez said.

"You can't swim thirty feet?" DeLuca asked him

"I can swim thirty feet," Vasquez said, "but not as fast as a crocodile can swim thirty feet."

"Jesus," DeLuca said. Hoolie had a point. "It's always something."

He surveyed the scene quickly.

"Get the bread from all the tables," he commanded.

He kept watch while Hoolie and Asabo filled a white tablecloth with rolls and bread scraps. Dari's men were retreating, their return fire abating. That meant whoever had fired on them was probably advancing. In the distance, DeLuca thought he heard the sound of jet engines approaching.

"Wait for it," he said. "On my signal, cast your bread upon the water, as far in that direction as you can."

The Hellfire hit the hillside, throwing up a spray of fire and smoke, the flames barreling up into the night sky, lighting up the trees.

"Now!" DeLuca commanded.

Hoolie and Asabo stepped out onto the remaining span of bridge and flung the bread in the direction opposite the shore.

"Wait a second," DeLuca said. He heard the sound of tilapia feeding on the bread, and then the louder sound of crocodiles feeding on the tilapia.

"Let's go," he said, diving into the water as the others joined him. He swam as fast as he could, pulling himself up onto the shore but not pausing there, running with his head down for cover until he reached a stone wall by the motel office. Asabo joined him there, and Vasquez a moment later, the three of them dripping wet.

"Boo-ya!" Vasquez said. "Man—I was walking across the top of the pond like a cartoon mouse."

"Love attracts love," DeLuca said. There was still considerable automatic weapons fire coming from the hill, and it was getting closer. "Let's go—that way!"

They sprinted for the cottages, taking cover behind one and pausing. Before them was the jungle, into which John Dari and his men had disappeared. DeLuca lacked flashlights or NVGs and was effectively blind. He was equally disappointed to learn his phone had gotten waterlogged during his brief swim and was not functioning.

"Use mine," Vasquez said, handing DeLuca a phone still inside a waterproof Ziploc bag.

"Are you okay?" Scott said when DeLuca managed to connect.

"So far," he said. "We got wolves at the door. Any suggestions?"

"There's a trail," Scottie said. "You're behind cabin four from the right, facing the pond. The trail head is behind cabin six, two to your left."

They moved. DeLuca thought he saw an opening in the bush.

"Where does it lead?" he asked.

"No idea," Scott said. "Away."

"Away is good. Stay on the line and keep my signal," DeLuca said, plunging headlong into the bush with the others close behind him as a squad of gunmen appeared near where they'd parked the Cressida.

They ran. There was no light, but all the same, DeLuca thought he could make out the gist of the trail, leading downhill, the going treacherous as they stumbled over roots and rocks. Now it was important only that they put some distance between them and the motel. He ran until he was thoroughly winded, perhaps half a mile, maybe less, it was hard to say. The smell was nothing like the "rain forest scented" shampoos his wife liked, floral and pleasant. It smelled like mushrooms, dank rotting vegetation, putrefaction, and decay. He saw the moon briefly through the jungle canopy above. He got back on the phone.

"What's happening?" he asked Scott. A jet streaked high overhead.

"Don't stop now," Scott said. "They're looking for the trail. Somebody behind you is using GPS. I've got his signal."

"Can you blind him?"

"Not easily," Scottie said. "Wouldn't you rather know where *they* are?"

"You have a point," DeLuca said.

"There's some sort of facility, three klicks down the trail," Scott said. "I'm looking at a map but it's not clear what it is. More to come. Get moving."

They stayed close together in the darkness, Asabo explaining that it was probably a trail made by forest elephants, judging by the width of the path they were on, or so he'd read—he'd never actually been in the jungle before now. They paused when a flare lit the sky, maybe a mile behind them. Whoever was chasing them had lights and would be able to make better speed. They followed the directions Scott relayed to them, stopping when he told them to stop.

"What's next?" DeLuca asked.

"You're there," Scott said.

"We're where?"

"Check your Fee-bee-cee-bee—I sent you the same map I'm looking at."

"My CIM took a swim—what are we looking for?"

"A research station of some kind."

"Where?"

"Right there. Exact coordinates. Milsat's accurate down to two meters."

"There's nothing here," DeLuca said.

"There has to be. You're right on top of it."

"We're on top of it? Negative. We see nothing."

"It's on top of us," Vasquez said. "Look."

He'd found a pair of climbing harnesses attached to ropes leading straight up into the air.

"The station's in the canopy," Asabo said.

"Can you climb?" DeLuca asked him. "You ever use one of these?"

"I've done some rock climbing," Asabo said. "In Vermont."

"Pretend this is Vermont," DeLuca said, helping Asabo into the rig and turning to Vasquez. "We can't outrun them. Once you're up top, drop a rig for me."

"How long do you think these ropes have been exposed to the heat and humidity?" Vasquez said, giving one a tug to test it as he snapped a carabiner onto the belt of his harness. "Somebody could take a whipper."

"Why do you think I'm sending you first?" DeLuca said.

"It's always something," Vasquez muttered.

DeLuca waited below as the other two ascended. He heard a clattering overheard, and then he heard nothing but the night.

He waited.

He saw another flare, closer now, perhaps half a klick off.

"Any time, Hoolie, any time," he said under his breath. He wondered what was keeping them. Had they run into trouble of some kind? He heard voices far off but growing louder.

"Now would be a very good time, Hoolie," he said. He considered his options. There was a layer of muck at his feet, damp decaying leaves and vegetation. He could lie in it and cover himself if he had to. He waited, counting to ten. At ten, he would burrow into the muck like a salamander in autumn. He heard voices again, closer now.

When the harness finally dropped, at the count of eight, he suited up and climbed as fast as he could. A platform had been built in the canopy, about three hundred feet above the ground, he estimated. He pulled the ropes up behind him, and then the three of them lay down on the platform, a wooden square about twelve feet across.

"Sit tight," Scott said. "We've got you on UAV. They're right below you. One of them has NVGs with infrared strobe."

They waited.

Another flare fired from a flare pistol lit up the night sky, the bright light hanging in the air as it drifted from its parachute. DeLuca doubted they were visible. The jungle canopy was too thick. Down below, they were guessing.

He heard a burst of machine-gun fire coming from directly beneath them, bullets ripping through the leaves all around them. They heard shouts, men below them, calling out into the bush, and then the shouts faded.

He listened to his own breathing, his heart thumping in his chest.

A few minutes later, Scottie told DeLuca it appeared that the troops looking for them had moved on down the trail.

"We'll stay here until the light comes up," DeLuca said. He turned to Asabo. "Could you hear what they were saying?"

"They said, 'Come out, John Dari—come out and get what's coming to you.' Things like that," Asabo said.

"Ligerian army," DeLuca concluded. "Probably Ngwema. How'd they find out about the meeting?"

"Dari's men?" Vasquez said. "Somebody flipped on him?"

"I doubt it. It wasn't from us," DeLuca said, thinking. "We're encrypted. LeDoux briefed CENTCOM if he briefed anybody. They briefed the Pentagon. They briefed the White House. The White House calls Bo? Bragging about how they had somebody meeting with Dari?"

"Maybe it's not that complicated," Vasquez said. "Maybe the clerk at the hotel opened the envelope. It wasn't sealed. Who compromised us isn't exactly the problem, though, is it?"

"No, it's not," DeLuca said. For Paul Asabo's sake, he stated the obvious. "The problem is that now John Dari believes we set him up. He was the target, not us. And he knows it. He thinks we tried to kill him."

Chapter Nine

WHEN SYKES CONTACTED HUBERT NKETIA IN
Kumari, Nketia assured him that if they could get to a village called Amagosanda, he would have troops meet them
there to take them the rest of the way. When he told Nketia that Ms. Duquette was hoping to meet with John Dari,
Nketia said that he would try to arrange it, but that
Mr. Dari was a very busy man these days. Sykes's bullshit
detector went off immediately, but he decided to reset it—
he was a stranger in a strange land, where the rules were
different. He wondered if Nketia was waiting for a bribe
to be offered. In the hotel lobby, he told Major Fewalla,
the officer heading Gabrielle Duquette's security force,
that they needed to go to Amagosanda. Fewalla returned
after talking to his men and said that given how the situation had deteriorated in the last forty-eight hours, the
dangers had increased proportionately, and his men were
going to need hazard pay, five hundred dollars a man.

"This is extortion," Sykes said. The major nodded and
smiled.

"Yes, that is right," Fewalla said.

When Sykes reported the news to Gabrielle and told
her they were shaking her down, he added, half in jest,

"For that kind of money, you could just rent a helicopter." She responded by saying, "All right then, do it," went into her bedroom, and returned with twenty thousand dollars in new one-hundred-dollar bills.

At the airport, he found a pilot named Kwame Mac-Arthur, a captain in the Ligerian air force, skinny as a pencil with aviator sunglasses, a thin mustache, a gold tooth in the middle of his smile, and a walk that made him look slightly like a marionette. After dickering over the price, MacArthur said he thought he'd be able to fly them, as long as they could be back that evening. The helicopter, a Chinook with Ligerian air force numbers and insignia on the aft pylon, was more helicopter than they needed, capable of carrying as many as forty passengers, but it would have to do. As they boarded the jolly, Sykes had further misgivings.

"There's no copilot or flight engineer," he told Gabrielle, as MacArthur settled into the right-hand seat. "We might want to rethink this."

"I don't want to rethink this," she said. "Can one man fly this thing?"

"I suppose," Sykes said. "I doubt he'd try if it wasn't possible. I've just never seen it."

"You've flown in these before?" she asked.

"Hundreds of times," he said.

"Ask him if we could hire a copilot and a flight engineer—tell him it's not a matter of money," Duquette told him. Yet when he walked forward and spoke to the pilot, MacArthur only shook his head, then returned to his preflight checklist.

Gabrielle made a circling gesture above her head with her index finger to tell the pilot they were ready, then buckled herself into a seat by the window. A minute later, they were airborne. Sykes had packed a pair of MAC-10s with as many ammo clips as he could carry in a backpack. Duquette carried only her silver Zero case, not daring to leave it behind. A .60-caliber minigun was mounted at the rear door of the jolly.

A greeting party was waiting for them in Kumari, including dancers in colorful costumes, drummers, singers, children with hand-lettered signs that said WE LOVE YOU GABRIELLE, a television crew, and a coterie of officials and men in dark suits. Her smile lit up the terminal, Sykes thought. Hubert Nketia was a well-dressed man of about sixty, with close-cropped white hair, a broad grin, and a hearty embrace for the famous actress, who introduced Sykes as her traveling companion. Sykes instructed Captain MacArthur to have the helicopter refueled and to wait for them in it with the engine running, adding that there would be a substantial bonus for him, pending their safe return to Port Ivory. If MacArthur was for sale, Sykes wanted to make sure he understood that Gabrielle Duquette was the highest bidder.

"Will Mr. Dari be meeting us?" he asked Nketia when he had a moment.

"Oh yes yes, I think so," the man said, smiling brightly. Too brightly, Sykes thought. Maybe working in counter-intelligence had made him cynical (DeLuca had warned him it would), but he didn't trust people who smiled too easily and told you what you wanted to hear.

They boarded limousines and were brought to a place called the Safari Inn, where a banquet had been prepared. On the way, Sykes checked his gear and made sure he had a round chambered in his automatic.

"What's that for?" Gabrielle asked him.

"You're usually most vulnerable during transport," he told her. "Are you absolutely certain about this guy?"

"Hubert is my son's godfather," Gabrielle said. "I'd say you're too suspicious, but I actually like that in a body-guard. We're okay."

He hoped she was right.

The resort catered to American and European hunters, but had been prepared to accommodate Gabrielle Du-quette's antifur, pro-PETA sensibilities. Sykes saw blank spots on the walls of the lobby and banquet hall where an-imal trophies had been removed—it was, after all, a hunt-ing lodge. He saw one of the kitchen staff shoo a small child out the door, the child attracted by the aromas of stewing meat, curry, and lemon grass—there was nothing intrinsically wrong about that, but it seemed to him that the cook had acted a bit too roughly, too rudely. When the food was served, the children from the airport performed on a stage, singing songs and playing music with a "bam-boo orchestra" that used truncated bamboo shoots of varying lengths and widths, which, when bounced on the stage, produced both a rhythmic pulse and musical notes. After the meal (a repast that struck Sykes as insensitive, given that they were in the middle of a famine), Nketia made a speech thanking the beautiful Gabrielle Duquette for coming and for calling the world's attention to the plight of the Ligerian people.

Sykes had heard speeches before, so he decided to have a look around. Something was wrong. Off. Didn't add up. Standing at the door at the back of the kitchen, he noticed the same children who'd been singing on the stage, a few moments before, being herded by a pair of armed men into a waiting passenger van. This was a job for armed men? When one child reached out a hand beseechingly, the soldier slapped it away and pushed the child forward with the barrel of his gun. They were still hungry? As far as Sykes could tell, the only children who were actually being fed were the two seated to either side of Gabrielle, each child with a nanny standing in attendance, but the nannies, Sykes noticed, had long, painted fingernails and looked more like prostitutes, frankly, than childcare providers.

People weren't who they said they were. It was a setup. But for what? His biggest fear was an abduction, that John Dari had lured Gabrielle here, using people she knew, or thought she knew, and that he planned to use her to get the attention he needed, the way his abductors had used Daniel Pearl to get attention. If you could seize the world stage, killing a journalist, think what you could do if you abducted an actress who already had the world's attention?

Sykes excused himself, saying he needed to use the bathroom, found a stall and locked the door. Using his CIM, he logged onto SIPERNET and plugged in the name Hubert Nketia. In the rush to arrange for transportation, he hadn't had time, and he'd trusted Gabrielle's judgment. Finally a file downloaded. What he read partially confirmed his suspicions, though it looked less like an abduction than a scam. They were still in danger.

According to his handheld, a man named Hubert Nketia had been arrested in Brooklyn in 1986 for running a long-distance telephone scam, selling stolen calling-card numbers to foreign nationals. In 1991, the same man, Hubert Nketia, had been arrested for credit theft, again heading a ring of criminals who this time pulled the un-shredded carbon copies from credit card transactions out of wastebaskets to get the numbers and then cloned the plastic—his people had worked as housekeepers in various hotels in New York City. When the photograph finally downloaded, Sykes saw that it was the same man, albeit younger looking, not as gray. Nketia had been extradited, sent back to Liger to serve his time in prison. It probably wouldn't be terribly difficult for a man with money to buy his way out of a Ligerian prison.

He saved the files to memory. He was 99 percent certain he knew what sort of scam this was. When he returned to the banquet, Gabrielle told him she was going to discuss business with her friend in private, and that he could wait in the lobby if he wanted. He told her he thought it would be a good idea if he accompanied her—a very good idea. She reluctantly agreed.

They adjourned to what Nketia said was the presidential suite, where cocktails awaited. A barman with a suspicious bulge beneath his vest asked Sykes if he wanted anything. Sykes declined, carrying Gabrielle's Zero case and staying close to his pack, unsnapping the snaps as inconspicuously as possible in case he had to reach his weapons in a hurry. Nketia poured champagne.

"This is a grand thing that you are doing, Gabby," he said to her, raising his glass in a toast. "It is unfortunate that in Liger today, we can do more good in private than we can do in public, but that is how it is. The good you do today will have a lasting effect for years to come. The children whose lives you will save will be forever in your debt."

In his pocket, Sykes pressed a button on his SATphone. He'd set it up, in the bathroom, to play a sample ring tone. His phone chirped in his pocket. He took it out quickly, apologizing, and "answered" it, pretending to listen for a few moments.

"Excuse me, Gabby . . ."

"Not right now," she said.

"I think you'd better take this . . ."

"Tell whoever it is that I'll call him back," she commanded.

"It's Wayne Gretzky," Sykes said. "He's out of backfat and he needs you to send him loonies."

She looked at him like he had a monkey growing out of his forehead. She was Canadian. He'd read that in *People* magazine. He didn't know much Canadian slang, but what he knew, he'd used, trusting that Nketia wouldn't understand. Sykes looked Gabrielle Duquette in the eye, unblinking, to stress the gravity of what he was saying. When she took the phone from him, she heard a message for her that he'd recorded in the bathroom, dialing his own number and retrieving the message he'd left in his own voice mail before handing her the phone.

"Gabby, you're not going to like what I have to tell you," his message said. "You should probably nod and argue and say things like 'yes' and 'no' and 'uh-huh' to pretend you're actually talking to somebody. This isn't what it appears to be. I have a handheld computer on me with wireless satellite access to a database called SIPER-NET that our intelligence agencies use to exchange information."

"Oh really?" Duquette said out loud. "That's interesting. I thought you were out of that business."

"I'm recording this message in the bathroom. I just re-searched Hubert Nketia. He was arrested twice in New York for scams, one involving stolen calling-card num-bers and another involving stolen credit cards. He was de-ported in 1992, but I'm guessing he bribed his way out of prison once he was sent back to Liger. His photograph came up as well. There isn't any doubt, Gabby. I can show you if you give me a chance. This man is a con man and a convicted criminal. Okay?"

"Uh-huh," she said, catching Dan's eye. She looked upset, as if she were about to cry, then instantly changed her expression. She was an accomplished actress.

"I know you think he's a cuddly old fart and he's your kid's godfather, but that's part of the game, gaining your confidence. That's why it's called a con. Now let me tell you what I think and you just nod if I'm right. I think you have money in your case. Probably a lot of money. Nod if I'm correct."

She nodded, looking at Nketia and smiling apologeti-cally for having to take the call. She looked at Dan, with an expression of surprise.

"Smile once in a while. Remember that they still think you think this is a happy occasion. Did Nketia tell you he needed you to bring money to Liger and that you had to do it in person?"

"Yup, uh-huh," she nodded, smiling brightly.

"Did he tell you that if you gave him the money in cash, he'd use it to bribe a government official to release an even larger amount of money? Or maybe food or something like that?"

She looked shocked, her eyes widening, as she nodded again.

"Uh-huh," she replied.

"This is called a 'Nigerian scam,' but Nigerians aren't the only ones who do it. It's done in person, in chain letters, or on the Internet—it works like this. They get somebody with a good heart and money, like you, and they tell them they can help somebody else. Usually the con says there's money in a bank, maybe an inheritance, but the bank manager won't allow them to withdraw it unless they pay a fee or bribe him, something like that. So the well-meaning person gives the con man the money, and they never see him again. How much money is in the case—is it over a million dollars?"

"Uh-huh," she said, still in shock.

"Is it over two?"

She nodded again.

"Uh-huh," she said cheerfully.

"Here's what we're going to do. I'll be the director. What I'm looking for is a sudden sickness, somewhere between Debra Winger in *Terms of Endearment* and that guy who had a snake burst out of his stomach in *Alien*. Your character's motivation is, you don't want to be killed. Okay? I will take you and your Zero case to the bathroom, once you get sick, and we'll leave from there. The women's room has a window. Okay?"

"Okey-dokey," she said. "I wish you'd said something earlier."

Sykes made a weak expression.

"I'm sure you would have if you could have," she said. "Thanks, Wayne—you're an angel. Bye-bye."

She hung up the phone, handed it to Dan, making contact with his fingers as she did, then returned to her seat.

There were four men in the room, not counting Nketia and including the bartender. Unfortunately, Nketia had brought one of the children with him, a little girl who was probably two or three years old, with big pleading eyes and a sweet soft smile. He said they'd decided at the orphanage to name the girl Gabrielle. Wasn't that nice? The girl's presence made shooting up the room and stepping over the bodies on their way out problematic.

"Now tell me," Gabrielle said. "This man who you say will help you release the relief funds for the food—you're sure that he can be trusted?"

"Oh yes, yes," Nketia said, gesturing with his hands. "He is my brother-in-law. If he were to do anything, my sister would not come to his bed for a year, and he is far too fond of her to allow that." Nketia laughed. "He will spread your gift around to the appropriate people. That is just the way business is done here in Liger sometimes. There is no avoiding it. Now, unfortunately, the hotel has been very kind to allow us to use their facilities, but I'm afraid—what's wrong?"

Gabrielle was holding her gut, her eyes bulging.

"Oh, my God," she said painfully. She raised a hand in the air, feeling her stomach with the other. "I think it's nothing. It's . . . Oh, Lord, please . . ."

She looked absolutely green. Her performance was remarkable as she sickened and fell to her knees, grasping the coffee table for balance. Sykes helped her to her feet. She said she had to go to the bathroom.

"My medicine," she said to Sykes. "It's in my case— would you bring it, please? I apologize. These things happen suddenly sometimes. Dan, could you assist me?"

Nketia gestured to one of his men to help her. Sykes took her other arm and threw it over his shoulder, and together, the two men helped Gabrielle Duquette to the bathroom. Sykes grabbed his backpack on the way.

Once inside the bathroom, he grabbed the other man by the hair and pounded his head against the wall. The man slumped to the floor, unconscious.

"Oh, my God," Gabrielle said, stepping back from the unconscious body. Sykes locked the bathroom door.

"He'll be all right when he wakes up," Sykes said, even though he didn't know that to be true. He kept his voice to a whisper, wary that someone was on the other side of the bathroom door. "Maybe a slight memory loss, but that's in our favor, too. Make some sick sounds while I open the window."

Behind him he heard a retching sound that was utterly realistic.

"Are you all right, Gabrielle?" someone on the other side of the door called out. "Would you like me to call a doctor?"

"I'll be out in a minute," she called back. "I think it might have been food poisoning. Can you give me ten minutes?"

They were out the window in one.

In front of the Safari Inn, beneath a broad, thatched portico, two limos waited. A single driver leaned against the fender of one of them, smoking a cigarette. Sykes told him Hubert wanted to have a word with him. When the driver was gone, Sykes disabled one of the limos by ripping out the ignition wires, then started the other, with Gabrielle in the backseat. He stepped on the gas when he saw two men in his rearview mirror, pointing rifles at them from the portico and firing. The bullets bounced harmlessly off the rear window.

"Well that's good news," he said. "I was sort of hoping these were bulletproof."

"I don't know why you had to hurt that man," she said.

"Why?" Sykes said. "Seriously? Because he would have killed us both in a heartbeat, that's why. It's not like in the movies, where the good guy always has to wait for the bad guy to draw first. The only reason they didn't just kill us and take the money right away was they probably thought they could get more out of you down the road."

They drove for ten minutes in silence. Sykes was afraid that Nketia was going to call ahead to have somebody meet them and rob them, so he took a side road, guided by Scott DeLuca on his SATphone and by the map that Scott downloaded to his CIM.

"Is that the thing you know that I don't?" Gabrielle Duquette said at length. "About killing people? You're not really retired, are you?"

"No, Gabby, I'm not," he said.

"So you lied to me, then," she asked.

"Yes," Sykes said. "I did."

The limo was running on fumes by the time they reached the airport, pulling onto the tarmac and stopping next to the helicopter hangar. They'd ridden the rest of the way in silence. When Sykes inquired about the whereabouts of his pilot, he was told by a mechanic that Captain Mac-Arthur had been arrested, for treason, the mechanic believed. Gabrielle Duquette waited for him by the chopper.

"Just tell me one thing," she asked him, "because I have to know. Are you on my side?"

"Are you kidding me?" he said. "The daughter of

Princess Leia and Han Solo? How could I not be? Unfortunately, I have more bad news, I'm afraid. MacArthur shan't return."

"What do you mean?" Gabrielle said. "Where is he?"

"Somebody took him," Sykes said, trying the door to the helicopter, which opened. "Let's get inside. I'm feeling a bit conspicuous, standing out here in the open."

Sykes closed the helicopter door behind him. It was cool inside with the air-conditioning running, which meant MacArthur had left the auxiliary power unit on. An alert on his CIM informed him that a convoy of LPLF trucks was speeding toward the airfield and would arrive in ten minutes.

"Can we take the limo?" Gabrielle said.

"Negative," Sykes said, trying to think. "It's out of gas." He saw a pair of Jeeps parked on the apron by the hangar door. It would take him a while to steal one.

"What about this?" the actress asked him. "Can you fly this?"

"Can I fly a helicopter?" Sykes said. "No, I can't."

"You said you've flown in them hundreds of times," she argued.

"In the back," Sykes said. "It's not like a car—Daddy doesn't let you sit on his lap and pretend."

"What are our alternatives?" she asked.

"Unfortunately, none," Sykes said. He eyed the cockpit's control panel, picking up the checklist he'd seen MacArthur referring to. It was written in a language he didn't recognize. The labels on the dials and instruments were in English. As far as he could tell, the fuel tanks were full. He dialed a number on his SATphone, then took a radio headset and wedged the phone next to his ear so that his hands would be free. The meter on the face of the telephone, indicating remaining battery power, was down to a single bar.

"Scottie," he said when he got through. "This is urgent. Patch me through, ASAP, with a chopper pilot—somebody who knows the Chinook. Forty-six, I think. Maybe forty-seven. I'm going to need some help."

Thirty seconds later, Sykes heard a voice, a pilot named Captain Evans who asked him what the problem was.

"The problem is, I'm not a pilot." Sykes said, "but we have no other means of evac.'"

"All right," Evans said hesitantly. "I suppose if we take it slow . . ."

"Let's take it fast," Sykes said. "We're going to have company soon."

"Okay," Evans said. "Why don't you start by telling me what you're sitting in?"

"I'm in a Chinook."

"What model?"

"I don't know," Sykes said. "Where would I find the model number?"

"Oh, Jesus," the actress said, rolling her eyes.

"It should be painted on the tail, on the aft pylon, below the service numbers," Evans said. "Why don't you get out of the helicopter and check? It's rather important."

When Sykes returned, he told Evans they were in a CH-47D, which Evans told him, sounding relieved, was a good model to fly solo, with a FADEC or Full Authority Digital Engine Control system that made it something like starting a car.

"I gather the APU is on and you're in ground idle. There are two levers on the console above you. Those are your engine condition levers. They're about eight inches long with knobs on the end. Advance them forward simultaneously until they lock. The rpm gauge on the instrument panel in front of you should read 100 percent. Do you see it? It's a white needle . . ."

"One hundred percent," Sykes said. The engines thundered as the aircraft began to vibrate.

"Next to the engine condition levers, to the left, you'll see three switches. These are your generators. Push the two leftmost switches forward to shut them off. You'll also see two switches to the right of the condition levers marked PTS—these are your power transfer switches. You need to turn them off to pressurize your flight controls . . ."

"What's he saying?" Gabrielle shouted above the roar.

"Be with you in a minute," Sykes told her.

"Now you can turn the APU generator off," Evans said. "That's the switch next to the two generators you already turned off. Now, on the center console, you should see a rotary knob marked AFCS in the off position. That's your Automated Flight Control System. I want you to look at the controls. Do you see the artificial horizon indicator?"

"Got it," Sykes said.

"Your airspeed indicator is to the left and your altimeter is to the right. The circle below it is your compass. Above it, you should see the Master Caution Panel. Do you see a pair of lights marked AFCS? I want you to turn the rotary knob to the position marked 'both on.' The two AFCS lights on the Caution Panel should extinguish."

"Got it," Sykes said. The rotors on the bird were turning at full speed, three in the front and three in the back, spinning in opposite directions. He gave Gabrielle Duquette one of the MAC-10s and told her to cover the hangar if someone came out and tried to stop them. She took the weapon reluctantly. He saw a line of white trucks in the distance, pausing at the airport gates.

"Now I need you to lock down the aft wheels," Evans said. "You should see a swivel switch on the rear left portion of the center console. I want you to pull that back . . ."

"Got it," Sykes said.

The trucks approached.

"Excellent," Evans said.

"Any way we could expedite would be appreciated," Sykes told Evans, watching the trucks as the gate swung open.

"There's a lever on your left, mounted to the floor," Evans said. "That's the collective. It changes the pitch on the rotor blades . . ."

"You can tell me everything you want about how helicopters work later," Sykes said, the trucks approaching. "We really have to be going."

"Pull up on the collective and hold it at the point where you achieve lift," Evans said. "When you're twenty or thirty meters up, you can nudge the cyclic forward a few inches. That's the stick between your legs. You'll feel the aircraft tilt slightly . . ."

Sykes throttled up as the massive aircraft rose clumsily into the sky. He saw below him where soldiers trying to aim rifles at them were knocked to the ground by the rotor wash. If anybody fired on them, it was too loud in the cockpit to hear it. Following Captain Evans's instructions, he turned the aircraft and accelerated just as the lead truck in the convoy chased them across the tarmac. Then they were fully airborne and flying, with the distance between them and the airport increasing.

"So far so good," Sykes said. "Captain Evans? Hello?"
The battery in his SATphone was dead.
It was going to make landing a bit tricky.

DeLuca, Vasquez, and Asabo had returned to the Hotel
Liger in Baku Da'al earlier that morning, spending the
night in the rain forest canopy and descending the ropes at
first light. The Park Motel was deserted when they returned to it, the bar looted, as was the lobby and all of the
guest cottages. On the banks of the pond, they saw three
crocodiles that had been shot to pieces and coarsely
butchered, their heads and claws taken, the rest bloated
in the sun and infested with flies and coprophagia. The
Cressida had been shot to pieces as well, the passenger
compartment filled with debris and broken glass, and it
had been set on fire, too, but the tires were intact and, to
DeLuca's amazement, the vehicle started when he turned
the key.

"You gotta love Toyotas," he said.

"The guy at the rental desk isn't going to like it,"
Vasquez said.

As they drove, they listened to the radio. They heard a
DJ who seemed to be ranting and raving, a lively reggae
tune playing in the background as he spoke. DeLuca
asked Asabo to translate.

"This is a Muslim station," Asabo said. "He is saying
to kill all the Christians and all the white people. That the
Ligerian People's Liberation Army cannot do the job
alone, so they need the help of every patriotic Muslim and
Kum and Da. He says the Fasori have oppressed them for
too long. Now is the time to strike and strike hard, until

your arm is weary, but Allah will give you new strength. That sort of thing."

DeLuca turned the dial until he stopped at a different station, where a different DJ was speaking with equal vehemence. Again, Asabo translated.

"This is a Christian station," Asabo said. "He's saying that the Fasori and the Da have been friends for a hundred years and that the Kum are cold-blooded killers who've tried to drive a wedge between them. He says the Da and the Fasori people must kill the Kum. And that the government will try to help them, but the government cannot do it alone."

Asabo stopped.

"I'm sorry," he said at last. "It's hard to listen to these statements. They're both saying the same thing. My country is insane."

When they arrived, they saw that the hotel's front courtyard was crowded with refugees, women and children crying and huddled on blankets beneath makeshift tarps, guarded by AU and UN soldiers who were too few to resist any sort of significant attack. There were two buses in the driveway, each painted white with the blue United Nations logo on the front, back, and sides and the letters UN large enough to be unmistakable. UN soldiers loaded whites and Europeans onto the buses for evacuation. DeLuca noted that Tom Kruger and Roddy Hamilton and the journalist he'd met at the poker game and knew only as Kurt had boarded the bus as well.

DeLuca was standing on the porch when a slender white man carrying a small suitcase approached him.

"Excuse me?" the man said. "Would you happen to know where I might find any American military personnel?"

"Military?" DeLuca said. "I don't think they're here yet. Is there something I could do for you?"

"I'm a bit confused," the man said. "My name is Andrew Rowen. I haven't been able to make any phone calls for over a week, and then I heard there was fighting. I'm not sure what's going on. I've been sitting at my house, waiting for someone to call."

"Join the club," DeLuca said. "Reverend Andrew Rowen, from Humboldt, Texas?"

"Yes," the man said, smiling. "I was hoping maybe there'd be some sort of transportation available."

DeLuca pointed to the buses in the courtyard.

"That's about all that's available," he said.

"Going to Port Ivory?"

"Straight to the airport, I believe," DeLuca said.

"Thank you," the man said

DeLuca knew he probably should have made special arrangements for the president's friend, but didn't—he could take his chances, with everybody else.

DeLuca found his weapons in his room where he'd left them. Both his phone and his CIM had succumbed to the moisture from submersion. He had backups in his room as well. He considered telling somebody that the president's personal guru was alive and well, but with all the journalists on the bus, the news would spread soon enough, and it was the kind of political media nonsense DeLuca stayed out of, whenever possible. He turned on his backup CIM. Once he was uplinked, he saw that there'd been heavy fighting in the northern suburbs, according to IMINT, government columns of tanks and troop transports meeting a force of rebels armed with RPGs that were effective against the armored vehicles. The airport had been taken, but the road south was still open. DeLuca could see plumes of smoke on the horizon from his balcony, and he heard the distant rumble of artillery fire.

"What've you got on my people?" he asked his son.

"I wish I had better news," Scottie said. "Sykes is on a Jolly Green, flying north to Kumari. Mack hasn't reported in and doesn't answer, but we have her signal, south of Kumari and moving. I think she's okay. We have Dennis's signal, but it hasn't moved since yesterday. That might just mean he dropped his phone. Or he could be hurt."

"Update me as soon as you hear anything," DeLuca said.

"What are your plans?" Scott asked. "I was worried about you."

"Spent the night in a tree," DeLuca said. "I need to brief the general at his earliest convenience. After that, unless he has any further need for us here, I was thinking maybe we'd mosey off into the sunset. I'm not sure what else we can do. But now I'm going to have to go get Dennis, unless he can move on his own power."

"I'll do my best," Scott said. "LeDoux's at a briefing, I believe. I'll pass your message on."

"Appreciate it," DeLuca said. "Pass this on, too—we strongly recommend taking out the radio stations. They're not doing anybody any good right now. We'll have to rebuild them, once this is over."

"I'll pass it on," Scott said.

DeLuca paused to send a brief e-mail to MacKenzie, tapping with his stylus on the tiny onscreen keyboard on his pocket computer. He'd been meaning to tell her in person. He wrote:

Mack,

Ackroyd does not check out. Be careful. No record of
publishing, etc. No Google. Past suspiciously blank.
I suspect identity a cover. CIA? MI-6? Just a thought.

D

DeLuca went to the lobby, a few minutes early—he
and Vasquez and Asabo were going to rendezvous there.
He hadn't eaten anything in twenty-four hours and had
ventured into the dining room to see if there was anything
left from the continental breakfast when he saw a familiar
face, a woman sitting at a table next to a man he didn't
recognize.

"*There* you are," Evelyn Warner said. "I was going to
give it a few more minutes and give up on you. Your
friend Mary Dorsey told me I'd find you here, and here
you are. Donald Brown, I'd like you to meet my ex-
husband, Hewitt Lloyd. Call him Hugh. But don't be too
nice to him because he's being something of a shit."

"Perhaps you could help us," Lloyd said. "We're trying
to settle an argument. I say it's a good idea, when you're
caught in the middle of a war about which you can do not
a thing, and the enemy troops are bearing down on you,
and if they catch you, they're quite certain to kill you and
quite possibly do any number of nasty things to you first,
to take flight and move to a safe place when you have the
chance. Evelyn, on the other hand, seems to think it's a
good idea to stay where you are, solely because the person advising her to flee is someone she's always had a
hard time admitting could ever possibly be right. What do
you think?"

"I think if I had to choose between which war I want to be in the middle of, yours or Liger's, I'd prefer to step out into the courtyard and take my chances," DeLuca said.

"Oh, well put," Evelyn said. "Don't worry, darling— Hugh was just leaving. Weren't you, Hugh? Remember how you said you were leaving? He's got to get back to his people at El Amin."

Lloyd stood up, looked at Warner, and sighed heavily.

"Forgive me, Mr. Brown," Lloyd said, "but if I could, I'm afraid I'd like to take your friend away from you. Evelyn, I can really only say this one more time. If you come with me now, you'll be safe. My car is waiting, but I really can't stand here all day and argue with you. If you don't come with me, God only knows what's going to happen. If you must make a foolish choice, so be it, but I think for once in your life you could be sensible and go along with someone else's idea for a change. I may not have many areas in life where I know more than you, but I'd think you'd have to agree that Liger is one of them."

"Oh, Hugh, please, you can go now—go with a clear conscience. You did your best, didn't you? You tried. That's all you can do," Warner said. "Besides, I've just met up with my old friend. We haven't had a moment to catch up, so why don't you just leave us? We'll be fine, won't we, Mr. Brown?"

"Perhaps Mr. Lloyd has a point," DeLuca said. "We could always meet another time."

"Nonsense," Warner said. "No time like the present. Good-bye, Hugh. See you at the Henley. Hugh's quite a rower. Always pulling his little oar."

"Evelyn," he said, then gave up. He turned on his heel and left, shaking his head as he went.

Evelyn gave DeLuca a terse smile.

"You're the intelligence expert," she said. "Tell me, David—what did I ever see in that man? Where was my intelligence when I needed it?"

"Intelligence and love have nothing to do with each other," DeLuca said. "If they did, nobody would fall in love more than once. I suppose he's good-looking, if you like that British square-jawed rakish devil-may-care sort of thing."

"Oh, he's quite good-looking," she said. "Just ask him, if you don't believe me. How are you?"

"I spent the night in a tree," he said. "Other than that . . . What are you doing here? You really shouldn't be here."

"Don't you start," she said. "Ms. MacKenzie said I could find you here. I was worried when they said you were supposed to return last night."

"Have you heard from Mack?" he asked.

"Not since she went to Kumari to talk to Imam Dadullahjid," Warner said. "Stephen and Claude are with her. Let me get right to the point, David, because Hugh is right—there isn't much time. I have eight hundred women and children living under plastic sheets and one or more armies about to land on us. I have twenty-five African Union troops with virtually no bullets in their guns to protect us and they're scared out of their wits. I have ten United Nations troops and we suspect two of them have been trading food for sexual favors with some of the girls. I also have four French doctors and six nurses, all of whom are white, and at least twenty or thirty people who are too sick to walk. I need your help. I need whatever help you can give me."

DeLuca looked at her.

"I don't know how much I have to offer," he said. "Right now, there's only three of us. Myself, Hoolie Vasquez, and Paul Asabo."

"Paul Mufesi Asabo?" she asked. "The king's son?"

DeLuca nodded.

"Is there anyone you won't use?" she asked him.

"It's my understanding that he volunteered," DeLuca said. "He wanted to help."

"Did he?" she said. "Well, you may have a greater asset there than you realize. You know, there's a persistent rumor that his father is still alive. One of those things people believe because they want it to be true."

She startled as an explosion sounded, closer than any they'd heard before.

"David, I'm afraid," she said. He was surprised to hear that word, coming from her. "Something terrible is going to happen. You're really the last hope I have to stop it. Is there anybody you can call? I'm not asking for a full division—a hundred men . . ."

"That's just not how we do it anymore," he said. "If we go, we go in force, with air support and the whole nine yards. They told me two days ago that I was on my own until Saturday. I'm sorry."

"You sent people to rescue your idiot ambassador," she said. "Are you saying you'd risk your lives for one white man, but not for eight hundred black women and children?"

According to the report he'd read on his backup CIM, the political fallout from the rescue mission was still shaking out, people, including members of the House and Senate, charging the president with acting unilaterally and going to war without the permission of Congress and even launching a crusade according to his own personal religious agenda—he'd used the word crusade three times in a speech defending the mission. He knew why Warner had said what she'd said, but he knew she understood his position, too.

"I'm sorry," she said. "That was unfair. Particularly given that you're here risking your life even as we speak— very bad form on my part. I apologize."

"What about your ex?" DeLuca asked. "I was told Ngwema released the mercs. Can't he send someone? He is with them, isn't he?"

"They only fight for what they're paid to fight for," Warner said. "You know that. They're called mercenaries. Not missionaries."

The UN buses were gone from the courtyard, as were the United Nations troops that were protecting them.

"I'll do what I can," he told her. "I can give you information. And we have UAVs in the air that are armed, but they're really not what you need. Right now my team is scattered all across the country, and I need to pull them in." He saw Vasquez and Asabo crossing the lobby toward him. When they arrived, he made the introductions.

"Evelyn Warner, BBC foreign service," she said, shaking Asabo's hand. She took out her business cards and handed one to DeLuca and another to Asabo. The card had her SATphone number. "Now you must grant me an interview when you have a moment. I knew your father, I have to tell you, met him when I was a young girl and not much of a reporter, through my husband's family, actually, but I liked him very much. Can we make a date?"

Asabo looked at DeLuca for guidance.

"It's all right," DeLuca said. "Nobody can keep a secret from Evelyn for very long."

"I've ordered a martini, but I don't know where the barman went," Warner said. "Can you stay a moment? I was hoping somebody could make me laugh today. That's another thing there's a shortage of in Liger."

Then a shell rocked the hotel, striking one of the upper floors, and immediately, a second explosion shook the building, hitting the roof somewhere near the banquet facilities. A third explosion followed, a mortar round sending up a spray of dirt and debris as it struck the center of the courtyard, where moments before, people had huddled.

Vasquez ran to the door. DeLuca could have kicked himself—the barman disappearing should have been a sign. How did he miss it?

"Incoming—convoy at the gates," Hoolie reported. "Six . . . eight trucks, maybe 150 troops."

DeLuca saw trucks in the driveway, rebel soldiers in the familiar red berets of the Ligerian People's Liberation Front, pumping their fists in the air and shouting, their eyes lit by the wild light of combat.

"Let's go," DeLuca said, taking Evelyn Warner by the hand and pulling her to her feet.

For the second time in less than twenty-four hours, he was running. They ran through the lobby toward the rear of the building, the kitchen in disarray, the doors swinging open. There was a service court at the rear of the building, a white wall with a wide gate in it to allow the passage of delivery trucks, a laundry building, a garbage facility, a storage building. DeLuca, Warner, Vasquez, and Asabo ran, following a crowd of people fleeing the troops assailing the front of the building. He heard a roar of gunfire behind him.

Behind the hotel, a cobblestone street ran uphill, with shops lining either side. He heard more mortar rounds landing behind them. Screams. People running everywhere.

At the top of the hill, the road came to a T. Across the street, he saw a church, St. Michael's Cathedral, according to the sign, a gold cross shining from the top of the cathedral dome. Terrified people crammed to squeeze through the wrought-iron gates that spanned a gap in the cement wall surrounding the edifice. He heard small-arms fire. Shouting.

"In there," DeLuca said, pointing to the church. "Quickly!"

Inside the gates, he saw perhaps five or six hundred people, filling every square inch of the churchyard, frightened children, mothers trying to quiet them, rocking them, hushing them, kissing their foreheads, and scared boys holding sticks, as if they could defend their families with sticks.

Someone was screaming above the din. DeLuca saw a priest running toward them, a short man in a clerical collar and black cassock, a large cross hanging around his neck on a gold chain, and he was shouting at them, pointing and gesturing.

"What's he saying?" DeLuca asked Asabo.

"He wants you to leave," Asabo said. "He says he wants no white people here. That if you stay, they will kill everyone."

DeLuca watched as a second priest, wearing a red surplice and white tippet, joined the first, handing him a machete. The two priests approached the gate, the short one holding the machete high above his head in a menacing way, shouting in English, "Get out, you go now, get out!"

Asabo stepped in front of the charging priest, holding his hand in the air to show the palm of his right hand.

"I am Paul Mufesi Asabo!" he called out. The priests stopped in their tracks. DeLuca watched as the crowd fell silent. A look of wonder spread across the faces of the refugees taking shelter, the news spreading by word of mouth, "Mufesi Asabo is here, it's him, the son of the king, he's here . . ." Asabo spoke briefly with the priests, and although DeLuca couldn't identify the language, he recognized the tone of chastisement and reproach, Asabo shaming the priests as they lowered their weapons. The priests were frightened, too. They spoke softly now. DeLuca heard a chant rising among the throng, *"Da-hene, Fasori-hene, Mufesi Asabo,"* which Evelyn Warner translated as "king of the Da, king of the Fasori."

"He says you can stay," Asabo said, turning to DeLuca. "I've told him his behavior is shameful."

"I gathered," DeLuca said, "but I also think he might be right. We may want to find other accommodations."

"I'll stay," Asabo said. "These people are frightened."

"If the rebels find you . . ." DeLuca began.

"No one will betray me," Asabo said. He turned to the crowd and put his finger to his lips to shush them. DeLuca was astonished to see that even in the chaos and confusion of war, the crowd turned silent at Asabo's command. "I'll be okay."

"We'll be back," DeLuca said.

They turned right out the gate and ran, trying every door they could to look for a place to take refuge, but all the doors and gates on the street were locked. DeLuca turned. He saw men standing on the roof of the hotel, observing the city below with binoculars. They came to another T.

To the right he saw people fleeing, several blocks away now. To the left, the street the hotel was on—they ducked quickly behind a wall as a truck carrying troops sped across the intersection. Had it turned, they'd have had nowhere to hide, and perhaps the next truck would turn.

DeLuca saw a mosque across the street, a stone wall, a door, and then the door opened a crack. He saw a bearded man, dressed in clerical robes, his head wrapped in a white turban. The man glanced down the street in both directions, then gestured for them to cross. DeLuca, Warner, and Vasquez ran, slipping through the door just as a troop transport turned up the street. The imam put his finger to his lips to indicate the need for silence, his back to the door as he waited. Once the transport had rumbled past, he opened the door again to check.

"You are safe here," he said in English, closing the door and locking it. He identified himself as Imam Ahmed Al-Shahab. DeLuca spoke to him in Arabic. The imam told them they could stay as long as they wished.

"We thank you for your assistance," DeLuca said in Arabic. *"We have Allah to thank that you were here to open the door."*

"The Koran requires that I help," the man said in reply. *"If you give me your weapons, I will give them back to you when you are ready to leave."*

Again, DeLuca trusted his gut, even though his instincts, as a cop and as a soldier, told him never to give up his weapons to anyone. Evelyn Warner was unarmed. He gave his MAC-10 to the holy man and instructed Vasquez to do the same.

They waited, listening to the sounds of artillery and gunfire, waxing and waning. After an hour, the tide of battle appeared to have turned. DeLuca followed the fight in real time on his CIM, alternating between satellite imagery and an iconographic display provided by IMINT using arrows and markers. IPAB/LPLF forces had not been defeated, so much as they'd passed through without leaving a rear guard. Ligerian regular army troops were currently making a stand south of town. A dozen villages north of Baku Da'al had been burned to the ground.

When Scott said it looked like it was safe to return to the hotel, DeLuca thanked Imam Al-Shahab, who gave them their weapons back and bade them, without a trace of irony in his voice, to go in peace. Paul Asabo had managed to turn aside an assault in the church when he was able to reassure the troops that the priests had given shelter only to women and children, after secreting the men and boys inside the chapel.

The hotel was riddled with bullet holes. DeLuca found the Toyota Cressida he'd rented tipped over on its side. He and Vasquez righted it, the car bouncing on its shock absorbers, but when he turned the key, again it started.

"Sweet," Vasquez said.

DeLuca searched the hotel and found Robert Mohl seated at the bar, drinking the last remaining beer on the premises, the rest of the booze supply having been looted by the rebels. He'd passed the attack hiding in the basement, he said.

"I think maybe it's time I packed my things and headed out," Mohl told DeLuca. "Time to call it a job."

"Why weren't you on the bus?" DeLuca asked him.

"If they stopped the bus and found a CIA agent on it, they'd have killed everybody, I think," Mohl said. "Best not."

DeLuca noticed that the door to the parrot cage was open.

"I let them out," Mohl said. "Unfortunately, I don't know where else they're going to find work. Perhaps I'm not the only one in need of a career change."

"We have a car," DeLuca told him.

"That's all right," Mohl said. "I've made other arrangements. Maybe after this, they'll start calling me an 'old Africa hand.' I always wanted to be an old hand somewhere." He finished his beer with a swig and staggered to the door, straightening both his tie and his posture as he made his exit.

Perhaps because of the Doctors Without Borders logo on the door, Evelyn Warner's Land Rover had been left untouched, a small miracle, she said. She told DeLuca she had to get to Camp Seven. He took her aside and showed her the map displayed on the screen of his CIM. A large contingent of hostile troops had paused north of a line between Camp Seven and Sagoa. At the estimated rate of advance, barring an encounter with unexpected resistance, enemy troops were anticipated to arrive at one or both places by nightfall.

"How many people in Sagoa?" DeLuca asked.

"I'm not sure," Warner said. "A few thousand. More than at Camp Seven. What are you going to do?"

"I'm going to do what I can," DeLuca said. "I need to find out what's happening with my team. Once I know that, I'll have a better sense of what's going on and what I can do."

"If I see Ms. MacKenzie, I'll tell her to call you," Warner said. "Take care, David."

Chapter Ten

DENNIS ZOULALIAN WOKE UP IN A HOSPITAL bed but had no idea where he was, or how he'd gotten there, or for that matter, that his name was Dennis Zoulalian. Words swam in his head, but not all of them in the same language. The television in his room was tuned to Al Jazeera, and he understood everything the announcers were saying, but he knew that Arabic was not his native tongue. His neck hurt, and his vision was blurred. His head throbbed. A doctor shone a small light in his eyes and spoke to him in French, which he also understood. He couldn't respond.

He was tired, so he went back to sleep.

The next time he awoke, his vision was better but his neck still hurt. He recalled being in a car, but the details of the rest of it simply weren't there.

"Patient X. Je m'appelle Claude Chaline et je suis avec Docteurs Sans Frontières. Parlez-vous français?"

"Oui," Vasquez said.

"Vous étiez dans un accident. Vous avez souffrit d'une commotion cérébrade. Savez-vous où vous êtes?"

The doctor said he'd been in an accident and was asking him if he knew where he was.

"Je ne suis pas sûr. Je suis dans un hôpital. A Liger."

"Vous vous rappelez comment vous êtes arrivé ici?"

"Do I remember how I got here?" Zoulalian said in English. The doctor seemed surprised, then concerned.

"Parlez s'il vous plait en français."

The doctor told him his dental work was American—had he lived in America?

"Oui."

"Qui êtes-vous?"

Who was he?

Excellent question. Something told him not to speak English again. The same voice told him he was in danger, and to be careful.

"Je ne sais pas. Je voudrais savoir."

I don't know—I wish I did.

"They found these on you," the doctor said in French. He was holding a satellite telephone and a small hand-held computer. *"Unfortunately, both require some sort of password to access. I don't suppose you remember what your passwords are? They might help us learn who you are."*

"I don't remember," Zoulalian said.

"You speak English without an accent. I also found a tattoo on your butt cheek when I examined you. A pair of green footprints. Do you know how they got there?"

Zoulalian shook his head.

"Let me tell you what I think, then. It might help you remember. A few years ago I taught a course in how to provide emergency medical treatment to undernourished and starving people. The course was at Lackland Air Force Base in San Antonio, Texas. My students were all members of the U.S. Air Force's para-rescue service.

When they graduate, to show that they are members of the team, they get a pair of small green footprints tattooed on their asses. Your own physical fitness is probably what saved you from the car accident, as much as the airbag. I think you are a PJ. Or you were, at one time. I have also never met an Arab who has a tattoo."

Zoulalian tried to remember. He recalled the training, running for what felt like hours beneath the hot Texas sun. He'd quit. No, he'd finished the program, done the job, for a while, but then he'd transferred . . . changed jobs. To what?

"Your memory will come back to you," the doctor said. *"The condition is temporary and quite common to head injuries. I think you will be sore, but I find nothing broken. Can you sit up?"*

Zoulalian sat up. His vision spun and his head banged like a drum, and the doctor was right, he was sore in his chest and neck, but beyond that, he felt relatively all right.

"So here is what happened. I was in a car. With some other people. You were in the car chasing us when you had the accident. I came back to see if I could help. I sent my friends on ahead. Everyone in your vehicle was killed but you. They brought you here, and they brought me here to treat you. There's a man outside the door with a gun, but he's not guarding you—he's guarding me. I'm a prisoner. They think you are one of them. I need to get back to my camp. There's only one man outside the door. I've prepared a syringe with a fast-acting barbiturate, but I need you to distract the guard. I don't know what you're doing here, but my sense is that if you are an American, you need to escape as much as I do, so if you'll help me, I'll take you with me. How does that sound to you?"

Zoulalian had to think? Was it a trick? No. He could tell from the doctor's voice that he was someone he could trust.

"Très bon," Zoulalian said.

Zoulalian called out to the guard in Arabic and asked him to enter the room. When the guard entered, he gestured with a crooked finger, inviting him to come close so that he could whisper something to him. When the guard leaned over, Zoulalian grabbed the barrel of his Uzi, to make sure it wasn't pointing at the doctor, then whispered, in English, "Nighty-night."

The doctor stabbed the guard in the carotid artery with the syringe. The man dropped instantly.

Zoulalian got to his feet, still a bit woozy, and helped the doctor lift the guard into the bed, where they covered him with a sheet. The doctor prepared an IV drip with enough sedative in it, he explained, to keep the guard unconscious until the following day. They removed the guard's identification papers and left him there. With any luck, it would be some time before anyone realized a different man was now lying in the bed of patient X.

Zoulalian held the guard's weapon on his lap, hidden beneath a blanket, while Dr. Chaline pushed him in a wheelchair to the front door of the hospital. In the drive, they saw a black Mercedes belonging to some local tribal leader or warlord, the driver leaning against the front fender. Chaline opened the back door and helped Zoulalian in, then snapped his fingers to command the driver to get behind the wheel.

"Your employer said you are to take us," Chaline said in English, getting in on the passenger side. "Quickly. There isn't much time. This man is not well."

216   David DeBatto and Pete Nelson

The driver sped away. Zoulalian looked out the rear window to make sure they weren't followed. Once they were out of town, Zoulalian pointed the Uzi at the driver's head and told him he could get out now, and thanks for the lift. They left him standing by the side of the road.

MacKenzie and Ackroyd tried to talk Dr. Chaline out of going back, telling him he'd be taken hostage if he did, but he insisted, arguing that Docteurs Sans Frontières also meant doctors who didn't take sides, and that if there were wounded people, he could not walk away. He would be safe, once it was understood which NGO he worked for, he told them.

Mack and Stephen drove across an open, barren landscape, aware that the dust kicked up by the Land Rover made them visible for miles, crossing a rickety trestle bridge that spanned a nearly empty river bed where three elephants wallowed in a water hole. They'd left the main highway, certain that traveling on it wouldn't be safe, and were quite lost, despite the map Stephen found in the glove compartment that he was hoping might help them navigate (she'd left her CIM at Camp Seven). They drove until they came to the Convent of St. Ann's, a compound of red brick, squatting in the dust, where the abbess told them it wouldn't be safe for them to stay, because men with guns had come every night, looking for somebody to kill. She'd sent her girls and her sisters in Christ to a convent in Ghana, across the River Liger, and she was the only one there, protected only by her advanced age and by her faith in God, which, she said, was enough. She gave them food and drink and suggested they drive another hour down the road to a village called Sagoa, where they might be safe. It would be dark soon, the abbess said, and it would not be safe at all for them to travel at night.

The setting sun bled across the western sky and turned the clouds to tongues of flame, and then the cobalt dome turned black overhead, the Milky Way glittering with an incandescence brighter than fireworks. MacKenzie was certain the abbess had given them the wrong directions, because ahead of them they saw only blackness, thick and opaque, but then she saw a light flicker. Foolishly, she'd expected to see a glow in the sky, the way the lights of a city might illuminate the horizon, but there were no lights in Sagoa, no electricity, only people sitting around charcoal fires or kerosene lamps in front of their homes, round earthen huts with roofs of thatch, each hut surrounded by massive clay storage jars and tin jerry cans. She saw children hiding inside their houses, fearful of whoever was in the vehicle, peeking out through the portals. They were Da, Ackroyd told her, identifiable by the distinct scars on their cheeks and by their humble, almost meek manner.

They stopped the car and parked beneath a large acacia tree at the center of the village, where they were met by a delegation led by a man who introduced himself as Father Ayala, a Spanish priest who'd been working in the village as a missionary. Stephen spoke some Spanish and conversed with the man for a few moments before telling MacKenzie what was going on.

"These people," Ackroyd said, "are LPF. Ligerian People's Front. They've come from up north, where, if I understand Father Ayala correctly, they tried to stop the rebels by sitting on the road to block it, and the troops drove over them. They're trying to get to Port Ivory. I told them it might not be safe there either."

Father Ayala spoke again for a few minutes. Ackroyd shook his head sadly.

"He's asking us if we have any food," Stephen told MacKenzie. "The people here are very hungry, he says."

Ayala spoke further. Ackroyd listened.

"He says there's food in a storage building owned by the government," Ackroyd told her, "but a powerful witch put a curse on the food so they can't eat it."

"Where?" MacKenzie asked.

Ackroyd asked the priest where, and the priest pointed to a tin warehouse, the size of a three- or four-car garage, at the edge of the common beneath a smaller tree, with a five-hundred-gallon fuel tank next to it, mounted on poles.

"There's food in that building, and nobody guarding it, but people are starving?" she asked. Stephen nodded.

"Juju," he said. "I know it sounds silly, but to them, it's totally real. A witch's curse is nothing to mess with. You do not want bad juju."

MacKenzie thought for a moment.

"Would they eat the food if I removed the curse?" she asked.

"I don't know," Stephen said. "Did you bring the curse-remover?"

"Ask him," she told Stephen, who relayed her question to the priest, who in turn asked the village elders standing behind him. The priest nodded to indicate that the people would indeed eat the food if the curse were lifted from it.

"What do you have in mind?" Stephen asked MacKenzie as she walked back to the vehicle. "This isn't something these people take lightly."

"I'm counting on it," she told him. "Don't forget—I'm a witch, too. I didn't get this red hair out of a bottle."

She'd noticed, in the back of the Land Rover, a set of emergency supplies in case of car trouble, including a full tool kit and a four-pack of emergency chemlites in an aluminum sleeve to protect them from exposure to sunlight. Some chemlites the Army issued were designed to emit a variety of lumens for different lengths of time, and generally the longer a chemlite burned, the dimmer it was. The chemlites she took from the car were formulated to glow very brightly for about thirty minutes. They were orange, two feet long, and each about the thickness of her thumb. She took a machete from the back of the truck and walked to the storage building, where she saw that the door was locked with a simple padlock. It seemed like half the village had followed her to see what she was going to do.

She bent the four-pack of chemlites across her knee, hearing each one snap, then shook the pack to make sure the chemicals mixed. A faint orange glow emanated through the foil wrapper. She held it up in the air in the darkness so that everyone could see the faint orange glow—Evelyn Warner had told her that people believed witchery took the form of light rising from the body—then she set the four-pack down on a wooden bench, raised the heavy machete blade high over her head, and brought it down with as much force as she could bring to bear, slicing the aluminum foil sack and the chemlites inside open, whereupon she quickly flung the liquid against the side of the building, daubing it on the door and on the padlock. Exposed to air, the chemophosphorescence would last only a few minutes more. The result achieved was better than anticipated, a kind of psychedelic Jackson Pollock/Peter Max effect.

"Tell them that once the light's gone, the curse will have been lifted," she said.

Ackroyd relayed the message to Father Ayala, who passed it on to the people of Sagoa. Ayala, MacKenzie surmised, understood the sham and saw right through it but didn't care, as long as the hungry people were fed.

A few minutes later, Stephen broke the padlock with a large maul. Inside, they found cardboard boxes and wooden crates with the letters IPAB stenciled on the side. The cardboard boxes contained U.S. Army issue MREs, enough to feed the village for perhaps a week. The wooden crates contained AK-47s and ammunition. When MacKenzie told Father Ayala, as Stephen translated, that she'd be willing to show his people how to load and fire the Kalashnikovs, he shook his head and refused, saying his organization was a pacifist organization—even in the face of death, they would not resort to violence. She showed them, instead, how to open and use the MREs, either beef stroganoff or chicken tetrazzini, how to crack the chempacks to heat the entrées, and she held up one of the cookies and took a bite to demonstrate that what appeared to be a thick piece of cardboard was in fact edible.

She expected a rush, but the people of Sagoa waited patiently as the meals were distributed. She'd expected cheers, or some kind of animation, but the people simply took their food and consumed it in silence, the children crouched around their MREs as if to protect them from raiding hyenas, fearful that someone was going to take them away.

Mack was starving, devouring her meal without thinking too much about it. Ackroyd picked at his meal and eventually handed what he couldn't eat to a child, who thanked him. They were sitting on the tailgate of the Rover.

"They're not very good," Mack told him, "but you really should eat something. You're too thin."

"You should have seen me in college," he told her with a smile. "I was downright roly-poly. I've been trying to lose weight my whole life. This is great. They say you can't be too rich or too thin—I'll work on being too rich later."

"Tomorrow," she said, "we should head back to Camp Seven. How far do you think it is?"

"As the crow flies," he said, "probably not far. The question is, how to drive there. The road we were on leads back to Baku Da'al, Ayala said. There's an oil facility at El Amin, but it might not be connected by road. The pipeline runs north and south but the oil workers patrol it with ultralight aircraft. There must have been a road when they built it."

"I'll call for directions in the morning," she said. "Unless my batteries give out."

"Call who?" Ackroyd asked. "Triple A?"

She'd almost said she'd call CENTCOM. To Stephen, she was still Mary Dorsey, with the United Nations. She'd dialed DeLuca's number earlier, but he wasn't answering. She'd been impressed, all day, by the way Stephen had watched out for her. She had to admit she'd developed a bit of a crush, as Evelyn Warner might have said. Nothing serious, of course.

"I'll call the CIA," she said. "Maybe they're watching us right now with their satellites."

He looked up at the night sky.

"It'd be just like the military to fuck up the Milky Way," he said.

"Are you antimilitary?" she asked him.

"Not at all," he said. "My father was in the military. A colonel, in fact. I'm just feeling very pro Milky Way right now."

"Me, too," she said.

"We should get some sleep," he told her. Most of the fires and lamps in the village had gone out now. They heard a woman singing softly somewhere. "There's blankets here. If you put the seat down, you can sleep in the back of the Rover. It's not bad, and you probably want to get up off the ground, where the no-see-ums won't get you."

He wrapped a blanket around her shoulders, then picked up a second one and wrapped it around his own before slipping down from the tailgate.

"So I guess I'll see you in the morning," he said.

"Where are you going?" she asked him. "Where are you going to sleep?"

"I don't know," he said, looking around. "I'll find a place somewhere."

"Get in the car," she told him. "I'm sure it's big enough in the back for the both of us."

The fact was, in the last three days, she'd grown enormously fond of the young writer, with his nimble intelligence and his quiet good looks, his gentle manner, his large heart. He was not, at all, the kind of man she was used to meeting in the military, and perhaps that was why she was so intrigued by him, or maybe it was just the old-fashioned stuff, the way he made sure she was taken care of before attending to himself, held doors open for her, listened to her closely when she spoke, and showed an interest in her. In the military, most guys (her team members the exceptions) still didn't know quite what to do with a woman who was also a peer and fellow soldier, except treat her like one of the guys, make coarse jokes, unless they felt threatened, and then they were complete assholes. Stephen was a good person. He told amusing stories. He found her stories reciprocally amusing. There was something mysterious about him, something he was withholding from her, and she wanted to know what it was. She'd had a fantasy, as a younger girl, of living in Hollywood and being an actress and living with a man who loved her and wrote fabulous screenplays for her to act in, sort of like Marilyn Monroe and Arthur Miller. The fantasy changed to living with a rock star who wrote songs about her, and then after a few years of dating actual boys, her fantasy was just that someday she'd meet a guy who wasn't a total dickhead. Stephen cared about what was going on in Africa, but not in a bleeding heart distant way—he was actually here, putting himself on the line, literally, though he didn't have to, trying to do something about it, to make things better, and she admired that.

When he lay down next to her in the back of the Land Rover, she felt her pulse quicken and wondered if she was falling in love with him. The idea struck her fairly suddenly, but just as suddenly, it made a kind of strange sense. It was an unlikely time and place to fall in love, but who could control the time and place when you fell in love? Maybe she wanted to fall in love, willed herself there, because of the hatred and horror all around them. Maybe the urge or need or wish to fall in love was some sort of survival mechanism, a thing the body knows it needs, the same way it knows it needs water or food. It wasn't the simple emotional release of sex she wanted, the way men wanted that, but something deeper and purer, a sense of connection and intimacy, where the bond came from knowing the utter truth about each other. There were men she trusted with her life, men like DeLuca, or Dan, but this was a man she trusted with her soul. That was how it felt.

She bunched her sweatshirt up beneath her head for a pillow and lay down next to him. They'd put a blanket down to lie on and used the second to cover themselves. He'd propped his head up on his backpack.

"I can't wait to read what you write about all this," she told him. "I'm sure it's going to be brilliant."

"I know this will sound strange," he told her, "but it is brilliant. I don't have any doubts. It might even win a Pulitzer. Sometimes I think the only thing that could stop it would be if Kruger and the others get jealous and sabotage me."

"How would they do that?" she asked.

"I don't know," Stephen said. "Accuse me of plagiarism, maybe. Hack into my computer, when I start writing it into my computer, and erase everything."

"I've been tempted to peek into your journal . . ."

"Don't ever do that," he said, flashing anger for the first time. "I'm sorry, but I really don't like people reading what I write before I finish it."

"I wouldn't," she said. "I only said I've been tempted . . ."

"Well just, please, okay?" he said, calming down. "I'm sorry. I'd rather wait to show you when I'm finished. I don't want to sound like a wuss, but that's how I feel."

"All right," MacKenzie said. "You have to promise. It's just that I see you writing in your journal and I get curious. I'll wait. I just wanted you to know that I believe in you. And as someone with whom I was recently shot at, I can tell you that I've been shot at before with other men, and you're not a wuss. Not remotely."

"Call me old-fashioned," Stephen said, smiling, "but I don't think I like hearing that you've been shot at with other men. I want to think I'm the only one."

"You're the only one, Stephen," she said. "I've never been shot at before with anyone like you. I mean that."

"Mary Dorsey . . ." he whispered.

"What?"

"I really have to kiss you now."

"I really want you to," she told him.

They made love quietly, her body pressed against his, which was thin and gaunt, she thought, but which she welcomed to hers. He was a surprisingly aggressive lover. They slept. In the morning, rising before anyone else was awake, he told her he wanted to remember this place always.

Telling him her true identity was out of the question. She knew the rules. It put you in greater jeopardy, and it put the people you knew in greater jeopardy, including both your fellow team members and the people who knew what your cover was. Evelyn Warner knew. Stephen would probably be upset if she told him. Perhaps when this was all over, the right moment would present itself.

Regarding more practical matters, she was hesitant to leave the enemy weapons cache they'd found intact. She spoke to Father Ayala again, using Stephen to interpret for her, and told him if the village was attacked, and he chose a passive resistance, there was a chance the enemy would use the weapons against him. She appreciated his commitment to nonviolence and respected the philosophy behind it, but, she told him, there were people working in Liger to terrorize the population by killing and raping and mutilating the innocent and (she decided not to spare the man's sensibilities, because it was too important that he understand the impact of his decision) by forcing people to watch or participate in acts of cannibalism—"Father," she said, "these guns can stop that from happening. Perhaps prayer will tell you whether or not you want to use them." There were six crates, each containing a dozen AK-47s, one of the simplest rifles to operate ever made, and one of the most reliable. She opened three crates and unpacked the weapons, loaded clips, and prepared the rifles for use. She and Stephen loaded the remaining three crates into the back of the Land Rover, along with extra ammunition, to bring to Camp Seven.

Before they left, she remembered to turn her phone back on. She'd turned it off, the night before, to shut the war out, if only for a night. She called CENTCOM Ops, out of Stephen's earshot, and gave the duty officer the GPS coordinates of her current position. He gave her directions back to Camp Seven. Stephen had been right, there was no direct route between Sagoa and Camp Seven, sixty kilometers apart as the crow flew but nearly two hundred by road. She felt the need to hurry, but at the same time, if it meant spending more time with him, she didn't mind the circuitous route, particularly because a small voice, one she tried to ignore, was telling her their time together was limited, a thing she did not want to be true.

He was a terrible driver, she discovered, turning left

when she said right and not paying attention. At one point, he stopped, confused, certain they were driving in circles. He was, she thought, adorable.

DeLuca had stopped to check in, paused at an intersection in the proverbial middle of nowhere. His map told him one road led to Sagoa, the other to Camp Seven. He was relieved when Scottie told him Dennis's signal was moving again, even though Scott said he couldn't say why Zoulalian had turned his phone off and left it off. He was in a black Mercedes, Scott said, owned, according to the license-plate number picked up by the cameras in the sky overhead, by a local warlord named Ali Khan who was believed to be aligned with IPAB.

"Is that satellite or UAV?" DeLuca asked.

"Actually, we have a U-2 up," Scott said.

"U-2?" DeLuca said. "From the sixties?"

"They started making them again in 1988," Scott said. "They stay in the air as long as a UAV but they fly a helluva lot faster, so they cover more ground. Do you want to call Zoulalian?"

"No," DeLuca said. "I'll wait for him to check in. How about MacKenzie?"

"On her way to Camp Seven," Scott said.

"Patch me through to LeDoux," DeLuca asked. "You okay?"

"I'm good," Scott said.

"Have you told your mother anything?"

"Just that we were keeping an eye on you," Scott said.

"You can tell her I'll be out in three days," DeLuca said, "if not sooner."

When LeDoux came on the line, DeLuca asked him for an update. LeDoux said the rules of engagement had not changed. The Marines were boo-ya and ready to fly. A G-2 with the 27th Infantry had complained that his men hadn't been given a chance to acclimate before heading directly into combat, the way troops invading Iraq had trained first in Kuwait. The colonel who'd expressed his concern for his men had been reprimanded for voicing his dissent. He'd gone rogue with the media after that, saying he had misgivings about sending his men into a conflict the undertones of which were more religious than strategic, at the whim of a born-again American president who was too willing to risk the lives of his troops in the service of his own personal religious vision. Needless to say, he'd been removed after that and reassigned, and would possibly face charges as serious as treason for his comments, though right now they were just trying to get him away from the microphones.

To make matters worse, LeDoux said, the evangelicals in Congress had led a group sing on the Senate floor of the song "Onward Christian Soldiers," the pictures on television showing the Republicans in full voice while Ted Kennedy sat tight-lipped with his arms folded across his chest. To rally political support, the White House was referencing evidence of new atrocities unfolding on an hourly basis, perpetrated by Samuel Adu and John Dari and various IPAB or LPLF forces.

"I thought one of the reasons I'm here was to verify Dari's participation in the atrocities," DeLuca said. "And, for the record, I can't."

"They need names," LeDoux said.

"How about Reverend Rowen?" DeLuca asked.

"Still debriefing that," LeDoux said, which DeLuca understood to mean they were trying to figure out how to spin it.

"What's the bottom line, as Kissick would say?" DeLuca said. "What can you do for me? I'm going to need fire support."

"Bottom line," LeDoux said, "no CAS. UAV only. I can give you what resources I have, but I can't increase or jump the dates."

"I figured. How many Predators can I have?" DeLuca said.

"We have six," LeDoux said. "Rotating in eight-hour shifts."

"Can you fly all six at once?" DeLuca asked.

"Not and give you coverage after they're returned to base," LeDoux said. "It's your call. Where are you?"

"At a fork in the road," DeLuca said. "About an hour out of Baku. You know what Yogi Berra said—'When you come to a fork in the road, take it.' Camp Seven is that-a-way and a village called Sagoa is this-a-way. I wanted your thoughts."

"Baku's gone bad," LeDoux said.

"*Gone* bad?"

"Gone worse," LeDoux said. "Government troops blew up a mosque. Near your hotel. We're in Iraq for two fucking years and we avoid the mosques. Anyway, that's behind you. Heavy fighting, door to door. LPLF, we think. According to SIGINT, we have rebels an hour or so north of Sagoa and the same for Camp Seven. Neither looks good. You can't just sit tight?"

"Negative," DeLuca said. Mack was headed for Camp Seven, where Evelyn Warner was waiting for help. He couldn't reach Sykes or Zoulalian. He couldn't divide his resources, nor did he really have resources to divide— even if his team was all together, there were only five of them, six if he included Paul Asabo. Sending one or two people to either Sagoa on Camp Seven didn't make sense. He had to choose one, a village of men, women, and children, or a smaller encampment of women and children. There were more people in Sagoa, but the refugees at Camp Seven were more vulnerable, protected only by a handful of African Union troops whose value as a deterrent was very much in doubt.

"Can we move government troops?" he asked.

"We can make recommendations," LeDoux said. "They don't have to listen. Bo's going to do what he wants. Ngwema will do whatever suits him. It looks like they're both concentrating their forces around the urban centers and abandoning the countryside to the rebels. With all the predictable results."

"Well," DeLuca said, making a decision. "We're going to Camp Seven. We should be there in about an hour. How long before the shit hits the fan?"

"About that," LeDoux said. "Maybe a little longer."

"We'll have to risk a speeding ticket then," DeLuca said. "Give me four UAVs now and two on standby. How long is turnaround? How far from base to Camp Seven?"

"Base is the *LBJ*," LeDoux said. "We can turn 'em around pretty quick. From home to you is about forty-five minutes. The new ones are faster than the old ones. What are you going to do?"

"Not sure," DeLuca said. "Still improvising. But like they say at last call, you don't have to go home, but you can't stay here."

When he reached Camp Seven, he found matters in complete disarray, or rather, complete disarray would have been a significant improvement. Evelyn Warner told him the United Nations troops had been recalled before she'd been able to return. The African Union troops had been ordered to pull back and regroup with a larger contingent of AU forces positioned thirty kilometers to the south. For now, Corporal Okempo was stalling, but he was getting pressure from above to move his men. He didn't want to defy his orders.

"I'm so grateful that you've come," Warner said. "I wish I had better news. I think maybe a hundred of my girls have already scattered or run off, thinking they'll be safer in the bush than here. Maybe they're right."

They were interrupted when DeLuca saw a trail of dust rising in the distance on the road from Sagoa, a single vehicle, a white Land Rover, making speed.

"That's Dr. Chaline's car," Warner said. "I was almost hoping not to see him again."

Hoolie tapped DeLuca on the shoulder and handed him his CIM. On the screen, DeLuca saw a map of the area, with Camp Seven at the bottom of the screen. Above the camp, to the north, a field of red dots representing troops marching south, perhaps five kilometers away, estimated strength, two thousand men, according to the attached dialogue box, led by Samuel Adu.

DeLuca looked at the sun, setting in the west. In another hour or so, it would be dark.

"We'll have to work with what we have," he said, surveying the surrounding landscape.

"Spoken like Davy Crocket at the Alamo. Remember the Alamo?" Hoolie said.

"Who could forget?" DeLuca said. "With one difference."

"Which is?"

"They had a fort."

Asabo looked puzzled.

"Famous American battle," DeLuca told him. "Nothing to worry about."

Chapter Eleven

"WHERE ARE WE?" GABRIELLE DUQUETTE asked Dan Sykes. She'd walked to the flight deck and was leaning over his shoulder after spending the first part of the trip staring disconsolately out the spotter's window. He'd maintained a hover of about a thousand feet. They were going to lose the light in another hour or so.

"What do you mean?" he shouted back, trying to sound positive. He didn't dare use the radio, but he was getting to the point where he needed to talk to someone who knew how to land a helicopter. He'd found a pair of helmets and plugged the com cords in so that they could use the intercom to communicate above the roar of the engines. She seemed to be in better spirits.

"What do you mean, what do I mean?" she said, pointing. "That way, toward the setting sun, is west, unless I'm mistaken. We're flying east. Port Ivory is south. I want to go to Port Ivory."

"The closest border is east," Sykes said. "I think we'd be safer if we left the country. Would you look in the cabinet where the flight engineer sits and see if you can find a manual or something?"

"Why do you need a manual?" she asked.

"See if there's a chapter that says how to land."

"Why?"

"Because I'm going to need you to read it."

"Why do you need me to read it?" she said. "Why can't you just ask your friend how to land?"

"My phone went dead," he told her. "About half an hour ago."

"*What?*" she said. "You're telling me this *now*?"

"I didn't want to worry you," he said.

"You didn't want to *worry* me?" she said. "Why did you take off if you didn't know how to land? I should think that would have been a fundamental priority."

"I didn't really have much choice about taking off," he said.

"We don't have much choice about landing either, do we?" she said.

"I understand why you're concerned—"

"Concerned?" she shouted into the headset. "CONCERNED?! I'm fucking more than concerned, Dan Sykes!"

He waited for her to calm down.

"I thought maybe I could figure out how to land, once we were in the air," he said sheepishly. "Keep your eyes open for a pipeline. It runs north to south, parallel to the eastern border."

She had her eyes closed, thinking. Finally she opened them and glared at him.

"Why are men like this? I know you hate to ask for directions, but this is insane," she said. "Stop the helicopter. I want to get out."

"Well, that's pretty much what I was getting at . . ." he told her.

She fished inside her purse and handed him a satellite phone of her own.

"All you had to do was ask," she said.

When he finally got through to the Pentagon, he explained the situation and said he needed to speak with Scott at Joint Intel, who told him, when they were finally reconnected, that he was afraid he'd hung up on him. Sykes said he'd had a dead battery and asked to speak to Captain Evans again.

"Got him right here," Scott said. "We've been talking, while we waited to hear from you, about diverting you south to a place called Camp Seven. We can vector you in if you're willing. It's not far. We have people on the ground who need evac. Let's go to 122.8 on the VHF. We won't have any privacy, but I don't think anybody is listening right now."

Once they were on radio, Captain Evans directed him to turn south. Gabrielle looked at him, wondering what was going on, now that she could hear the transmissions in her headset.

"Not a problem," he told her. "We're going to swing south a bit and pick up some friends of mine. They tell me landing should be a piece of cake."

His mother had always encouraged him to think positively. He wondered which was a stronger force, positive thinking or gravity? Probably gravity, but he didn't want to let on that he thought so. Captain Evans asked Sykes to read the gauges out loud to him. They had enough fuel to fly for another hour or so.

As they approached Camp Seven, Scott came back on the line.

"We're having a thought here—tell me," he asked, "if you can see below you, what do you see?"

"Trees," Sykes said. "Grass. I see Africa."

"I'm going to ask you to bank left to get a look down," Evans said. "Gently, with your right hand . . ."

Sykes saw men marching across open land, scattered in no particular formation. He told Scott.

"In what strength?" Scott asked.

"Can't say," Sykes said. "More than five hundred and less than a thousand."

"Those are the bad guys," Scott said. "Anything you can do to slow them down would be appreciated, but watch for triple A. Are you taking fire?"

"Negative," Sykes said. "Who are they? Dari?"

"Adu's unit," Scott said. "We think."

"I got a mini in the tail," Sykes said. "But nobody who can use it." He looked Gabrielle in the eye. She shook her head. "Unless I could set this thing on autopilot . . ."

"Negative, negative," Evans said. "That's not a Cessna."

"What is this?" Duquette said, pointing at a hatch in the floor of the passenger cabin.

"That?" Sykes said, looking over his shoulder. "That's the hell hole."

"What is it?" she asked. "Is it a trapdoor?"

"More or less," Sykes said. "It's a rescue hatch. Winching men up, or down. Why?"

"Can you open it?"

"There's a button next to the hatch that opens it. You have to pull the bar back manually. Why do you want to open it?"

He looked over his shoulder and saw that she'd opened her Zero case and was holding a stack of one-hundred-dollar bills in her hand. She pointed with her other hand toward the hell hole at her feet.

"I think we might have figured out how to slow them down a bit," Sykes told command. "How low can I fly before they shoot me?"

He turned, banking back into the sun as Evans instructed, and brought the helicopter to five hundred feet. Gabrielle Duquette propped her silver Zero case on the floor next to the hatch, opened the hatch, flipping it on its hinge until it lay flat, and then, as fast as she could, tossed fistfuls of American currency out of the helicopter, ripping the rubber bands that bound them and setting the binders aside, the cash dispersed by the rotor wash in a downward vortex, the money falling like so much green snow on the advancing rebel troops. They saw soldiers looking up, and then they saw men running everywhere, scrambling to recover the pieces of paper that fell from the sky, the rebel troops' forward movement momentarily halted.

"Whaddaya know?" Sykes said. "You *can* throw money at a problem. I wish my father was here."

"Why? Is he a pilot?"

"No," Sykes said. "He's a Republican."

Camp Seven was a frenzy of activity. Everything seemed to be happening at once.

When DeLuca saw MacKenzie step out of the Land Rover, he couldn't have been happier. She introduced him to her friend, Stephen Ackroyd. It was none of his business, but somehow DeLuca sensed immediately that something had passed between them.

"The fifth estate was talking about you back at the Hotel Liger," DeLuca said.

"Well, don't believe everything you hear," Ackroyd said.

"We have some surprises for you in the back," Mack said, pointing to the arms cache. DeLuca gave them a brief inspection.

"Did you read the e-mail I sent you?" he asked her.

"Haven't had a chance," she said. "Why? What'd it say?"

Ackroyd was standing right next to them.

"Read it, when you get a chance," DeLuca said. Mack crossed to where Evelyn Warner was standing, giving her a big hug and receiving one in return.

"Bill Murray went to my high school," DeLuca said to Stephen, asking him flat out. "Did anybody famous go to your high school?"

"Mine?" Ackroyd said. He looked genuinely puzzled. "I don't know. I don't think so. The guy who draws the cartoon *Garfield*, but he's not famous."

"You're a writer, right?"

"That's right," Ackroyd said. He seemed suddenly suspicious.

"What have you written that I might have read?" DeLuca asked him.

"Oh, I don't know," Stephen said, his eyes blinking rapidly. "Probably not much. I haven't really published too much."

He moved to help Vasquez unload the Land Rover.

DeLuca let it go, for now.

"Are you all right?" Evelyn Warner asked MacKenzie.

"We're good," Mack said. "We had to leave in a hurry."

"Where's Claude?" Warner asked.

"There was an accident," Mack said. "Dr. Chaline went back to help them. I'm sorry. We couldn't stop him."

"Of course you couldn't," Warner said, disconsolate that her friend was lost.

"Evelyn," DeLuca interrupted, watching as an unidentified Chinook helicopter turned in the air perhaps one or two kilometers north of them. He'd ordered Vasquez and MacKenzie to break out the AKs and load them. He'd sent for Corporal Okempo as well. "Everybody has to leave, now. There's no time for discussion. My CIM says there's a road along the river, going south. Where does it end?"

"There's a ford, about five miles from here, where the river is shallow enough to cross. Until it rained two weeks ago up north, both branches were down to a trickle."

"What's on the other side?" DeLuca asked her.

"Another road," she said. "For about five miles. This is the West Liger. The western fork. The road comes to the East Liger, just above where the two branches meet."

"And on the other side of that?"

"That's the border," she said.

"If you cross, you'll be safe?"

"Safe's a bit relative, isn't it?" she said. "Safer, I suppose. Bo's posted troops at the borders to stop people from leaving the country, but God only know if they'll still be there. I don't think the rebels would follow us across."

"Take your people there," he told her. "Don't let the border guards stop you. If you tell them two thousand rebel troops are chasing you, I suspect they'll escort you across the river personally. Corporal Okempo, I'm going to give your men real guns with real ammunition. Agent Vasquez will show your men how to use them, but it's the world's simplest rifle. Point and shoot, just like Kodak. Keep the people in order and keep them moving. I'm hereby authorizing a field transfer to the United States armed forces, all right? If somebody gives you any trouble for following my orders, I'll fix it later, okay? I promise you. You won't get in trouble."

Okempo nodded uncertainly. DeLuca wondered just how much he understood.

"I'm not sure these people can go ten miles," Warner said. "They're scared. They've been through so much already."

DeLuca saw the Chinook approaching. He was about to order Vasquez to fire on it when his SATphone rang and Scott told him the Chinook was friendly. He asked Scott to stay on the line.

"It looks like help may be arriving, but you still have to evacuate. You have to do what you can," DeLuca told Evelyn, holding his hand over the phone. "Leave everything. You have to go, now."

Warner spoke to Cela, who began the evacuation. Some people ran, some walked, carrying what they could. Some children thought it was a game.

"David," Warner said, "I have fifty people in the infirmary who can't even stand."

"We'll take care of them," DeLuca said, though he wasn't sure how.

He found Asabo.

"Paul, I want you to help Evelyn get the women and children to safety. Tell them who you are. They'll follow you. They'll calm down if they know you're leading them. Okay?"

Asabo nodded.

DeLuca watched as the helicopter attempted to set down in a nearby field, moving up and down three or four times and rotating in place at least half a dozen times before settling in, nearly backing tail first into the earth before finally correcting and dropping with a loud thud from a height of three or four feet, teetering momentarily on two wheels before settling in a cloud of dust.

"That's the worst landing I ever saw," Vasquez said.

When Sykes emerged from the pilot's door, DeLuca understood why. With him was the actress, her beauty as out of place here as a rose in a toilet bowl.

"I didn't know you knew how to fly jollies," DeLuca said to Dan.

"Neither did I," Sykes said. "This is Gabrielle Duquette. Gabby, this is my boss."

"Pleased to meet you," DeLuca said, turning to Dan. "How much fuel do you have left?"

"I'm not sure," Sykes said. "Maybe a third of a tank. The bad guys are one or two klicks north. You need a lift?"

"Not me," DeLuca said. "How many passengers can you carry?"

"You're asking me?" Sykes said. "Hang on." He spoke into Gabby Duquette's SATphone. "Captain Evans, how many passengers can I carry?" He turned to DeLuca. "He says thirty-six, including the crew. Fifty thousand pounds, gross weight."

"Thirty-six grown men?" DeLuca asked. Sykes repeated the question for Captain Evans, then nodded to DeLuca.

"We have fifty immobile women and children," DeLuca said, doing a bit of math in his head. "That ought to equal about thirty-six grown men. Evelyn, get your sick people on the helicopter. Agent Sykes will help you."

"I'll help, too," Gabrielle said.

"Thank you," DeLuca said.

"There's a minigun in the back we don't need," Sykes added. "We could lose the weight, too."

"Hoolie," DeLuca said, pointing at the chopper, "can you get the mini and mount it on the Rover?"

"I'll have to punch a few holes in the roof, but yeah. Give me ten minutes."

"Do it. You have five," he said.

A pair of headlights approached from the south.

"Jesus," DeLuca said, "what next?" He scanned the terrain again, keeping his eye on the car that would soon arrive, then got his son on the SATphone. The approach from the north was guarded by a pair of hills with a gap of perhaps five hundred yards between them. If the rebels seized the high ground, anyone remaining in the camp would be easy to hit with mortar, RPG, or rifle fire. He needed to keep the enemy inside the chokepoint. "Scott, I need fire on the mountains. How many Preds do we have?"

"Two on scene and two will be there in about ten minutes," Scott said. "The Hellfires can be there sooner than that—they're in range."

"Do you see the two hills north of my position?" DeLuca asked.

"Roger that," Scott said.

"You got the bad guys on infrared?"

"Got 'em."

"When they cross the line at the chokepoint, light the hills," DeLuca said. "First one, then the other. I want them to think it isn't safe up there."

"Roger that," Scott said.

In the distance, DeLuca thought he heard the sound of

loud music, boom boxes, chanting. Apparently the rebels were in something of a party mood, and not interested in gaining the advantage of surprise, but then, it was a war where terrorizing the opponent seemed more important than killing him.

Sykes interrupted him.

"We got a problem," he said.

"You have your people loaded?"

"Just about," Sykes said. "You want me to fly across the river and out of country, right? To where the others are walking?"

"Yeah," DeLuca said. "Keep everyone together."

"Evans thinks I'm going to need an LZ. Something lit so I can see it. It'll be dark in fifteen minutes. I had enough trouble landing that thing in daylight. We have zero NVGs."

"Scott," DeLuca said. "Check your topos. We need an open space where the river road south turns east and crosses out of Liger, ten to fifteen klicks from here. What have you got?"

"Hold on," Scott said. "On your CIM. Got it?"

"Roger—what's the terrain like? Wooded?"

"Semiwooded. It looks like some sort of refugee camp on the other side."

"Room for an LZ for the jolly?"

"There's room."

"What can you do to light it? We have zero NVG capabilities. Sykes is flying the jolly—he needs a safe place to land. We have fifty people on board."

"I can't get command and control in that fast," Scott said. "The closest FOP is still too far south."

"How much fuel do your Predators have on them?"

"Two hundred gallons av gas at full," Scott said.

"They fly about the same speed as a chopper, right?"

"About," Scott said.

"Here's what I want you and Captain Evans to do—when Dan is up, send a Pred and lead him to a safe LZ. When you get there, crash the Pred to give him a target. Tell LeDoux he can put the cost on my tab."

"Not a problem," Scott said. "At least not right now."

"I got you an LZ," DeLuca told Sykes. "Go now—Evans will explain."

"See you on the *Johnson*," Sykes said.

"You got it," DeLuca said.

Gabrielle Duquette approached them.

"Let's go," Sykes told her. "Get on the jolly—it's going to get hot here in a minute."

"I gave up my seat," Duquette said. "I can walk."

"Gabby . . ."

"I can walk," she said firmly. "I'm able-bodied. They need it more than I do."

"Gabby . . ."

"Take the money," she said, the Zero case still on board. "Use the rest when you're safe. These people are going to need a lot of things. You should go."

Sykes put a hand on her shoulder.

"I'm still going to get you home safe," he said.

He turned and ran to the helicopter.

Only a few refugees remained in camp. Evelyn Warner was hurrying them down the river road, women shuffling in the dust with their babies strapped to their backs, what few belongings they could bring with them piled on their heads.

"Ackroyd," DeLuca said, pulling the man aside. "Time for the civilians to leave. I need to know who you are.

Who you work for. My name is David DeLuca and I'm with U.S. Army counterintelligence. Who sent you here?"

"No one sent me here," Ackroyd said. "I came because I heard they needed people."

"Who are you working for?" DeLuca insisted. "Don't say a magazine because we checked. Did David Letterman go to your high school?"

"Why are you asking me about my high school?"

The man appeared to be confused. DeLuca simply didn't have time to take apart Ackroyd's story. If he was CIA and needed to maintain his cover, DeLuca would learn the reasons later. He could be DIA, NSA, DHS, Special Forces, any number of things, or he could be a foreign national who spoke perfect English with an American accent. Or none of the above. DeLuca needed him to leave, to eliminate the variable. He looked Ackroyd in the eye and made a decision.

"Would you be willing to carry one of these?" DeLuca held up an AK-47. Stephen Ackroyd nodded. DeLuca gave him the weapon. "Take Ms. Duquette with you and join the others."

"What about me?" Gabrielle Duquette said. "I've had gun training. They give it to you when you have to handle them in films."

"You want one, too?" DeLuca asked. She nodded. They needed every able-bodied person they could get. "All right," he said, handing her a Kalashnikov.

MacKenzie caught up with Stephen before he joined the exodus and told him to be careful.

"Some day when this is all over, maybe we'll look back on it and laugh," she said. He just looked at her. He didn't get what she was trying to say.

"Just a joke, Stephen," she said.

"Oh," he said. "Okay."

"What's wrong?"

"Nothing's wrong," he said, smiling. "Everything's peachy. I guess it never occurred to me that some day this would be over."

"I meant the war," she said, kissing him. "Not us."

"Whatever," he said, walking off.

It was an odd response, she thought. She didn't have time to worry about it.

The headlights approaching from the south loomed into view, a black Mercedes, driven by a man with white hair. Hoolie reported that he'd finished mounting the minigun on the roof of the Land Rover. DeLuca recognized Dennis Zoulalian as he got out of the car, accompanied by the older man, who introduced himself.

"Do you know this man?" Claude Chaline asked him. "Who are you?"

"Agent David DeLuca, United States Army counterintelligence," DeLuca said. "I know him."

"This man has had a brain injury," Chaline said. "I need to get him to safety. He had no identification on him."

Zoulalian looked at DeLuca, and then at Vasquez, as if he recognized them both.

"Whussup, Zoo?" Vasquez said. "You look like you swallowed a turd."

DeLuca looked at Chaline, then at Dennis. He put his hands on Dennis's shoulders and looked him in the eye.

"Your name is Dennis Zoulalian," DeLuca said. "You're a sergeant first class and a special agent in the United States Army, counterintelligence. You work for me. You were working undercover."

"Is that a cool job?" Dennis asked.

"Not today it's not," DeLuca said, turning to Chaline. "You say he's injured?"

"Right now, I think it's just his long-term memory," Chaline said. "His short-term is fine."

"He can walk?"

Chaline nodded.

"It's good to see you, but you couldn't have come at a worse time. Here," DeLuca said, handing Dennis a rifle. "It'll come back to you. It's like riding a bike. Dr. Chaline, your people went that-away. Stephen, Gabrielle, take Dr. Chaline with you. Evelyn, you, too."

"I'll come with you," Warner said.

"We're not going anywhere," DeLuca said. "We'll try to hold them here for as long as we can and then lead them west. There's an oil facility about ten kilometers from here . . ."

The rock and roll music in the distance was louder now, some sprightly world-beat tune that jittered in the darkness.

"David," she began.

"Go, now!" he said. "That's an order, Evelyn."

"Remember the Alamo?" Hoolie asked Zoulalian.

"The car rental company?" Dennis replied.

Then the hillside west of the chokepoint was lit by a large explosion.

"Go!" DeLuca shouted to Warner and the others. "Run!"

A moment later, the hill to the east of the chokepoint was rocked by a second explosion. DeLuca heard small-arms fire in the distance as a flare lit the night sky, half a kilometer from them.

The rotors of the helicopter turned faster and faster, churning up the dust in a furious roar, but the overloaded aircraft wasn't moving. DeLuca considered boarding and pulling passengers off until it was light enough to ascend, a task somebody had to do, better to lose five than lose fifty . . . then the massive helicopter rose from the ground, turning slowly and soaring over their heads, close enough that they had to duck. The helicopter climbed into the sky, gaining speed as it turned south.

The rebels were closer now, firing.

DeLuca fired back. He signaled to Hoolie, who turned the minigun toward the gap and opened up, the deafening roar of the .60-caliber weapon still one of the most awesome things DeLuca had ever witnessed, five thousand rounds a minute, every tenth round a tracer, creating a blaze of fire that chopped down trees and shot through cement walls and demolished everything in its path. MacKenzie and Zoulalian opened up as well, spread out along a line in a formation DeLuca hoped would make Samuel Adu's troops believe there were more of them than there actually were.

He heard shouts in the night, men screaming.

Hoolie opened fire again with the minigun. The magazine contained twenty thousand rounds, and after it was spent, there'd be no way to reload it.

A grenade exploded, near where the infirmary had been.

They saw and heard more small-arms fire, directly in front of them.

There were more rebels than DeLuca had first thought. In another minute, they'd be overrun. He signaled to Dennis and Mack to pull back, as Hoolie opened up with the minigun for the third and last time, firing in a sweeping arc until the magazine was empty, the superheated barrel of the gun glowing orange in the night.

DeLuca was about to order a retreat to draw the rebels west when he heard, in the sky directly above him, another burst of machine-gun fire, then a second, and a third, the sky lit by what appeared to be a thousand green chemlites. He thought of fireflies. A few seconds later, a man flying a square parachute flared his toggles and landed on two feet between DeLuca and Zoulalian. He was dressed in an insulated "Mr. Puffy" suit that indicated he'd dropped from a considerable altitude. The man took off his helmet and his pressure-demand oxygen mask.

It was Preacher Johnson.

"On the money, boys," Johnson called into his radio, immediately stripping himself of his jump gear. "You can pay me later. Deploy and press 'em back while I talk to the chief."

DeLuca saw other members of the group he'd known in Iraq as Task Force 21 landing all around him, flaring and dumping their square parachutes all in a single motion. They were human monsters, genetic freaks, most the size of NFL defensive linemen, bodybuilders trained in the martial arts and perhaps, man for man, the most deadly killing force ever assembled in the history of warfare. Other than that, they were a fun bunch of guys to hang out with. He was glad to see them.

Johnson approached with a salute, unzipping his down-filled suit to reveal the DCUs and the full battle rattle he wore beneath them. He saluted.

"How you doing, Chief?" Johnson said. "Got your message. Isaiah thirty-six verse twelve. Thought maybe you could use a hand."

"I wasn't expecting you. What are you doing here?" DeLuca asked him.

"Our shit up north went to fuck-all," Johnson said. "We were on a 130 headed home when we heard you were having a party, so we broke out the toys."

"I didn't hear a plane," DeLuca said. It didn't surprise him that Scottie hadn't told him. TF-21 was an autonomous unit that rarely asked permission or filed reports about half the things it did.

"We hahoed in from about forty klicks upwind of here," Johnson said, referring to the HAHO or High Altitude High Opening technique of incursion where paratroops pulled their chutes at thirty-five thousand feet (normal sky divers jumped at about five thousand feet) and then sailed the winds aloft on steerable chutes for distances as great as a hundred miles. It was a form of parachuting that only the most expert troops could pull off, but TF-21 certainly qualified as that. They also came armed to the teeth, with as many different forms of arms and weapons as each man could carry. DeLuca saw a rocket-propelled grenade launch from their side, streaking low across the landscape to explode five hundred meters off.

A single green chemlite landed at his feet, attached to a two-foot-square sheet of plastic.

"We were hoping they'd think there were thousands of us," Johnson said. "Soon as they come across one of those, they might figure we're full of shit."

There was weapons fire all around them, most of it headed north now as the rebels retreated and regrouped. One of Johnson's men approached, panting.

"Everybody's down," the man said. "Awaiting orders."

."You remember Sergeant Green from Iraq?" Johnson said to DeLuca, turning to his man and screaming in his face, "Why are you panting, Sergeant Green? Are you out of shape, Sergeant Green? Have you been slacking on your PT, Sergeant Green? Drop right now and give me twenty!"

"Boo-ya," Green said, dropping and doing twenty quick push-ups before jumping to his feet.

"Take three men and set Claymores along a line from there to there," Johnson told Green, glancing at his own CIM for a read of the battlefield. "And stand by while I talk to the chief." Green ran off. "They love but fear me," Johnson said. "I been slacking off on the fear part lately. So, you got a plan, or do you just wanna stay here and blow the shit out of stuff for a while?"

"I have seven hundred people down the road that way," DeLuca said, pointing. "I want the bad guys to follow us this way." He pointed a second time. "There's some sort of oil facility ten klicks down the trail where we might be able to make a stand. This place is definitely not suitable. You got goggles?"

"Plenty," Johnson said.

"We should go before they flank us," DeLuca said.

"Let us go then, you and I, to where the evening sky lies etherized, like a patient upon a table," Johnson said.

Before they left, Johnson had a man booby-trap the Mercedes with a charge of C4 explosive rigged to a motion sensor, set to detonate at the first disturbance. Any rebel soldier who thought he'd just found himself a new Mercedes was in for a rude awakening.

Another parachute flare lit the night sky. A rebel soldier in a red beret, wearing a brightly colored tie-dyed

T-shirt, ran from the bush, screaming and waving a machete over his head. DeLuca cut the man down with a burst from his MAC-10, as a second and then a third man charged, each to be cut down and killed in a similar fashion.

"Looks like they're sending all the stupid people first," Johnson said.

Then the rebels charged in greater numbers, the night split with the sound of a thousand rifles firing.

But DeLuca and his team were gone.

Johnson's men led the controlled retreat, running double time down a path worn into the sand by thousands of feet over perhaps thousands of years. DeLuca heard, behind him now, the Claymores detonating, and then a massive explosion as the Mercedes went up.

"We must have had something we didn't know about in the trunk," Zoulalian said.

MacKenzie and Vasquez stayed with DeLuca. They fired bursts behind them, more or less at nothing in particular, to let the enemy know which direction they were headed. DeLuca expected the enemy to follow, but cautiously now, aware that the path might be mined or booby-trapped. The read he got from his CIM indicated he was right, dots taken from an infrared image from a camera in the U-2 ninety thousand feet above them showing the positions of the enemy troops behind them. They'd taken the bait, and now followed from a distance of about a mile.

The terrain leveled into barren sand and scrub brush as the trail climbed a hill, then dropped again to a plain of sparse grass and widely spaced acacia trees, the night sky a dome of stars with a quarter moon rising in the east.

They ran. DeLuca kept an eye on his CIM, watching the enemy, who were neither gaining nor losing ground.

They came at last over a hill, where they looked down onto a large pipeline, twin parallel conduits each about five feet in diameter, mounted on concrete support pillars to elevate the line six feet off the ground. The pipeline ran south, carrying oil from the northern oil fields to the storage facilities in Port Ivory, where the crude was loaded onto tankers to be taken to refineries around the world. They saw, in the moonlight, a group of small buildings about half a kilometer to the south. DeLuca could have used a breather, and Mack looked a bit weary herself. Dennis had a kind of bewildered smile on his face. His memory wasn't back, he said, but he was adjusting to the ambiguity.

They moved again at double time and stopped running when they reached the compound, a maintenance camp that appeared, upon initial inspection, to have been abandoned quickly. They found a large tool shed, a cook shack, bunks, a supply shed, computers that had been smashed, a TV with a DVD player and a collection of porn DVDs, and a garage where a single ATV sat disabled with its wheels missing. The buildings were made of tin, with tin roofs, and would offer little if any protection to anyone foolish enough to hide inside one of them. Johnson had twelve men with him. DeLuca's team brought the total to sixteen. According to his Critical Information Module, about a thousand enemy soldiers had followed, marching along the trail behind them, about twenty or thirty minutes away.

"I'm interested in hearing your thoughts," DeLuca told Johnson.

"No you're not," Johnson said, "because I'm thinking

of the hereafter. I don't know if you've had a chance to get right with God, but now might be a good time to begin."

"I didn't know you were such a pessimist," DeLuca said.

"Not pessimistic at all," Preacher Johnson said. "No man with faith can truly be a pessimist. Which isn't to say it don't look like we are truly fucked. I do have one thought."

"Which is?"

"We blow the pipeline and leave a two-hundred-mile-long fence of fire between us and them. Something like that. Might be hard on the average American's pocketbook at the gas pump."

"I think the average American will understand," DeLuca said. "If they don't, the above-average Americans can explain it to 'em. Do it."

While Johnson's men set explosives along the pipeline, using C4 plastique charges, Vasquez rushed to tell DeLuca he'd found something. DeLuca ducked under the pipeline. On the other side, Vasquez led him to a large hangar where, inside, he showed him his discovery, a fleet of Flightstar Spyders, open-cockpit single-seat three-hundred-pound ultralight aircraft, twenty of them, with sailcloth wings and ten-gallon tanks, each aircraft powered by a forty-eight-horsepower air-cooled engine, Vasquez explained.

"These'll do about seventy-five miles an hour," Vasquez said. "I flew one in California last summer. These must be what they used to patrol the pipeline. You can land almost anywhere."

"What's the range?" DeLuca asked.

"About two hundred miles," Vasquez said. "Give or take."

"What's the payload?"

"I'm not sure," Vasquez said. "It'll get a normal-sized man up fine, but these guys are huge. It won't go as far with a big guy in it as it would with somebody like . . ."

"Like me?" DeLuca said.

"No offense," Vasquez said.

"None taken," DeLuca said. "Can they fly?"

"They look ready to me," Vasquez said. "They're all gassed up. I'll bet the only reason whoever abandoned this station left them behind was that they didn't know how to fly them."

"Is it hard?" DeLuca asked.

"Not really," Vasquez said. "You got a side-mounted control stick. You just pull back on it once you're doing better than thirty miles an hour or so and up you go."

DeLuca checked his CIM again. The rebels were half a mile off.

"Get 'em rolling," he said. "Now. What's the range again?"

"About two hundred miles?"

"And how far is the coast?"

"About two hundred miles," Vasquez said.

"I'll call ahead and see if we can get them to move the coast a little closer."

Johnson assembled his team at the hangar. Each ultra-light featured a cockpit about the size of a small baby carriage, where the pilot sat beneath the thirty-inch-deep wing, the engine centered and mounted atop the wing, so that the pilot looked through the propeller to see where he was going. DeLuca borrowed a radio headset from one of

Johnson's men to stay in touch with TF-21 and gave a second headset to Vasquez, who would lead the way. One of the ultralights was a two-seater, which MacKenzie and Zoulalian shared, the lightest possible pairing, and because DeLuca didn't quite trust that Dennis's head was entirely right yet. They heard music again, as a flare soared above the maintenance camp, on the other side of the pipeline.

"Gentlemen, start your engines," Johnson said.

DeLuca's propeller jumped to life as he turned the ignition. He waited for the others to take off, then throttled up as the small aircraft began to roll forward. DeLuca had a lifelong fear of flying, but in this case, it was overmatched by his lifelong fear of being killed and eaten. The Spyder rumbled and shook as if it was going to rattle into a million pieces, but then he pulled back on the control stick, and he was airborne. They took off at 160 degrees, climbing at a rate of about one thousand feet per minute. He wished he had a parachute, but then, that was pretty much what he was flying, a powered parachute. He throttled forward as men fired at him from the ground, one round striking his landing gear, he guessed, rattling the small aircraft but doing no other damage, and then the tracer rounds were all streaming below him, arcing back to earth, and he was out of range. He wondered how he was going to set down, with a damaged landing gear. He'd deal with it when the time came.

"This is awesome," he heard Preacher Johnson say, with the enthusiasm of a teenager behind the wheel of a car for the first time. "Eyes below, people, and watch out for flying shit."

Johnson triggered the detonators, and the two crude-oil pipelines blew in a massive display of pyrotechnics, huge clouds of smoke and fire rising high into the sky behind them. DeLuca banked left to get a better view and felt the heat rising until he had to briefly cover his face with his arm. The explosions spread down the pipeline, racing south like an old-fashioned gunpowder fuse before extinguishing itself where the pipeline dipped below the surface of Lake Liger in the distance.

"Well done," DeLuca said.

"You know our motto," Johnson said. "Task Force 21— when you need shit blowed up good, but you don't have time to blow it up yourself . . ."

They flew for a few minutes. It was almost peaceful, once you got used to it.

"Hoolie," DeLuca said. "I'm thinking if we throttle back we could save—"

His question was interrupted by a stream of bullets that flew just below his left wing, including bright red tracers that made him turn his stick instinctively to the right. He looked behind him and saw, in the moonlight, one of the ultralights they'd forgotten to disable, piloted, apparently, by one of the rebels who was shooting at him, the muzzle flash of his weapon showing his position. DeLuca swerved again, rather than give him an easy target. They'd fastened green chemlites to their wingtips to make their aircraft visible to each other, lights that were relatively dim to the naked eye but glowed brightly when seen through night vision goggles.

"Who's this guy think he is?" Preacher Johnson said. "Baron von Richthofen? Who wants to be Snoopy and go get him?"

"Sergeant Green volunteering," DeLuca heard over his headset.

"Hold on, Green," DeLuca said. "I might have a better idea. Scottie, you there?"

"I'm on you," Scott said. "What do you need?"

"We have two more Predators, fully loaded, right?"

"Three, six o'clock high, following you home," Scott said. "But only one is loaded. You crashed the fourth. What about 'em?"

"Do Hellfires work air-to-air?"

"Not like Sparrows or Sidewinders, but they'll work if you paint the target. Do you have lasers?"

"Negative," DeLuca said. "Can you paint the rearmost ultralight with Pred one or two and fire on it with Pred Three? He's being a pain in the ass. Literally."

"Absolutely," Scott said.

"He's not too small?"

"Not a problem," Scott said.

"Then do it. And remember, I said *hind*most," DeLuca repeated, swerving again. "Not the second-to-the-last guy, because that would be me."

"Roger that," Scott said. "You're penultimate. Hang on one second. Target acquired. Locked on, and . . . firing."

DeLuca looked behind him. He saw nothing, then a streak of light, and then the last ultralight exploded, the missile striking it dead center, creating a ball of flame and a blossoming burst of debris that fell from the sky like fireworks.

A moment later, a strange-looking aircraft appeared about a hundred feet off his right wing, a white bulb-nosed torpedo-shaped plane, something like a spoon turned upside down, with broad thin wings, the tail an inverted V. DeLuca had seen Predator B-001s on the ground, but seeing one in the air seemed nevertheless odd and other-worldly. The pod in the nose contained the aircraft's forward-looking SAR, electro-optical and infrared sensors, GPS-INS guidance systems, and laser-target designator, as well as the TV camera the remote pilot used to fly it, with a twin-blade turbo-prop mounted at the rear, above the tail fins. Perhaps what made it so eerie was that the Pred was completely silent, or at least DeLuca heard nothing above the sound of his own engine.

"You mind if I take your picture to e-mail to Mom?" Scott said. "Smile."

DeLuca raised his right hand and touched it to his forehead.

"She's going to like that one," Scott said.

"It'll give her a good idea of how much fun we're having," DeLuca agreed.

They followed the pipeline, easily visible in the moonlight to the naked eye, flying south from where the conduit emerged from Lake Liger. The flying part was, once you got used to it, okay. DeLuca tried again not to think about how, or for that matter where, he was going to land. Scott told him Sykes had made it, and that without knowing the details, it appeared that Evelyn Warner and the others had reached the border and crossed successfully.

Even in darkness, DeLuca could see evidence of the miseries below. They flew at perhaps a thousand feet, he couldn't be sure, passing over a village where the thatched houses below were burning. They were low enough that they could make out, by the light of the flames, troops running from hut to hut, and men firing back at them, men hacking at other men with machetes, and men pleading for their lives, begging on both knees before being destroyed, a vision of hell, DeLuca thought, worse than anything envisioned by the painters he'd studied in his art history class in college, those right-hand panels in the Renaissance triptychs depicting hell as the artists envisioned it then—hell had gotten a lot worse in the intervening years. They saw a line of vehicles moving away from the village in single file on a road below, some sort of convoy, DeLuca assumed. Scott told him he thought it was a division of Ngwema's men, closing on the capital. In the distance, DeLuca saw a faint glow on the horizon and asked his son what was happening to the south.

"The orange glow is Port Ivory," Scott said. "The city itself is blacked out. LPLF blew up the tank farm at the refinery yesterday and it's still burning. Circle west if you can—the wind is southwest to northeast. There's a lot of black smoke that you're not going to want to fly through."

"Hoolie, vector right of the flames ahead," DeLuca told the leader of the formation.

"Roger that," Hoolie replied.

"We're going over the city, boys," Preacher Johnson said. "Watch for triple A—we're well in range. We probably look like a flight of geese on anybody's radar. And sound like a swarm of bees. You know why when you see a bunch of geese in the sky and one side is always longer than the other—you know why that is, Agent DeLuca?"

"Why is that, Sergeant Johnson?"

"There's more geese on that side," Johnson said.

The northern suburbs of Port Ivory seemed quiet. Yet the vision of hell DeLuca had seen, passing over the village earlier, was multiplied a thousand times as they approached the center of the city. He saw houses and buildings on fire, cars and buses overturned and in flames, a crowd of men with machetes chasing a single man who stumbled as he fled, rooftop machine guns mounted in sandbagged nests firing on crowds of rioters below, a line of tanks in a park firing on a row of apartment buildings, people looting, people dying. He smelled smoke, and cordite, and something else, a faint chemical smell that burned his nostrils and made him pull up on his control stick to get away from it.

"What was that?" he asked.

"Mustard gas," Johnson said.

"Who's using it, I wonder?" DeLuca asked.

"Could be anybody. You can make it yourself out of bleach and ammonia," Johnson said. "People poison themselves all the time, mixing the two to clean their bathroom floors."

He felt the heat rising from the fires below, smoke in the air that made his eyes sting. Then, finally, he smelled the ocean, a vast black expanse beyond the city. On the horizon, he saw a beacon suddenly shine straight up into the sky, a beam of light like the searchlights DeLuca's old man once chased in the family station wagon on Long Island when a new supermarket or car dealership used them to advertise a grand opening.

"Suggest you head for the *Johnson*," Scott said. "That's the light you see ahead of you. I told them to clear the decks for you. You got a clear night with no cross winds and calm seas, so it shouldn't be a problem."

"What are my other options?" DeLuca asked. "I've only been a pilot for a couple hours. I'm not sure I'm quite ready for a carrier landing."

"We're out of other options, unfortunately," General LeDoux said, his voice coming in on the headset. "The airport is a free-fire zone, and there's nowhere else to send you, I'm afraid."

"Carrier it is then," DeLuca said, gazing below as he realized he was now flying over open water, the beach behind him.

"It might be a moot point," Vasquez said. "I'm out of gas. I'm on fumes. I don't think I have enough to make the carrier."

"Ditto that," Johnson said. "Boys, check your gauges. How we doing?"

One by one, Johnson's men reported in. They were all running low on fuel.

"Make the carrier deck if you can, straight ahead, but if your engine shuts off, I suggest you make a water landing," Johnson said.

"And just how do I do that?" one of his men asked.

"You'll think of something," Preacher Johnson told him.

"That's an oxymoron," someone else said.

"What is?"

"'Water landing.'"

"General," DeLuca said, "if you don't mind, could you tell the *LBJ*'s search and rescue to get their swim fins and meet us halfway?"

"Already in the air," LeDoux said. "We've got you on visual."

"This is Captain Evans," a new voice in DeLuca's headset said. "I'm a pilot here at flight control and I'm going to talk to you all about how to do this. You people really should leave the flying to the professionals, you know. All right. I want you to slow your forward airspeed. Also jettison anything you might be carrying that adds any weight, weapons, etcetera—you don't need 'em anymore. We're going to put you all in the water in a controlled ditch, rather than risk having your engines fail you into a stall before you reach the ship. If they cut out, we believe you'll still have glide. Take your shoes off if you can, because you're going to have to swim, and unbuckle your harnesses because you don't want to go down with your birds. We're going to try to make a belly landing, as if you were flying an old-fashioned dumbo. You may or may not flip forward, depending on how you hit it. You have great seas to do this on, boys, really smooth—you couldn't have ordered anything better . . ."

DeLuca realized that without a radio, MacKenzie didn't know what was going on. He called her on her SATphone.

"They want us to land in the water," DeLuca told her. "Listen to me carefully. Slow your forward airspeed. Jettison your weapons and take off your shoes—you might want to remind Dennis that he crossed-trained from pararescue and still owns two of the swim records in the pool at Lackland. Control wants you to fly as low as you can . . ."

He saw, ahead, the searchlights from a fleet of rescue helicopters approaching, shining on the water to let everyone know they were coming.

"I'm out of gas," he heard someone report. "Going in."

And then he heard his own engine sputter for a few moments and cut out. He was about ten feet above the surface, the water racing past beneath his feet.

"If you cut out, wait until you're nearly down and pull back . . ." Evans said, as DeLuca followed his instructions, and then he was down, the water shaking him with a jolt that bounced him in his seat, his head cracking against the brace overhead as the machine tumbled forward and flipped upside down.

Suddenly there was water everywhere.

Blackness. He was upside down.

His foot was stuck. He couldn't move it.

He held his breath and freed his foot.

Tumbling.

He was underwater.

He swam for the surface, kicking as hard as he could, his lungs about to burst.

He made the surface, gasping for air, and treaded water. He saw, floating about ten feet from him, a small green chemlite, six inches long and no thicker than a finger, so he swam to it and waved it overhead.

He saw a helicopter, maybe three hundred meters off, holding position above a crashed vehicle. No one saw him, so he decided to swim for the helicopter.

Then he was bathed in a wash of bright light as a second chopper approached from the rear and slowed to a stationary hover. He saw a pair of divers bail out the back as the HH-60 low-slowed in a circle. The divers swam to him. The first one to reach him took off his facemask and left it on his forehead.

"Are you hurt?" the swimmer asked.

"I'm all right," DeLuca said.

"Sergeant Mark Lewis," the diver said. "This is Sergeant Cliff Eberhardt. We'll be your rescuers tonight."

DeLuca was distracted when a marksman on the HH-60 began firing at them, the bullets zipping into the water all around them.

"Why's he shooting at us?" DeLuca said as the flight engineer aboard the HH-60 lowered a penetrator on a steel cable. The SEAL didn't answer, straddling the paddles at the bottom of the penetrator and instructing DeLuca to put his legs over his own and buckle on. The marksman continued to fire as DeLuca was hoisted up into the helicopter. They waited a minute longer to extract the remaining SEAL.

"What were you shooting at?" DeLuca asked the marksman, once he'd caught his breath. The shooter handed him a pair of infrared goggles and invited him to have a look for himself. DeLuca donned the goggles, built to reveal the body heat of anybody or anything within its field of vision. When he did, he saw, swimming below the surface, seven or eight large sharks, though it was hard to count them because of how they kept moving on top of each other.

"Probably wondering where their dinner went," the marksman said. "Bull sharks, I think."

"I know some crocodiles they should meet," DeLuca said.

Once aboard the USS *Lyndon Johnson*, DeLuca and Preacher Johnson took stock. Johnson collected a hundred dollars each from the men he'd bet that he could land his HAHO jump within ten feet of DeLuca, and another hundred each from three men who'd gone double or nothing that they weren't going to get out alive. Two of his TF-21 team members had broken limbs and one cracked out six of his front teeth when his face hit the windshield when he ditched, but these were things Johnson considered minor injuries.

Mack and Dennis were good, and in fact, the ultralight they'd ditched in had stayed upright and actually floated long enough for the SEALs to pull them out with little trouble. Vasquez had ignored Captain Evans's advice and landed safely on the flight deck, where some of the Hornet and Prowler pilots were pointing at his aircraft and laughing at it before pushing it over the side.

Crew members brought them dry clothes to change into and hot coffee to warm them—Mack asked for a Venti half-caf soy vanilla latte—and then the crew members showed them to quarters where they could clean up.

An hour later, the vertical takeoff V-22 Osprey that Captain McKinley had sent to retrieve Dan Sykes returned. He was given fifteen minutes to relax before the debriefing.

They met in the conference room off the flight deck. General LeDoux brought them up to speed on what was happening in country, showing them a map of where the fighting was taking place, the conflict spread across all of southern and much of central Liger. When Mack asked him specifically what had happened in the village of Sagoa, LeDoux clicked the mouse on his computer, summoned the falcon view, and explained that there'd been reports of extremely fierce fighting in Sagoa, with heavy casualties. He zoomed in close enough for MacKenzie to see that the village had been destroyed. A large number of people lay dead in the village square.

"Are those civilians?" she asked.

"We can't tell," LeDoux said. "We're going back for better pictures in the morning. I'm not sure when we'll get around to processing the data, frankly. It's a pretty big theater right now."

"I know it's not my place to ask, General," MacKenzie said, "but is there any way we could expedite on Sagoa? I need to know."

DeLuca was surprised to hear MacKenzie speak up.

"I'll see what I can do, Agent MacKenzie," the general said. She thanked him.

DeLuca asked Sykes what had happened to the refugees.

He'd set down, Sykes said, in a field marked by the crashed UAV. There was a large refugee camp, a shanty-town thrown together in the last few weeks that they were calling Camp Cobra, across the border from Liger, where Evelyn Warner and Dr. Chaline managed to move all of the women and children evacuated from Camp Seven. Soldiers at the border were charging exit fees, which had to be negotiated, given the large number of people who had to cross. There'd also been an outbreak of both septi-caemic and pneumonic plague in Camp Cobra, *Yersinia pestis* bacteria carried by the vermin infesting the camp, and not enough medicine or doctors to treat everyone, at which point Sykes had handed the silver Zero case to Gabrielle Duquette, who handed it to Dr. Chaline, telling him what was inside. Once Dr. Chaline had passed the ap-propriate amounts of United States currency to the appro-priate officials, all went smoothly. The sick and injured from the Chinook had been taken by bus or ambulance to a hospital facility near Accra. Warner and Duquette de-cided to stay in Camp Cobra with the refugees.

"So no casualties then?" DeLuca said.

Sykes hesitated.

"Just two," Sykes said. "Paul Asabo was arrested by government troops when he tried to get them to waive the exit fees. They took him away when they recognized him. I couldn't tell you where. We tried to bribe them to let him go, but they were too afraid to take the money."

"Who else?" DeLuca asked.

Sykes turned to MacKenzie.

"We couldn't find your friend Stephen," Sykes said. "We looked everywhere. He must have dropped out somewhere along the way. That's what Evelyn Warner thought. Or he got lost in all the confusion. We looked."

"Well then," DeLuca said after a very long pause, during which he was certain everyone was thinking the same thing he was. "I guess that means we'll just have to go back and get them."

Chapter Twelve

"YOU'RE UP EARLY," LEDOUX SAID. "I THOUGHT you could use a good night's sleep."

Dawn had come cool and clear. In forty-eight hours, Operation Liberty was due to launch, and activity on the USS *Johnson* was ramping up accordingly. Aircraft were prepared. Ordnance was readied for loading. Flight plans for the first thousand sorties were redrafted, reanalyzed, and filed. Pilots wrote letters home or sent digitized video clips over the Internet.

"You're right, I could," DeLuca said. He'd risen early and joined a group of sailors who were doing calisthenics on the flight deck. It wasn't so much that he felt in need of PT but rather that exercise helped him clear his mind. "Right now, I'm marginally more useful when I'm awake."

LeDoux handed him the second cup of coffee he'd brought with him.

"Come on inside, if you have a minute," LeDoux said. "There's something I want to show you."

A young Marine lieutenant was reading the *New York Times* on the large plasma screen in the flight deck conference room when LeDoux and DeLuca entered. The man jumped to his feet and saluted when the G-2 approached.

"As you were, Lieutenant," LeDoux said. "Dim the lights, please, and run the sequence we were looking at for Agent DeLuca, if you would."

The headline read: HEAVY FIGHTING IN LIGER, PORT IVORY. SIX AMERICANS KILLED.

"Who was killed?" DeLuca asked.

"A family of missionaries, from Indiana," LeDoux said. "They're spinning it like if we'd have only acted sooner, we could have saved them. We had three different teams, including one two days ago, try to talk them into evacuating, but they thought God would save them. They said this was a holy war and they knew their God was bigger than the enemy's God."

"You know the one about the guy on his roof in a flood?" DeLuca asked his friend. "First a fire truck comes when the waters are up to his windows and extends the ladder, and the guy says, 'Go away—the Lord will save me, I believe in the Lord.' Water's up to the eaves, so the Coast Guard sends a boat, the guy says, 'Go away—the Lord will save me, I believe in the Lord.' Finally the water's up the chimney, so they send a helicopter that lowers a rope, but the guy says, 'Go away—the Lord will save me, I believe in the Lord.' So he dies, and he goes to heaven, and he gets up there and he says, 'What happened, Lord—I thought you were going to save me?' And the Lord says, 'What do you want, moron? I sent you a fire truck, a boat, and a helicopter.'"

"Tell that one to the White House," LeDoux said. "I've been a Republican since I was sixteen years old, and I voted for the president, because he's a good man, but I swear, some of these evangelicals who've been whispering in the president's ear ought to be seriously beaten with hoses. You know what they were debating today? One of the Democrats showed up with a bumper sticker that said, 'Who Would Jesus Bomb?' So one of the Republicans cited how Jesus was not entirely nonviolent and got physical when he had to drive the money-changers out of the temple, and how if he were around today, he'd use any means necessary, including smart bombs that only kill the bad guys. He said Jesus would love smart bombs. They spent the rest of the day, swear to God, arguing about what Jesus would or would not have bombed. It's insane."

"I think I prefer the line from *Hannah and Her Sisters*," DeLuca said, "where Max von Sydow says, 'If Jesus Christ were to come back today, he would not be able to keep himself from vomiting.' Has the schedule changed?"

"So far, we're still holding," LeDoux replied. "That wasn't what I wanted you to see. Lieutenant."

The lights dimmed and on the plasma screen, an overhead view of a place that seemed vaguely familiar appeared.

"It's a good thing MacKenzie spoke up last night," LeDoux said. "I put through the request to expedite and your son and his friends stayed up all night to do it, so let him know we're grateful. This is Sagoa. It's also a good thing the artificial intelligence program that tells the computers what and what not to look for isn't all that intelligent yet, because we wouldn't have these pictures if it hadn't screwed up. It programs the birds to watch our people and it locked in to Mack's signal when she called in the morning to ask for directions to Camp Seven, but it didn't figure out that probably meant she'd be leaving Sagoa and driving to Camp Seven, so the bird stayed on Sagoa."

"Another argument for women in the military," DeLuca said. "Men wouldn't have asked for directions."

"We'll time lapse the sequence for you. This is 2000 hours. Everything looks good."

The image on the screen moved forward, flipping from a natural-light image to infrared.

"At 2042 hours, as the darkness settles in, men in trucks arrive. You can't tell, but the lead vehicle there is an H2, the civilian version of a Hummer. Blood red. We cross-checked and learned the vehicle was seized by Samuel Adu's men two days ago in a village where WAOC had made a gift of it to a tribal chief who was sitting on land they wanted to develop. Anyway, unless somebody took it from Adu, we can reasonably expect this is Samuel Adu and his men."

The image clicked forward again.

"Twenty-one ten, Adu's men have begun to round everybody up into the village common. This bright orange spot here is a large fire, and the black spot in the middle is a cook pot. Just like in the old missionary jokes. This is the pattern the cannibal gangs in Sierra Leone established. They'd come into a place, round the people up, butcher a few in front of everybody else and put the pieces in the pot and eat them, for effect. I wish to God I was kidding. If we tried to talk about this in the media, we'd be lynched for stereotyping. Okay, now we're going to shorten the sequence and zoom down a level or two. Lieutenant."

The Marine lieutenant tapped his keypad.

"Here you see some sort of resistance. The people decide they're not going to stand for it, I guess. This guy steps forward and gets shot. These two guys try to run away and they get shot, too. Now watch."

The image clicked forward again, the numbers in the corner of the screen saying it was 2114 hours.

"These guys outside the circle are Adu's men. They rounded the villagers up and put them in the middle. So boom, boom, boom, and over here, bang bang bang, all of a sudden, Adu's men start to fall. Zoom out a level, Lieutenant."

The Marine complied.

"Dot dot dot dot dot," LeDoux said. "Somebody's coming in, in large numbers, from the northeast, moving cross country at a pretty good clip. And . . . bang bang again, and now it's armed forces against armed forces. Bang bang bang. There's collateral damage as the villagers scatter. Forward again, the new force has driven Adu and his men out, there's the H2 leaving . . . the trucks . . . a few scattered soldiers firing back, down they go . . . some clean-up action there and there . . . now it's 2205 hours and Adu's men are gone and these new guys are in their place. There's only fifty of them, but they took ground from a significantly larger force and drove 'em out. If you ask me, these guys are heroes."

"So who are they?" DeLuca asked.

"At first we thought it was the mercenaries from the El Amin facility, for a few reasons, but we were wrong about that," LeDoux said. "The icon in the bottom of the screen indicates correlated SIGINT, so Scottie cross-checked and pulled it up. In an urban environment where more than one person had a cell or SATphone, we might have lost it in the snow. I don't have the audio. Zoom down, Lieutenant, center on this man here. This is the guy making the call out. We don't know who he called, but we can ID the caller with good confidence."

"And?"

"It's John Dari," LeDoux said.

DeLuca was not surprised.

"I forwarded all this to the Pentagon, since getting intel on Dari was the original mission," LeDoux said. "They think it's a power play between rivals. They want to know what you think."

"Do they really?" DeLuca said. "I'm the one who gave Dari the information we had on Adu. He asked me specifically where we thought he was, and I showed him on my CIM. Dari took on Adu because Dari knows, as well as you or I do, that Adu is as bad a piece a shit as any of us have ever seen. The Pentagon thinks they're jostling for power?"

"The Pentagon is going on prior assumptions," LeDoux said. "Strictly if then, go to. The guy I talked to told me they intend to rely on the operant paradigms until there's a shift."

"Operant paradigms?" DeLuca said. "That sounds like it comes directly from General Kissick. Remind me to shift his paradigms with my boot up his ass, next time I get a chance."

"Can I tell them your thoughts?" LeDoux said.

"You can tell them," DeLuca said. "You could buy 'em books, too, but they'd just chew on the covers."

"Now I've got some bad news," LeDoux said. "I told them you had a man who was left behind and you wanted to go get him. They've denied permission."

"Denied?" DeLuca said. "Why?"

"They're saying he's not really your man," LeDoux said. "He's a civilian."

"And he's black," DeLuca said.

"I'm not sure I'd play the race card here," LeDoux said. "These guys are old school. They still have the old the-Army-was-integrated-long-before-the-rest-of-the-country-ever-was mentality."

"So Scott O'Grady goes down in an F117 outside Belgrade, and Wesley Clark scrambles half the Army to get him, but we leave one black guy in Liger, and we say fuck it?" DeLuca said. "Is that really how they want to play it?"

"Asabo isn't an Air Force pilot," LeDoux said. "Scott O'Grady was. That's the way they see it."

"That's not how I see it," DeLuca said. "I had thirty-five informants working for me in Iraq and last I checked, thirty-four of them were still breathing in and breathing out. And you know what happened to the last one." DeLuca referred to an informant named Adnan who'd voluntarily stayed behind in a bunker that was about to be destroyed, to settle some personal business with a man named Mohammed Al-Tariq who'd been hiding there. "If I don't take care of people, I don't have people. If you think . . ."

"You're preaching to the choir, David," LeDoux said. "In this particular instance, my hands are tied."

"This is crazy," DeLuca began.

"However," LeDoux said, interrupting again. "That said, what I *can* do is send in a team to observe the peace talks. Which may be a ways off, but we need to be prepared. You'll probably want to get to know some of the people who're going to be negotiating, once everything settles down. President Bo has moved his government to the Castle of St. James, for the time being. I suggest you take your team and Preacher Johnson and some of his men and arrange transportation with Lieutenant Riley and some of his SEALs. You might want to go at night, so as not to cause a disturbance on diplomatic fronts. And watch out for mission creep. You know how easy it is for one mission to turn into something else."

"We're going back strictly to observe?" DeLuca said.

"That's right," LeDoux said. "The ROEs are, of course, yours to determine. I would think Paul Asabo would be welcome at the peace talks, when they happen, representing the monarchy and all that. You might want to get in touch with him first."

"That sounds like a plan," DeLuca said. "I'll see if I can track him down. For the peace talks."

"Provisional. It's not a plan," LeDoux said, "unless you get some hard intel between now and midnight tonight on Asabo's whereabouts. Use whatever you have, but I can't authorize a fishing expedition, observers or otherwise. David, you can't just go back and poke around a little bit. Not the way things are. If you can come up with something reasonable and concrete, I think we can work together on it. But you have to prove it to me, all right?"

"Fair enough," DeLuca said.

He was talking to Scott when MacKenzie knocked on his door. Scott had had a team poring over the image intelligence available from the border crossing the night before, but it was too confusing. Dozens of trucks and vehicles had come and gone in the hours before or after Paul Asabo had been seized, and it wasn't possible to pinpoint exactly when that had happened, so he could have been in any of them. SIGINT had nothing, no reports on the few radio stations that were still broadcasting, no intercepted e-mails, no Internet activity on the various Liger-watch Web sites, save one that reported that a very important person had been captured and would be tried for treason.

"Got a minute?" MacKenzie asked.

"Sure," DeLuca said. She'd been trying to reach Evelyn Warner, who'd been there when Asabo was arrested, and, by the look on her face, having little luck. "Anything?"

She shook her head.

"It's not going to happen," she said. "I think the only way to reach her would be to go in person. There's no land lines and the unhappy neighbors are jamming the wireless frequencies to stop the rebels from talking to each other across the border because they're afraid spies have infiltrated the camps. I need to talk to you. I have a conflict."

"What's that?" DeLuca asked.

"I understand why you want to get Paul, and I'm right there with you if you need me, 100 percent," she said.

"I know that," he said. "But?"

"I want to find Stephen," she said. "I read the e-mail you sent."

"And?"

"And I don't think he was CIA," she said. "Or anything else."

"He said he was a writer," DeLuca said. "A journalist. We can't find a record of anything he ever published."

"I respectfully disagree with your conclusion," Mack said. "I know you're the team leader, but you didn't know him. You tell us to trust our instincts, right? Well I trust mine. He was a member of my team, as much as Asabo was part of yours. Just because you can't be Googled doesn't mean you're lying."

She was digging her heels in. DeLuca could have over-
ruled her but chose not to.

"What do you have in mind?"

"I thought I could fly in through Ghana and start from
Camp Cobra and see if anybody there knows anything,"
she said.

"And if nobody does?"

"Well, the least I could do is trace back to Camp Seven.
It's not that far."

"Alone?" DeLuca asked.

"I could try to arrange for something," she said.

"I don't want you traveling in country alone," DeLuca
said. "That's my one stipulation."

"I hear you," she said. He hoped that she did.

"Do you know who to talk to about transport?" he
asked. She nodded. "Make the arrangements and then
leave me a flight plan."

Sykes and Vasquez were digging up information about
Daniel Bo's prison system, the gulag where Paul Asabo
might be found, if he was still alive. For a man who por-
trayed himself as a devout Christian with close ties to the
Catholic church, Bo's prisons and jails were conspicu-
ously lacking in Christian charity. Conditions, according
to the antigovernment Web sites maintained by expatri-
ates, ranged from horrible to hideous, "rehabilitation centers" where men were shackled to stakes in the sun for
punishment, or confined with twelve or fifteen men in
cells meant for one or two. The prison population was 62
percent Da, 33 percent Kum, and 5 percent Fasori, and 92
percent of the guards and administrators were Fasori.
Prisoners were, it appeared, one of the main labor re-

sources for government projects, and had built the soccer stadium, the Lions' Park Casino, the presidential palace and many of the prisons. Officially, Liger was a country that did not have capital punishment. Unofficially, Liger was a place where people who were arrested frequently disappeared. Bo's favorite method of execution was throwing people out of helicopters, dropping them into either the ocean or the desert, places where the bodies would never be found.

"A lot of the prisons have been liberated, it looks like," Sykes said. "Not that Bo would have taken Paul to one, necessarily, but we can narrow down the ones he still has control over."

DeLuca asked for a briefing with Robert Mohl, who'd managed to fly out of the country on a WAOC helicopter. Wes Chandler, his boss, had flown to Langley. Mohl was surprised to hear that Paul Asabo had come back.

"He was sitting in the bar with us when I talked to you," DeLuca said, "at the Hotel Liger."

"*That* was Paul Asabo?" Mohl said. "I must have missed it."

"Why do you think he was arrested?" DeLuca asked.

"Why?" Mohl repeated. "Well, I suppose the fellow at the border made a phone call of some sort to somebody. I don't expect there was a standing arrest warrant posted. They wouldn't have been anticipating his return."

"Called who?" DeLuca asked. "Best guess."

Mohl thought.

"I suppose it could be a simple kidnapping for ransom," Mohl said. "There's an awful lot of that going around. That's how the Lord's Republican Army in Uganda has been funding itself for years. Maybe the guards saw an opportunity. Seize somebody important, and then either ransom him themselves or sell him over to somebody else who knows how to do that sort of thing."

"Who would that be?"

"A local warlord," Mohl suggested. "A tribal chief, maybe. Or else the government itself. They could have taken your man to a third party who'd sell him back to the government and split the take with the border guards. Or maybe it was straighter than that. Maybe the guards called their superiors, who called theirs, who called theirs, and the word came back from on high to arrest him."

"And bring him where?"

"Who can say?" Mohl asked. "A jail? Somebody's house? The presidential palace? There's been a story for a long time that Bo had a private prison there in the basement. Do you remember the stories of Idi Amin having a freezer full of the heads of his enemies? I think Bo might have a similar mentality, without the freezer, keep his enemies close, where he can keep an eye on them."

"Close and alive?"

"I don't know," Mohl said. "It was never more than a story."

"Asabo is a threat to Bo?" DeLuca asked.

"Oh, yes, I should think so," Mohl said. "People look back at the king as the last unifying benevolent leader of Liger. The man who got rid of the British, or made a deal with them to leave, but either way. He wasn't just king of the Fasori. The Da loved him, many of the Kum did, too. Any heir to all of that would be a huge threat. What was the region?" Mohl asked. "The place where this happened?"

DeLuca showed him on the plasma screen.

"I could ask a few people," Mohl said. "Call in some favors, I guess. I don't even know that the phones will work."

"Do what you can," DeLuca told the CIA man.

Preacher Johnson said he had a few angles to work as well. Deluca had even e-mailed Walter Ford and asked him to track down any properties that Bo might have owned outside Liger, on the chance that he'd simply wanted to hustle Paul Asabo out of the country and stash him somewhere for later disposal. The breakthrough came when DeLuca's cell phone rang, and on the other end, John Dari.

"I told you I would call you," Dari said.

"So you did," DeLuca said. "How can I help you?"

"Paul Asabo has been arrested," Dari said. "I was hoping you could ask President Bo to spare his life."

DeLuca covered the phone with one hand and asked Vasquez to contact SIGINT and see if they could get a lock on Dari's signal.

"All our people are out of country," DeLuca said. "Including Ambassador Ellis. We pulled them out days ago."

"You have channels," Dari said.

"We *had* channels," DeLuca corrected him. "We haven't been able to get through to the president lately, but there's a chance we still could, yes. Why, may I ask, are you asking for intervention?"

"Why?" Dari said. "Simple. Paul Asabo owes me a favor. I'm not going to be able to be repaid if he's in prison."

"After this call, he owes you two," DeLuca said. "I'm glad to hear you're all right. I was afraid you'd think I gave information to Ngwema about our last meeting."

"I thought so at first," Dari said. "But then I thought harder about it. It would not make any sense for you to have brought violence to me. Not without using the threat of it for leverage first to corrupt me."

"Wrong department," DeLuca said. "My business is trading favors, not making threats. I'll be honest with you, John. We don't know where Paul is. We can't do anything until we find that out. And even then, our options may be limited."

"He's being held in the castle," Dari said after a pause. "The Castle of St. James."

"Are you sure?"

"I am certain," Dari said. "I have a man in the castle. He has seen him. He might be able to help you, but we cannot contact him. He can only call us."

"What's his name?"

"Henry," Dari said. "Henry Mkembasasso."

"I have a favor I need from you in return," DeLuca said. "I'm putting a woman into the shantytown across the border from Camp Seven. She's going to be looking for a friend. I want her to be safe. Her name is Mary Dorsey."

"I can help you," Dari said. Vasquez held up a sign to tell DeLuca Scott had the coordinates of Dari's SAT-phone, a northern suburb of Port Ivory. DeLuca put his hand over the phone again.

"Let's keep this to ourselves," he said to Vasquez. "I don't want some asshole sending a Tomahawk into our business."

He returned to Dari.

"We know what happened in Sagoa," DeLuca said. "If there's anything we can do to help you along similar lines, you let me know."

There was another pause.

"I'll give you my number," Dari said. "Unless you've already traced it. You can tell me if you know anything. Like where he has gone."

"We'll do that," DeLuca said. "I'll tell the birds to look for a red Hummer. There can't be too many of those in Liger."

MacKenzie could find neither Evelyn Warner nor Dr. Claude Chaline when she reached Camp Cobra, around 1400 hours, arriving on a CH-47 from the USS *Cowper* carrying medical supplies as well as twenty U.S. Marines brought in at the request of the Ghanaian government to help keep order at the border and prevent armed marauders from robbing the refugees. The fighting in Liger had swelled the numbers of refugees in Camp Cobra beyond the breaking point, but international relief had begun to arrive, white SUVs and trucks from UNHCR, Oxfam, the World Food Program, the Red Cross, United Way, the Red Crescent, Catholic World Relief, and the Gates Foundation bringing in workers and supplies.

MacKenzie found Cela in the crowd as she was helping a USAID official talk to the queen mother about setting up a school for the children in Camp Cobra. Sara Ochora was at her side, helping her. Cela threw her arms around MacKenzie and screamed and hugged her when she saw her.

"I am so glad to see you," Cela said. "How are you? Are you well?"

"I'm all right," MacKenzie said. "The others are, too."

"I was so worried," Cela said, pulling at her hair and tucking it behind her ear. "Forgive my appearance. There's not enough water here yet for adequate bathing for the adults. Not even enough for drinking, really."

"You look beautiful," MacKenzie said. "Where's Evelyn? Where's Dr. Chaline?"

"They went with Ms. Duquette to talk to the local governor about the water," Cela said. "The local governor is a big fan of American movies."

"I was actually wondering," Mack said. "I'm looking for my friend Stephen Ackroyd. Have you seen him? I was going to ask Ms. Warner if she knew where he was."

Cela looked puzzled.

"I have not seen him," she said. "But there are so many people."

"But not so many *Obroni*," Mack said. "Thank you, Cela. Are you all right?"

"I am fine," the translator said. "A little hungry."

MacKenzie recognized one of the journalists DeLuca had said was at the Hotel Liger in Baku Da'al, filming a report and squinting into the sun in front of a cameraman, with the shantytown in the background and the American troops mingling in the crowd in full battle rattle, smiling and shaking the hands of the children who were beseeching them for food. She waited until the cameraman put down his camera, then approached the journalist.

"I'm Mary Dorsey, from the United Nations Women's Health Initiative," she told the journalist. "Do you have a minute?"

"Sure," the man said, smiling. "Tom Kruger, Fox News." He gestured to his cameraman to keep filming and pointed to MacKenzie, who ignored the intrusion.

"I'm looking for someone," she said. "A magazine writer named Stephen Ackroyd—do you know him?"

"I met someone named Stephen Ackroyd," Kruger said, "but he wasn't a magazine writer. I suppose that must be who you mean."

"He was on assignment," MacKenzie said. "Maybe his editor would know where he went. He said he was working for *Men's Journal*."

Kruger shifted his gaze briefly, moving closer.

"*Men's Journal*? Well, he told me he was working for *Esquire,* but when I called an editor friend of mine who works there, he told me they'd never heard of him. I figured he was one of those blog people filing to their own Web sites and bragging about how many hits a day they were getting."

"If you see him," Mack said, "tell him Mary Dorsey is looking for him."

"I will," Kruger said, "but more to the point, where do you and I go from here?"

"Excuse me?" she said.

"Where are you staying?" he asked her. "A bunch of us white folk have taken over a motel down the road. There aren't any rooms left, but you could stay with me, and just so you know, I'm huge. I'll make you happier than any man ever has before."

MacKenzie stared at him for a moment.

"If your estimation of your penis size is as accurate as all the other facts you people at Fox News disseminate," MacKenzie said, "I think I'll have to pass."

The cameraman guffawed. As MacKenzie left, she could hear Kruger insisting that the cameraman delete the previous segment.

She moved to the large wall tent that served as the administrative offices for Camp Cobra, but no one there had seen or met anyone named Stephen Ackroyd. She toured the camp briefly, but she suspected she was wasting time. She couldn't stop herself from thinking that Stephen was hurt somewhere and needed help, lying off the side of the road from Camp Seven, or on a trail somewhere. She didn't like the idea of defying one of DeLuca's direct orders, but she needed to go back to Camp Seven, alone if necessary, so she headed to the camp gate leading to the road to the border. At the gate, she saw a group of African Union soldiers posted there, and a familiar face. Corporal Okempo recognized her and asked her how she was.

"I'm good," she told him. "It's good to see you, George."

"Where are you going?" he said. "You don't want to go that way—that way is Liger."

"I know," she said. "I have to go back to check on something."

"Alone?" he said. "You cannot go alone."

"I'll be all right," she said. "I have to go."

"Wait, wait," he said. "You are on foot?"

"I'll be fine," she told him. "I run marathons—I'm used to being on foot."

"Wait, wait, no no no," Corporal Okempo said. "No no, you cannot. I will go with you. Please. You must let us."

"It's dangerous," she insisted.

"No no," he said. "You cannot go alone. Please. It would be dark before you could return. Please, I have a Jeep—we can drive. It's my job. We will go with you."

She considered his request.

"All right," she said. "Thank you."

Corporal Okempo picked three men to accompany them, and a minute later, they were off.

At the border, after they showed their papers to the guards on the Ligerian side of the river, MacKenzie paid their entrance fees in U.S. currency. Every thousand yards or so on the way back to Camp Seven, they saw stragglers or lone refugees heading for safety, gaunt, hollow-eyed people with barely the strength to move, mothers with children in their arms, kids wearing handed-down charity T-shirts with Domino's Pizza logos or Teenage Mutant Ninja Turtles characters on them, families walking silently, old women carrying plastic shopping bags containing all their remaining worldly possessions. "Have you seen an American?" MacKenzie asked them. "Have you seen an *Obroni*?" The sun was fierce. MacKenzie occasionally stood in the Jeep, hanging on to the roll bar, to survey the countryside. Each time they came to a grove of trees, her hopes rose, thinking she'd find Stephen resting beneath them with a broken ankle, perhaps, or maybe he'd stopped to assist someone in need and was staying with them until help arrived. She pictured him smiling and saying, "Thought you'd never get here," or making some lame joke about how women were always late. At one point, her hopes rose again when she thought she saw a white man walking toward them, but she was mistaken. It was only a fair-skinned African man who seemed half-dazed.

The scene at Camp Seven was one of desolation and destruction, as if the men who'd come to kill the people there had taken their frustrations out on the camp itself. Buildings and tents had been burned, solar cook stoves and water pumps destroyed. The infirmary had been slashed by machetes, beds and IV drips smashed and tossed to the ground, tables overturned, ration cards burned, as if to bring some further measure of hell to the people already visited by so much suffering, should they try to return. With Okempo and his men, they drove the lanes of the camp in silence, witnessing the devastation, and at one point MacKenzie called out Stephen's name, several times, as loud as she could, not because she expected him to answer but because she had to.

"Miss Dorsey," Corporal Okempo finally said. "I think we should go. There is no one here. Please. It will be dark."

Then trouble.

A troop convoy appeared in the distance, pausing on a far hill at a crest in the road and stopping.

MacKenzie noted that her three escorts from the African Union were equipped with the AK-47s that DeLuca had given them. They held their weapons uncertainly, the way a new father might hold his first child. Okempo seemed to be about twenty, and the two men who'd volunteered to come along were younger than that. MacKenzie had a MAC-10 in her shoulder bag, as well as her service Beretta. She opened her bag but left the weapons inside it, where she could reach them quickly. The truck approached slowly, stopping again about fifty yards from where the AU jeep was parked. A man in a red beret got out of the truck and gestured for someone to come forward.

"I will go," Corporal Okempo said softly. "Perhaps there will be no problem."

She could sense, in the way he walked, that it was only with some effort that he was able to place one foot in front of the other and proceed, checking back over his shoulder and straightening his posture to make himself look as large and as important as possible. A second rebel jumped down from the truck and pointed his rifle at the corporal, who raised one hand in a gesture of peace.

MacKenzie watched apprehensively as the two men, Okempo and the leader of the rebels, spoke for a few minutes, and then Okempo returned, a smile on his face.

"You see?" he said. "I told you it would be all right. They are SJD. They say they will drive with us to the border to protect our rear. Okay then? Not a problem. But they say there are marauders in this place still who are not part of any army but who have been causing trouble anyway. We can go."

Mack took one last look around the camp, then got back into the Jeep.

It was dark by the time they crossed first the West and then the East Liger rivers to re-enter Camp Cobra. She found Evelyn Warner in the administration tent. Dr. Chaline was in the infirmary. Warner wore a haggard look on her face, managing a brief sad smile to see MacKenzie again.

"Wasn't sure you were still with us," Warner said. "I'm glad that you are. I heard you went back to Camp Seven."

"It got a little sketchy, for a while there," Mack said. "Fortunately, we found some transportation when we needed it."

"I can't tell you how grateful we are," Evelyn said. "To you and to David and all the rest. Someone said some men parachuted in to lend a hand."

"It was a pleasant surprise," MacKenzie said. "Have you heard anything about Paul Asabo? We know he was arrested, but we don't know much more."

"I wish I had something to tell you, but I don't," Warner said. "He was telling the soldiers at the border to behave themselves. I was trying to intercede, but when they said to him, 'Who do you think you are?' he told them. Two minutes later, two men came and forced him into the backseat of a government SUV, and that's the last we saw of him. Do you know where he is?"

"We're trying to find out," MacKenzie said. "I actually came back to look for Stephen."

"Oh, dear God," Warner said, a look on her face of sad surprise. She put her hand lightly on Mack's arm. "Hasn't anyone told you? Stephen didn't make it."

MacKenzie felt her heart suddenly breaking, beat by beat.

"What do you mean?" she asked. "That he isn't here? He didn't come back with you?"

"He's here," Warner said. "His body is. But he didn't make it, Colleen. We've been trying to notify his next of kin."

"Show me," MacKenzie said.

Dr. Chaline stepped out of the infirmary just as they passed. When Evelyn Warner told him she was taking MacKenzie to see Stephen's body, he nodded grimly and volunteered to go with them. He cautioned MacKenzie that it was the practice in refugee camps to bury people quickly, given what the lack of refrigeration and the hot African sun could do to a body after the life had gone out of it and circulation no longer cooled it. The morgue was a large tent, kept apart from the camp and downwind, because the smell could be quite strong. There was a cemetery beyond the morgue where the bodies were moved as soon as an identity could be determined, communal graves

dug by a backhoe, with the attempt made to bury people
with their own tribal members. Bodies that had been either identified or determined to be unidentifiable were
taken from the morgue and stored on the ground, sprayed
with chlorine, and then covered with lime to slow the
decomposition until the burial crews could get to them.
There were outbreaks of cholera and dysentery from soil
and water contaminated with *Vibrio cholerae* and *Shigella
dysenteriae,* Chaline said, an epidemic of cerebrospinal
meningitis, one latrine for every six hundred refugees because the camp was on volcanic rock where latrines were
impossible to dig, and no mosquito control programs in
place to prevent the spread of malaria or lymphatic filaria-
sis. Things were barely in control, he told MacKenzie. He
hoped she could understand.

The smell was indeed overpowering. Stephen's body
lay on a table all by itself, covered in a white sheet. When
Claude Chaline pulled the sheet back, Mack felt her knees
buckle slightly. It was Stephen, but it wasn't Stephen. She
tried to harden herself and tell herself she was a soldier,
and soldiers were tough and didn't feel things, but her at-
tempts were unsuccessful. She took a deep breath and
turned to leave, walking away as fast as she could walk,
until Evelyn Warner caught up to her and put her arms
around her and held her. Soldiers weren't supposed to cry,
that's what they said, but in her experience, soldiers cried
all the time. For some, it was all that got them through.
They did it privately, when they thought no one else was
looking, but they all did it. Now it was her turn.

When Dr. Chaline reached them, she asked him how it
happened. Why? What was the cause of death? She said

she wanted a complete explanation, and not to spare her. She'd had EMT training, she reminded him.

"Starvation is one of the oldest things that people can die from," Chaline said softly. "People have starved to death since the beginning of time, but we still can't always pinpoint how it causes life to end. The causes are often multiple. Stephen would not eat. We all noticed how thin he was getting—did you know that this happens from time to time among relief workers, who feel so guilty eating in front of starving people that they can't eat themselves, and give away all their food to those they think are more deserving? Sometimes we have to assign minders and eat on the buddy system, to watch each other to make sure it does not happen."

MacKenzie was aware of the phenomenon. She felt Evelyn's arm around her shoulder.

"When he first came to us," Chaline continued, "he was quite overweight. I think he lost perhaps 30 percent of his body mass. He told us he felt better than he had in years. At a certain point, early in the process, sometimes a kind of contentment settles in. The psychological changes come later. I had spoken to Stephen about it. Starvation is a catch-all diagnostic. There is a final wasting away where the body depletes all its resources, but when you become extremely malnourished, long before that point, you become susceptible to a number of other things. He could have been hypoglycemic, or have had low blood sodium from dehydration. The body can't fight infections. Your heart loses muscle mass, which makes exertion difficult. There are electrolyte imbalances. If I had to guess at cause of death, I would say his heart failed. We've had cases of critical orthostatic hypotension, myofibrillar damage, ventricular arrhythmias, low QRS voltage—all of this can lead to sudden cardiac death. It's a combination. One thing occurs and then there is a sudden cascade to failure. I am sorry."

"If you knew he was starving himself, why didn't you do something?" she asked him. "You're a doctor. You could have force-fed him."

"A doctor cannot treat a patient against his will," Chaline said. "That is assault, from a legal definition, unless the patient isn't competent to make decisions for himself. With starvation, people are often completely lucid, right up to the end. It's a problem. Tell me—did you see any signs of megalomania or persecution?"

She thought, then nodded, remembering when Stephen told her he thought he was going to win the Pulitzer, unless the other journalists in Liger sabotaged his work.

"Anger or aggressiveness? Impulsiveness, perhaps?"

"Just once," she said, recalling how he bristled when she said she wanted to peek at his journal.

"Did he ever seem confused or disassociated?" Chaline asked. "As if he didn't quite know where he was? Or indifferent to the future?"

She remembered what a bad driver he was, and how, in the chaos of exiting Camp Seven, he'd seemed a bit lost, or distracted, but war was nothing if not disorder—feeling lost was normal, she'd concluded at the time. She remembered him not getting her joke, and saying, "It just never occurred to me that this would be over," and his last word to her, "Whatever." She'd missed all the signs. MacKenzie understood that to the doctor, Stephen's was just one of a thousand deaths he saw every week. It was different, but it was the same.

"I wish you'd told me," she said.

"He made us swear to say nothing," Chaline said. "I'm sorry."

"We're having some trouble contacting his next of kin," Evelyn Warner said. "We've tried the emergency contact listed on his passport, but there's no answer—the information appears to be out of date. This is horrible, but there simply aren't the facilities to handle this properly. Under these conditions, prolonging burial endangers everyone else . . ."

"I'll take care of it," MacKenzie said. "He can come with me. I'll contact his next of kin."

"We have his things," Warner said. "I'll get them for you."

MacKenzie contacted the USS *Johnson* and asked for a helicopter to come get her. She added that they would need to bring along a body bag for a team member whose remains needed to be stored and shipped to Evansville, Illinois—she'd furnish the details later.

Stephen's belongings all fit into a large knapsack. She went through them, hoping it would tell her who he was. In addition to a few changes of clothes, he carried with him a paperback volume of *The Catcher in the Rye,* a well-thumbed collection of poems by an Israeli poet named Yehuda Amichai, two paperback references on the flora and fauna of West Africa, and a well-thumbed dictionary, with words in it underlined that he'd intended to learn and use. *Apodictically: beyond contradiction, clearly proving. Probity: virtue, integrity. Contretemps: an inappropriate/confusing/awkward moment.* He had a toilet kit containing a razor that lacked the blade cartridge, a bottle of aspirin, a toothbrush but no toothpaste, a small flashlight with dead batteries, a fingernail clipper, and a comb. She found an empty prescription bottle for mefloquine, an anti-malarial medication, and another for sleep disturbances. In his wallet, an Illinois driver's license, an Evanston, Illinois, library card, an ATM card, and a card from his local grocery store that doubled your coupons, but no credit cards and nothing that helped her understand who he was.

When she opened his journal to see what he'd written, feeling that it would be okay now, saving this for last, she was stunned.

She founds words only on the first page. She'd seen him sit down with his journal on multiple occasions and had always been tempted to peek over his shoulder, but he'd always protected his writing from her, and she'd always respected his privacy. She hesitated opening the journal now, but she did it, in the hope of finding some kind of explanation. She found the reason why he'd chosen to starve himself, but she found also a greater mystery. He'd written:

I have come here to be a writer but so far, I am unable to produce anything. It's all worthless shit. My first instinct is to think this is ridiculous, one more ridiculous chapter in my pathetic and ridiculous life, but that's just me, getting down on myself, and nothing has become clearer, since my arrival, than that this is not about me. This country, this war, this famine, these poor people—this is not about me. I am not equal to this challenge, but who is? The other professional journalists at the hotel have laughed at me and called me a joke, and in a way they're right, but in another way, I can prove them wrong. They write about hunger

*and starvation, but they never get out of the fucking
car, or they file their stories from the bar, and they're
all overweight, and each night they go back to the
hotel and have a big meal and drink and joke about
how pathetic the people in this country are. It's they
who are pathetic. They know nothing, and never will.
The only way to understand this experience is to live
it, and then write about it, so that's what I've decided
to do. I will make myself as hungry as the people in
these camps, and then I will know what it's like. And
then I will write, once I've come through the other
side. That's my plan, anyway. I am a great writer. This
is the big one. This is the book that will be my legacy,
I think. I can't wait to get started.*

The other pages were either blank or contained doodles,
chains of boxes or scribbled geometric designs. On one
page, in the middle, she found a picture, a rather crude
drawing of herself, rendered in pencil, a portrait of her
with her eyes closed. He must have sketched it while she
was sleeping. Above the face was the name, Mary Dorsey,
and below it the words, "She will be my muse."

MacKenzie closed the notebook and put it in the backpack.

When the helicopter arrived, she showed the flight
crew where they'd find the body and watched as they
loaded it onto the HH-60. She found Cela and gave her a
hug good-bye, and then she found Corporal Okempo and
gave him a hug as well, promising him she'd never forget
his bravery and his courage. Dr. Chaline had finally allowed himself to fall asleep, so she didn't dare disturb

him to say good-bye. Evelyn Warner walked her to the helicopter.

"Tell David I intend to thank him in person when I see him," Warner said. "For last night. I know he could have made other choices and he chose to save us."

"I'm not sure he could have made other choices," MacKenzie said, "but I'll tell him. Can I ask you a personal question, Evelyn? When you and David were in Iraq, did you and he ever . . . become involved?"

Warner shook her head.

"I certainly gave it some serious thought, but I don't think he ever did," Warner said. "Inappropriate to bring it up, him being happily married and all that. It's a line I don't cross."

"Just wondering," Mack said.

"I'm always astonished that love can exist in places like this," Warner said. "You'd think we'd have higher priorities. But what do I know anyway?"

"You know a lot," Mack said. "Thank you."

DeLuca, Sykes, Vasquez, Preacher Johnson, and three of his TF-21 men sat two thousand yards offshore in the darkness in the second boat, awaiting Riley's signal. DeLuca felt lucky in a number of ways. First, knowing Paul Asabo's location eliminated the search part of what was a search and rescue mission. Robert Mohl had heard from a contact a similar rumor, that Paul Asabo was being held at the Castle of St. James. It was enough of a confirmation to persuade General LeDoux to green-light the operation. Second, detailed plans for a covert insertion into the Castle of St. James had already been drawn up—it had been the original plan to evacuate the ambassador,

a night mission that was scrubbed only after DeLuca
came up with a proposal to rescue the ambassador in broad
daylight and move the evacuation up twelve hours in the
schedule. They were favored by an overcast sky that made
the night even darker, the city of Port Ivory without
power, the fires to the west still burning. "We have flow,"
Preacher Johnson said. "We're in the blessing zone." High
tide was at 2113 hours, an hour after last light. Lieutenant
Riley and his SEAL team had gone ahead.

The Castle of St. James had been fortified, when it was
originally built, to protect the occupants from threats
from land and not from the sea, both because the likelihood of an attack from land was greater and because the
sea side had its own natural fortifications, the castle
mounted on a rocky cliff thirty feet above the water at
high tide, with a surf strong enough to dash even the best
swimmers to pieces against the rocks. When the castle
had been part of the triangular trade operation between
Europe, Africa, and the Americas, there'd been a wooden
pier connecting the "door of no return" with the sea.
Slaves were marched down a series of steps and onto the
pier, where they were loaded onto ships for transportation
to plantations in the Caribbean originally and later in
America. The pier and the wooden steps had long since
fallen into the surf, leaving only a lone door, high above
the water, set into walls that were twenty-five feet thick at
the base. There'd been talk, briefly, of putting a BLU-136
laser-guided "bunker buster" ordnance into the door and
taking the ambassador out through the hole.

Riley and three SEALs had entered the water from a
thousand yards out and executed a compass dive, swimming underwater and following illuminated compasses,

emerging unseen in their matte black scuba suits on the rocks below the door. They'd survived the surf and climbed the rocks, and then a pair of SEALs scaled the wall, setting bolts and rigging ropes as they went, until they'd reached the portal. The actual "door of no return" itself was the original item, made of thick wooden planks and cast-iron sheathing, but it had been designed to keep people in, not to keep people out. The additional work done over the years to reinforce the door had done little to alter that function. It took the SEAL at the door no time to cut the bolts holding the door closed with the portable oxyacetylene torch he'd brought with him.

"Ready when you are," DeLuca heard Riley say over his radio.

The SEAL driving the Zodiac switched to electrical power, the boat moving silently forward in the darkness. The castle had its own generator, with electric lights illuminating the walls and courtyards, but no lights shone on the sea far below. The falcon view showed Presidential Guard troops manning the parapets on the land side, with only a handful assigned to watch to the south. There'd been talk of creating some kind of diversion or distraction, but neither were necessary, given that armed rebels were already providing the service, attacking the castle from town with sporadic RPG, mortar, and small-arms fire. Ambassador Ellis had managed to telephone President Bo, who informed the ambassador that all was going exceedingly well, and that he and his cabinet were preparing, with complete confidence, to reoccupy their offices in the morning. Both SIGINT and IMINT confirmed that Bo and his cabinet were holed up in the castle keep. To DeLuca's surprise, General Ngwema was in the castle as well, rather than leading his troops from the field. Bo's personal Chinook helicopter sat in the east courtyard, ready to relocate the president and his administration if the castle were to fall.

DeLuca rechecked the falcon view on his CIM. He looked at the castle through his NVGs.

"I still say we oughtta get us a catapult and do this the old-fashioned way," Preacher Johnson said in a soft voice.

The risk factors were twofold. One was that they'd be seen. The second was that they'd be dashed against the rocks by the surf and drowned. At one point DeLuca nearly lost his balance, stepping out of the boat onto the rock, his arm caught in the tight grip of a SEAL who pulled him quickly to safety. The SEAL driving the Zodiac tossed them their gear and motored offshore to wait until he was called back.

A short, quick scramble up the wet rocks led to the climbing ropes the first pair of SEALs had rigged. At the top, the team assembled out of view, where the portal had been hollowed into the wall. Thermal imaging revealed nothing on the other side of the door. Imaging through the fifteen-foot-thick stone walls was, of course, impossible. Two SEALs held the door by the hinge side while two of Johnson's men, both of them African-Americans, DeLuca noted, grabbed the door by the opposite side. On a count of three, they pulled the door off its hinges and set it aside.

"Permission to throw this motherfucker into the sea," one of Johnson's men asked.

"Denied," Johnson said. "All political statements or gestures may be posted to the TF-21 Web site."

On the other side of the door was what appeared, viewed through night vision goggles, to be a short tunnel, not quite tall enough for any of them to stand upright in, perhaps twenty feet long. Johnson's men took the lead, moving quietly to the end of the tunnel, then gave the clear signal.

The tunnel opened onto a large room, the size of a barn, with a high ceiling, walls of cobbled stone and brick, and a dirt floor that sloped uphill away from them, a four-inch-wide gutter running down the middle of the sloping floor.

"That gutter served as the only toilet for the slaves they kept in here," Johnson whispered. "This room held maybe five or six hundred men. The women's quarters were up ahead. There's a trapdoor in the ceiling of the women's quarters where the governor used to climb down and pick the girls he wanted to have sex with. It was the only other way out of the dungeon. Girls who got pregnant were released because they figured a slave that was half white wouldn't work as hard as one that was all black. I believe the irony therein was lost on the colonial fathers."

"How do you know this stuff?" Vasquez asked him.

"I took a tour," Johnson said. "Back when I was still undercover."

Small windows, perhaps eighteen inches square, were set into the walls about twenty feet above the floor. An aluminum stepladder led to one, where there appeared to be a machine-gun mount, currently unoccupied. At the top of the slope, a large corridor turned left, and at the end of the corridor, a single dim yellow light bulb hung on a wire from the ceiling. The corridor was lined with boxes and crates containing, a quick inspection revealed, weapons, food, and cash, a block of U.S. hundred-dollar bills similar to the stash of U.S. currency they'd found in Iraq.

DeLuca had found, in Iraq, a stash that he later learned came to $22 million American. This stash was, he estimated, even larger. The weapons were brand-new U.S. Army issue M-16Bs and AR-10s. The food stores included caviar, pâtés, smoked fish, expensive cheeses, even a case of wine that Sykes, an amateur oenophile, said would fetch perhaps as much as three hundred dollars a bottle in a typical New York restaurant.

"Let them eat motherfucking cake," he said.

They found a set of stairs at the end of the corridor, uneven stone risers leading up to the lower levels of the keep, another bare bulb at the top of the stairs lighting the way. They heard the drone of a two-stroke engine behind a closed metal door and opened it to find the generator that was powering the castle, a large gas-powered nine-thousand-watt Honda on wheels, jury-rigged to a junction box. They were about to ascend the stairs when DeLuca heard someone behind him. He turned to see the door to a cell, iron bars, with only darkness within, and then, out of the darkness, he saw the face of Paul Asabo.

"See what I mean by flow?" Preacher Johnson said.

"I'd have to agree," DeLuca said softly, turning to Paul. "Are you all right?"

"I'm all right," Asabo said. "How did you get here?"

"Same way we're leaving," DeLuca. "We've got a boat waiting. We'll get you out of there in a second." He gestured to the SEAL who'd brought the torch to see what he could do about cutting through the lock on the door. "Can you walk?"

One of Johnson's men shone a flashlight into the windowless cell where Asabo was being held. DeLuca saw an old man squint at the light and cover his eyes with his hand. He was clean-shaven, with gray close-cropped hair, and he was dressed in pajamas.

"I can't go anywhere," Asabo said. "This is my father. He can't walk."

DeLuca moved to the cell door, shining his own flashlight on the ceiling. The old man was skin and bones, his legs as thin as a child's arm, but there was a light in his eyes.

"My name is Special Agent David DeLuca," he said. "I'm with United States Army counterintelligence. We've come to help you."

"Take my son and go," the old man said, coughing. "You can leave me here."

"No, Father," the younger Asabo said. The next thing he said was in Fasori, at the end of which the old man nodded.

DeLuca waited. He appreciated that decisions needed to be made with due deliberation, but the idea that they could find themselves in the middle of a firefight at any second made it difficult to remain patient.

Finally, Asabo finished speaking to his father.

"Thank you for coming to get me, David," Paul Asabo said, "but after all these years, I won't go back. Even staying here, in this cell, with my father, would be better. If I'm going to die, I want to die in Liger. Please. You should go, before someone comes down. The guards come every once in a while to check on the generator, or to get something."

"No one's going to die," DeLuca said. "We'll take your father, too."

"He can't walk," Asabo said.

"Then we'll have to get out some other way," DeLuca said, thinking. DeLuca didn't see how the old man would be able to negotiate the ropes at the door of no return, or any way to lower him down. If they couldn't go down, then they had to go up.

"What's at the top of the stairs?" he asked.

"I think there are guards," Asabo said.

"How many?"

"I don't know. Every now and then, I can hear men talking."

"Preacher," DeLuca said. "You said there was a trapdoor leading to the governor's quarters. Think it still works?"

"Couldn't say," Johnson said. "On the other hand, most things in this place appear to have been built to last."

"Scottie," DeLuca said, speaking into his radio. "Thermal imaging on the governors' quarters. Have you got it?"

"Through the roof only. The administrative offices or his living quarters?"

"Living quarters," DeLuca said. "Bedroom. Anybody in it?"

"It appears to be empty," Scottie said. "But getting thermals is sketchy."

"Nobody sleeping there?"

"Not that I can find. It looks clear."

"Good enough for me," DeLuca said. "Preacher, I saw an aluminum ladder in the men's dungeon. Send one of your men to get it, then show him where the trapdoor is and set it up. Your other man is going to need to carry the king up the ladder fireman style. Dan, we're taking the president's helicopter. You're going to have to fly it."

"I might as well just join the Air Force," Sykes said. "I hope all the buttons are in the same locations."

"Get Captain Evans back on the horn and tell him to stand by," DeLuca said calmly. He studied his CIM for the latest falcon view of the castle, showing him where Bo's men were positioned. He clicked over to a graphic view of the structure, showing him the layout, the doors, the exits, ramparts, towers, and barbicans. "I think it's fair to guess the president keeps his helicopter ready to go at a moment's notice."

The SEAL's torch cut through the last part of the lock. He shook it a moment, and then the cage door swung free. Paul Asabo stepped out as Lieutenant Riley and the third SEAL entered the cell to help the elder Asabo to his feet, wobbly as a newborn calf.

"Hoolie," DeLuca said, flipping his NVGs down, "on my signal, kill the generator. It's time we enjoyed our American God-given right to technological superiority."

DeLuca allowed the others to go up the ladder ahead of him, then gave the signal to Hoolie. The castle lights went out. Hoolie ran to the ladder in the pitch black and climbed up behind DeLuca, in whose NVGs the place seemed bright as day.

Climbing up through the trapdoor was stepping back into the seventeenth century. The governor's quarters were part of the Ligerian Historical Museum, and featured the original furniture, wall decorations, and historical details, a pair of men's slippers beside the bed, a Bible opened on the end table. The bed was a large four-poster, and there were marks that clearly indicated where chains had been used to fasten someone to it.

They moved aside the velvet rope and crossed to the hall, which opened onto a small balcony overlooking a courtyard below, where DeLuca saw four iron balls, each the size of a basketball, to which, Johnson explained, prisoners had once been chained as punishment, or to simply die in the sun for the viewing pleasure of the occupying powers. The courtyard was also where prisoners were occasionally drawn and quartered.

Beyond the balcony was a hall leading to the administrative offices, opening onto the castle's main courtyard. DeLuca saw a black Chinook, guarded by a pair of soldiers, and beyond that, the main castle keep where the Historical Museum's large exhibit hall was located. DeLuca saw candles being lit in the exhibit hall, where Bo's Presidential Guard had taken positions, men gesticulating and shouting. He saw soldiers manning machine guns in the towers and at the parapets facing town.

He checked his CIM again, zooming out for a larger view. Rebel forces appeared to have the castle surrounded, but there was something of a lull in the fighting. He clicked for the location of John Dari and found him nearby, moving approximately from City Hall toward the castle gate.

"Scottie," DeLuca said. "What's going on outside the gates?"

"See for yourself," Scott said. "I'm patching through a live feed. This is Al Jazeera."

DeLuca saw the captured digital imagery in real time, the streets of Port Ivory awash in rebel troops who seemed to have taken full control of the city.

"How many UAVs do we have right now?" DeLuca asked.

"All five," Scott said. "Locked and loaded. You crashed the other one."

"I'm going to need some shock and awe," DeLuca said. "Can you put something somewhere where the collateral damage will be minimal? Maybe between the outer and inner walls?"

"I can do that," Scott said.

DeLuca turned to Paul Asabo.

"Paul, I want you and your father to wait here until we come to get you," DeLuca said. "Lieutenant Riley, you're free to take your men back out the way we came if you want. It's your call."

"And miss all the fun?" Riley said. "I've never done a mission with CI before. Usually, SEALs like to think things through first."

"It's all a state of mind, Lieutenant," DeLuca said.

"Preacher," DeLuca said. "Have you got a plan to take out the guards?"

"Oh," Johnson said. "I'm sorry. Did you want me to wait?"

DeLuca looked out at the courtyard again, where Johnson's men had subdued the guards and were dragging them off to the sea wall. A moment later, Johnson's men had taken the guards' place, donning their helmets and flak jackets.

"No, I guess not," DeLuca said. "Dan—how long does it take to get one of those things ready to go, from cold start to liftoff?"

"Why are you asking me?" Sykes said. "I keep telling you, I'm not a pilot."

"Oh, come on, Dan," DeLuca said, smiling. "Be all that you can be."

"About three minutes," DeLuca heard Captain Evans tell him on his headset. "According to our thermals, the APU is hot."

"Any time you're ready, Scott."

"Firing," Scott replied.

DeLuca counted in his head, a thousand one, a thousand two.

On four, the night was split by the sound of a Hellfire slamming into the castle's inner bailey, and a moment later, a second missile hit. The Presidential Guards in the towers opened up with their machine guns, firing on the city below.

DeLuca led the way, crouching low and crossing to the helicopter. They'd gotten halfway there, in the open and completely exposed, when the courtyard was lit by the light of a flare fired from the castle keep. DeLuca saw men running into the courtyard, soldiers as well as men dressed in suits and ties. He straightened from his crouch and walked briskly toward them.

"Plan B," he said into his radio.

"Which is?"

"I'm not sure yet," DeLuca said. "Scottie, a couple more if you will."

DeLuca walked toward President Bo and his party as if he belonged there. He debated, briefly, telling Bo he was going to have to confiscate his helicopter in the name of the United States Army, when he had what he hoped was a better idea.

"President Bo," DeLuca called out, coming to attention and snapping off his snappiest salute. Sykes, Vasquez, Riley, and Johnson did the same. "General David DeLuca, United States Army. This is Colonel Johnson, Major Riley,

Captain Sykes, and Captain Vasquez." He was trusting
that no one noticed they'd come in sterile without any
identifying insignia on their uniforms to indicate rank.
"Ambassador Ellis sends his warmest regards, as does the
president of the United States."

"What are you doing here?" President Bo asked. He
was shorter than DeLuca had expected, dressed in a black
suit, white shirt, and red tie, the Kevlar helmet on his
head making him look something like a dictatorial bobble-
head doll.

"Your situation is untenable," DeLuca said. "Let me
show you."

A third missile struck the castle walls, a harmless but
impressive display of pyrotechnics. Scottie had heard
DeLuca's words, "Let me show you," and was following
his father's play. When DeLuca showed the Ligerian president his CIM, Scottie filled the screen with as many
blinking red dots and swooping green arrows as he could.
DeLuca saw where, at one point, Scottie even layered in
the weather forecast.

"As you can see. you really shouldn't stay, sir. My pilot
will take you and whoever you want to bring with you to
our carrier offshore."

"I'm General Ngwema," a tall man said, stepping forward and saluting. "I will stay here."

"Not a good idea, General," DeLuca said, trying to
sound crabby and wise, like a general should. "We've got
sixty-four B2 bombers that flew all the way here from
Missouri, and they're set to arrive and drop their payloads
in about ten minutes, accompanied by Tomahawks and
JDAMs and JSOWs and you name it—we're going to flatten this place for you and then bring you back to pick up

the pieces. No charge, compliments of the United States military."

He showed Ngwema the CIM. Scottie quickly added small airplane icons to the display.

"I will come back afterward," Ngwema said. "Our work here is not finished."

"My pilot will take you," DeLuca said, gesturing to Dan Sykes.

"I have my own pilot," President Bo said. DeLuca looked at Sykes, who nodded vigorously.

"All right then," DeLuca said. "This place is going to fall apart—you have to leave now. We'll follow you in our own chopper."

He pulled his men aside and circled them together in conference. A fourth missile slammed the castle for effect.

"What are we doing?" Hoolie asked.

"I don't know," DeLuca said. "Look important."

"What next?" Preacher Johnson asked, pointing vehemently to his SATphone, as if there were something important about it.

"We'll just have to wait and see, won't we?" DeLuca said.

"I thought there were too many RPGs and shoulder-fireds to fly helicopters out of here," Lieutenant Riley said.

"I heard that, too," DeLuca said. "In all things, there's an element of risk."

DeLuca watched as President Bo loaded two suitcases, filled with cash, no doubt, or diamonds, into the helicopter and told two of his wives or mistresses they could come with him, telling the other two they had to stay. The women left behind didn't seem to like it much. DeLuca

and the others saluted as the big black Chinook carrying
Bo, General Ngwema, Bo's cabinet members, and as
many of his guards as the aircraft could carry rose and
flew over the seawall, staying low as it cruised above the
open water, heading out to sea.

Soon it was far offshore and safe.

"Don't you wish we could have done that to the Clinton administration?" Sykes said.

"Scottie, you wanna tell the *LBJ* to get their guest
quarters ready?" DeLuca said.

"It's under discussion," Scott said. "People here in
Washington aren't quite as quick on their feet as you are.
The view from here seems to be that there are no vacan-
cies on the carrier."

"Well hey," DeLuca said. "Don't look at me. I just suggested they take off. They don't have to land if they don't
want to."

In the exhibit hall, he saw, by the light of the candles
that had been lit there, three of Bo's Presidential Guards
changing into civilian clothes. The men ran off in their
boxer shorts when they saw they weren't alone. DeLuca
saw piles of uniforms and weapons elsewhere, where other
guards had done the same. The machine guns atop the
towers had been abandoned as well. On his CIM, DeLuca
saw images of men slipping over the wall by the service
entrance and running from the castle. In the hall, DeLuca
saw that the stuffed lion had been removed from its
pedestal, and someone had cut the ivory tusks off the
elephant. A glass case containing examples of Da gold-
smithing had been looted, as had a case containing the
royal crown and scepter, but the Royal Sun Robe was intact. When he turned, he saw that Paul Asabo had come to

the hall with his father, who walked stiffly and slowly now but under his own power.

"John and I took a class together at Mill River Academy," Asabo said, looking at the Royal Sun Robe, "on the meaning and uses of symbolism. I remember telling the teacher that Africans don't separate symbol from meaning. That's what animism is. The spirit, the meaning, literally inhabits the thing. It was hard to make him understand."

Throngs of people pressed at the gate, where music played. A television crew was filming in the crowd, their lights bright in the night. When DeLuca's SATphone rang, the internal caller ID told him it was John Dari, who was, according to DeLuca's handheld, just outside the gates.

"You might want to take this," he told Paul Asabo, handing him the telephone. "I think it's for you."

Chapter Thirteen

● Liger Falls

Liger has a new government. President Bo flees. Asabo and Dari announce copresidency. Elections promised.

❑ In a surprise move, a new government was formed peacefully last night in the war-torn West African nation of Liger. Rebel factions (more ►►)

❑ Ex-Liger president Bo flees to Libya and seeks asylum when USS *Johnson* refuses landing (more ►►)

❑ Asabo president, Dari vice-president. Former high school friends to lead nation. "This is not the monarchy . . ." (more ►►)

❑ Instead of expected violence, Port Ivory sees joy, dancing in the streets (more ►►)

❑ Nation lays down arms as rebel leader throws weapons into sea through "Door of No Return." Widespread disarmament (more ►►)

❑ Free elections in six months, monitored by the UN, ECOMAG, and AU (more ►►)

❑ Celebration (see pix ►►)

❑ Royal robe (see pix ►►)

Related stories: ▣ Oil prices fall; ▣ Relief floods into country as U.S. troops, aid workers assist; Asabo's father freed; ▣Evidence of atrocities as Adu flees; ▣ Adu caught in firefight?

DELUCA WAS STANDING WITH SYKES WHEN HIS
SATphone rang. It was Scottie, telling him he needed to
check his CIM. On the screen, DeLuca saw a red H2
Hummer leaving town as part of a caravan of trucks and
SUVs. It was confirmed that the H2 contained Samuel Adu.

He consulted briefly with Asabo, who requested any
assistance the U.S. could give. DeLuca said he needed
transportation. Dari summoned his number two in command, a man he introduced as Captain Oscar Kudzimtuku, and told him to give DeLuca whatever he needed.

It took a while to clear the crowds still thronging the
castle, and a while to pass along the streets where the citizens of Port Ivory were celebrating, dancing, holding signs,
Christians and Muslims alike, playing loud music and
drinking beer, now that the war was over. DeLuca watched
a real-time data feed of video footage from the UAV flying above Samuel Adu's caravan, clicking between that
and a map showing the road Adu was on and where it led.
When Adu turned north onto the Baku Da'al highway,
DeLuca saw a shortcut and showed it to Captain Kudzimtuku, who got on his radio and told two of his trucks to
take the shortcut and set up a roadblock. The two leaders
watched the real-time feed as, fifteen minutes later, Adu's
red H2 stopped short of the roadblock, where a firefight
broke out. They watched as Adu's driver wheeled the H2
around and sped toward a cinderblock building, just as
DeLuca and the remainder of the SJD forces arrived. Scott
told his father that a biometrics analysis confirmed that
Samuel Adu had fled the H2 and had taken refuge in the
cinderblock building, an abandoned warehouse, Scott said,
perhaps twenty by thirty feet, not large. Inside it, thermal
imaging revealed, were perhaps fifteen or sixteen men.

The terrain was flat, with little to take shelter behind, forcing Kudzimtuku's men to find cover at a greater than desired distance, but at least Adu wasn't going anywhere, with SJD troops surrounding the building. Adu's men fired from the windows, and SJD forces fired back. Adu was trapped, and he knew he was trapped.

DeLuca phoned General LeDoux, who said he'd call Washington and get right back. When LeDoux called back, DeLuca listened, then got Scott on the line. Scott said he had the scene from the UAV but wanted to know the situation on the ground.

"It's a standoff," DeLuca said.

"Well then," Scott said. "You going to turn it over to the locals or stick around?"

"Washington thinks it's best if we finish it. I'm sorry to have to ask you to do this, Scott," DeLuca said. "We need to take the building down. We might take casualties if we do it from ground."

There was a pause. DeLuca knew what he was asking his son to do, pull the trigger on a man who wasn't going anywhere and was, if not defenseless, and hardly innocent, then more or less a sitting duck. This was not an American court of law, where a person was presumed innocent until proven guilty. This was war, where threats were assessed, and then countermeasures were taken. Sometimes, one arrived at a "gray area" where the distinctions between right and wrong were blurred, at which point men could exempt themselves from responsibility or recuse themselves from living in a moral universe and say they were just following orders, and then, like Captain Ernie Tibbets and the crew of the *Enola Gay*, the airplane that dropped the first atom bomb on Nagasaki, or any number of military men in similar but less notorious roles, a man could do harm in the name of preventing greater harm and live with a clear conscience for the rest of his life. Yet every officer knew how difficult it was to tell someone to kill someone else. It just was, despite the adrenaline rush of combat, or the obvious need to protect one's friends, or one's country, or the idea of freedom itself. Even if Scott was sitting at a computer screen five thousand miles away, DeLuca was still asking his own son to kill someone, to "lose his cherry," as some said. It was why DeLuca had been less than overjoyed when Scottie told him he'd been promoted. He'd hoped it wouldn't come to this. Samuel Adu was as bad as they come—there was no gray area there. Samuel Adu had literally butchered people in Sierra Leone and in Liger, and he'd commanded parents to eat their own children—it was as black and white as it got, and still it was hard.

"Not a problem," Scott said. "Bringing the bird around. What's he doing now?"

As Scott spoke, Adu emerged from the building with his shirt off, a machete in his right hand, which he held high above his head as he danced in a circle and sang. Captain Kudzimtuku told his men to hold their fire.

"I'm going to kill you all!" Adu shouted, laughing. He was clearly insane, DeLuca realized. "I'm going to fuck your wives and eat your babies. I am Samuel Adu . . ."

DeLuca had seen it before. In police parlance, it was called "SBC" or "suicide by cop," behavior some criminal suspects exhibited when they realized they were surrounded with no way out, one last fantasy about going down in a blaze of glory, in hopes of becoming famous in death if not in life, or, sometimes, in hopes of taking somebody else with them.

"I will slaughter you all," Adu said, dancing, laughing. Were it a betting matter, DeLuca would have bet money Adu was high on something. "Man, I the baddest killer you ever seen! I am . . ."

"Making it easy for us," DeLuca said, as if to finish the man's sentence, in more ways than one. "Hold off, Scott. He's out in the open. We'll take it from here."

There was no reason to make anyone else do it, and every reason to do it himself, to rid the world of someone who didn't belong. He drew his Model 66, aimed carefully, and fired a bullet that struck Samuel Adu between the eyes. The man dropped where he stood, and DeLuca knew, without having to inspect the body, that the man was dead.

On their way back to Port Ivory and the Castle of St. James, hoping to make better time through the crowds by taking a broader street, they found themselves on Presidential Way, passing the presidential palace, where DeLuca saw, somewhat to his surprise, a fleet of white SUVs. He asked Captain Kudzimtuku to turn in the drive, and to block any of the SUVs from leaving. Two soldiers, both white, stood guard by the vehicles but made little effort to halt or challenge the visitors. DeLuca got out of the truck and was met on the steps of the presidential palace by Hugh Lloyd and by a man DeLuca assumed was Simon Bell, an assumption confirmed when Lloyd made introductions.

"Though by the look of you," Lloyd said, "I gather your name isn't Donald Brown and you do not actually work for the World Bank. Correct?"

"What are you doing here?" DeLuca said. As he spoke, he glanced up to a second-floor window where he saw a man, catching a brief glimpse, but it was enough to see that the man had duct tape across his mouth, and that his hands had been bound behind his back. It was enough of a glimpse to know, as well, that DeLuca had met the man somewhere before.

"Waiting to leave this godforsaken country," Lloyd said. "In which case immediate would not be too soon. To what do we owe the pleasure of your visit, Mr. Brown?"

"Why are you waiting here?" DeLuca asked, ignoring Lloyd's efforts to charm him. He remembered where he'd seen the man in the window before. "And why do you have Hans Berger upstairs with duct tape across his mouth?"

Lloyd looked at Bell, who looked at Lloyd.

"That is an excellent question," Lloyd said. "It really cuts to the heart of the matter. You see, some of our South African colleagues seem to feel it's quite urgent that they be paid now, before we leave the country, and not later. Seems the person who was going to pay them is no longer able to. I've been trying to arrange for funding, but they've asked Mr. Berger to stay with them as collateral until I accomplish that task."

"Here?" DeLuca said. "At the presidential palace? Was Daniel Bo . . ." Then he put it together. "Not Bo—Ngwema. He was paying you. He hired you to help him overthrow the government. Your job was to secure the palace."

Lloyd said nothing.

"And Ngwema was in bed with the West African Oil Consortium," DeLuca said. "That's why your men are holding Hans Berger. They want WAOC to make up the difference."

"I think you've read too many Tom Clancy novels, Mr. Brown," Lloyd said.

"I don't read Tom Clancy. And you're an asshole," DeLuca said. "You had an opportunity to save your ex-wife's life and you didn't lift a finger, because you were too busy guarding a bunch of gas pumps. You kill people for money. You're also an international criminal for participating in a coup d'état. Your father will be so proud of you when he learns what you've been up to."

"I'd prefer to keep my father out of this," Lloyd said.

"Then tell him not to watch the news," DeLuca said. "Especially your ex-wife. She's going to love this." He glanced up at the second-floor window again, where he saw a rather mean-looking merc with a machine gun. "But you're busy now, so I'll leave you to your negotiations." He turned to Simon Bell. "They just don't have the same level of commitment as real soldiers, do they? Nice to see how you've whipped them into shape. By the way, you all should smile," DeLuca said, pointing up in the sky. "You're all on satellite cam. And stand up straight, Hugh—it looks better on the nightly news when you don't slouch."

Back aboard the *Johnson,* DeLuca and his team were finally able to ramp down. They showered, changed, called their families, ate. In the conference room, DeLuca learned that Wes Chandler had been canned as the head of CIA operations in Liger and that Robert Mohl had been appointed in his place. Mohl appeared to be taking his new responsibilities seriously. His dress was sharper, his shirt tucked in now, his shoes polished, and there was more evidence of the keen intelligence DeLuca had sensed lurking beneath his furrowed brow.

DeLuca found a private moment with Mohl and congratulated him.

"It's a big job," Mohl conceded. "Maybe more than I can handle, just between you and me. Given all the new changes."

"You'll be all right," DeLuca said. "Can I ask you a question?"

"Certainly," Mohl said.

"How long has it been since you had a drink?"

"Two days," Mohl said. "Almost exactly."

"How long before this that you'd gone two days without a drink?"

"I don't remember," Mohl said.

"So you're what, sixty-two or -three?"

"I'm fifty-one," Mohl said.

"Sorry," DeLuca said. "So you started drinking when? When you were eighteen or so?"

"About that," Mohl agreed.

"And how many drinks a day have you averaged?" DeLuca asked. "Be honest. I don't give a shit, so don't lie."

"Six?" Mohl said. "Some days more, some days . . . Maybe six."

"Let's say six," DeLuca said. "Thirty-four years, times 365 days, that's 12,410 days, times six, that's about 75,000 drinks. I don't know about you, but 75,000 drinks is over my limit. You gotta know when to say when."

"I've said when," Mohl said. "I'm not drinking anymore."

"Probably a good plan," DeLuca said. "Just remember—you were born sober. You know how to do it."

"Ambassador Ellis is looking for you," Mohl said. "He seems pretty upset about something."

"You piece of shit," were the ambassador's first words when he managed to take DeLuca aside, confronting him on the flight deck. He was wearing his traditional red bowtie over a short-sleeved white shirt and linen pants held up with suspenders. "Who the hell do you think you are? Who gave you the authority to tell President Bo he could come here? Or to tell Ngwema we'd be dropping bombs in ten minutes?"

"Did he think I said ten *minutes*?" DeLuca said innocently. "I told him ten *days*. No wonder they were acting so nervous. Did I say *minutes*? Well that explains it."

"Don't be coy with me, Agent DeLuca," Ellis said. "I was going to go easy on you because you saved my life, but who do you think you are? You think you're a one-man regime change? On whose authority did you—"

"Mr. Ambassador," DeLuca said, "blow me."

Ellis looked shocked.

"No one speaks to me like—"

"And shut the fuck up, while you're at it. I found a videotape in your office. I know you thought you shredded or burned everything, but you missed one. Guess what's on it? Did you know they passed a law to prevent sexual tourism that says an American citizen can be tried under American age-of-consent laws for acts committed abroad where the age may be lower or nonexistent?"

To DeLuca's knowledge, they hadn't, but it was something he'd always thought would be a good idea. When he'd seen the videotapes burned and melted in the wastebasket in the ambassador's office, he'd thought little of it. When Preacher Johnson told him the rumors that Ellis had made tapes of himself having sex with young girls, he dismissed it, but when he saw with his own eyes how widely the moral decay emanating from the Bo administration had spread, reaching from top to bottom, he reconsidered the rumors. He was bluffing now, because he had little to lose, but he could see by the look on the ambassador's face that he was guilty of something.

"This is preposterous," Ellis said. "This is blackmail."

"You can call it what you want," DeLuca said. "But here's what's going to happen. I keep secrets for a living, Ambassador, and I'll keep this one, because I know you have a wife and kids back home, and I don't want to hurt them, but I will if I have to. You're going to resign. You're going to say something about how it's time for new blood to help the new government get on its feet and that you need to step down. Say whatever you want to say, but do it today."

"You can't give me orders," Ellis said.

"Yes I can," DeLuca said. "See you at the briefing."

They met again, half an hour later, sitting at a conference table with Ellis and with Captain McKinley from the *LBJ,* Robert Mohl, General Kissick representing the Joint Chiefs, Admiral Webster, Admiral Pulaski, Captain Long, Captain Gates, Hanson Sedu-Sashah, General Rene LeClerc from the United Nations, Lionel Ayles-Kensey representing British interests, and Colonel Suarez from the 27th Infantry, as well as with Phil LeDoux, who was conversing with LeClerc in French when Kissick called the briefing to order. They asked DeLuca for his opinions on a variety of issues. IPAB? "Minimal influence," DeLuca said. "Some traction in the north, but mostly a small number of disorganized imams and dispersed terrorists struggling for power within the organization."

"Dadullahjid?"

"Windbag."

"John Dari?"

"Someone we can and should work with," DeLuca said. "The Robin Hood image is true. And it's not just a myth he perpetuates. He's the real deal. A natural leader."

"Paul Asabo?"

"Probably the single most unifying force in Liger," DeLuca said. "He pulls together all religions, tribes, and political factions. I think the likelihood that power will corrupt him is minimal."

"Do you think he's really going to hold general elections in six months?"

"Absolutely," DeLuca said. "Just like Jerry Rawlings did in Ghana. I also predict Asabo will be elected in a land-slide with Dari as his running mate, but I've learned my lessons about predicting elections from living in the U.S."

"What about the Ligerian People's Liberation Front, and General Mfutho?"

"I saw about a hundred LPLF troops running down the road in their underwear," DeLuca said. "I only know they were LPLF because we found a big pile of uniforms up the road from where we saw them. Weapons, too. My sense is, what they're saying on the news is correct. These people just don't want to fight anymore. Certainly not each other. They're desperate for help, but they're also desperate for peace."

"Recommendations?" Kissick asked.

"Can I give a personal opinion?" DeLuca said.

"Absolutely," Kissick said. "We're all just scrambling for purchase here. I want a brain dump, and we'll sort it out later."

"Brain dump it is, sir," DeLuca said, having to chew the expression a while before spitting it out. "It's my understanding that in this circumstance, unlike in Iraq or Afghanistan, Civil Affairs has been putting together a massive supply of men and material to assist in the reconstruction of Liger, after Operation Liberty's first phase was completed. We have food, medicine, water, hospital equipment and CASHs, engineers and all that, close at hand and in place to suppress any possible post-phase-one insurgencies. Do I have that approximately correct? The practical applications, if not the political interpretations?"

"You do," Kissick said.

"Then my recommendation would be that we skip phase one and go straight to phase two," DeLuca said. "A massive and immediate projection of soft power. Both because they need it now, and because it's a void that someone else is going to fill if we wait. That was how IPAB had gained a foothold in the north to begin with, by assisting the people there on the local level. They're still there, and the void is bigger than ever, and they're in the best position to fill it, unless we jump. I say send in the Marines and the 27th immediately, and make sure they're armed and trained to protect themselves and provide security, but make sure they all know how to change diapers and build schools, too, because I believe we would be both welcomed and respected if we did. It was not my sense that there's a strong anti-U.S. or antiwhite sentiment in Liger. There's not going to be an insurgency, unless we start blowing stuff up. They just want help. But what do I know? I'm just a lowly spook."

"We'll take it under advisement," Kissick said.

"The thought has merit," Ayles-Kinsey said. Sedu-Sashah and LeClerc nodded in support. "I see it as a time when might makes wrong. The Ligerians have seen how the West supports a regime with arms. If they see Asabo changing that arrangement and bringing in food instead of guns, it would certainly shore up support for him. Particularly in the north, where the need is greatest. I think . . ."

DeLuca listened, but he knew his contribution to the discussion was done.

Six hours later, the airlift began, Operation Manna, the White House had dubbed it. In the next twenty-four hours, over three thousand relief sorties were flown by U.S. C-141s, C-130 Hercules, and C5 Galaxies, bringing in water pumps, water purification units, solar cook stoves and windmills, construction materials and engineers, field kitchens and field hospitals, doctors and medical personnel, along with all the TV crews and newspaper reporters they could muster, after the White House determined they would use Operation Manna as an opportunity to tweak America's image abroad. As the planes flew, the White House announced its intention to release over $500 million in aid to West African countries, in addition to funds committed to rebuild Liger, and dismissed $35 billion dollars in prior debts accrued by Liger and its neighbors. A White House spokesman said plans were being made to hold a rock concert on the White House lawn to benefit the victims of the war.

Gabrielle Duquette had stayed in London, though she'd been invited to participate in the relief effort. One London newspaper had called her a hypocrite for refusing to go, and said that when push came to shove and she was really needed, she wasn't willing to put her money where her mouth was.

Dan Sykes considered bringing flowers with him, but he knew she'd received enough flowers in her lifetime to fill a stadium. When he knocked on the door to her hotel suite, after using a few CI techniques to discover the name she'd registered under, he was surprised again to see her answer it. She was wearing a thick white bathrobe over flannel PJs. She didn't have any makeup on, and she had bed-head, but her smile was lovely. "What are you doing here?"

"I was in the neighborhood," Sykes said. "Flying stateside, but I had a layover. I thought I'd check in."

Sykes noticed Band-Aids on her feet.

"Blisters," Duquette said. "I don't think anybody was meant to walk twenty miles in Prada sandals. The problem is, if I go out, somebody is bound to take a picture of my feet, and then everyone will want to know how I got them. Can I get you anything from the minibar?" she asked.

"I never use the minibars," Sykes said. "Too expensive."

"It's on me," Duquette said.

"I'm fine," he said. "I just wanted to see how you were doing."

"How'm I doing?" she said, sitting on the couch. "I guess I'm all right. Thanks for sending the helicopter to come get me. And thanks for not being the person flying it, too."

"I told you I'd get you home," he said. "I was hoping to meet your son."

"My nanny and my son Jonathan are flying in tomorrow," Gabrielle said. "It's been far too long since I've seen

him. I feel like I'm a terrible mother. But other than that.
How are you?"

"Not a scratch," Sykes said, holding out his arms to
show her. "It got a little sketchy there for a while, but I
think we straightened it out. I was worried about you."

"About me?"

"Yeah," he said. "Sometimes you see things, in a war,
that you're not meant to see. Or you do things. It can
change you. Particularly if you don't have anybody to talk
to about it. In my business, they train you to hold your
emotions in, to get you through and out the other side, but
they never talk about what you're supposed to feel afterward."

"I'm an actress," she told him. "We're trained, too.
Emotions on demand. Also to keep smiling, because you
never know where the cameras are."

"Yeah," Sykes said. "Well, there's no cameras here. In
the military, if you don't have friends to talk to about it,
you can go crazy. And since the only people you can talk
about it with are the people who've been through it with
you, you stick together. That's why nobody talks about
war, except with other veterans. Nobody else would ever
understand."

"Okay," she said, looking at him. "I think I get it."

"So anyway, I came by, in case you needed somebody
to talk to. Because if you try to hold it in, it's just going to
hurt you more."

She looked at him for a second, and then her façade
began to crack, and she began to cry, softly at first, but
then she was overwhelmed. Sykes sat next to her and held
her, stroking her hair and doing what he could to comfort

her. She cried for fifteen minutes. It was the first time that Sykes had seen her lower her guard. She was silent for another fifteen minutes, her head pressed against his chest, her eyes closed.

"You must be hungry after your flight," she said at last, drying her eyes. "Why don't you let me whip you up some waffles and bacon, Canadian style?"

"Well," he said. "I'm not really ready for waffles and bacon, just now."

"I didn't mean just now," she said.

"Oh," he said, not getting what she meant.

"Oh!" he said, getting what she meant.

She smiled at him.

"Dan," she said, closing her enormous eyes and kissing him. She looked at him, their eyes three inches apart. He felt like he was sitting in the front row at a multiplex before a full-screen closeup. "Turn off your phone," she whispered. "You're going to be busy."

MacKenzie made the arrangements with a sergeant named Rodriguez in the 14th Mortuary Services Battalion for the storage and transportation of Stephen's remains. Rodriguez was glad to assist, saying he'd expected to be busier than he was.

She could only learn, with Walter Ford's help searching all the available computerized databases, the name of one of Stephen's distant cousins, a man named Roy who lived in Santa Cruz. The cousin hadn't talked to Stephen in over ten years and hadn't a clue that Stephen had gone to Africa, or even that he'd ever entertained dreams of being a writer. Stephen's parents were both dead, Roy said, killed in a car crash when Stephen was sixteen. Stephen's father had been a machinist, the cousin thought, though he wasn't sure, and not a military man. Stephen had gone to a junior college for a few years, Roy recalled, but beyond that, the cousin had lost touch and couldn't be of any further help. He said he didn't want to have anything to do with funeral arrangements and wouldn't know who might. There was no next of kin. That's all he had to say.

Ford also discovered that for a while, Stephen had attempted to maintain a Web site, where he'd posted his blogs and his thoughts, but the Web site had gone down years earlier, and nothing of it remained. Stephen had sublet his apartment in Chicago to a stranger he'd met from a flyer he'd posted in a Laundromat, and he'd removed his things before the sublettor moved in. A neighbor MacKenzie managed to contact said he believed Stephen had sold all his worldly possessions to pay for the trip to Africa. The neighbor had bought a piano from Stephen, an upright, for three hundred dollars. The neighbor described Stephen as a loner, a really nice guy who nevertheless didn't seem to have that many friends.

Mack didn't know Stephen played the piano.

Examining his belongings more closely, she discovered that the ticket he'd bought had been one way. An ATM transaction receipt showed that he'd withdrawn $2,000 in cash a month earlier, and that he still had $6,217.23 in the bank. She called the bank to say she'd be acting as executor for the estate, and that Stephen would have wanted his money donated to charity, Oxfam, she decided. The bank said there'd be paperwork. She gave them her stateside mailing address. She was unable to turn up any will, note, or indication of what Stephen might have wanted to have done with his remains upon his demise. He'd said only, after their night together, "I know this is going to sound crazy, but as bad as everything in this country is, I wish I could stay right here with you forever. I don't think I've ever felt happier or more alive."

So she made arrangements for that to happen, for him to stay there forever. She had him cremated in a mortuary in Accra, Ghana, and then she arranged with a C-130 pilot flying a relief mission to take her over the GPS coordinates she'd marked and noted, the morning they'd awoken together. She put Stephen's ashes in a clay bowl, of traditional Fasori design, with an etching of a lion on it. When the pilot lowered the C-130's cargo door and the cargomaster gave her the go signal, she dropped Stephen's ashes out the back, where they would mingle with the African dust, and help redden the African sunset for a day, and return to the land where humans first came down from the trees and walked upright. She'd decided, beyond what she had done already, that she would allow the mystery of Stephen Ackroyd's life and death to end there. She didn't know quite what to say, but she'd memorized something she thought might be appropriate.

"Kwa maana jinsi hii Mungu aliupenda ulimwnegu," she said. *"Hata akamtoa Mwanawe pekee, ili kila mtu amwaminiye asipotee; bali awe na uzima wa milele."*

Her words were lost in the wind, but perhaps the wind was where they belonged.

She had two remaining tasks. One was to make sure that Corporal Okempo received a commendation for bravery under fire from the African Union, if not a promotion as well. The second task was to order the largest birthday cake she could find, chocolate with lots of frosting and colored flowers, and all the birthday candles it could hold, delivered to the orphans at Camp Seven, which was still under reconstruction. The cook she talked to on the USS *Lyndon Johnson* told her he'd worked in a bakery stateside. She found a relief pilot willing to make the delivery. On the cake it said, in bright red letters made of frosting, THIS CAKE IS ONE HUNDRED PERCENT MONSTER-FREE.

DeLuca returned to Washington. He was summoned to the Pentagon, where he was read the riot act, loudly and at length, for overstepping his authority and allowing, once again, his mission to expand beyond its original parameters. General LeDoux was at the meeting and took DeLuca's side, but the heat was intense. At the end of the dressing down, DeLuca was told he and Team Red were suspended from duty, pending further review, and that a letter of reprimand would be added to his file. They asked him to write up a full report, and he said he would, though he knew no one would read it. LeDoux assured him, after the meeting, that the suspension was only temporary, and that the letter of reprimand would be revoked, and that the bureaucrats were only covering their asses, in case someone from above, or someone from the media, got wind of what had happened.

"I know," DeLuca said. "I may be extraordinarily youthful in appearance, but I wasn't born yesterday. Frankly, I don't give a shit, as long as I can still do my job."

"You can," LeDoux said. "I'll make sure of it. I'm going to take some heat myself for this, but I think I can square it. Can I ask you one question?"

"Sure," DeLuca said.

"This goes no further than us," LeDoux said. "Did you

suggest that Paul Asabo put on the robe and then open the gate, or was it his idea to assume power?"

"Come on, Phil," DeLuca said. "You know I'm not smart enough to do something like that. I'm not even a commissioned officer."

"Stay by your phone," LeDoux said. "By the way, do you remember how I went through channels with your request to rescue the ambassador by posing as a car bomber?"

"Yeah?"

"I finally heard back from command," LeDoux said.

"And?"

"Request denied," LeDoux said. "Too high risk."

"Shit," DeLuca said. "I guess we'll just have to think of something else."

"Don't worry, though—you still have friends in high places. Matter of fact, the White House thinks very highly of you. Apparently there's talk of giving you some kind of medal for rescuing Reverend Andrew Rowen."

"Rescuing Rowen?" DeLuca said in disbelief. "I pointed to a bus."

"Yes," LeDoux said. "Promptly and with great accuracy. And for that, the president is extremely grateful."

"Can I go now?"

"Yes, you can," LeDoux said.

About the Authors

DAVID DEBATTO has served in the active-duty Army, Army Reserve, and Army National Guard as a German linguist, counterintelligence course instructor, and counter-intelligence special agent. He served in Europe at the height of the Cold War in the late 1970s to early 1980s and in Iraq during Operation Iraqi Freedom in 2003 where his Tactical Human Intelligence Team (THT) hunted Saddam, WMD, and top Ba'ath party leaders. He is currently writing further books in this series for Warner Books along with Pete Nelson as well as articles for major publications such as *Vanity Fair, Salon,* and *The American Prospect*. He is also a frequent guest on major television and radio news programs giving his analysis of breaking stories in the global war on terrorism. David lives in Florida.

PETE NELSON lives with his wife and son in western Massachusetts. He got his MFA from the University of Iowa Writers' Workshop in 1979 and has written both fiction and nonfiction for magazines, including *Harper's, Playboy, Esquire, MS, Outside, The Iowa Review, National Wildlife, Glamour,* and *Redbook*. He was a columnist for

Mademoiselle and a staff writer for *LIVE* magazine, covering various live events including horse pulls, music festivals, dog shows, accordion camps, and arm-wrestling championships. He's published twelve young adult novels, including a six-book series about a girl named Sylvia Smith-Smith, which earned him an Edgar Award nomination from the Mystery Writers of America. His young adult nonfiction WWII history, *Left for Dead* (Random House, 2002), about the sinking of the USS *Indianapolis,* won the 2003 Christopher Award and was selected for the American Library Association's 2003 top ten list. His other nonfiction titles include *Real Man Tells All* (Viking, 1988), *Marry Like a Man* (NAL, 1992), *That Others May Live* (Crown, 2000), and *Kidshape* (Rutledge Hill, 2004). His novel *The Christmas List* was published by Rutledge Hill Press in 2004.

DeLUCA WAS ABLE TO GRAB THE RINGING TELEPHONE at his bedside before it woke his wife. He slept more lightly than she did, a habit he'd picked up in Iraq, if not before then. He glanced at the clock on his bed stand. It was twenty minutes after five. Nobody calling at that hour would be calling with good news.

"DeLuca," he said.

"Good morning," the voice said. "Captain Martin with General LeDoux's office."

DeLuca had spoken with Martin a hundred times before, but Martin was the sort of guy who needed to give himself a full introduction each time he called, a formal military sort who followed the book at all times, but an okay guy.

"What can I do for you, Captain?" DeLuca said. He took the mobile handset into his study. The sky was becoming light in the east, overcast after a night of rain, the air coming through the window screen fresh and damp and full of ozone. Glancing out the window, he saw a pair of deer, sniffing at the tulips his wife had planted in the garden. He'd made a slurry from raw eggs and painted the flowers, upon the advice of his friend Walter, who knew about such things. The slurry was working—the deer turned away. Some people thought they were cute. He thought of them more like rats on steroids.

"Bad news, I'm afraid," Martin said. "There's been some activity. All in the last twelve hours or so."

"What kind of activity?" he said. "Where?"

"Minnesota, South Carolina, Florida and England," Martin said. "Three retired generals and an admiral have been attacked. And possibly something in your neighborhood. I can't really give you a full briefing, right at this moment. We're still gathering intel, but we only now got word. General LeDoux wanted to schedule something for later in the day, but it looks like some of our retired stars are being targeted. And/or their families."

"In my neighborhood?" he asked. "In Boston?"

"We're not sure," Martin said. "We've gotten news there's been a homicide. No details yet. We were hoping you could look into it."

"A homicide?" he said. "Why are you calling me?"

"It's military," Martin said.

"The M.P.s handle crimes by military personnel."

"We don't know the killers," Martin said, "but it appears to be a terrorist attack on U.S. soil against a military target. Global coordination has been suggested. The Pentagon wants to get CI involved. They're still discussing to what extent, but they want you to scramble, I'm afraid."

"Okay," DeLuca said. "Who and where?"

"Boston Common parking garage," Captain Martin said. "It's Katie Quinn. General Joe Quinn's daughter. We can tell you more at the briefing but right now, we'd like to get you on the scene ASAP. We just picked it up a little while ago, so it's pretty fresh."

"I'm about twenty minutes away," DeLuca said.

"We'll talk to you after you've had a look," Martin said. "We sent a car to General Quinn's house too. We might want you there as well, but we'll let you know. First things first. Sorry to have to wake you."

"It's all right," DeLuca said. "I had to answer the phone anyway."

DeLuca grabbed an armful of clothes, dressed quietly in the downstairs bathroom and left his wife a note on the kitchen table to tell her something had come up and to call him on his cell.

He found his Bs and Cs in the drawer of his desk where he kept them, then took his service Beretta from underneath his mattress and donned his shoulder holster, the weapon concealed beneath his jacket. A familiar feeling came over him. In the fifteen years between getting out of the Army the first time and re-enlisting after 9/11, he'd served with the Boston Police Department. He knew the drill, too well.

He was on the road minutes after hanging up the phone, on a steamy summer morning where the humidity and the temperature were both already in the low eighties. Traffic at that hour was light. He took the Northeast Expressway over the Mystic River Bridge and then 93 south into "The Big Dig," the massive reconstruction effort that, over the past fifteen years, had successfully taken interstate 93 and sunk it into the ground, the expressway now a tunnel beneath downtown Boston costing the city a mere $14 billion, which was only $12 billion more than they originally thought it would cost. He emerged at the Summer street exit and took it to Tremont, circling The Common once to see where a squad car blocked the garage entrance on Charles street, and parked finally on Boylston at a meter, walking across the park to a kiosk where an elevator and a stairway led down into the garage.

He'd walked the Boston Common a thousand times as a detective. The rain had stopped, but the sidewalks were still puddled. He recognized a homeless guy he'd known only as Marvin the Moon Man, who liked to sleep in the cemetery and who was, at this early hour, sitting on a bench in a thorazine haze, talking to himself. In another hour or two, Crazy Larry would be playing the bongos by the baseball fields. There were probably already Emerson College students, smoking pot in the Public Gardens. DeLuca noted the irony—the last time he'd visited the Boston Common had been to attend a political rally for retired U.S. Army General Joseph Quinn, who'd been running for president. General Quinn had spoken of how he'd come from Boston originally, traveled the world to serve his country and come home to Back Bay, and how he would nevertheless be willing, if called upon, to move to the White House to serve his country again. DeLuca had known General Quinn since Gulf One. He'd always liked and respected the General, for how he'd carried himself in Desert Storm, for the way he'd led the coalition of forces in Kosovo, and for how he'd always respected and stood up for the common soldier. DeLuca would have voted for him in a heartbeat, had General Quinn won his party's nomination, but he hadn't. Now, if Captain Martin's information was correct, the body of the General's daughter lay dead in the garage below.

He found the crime scene on level two, in the northwest corner of the garage, four squad cars with their flashers flashing, a forensics van and a number of un-marked. At this hour on a Saturday morning, the garage was nearly empty. A uniformed officer stopped him as he approached and told him no one was allowed to get any closer. DeLuca showed the officer his Badge and Credentials and asked him who was in charge. The uniform told him Lieutenant Morrissey was in charge but that Captain Wexler was there too.

"The Army is involved in this?" the cop asked.

"You got it. You said Billy Morrissey?" DeLuca said. "I thought he'd be up in New Hampshire ridding the rivers of unwanted trout by now."

"No sir," the uniformed officer said. "He's still with us."

Morrissey was talking to a junior officer. DeLuca approached and waited for Morrissey to look up. He smiled when he did.

"Hey Billy," DeLuca said, shaking the hand of his old friend. "Thought you did your twenty."

"Hello Lieutenant," Morrissey said. "Long time no see. Or what was it when you were in the Army? Sergeant?"

"I'm still in," DeLuca said. "Promoted to Chief Warrant Officer, if you gotta know. Who else is still around besides you?"

"Couple guys," Morrissey said. "Me, Doyle, Finn, Kaz Takata, Difranco, Lapinski, a couple others. And Wexler, of course."

He nodded toward the man standing by the garage tollbooth.

"Why's Wexler here?"

"I don't know," Morrissey said. "Scoring points. I'm just trying to stay out of his way. Maybe he was in the area."

"At five A.M.? He still an asshole?"

"Did the Sox win the Series?" Morrissey said. "Yeah, he's still an asshole."

"You know what I heard about how the Sox won the World Series? Their lucky charm?" DeLuca asked his friend.

"What?"

"They had Ted Williams' head in the cooler," DeLuca said. "Keeping the Gatorade cold."

"I bet it was smiling too," Morrissey said. "You here on Army business?"

"I'm afraid so," DeLuca said. "Counterintelligence."

"What the fuck's that mean?" Morrissey asked. "You're against intelligence?"

"Don't make me sound like Frank," DeLuca said. "CI is sort of the Army version of the FBI. Except with more toys. Something goes wrong inside the Army, we look into it."

"Like internal affairs?"

"Not exactly, but sort of," DeLuca said. "We're also who they send into the fifth world to find the guy who knows the guy who knows the guy who's causing problems. Sort of like working a drug gang from the street up. Except with bombs. Katie Quinn?"

"Behind the car," Morrissey said. "I didn't think the Army got involved in civilian matters."

"We do since 9/11," DeLuca said. "The Patriot Act gives us a bit more leeway. To be honest, they haven't told me yet why I'm here. There's apparently some question as to how civilian this is. I think they also wanted me because I know the father."

"General Joe?" Morrissey said, walking slowly.

"I worked his security detail, Gulf One," DeLuca said, walking with him.

"Yeah?"

"They knew he wasn't going to sit behind a desk at HQ when the ground game got going. He was out there in the dirt with everybody else, but they wanted me to make sure he didn't fall into the wrong hands."

"You like him?"

"Yeah, I liked him."

"He talk much about his daughter?"

"Not much, actually," DeLuca said. "What can you tell me?"

He knew that to Morrissey, even though they were friends, Morrissey nevertheless saw him as a fed, and cops didn't like feds, for a wide variety of reasons, mainly for how they took credit for everything and treated cops like scum.

"Not much," Morrissey said. "She got off work at four-fifteen and walked to her car."

"Working where?"

"You obviously don't have any trouble sleeping," Morrissey said. "If you did and you were awake in the middle of the night, you'd have heard her radio show. Sports Nation. They do it here but it's syndicated nationally. 6.90 AM, WSPO. It's her, a guy named 'Dan the Man,' and the producer."

"She was on air?"

Morrissey nodded.

"Reporting the nightly scores, but she also used to join in all the chitchat for the female perspective. The show goes until five, but her last segment is taped so she leaves at four-thirty. They talk about whatever's going on in the sports world and steroids or whatever and they take calls."

"Anything unusual about tonight's show?" he asked as they approached the body.

"We're getting a transcript, but no, we don't think so. She was shot about a quarter to five. The shooter was waiting for her, here."

"He didn't follow her across the park?"

"Doesn't look like it," Morrissey said.

"So he knew her," DeLuca said. "And he knew her car. He knew where to wait."

"Maybe," Morrissey said. "Probably."

"Robbery?"

"Her money is missing from her purse but her credit cards are there. She isn't wearing any jewelry, but we don't know that she wore jewelry, so that don't mean it was taken."

"Security cameras?"

"Disabled."

"Disabled?" DeLuca said. "When?"

"Last night."

"How?"

"I'll show you," Morrissey said. He led DeLuca to the cement pillar in the center of the garage's northern end where the security camera was mounted. DeLuca saw that someone had used a short length of plastic rod and duct tape to hang a small mirror in front of the camera lens, one end of the rod wedged into the gap at the top between the lens-body and the camera housing. The rod was bright red, and a cross-section of it would have revealed the shape of a four-leafed clover.

"What is that?" DeLuca asked.

"They're called KNEX," Morrissey said. "It's like the new Tinker Toys. They sell sets for kids in practically every toy store. I got some for my grandchildren."

"You got grandchildren now?" DeLuca asked.

"Two," Morrissey said. "Twins. Cameron and Maeve. Born right around when you left. Anyway, you can make any shape you want with 'em and they're pretty strong. Once the mirror was in place, you'd still see the garage, but from a different angle. You'd have to be paying wicked-close attention to even notice the view had changed. I got guys in the security office right now looking at the video. The license plate numbers all start to reverse around three thirty. We oughta be able to get it exactly. The downtown bar traffic is pretty much over after two-thirty or three—the guy in the booth said nobody comes in between three and five."

"Stairwell cameras?"

"We're looking," Morrissey said. "It rained last night, so all you had to do was keep your umbrella up and no one would have seen a thing. We're trying to figure out what car might have been parked under the camera—whoever rigged it would have had to stand on something. If we find the car, maybe we get shoe prints on the hood."

"So it wasn't random," DeLuca said. "The shooter knew."

"Maybe he knew what he was going to do, but not who to," Morrissey said. "To whom," Morrissey corrected himself. "How about Scott—you got grandkids yet?"

"Scottie was serious about a girl a while back, but she didn't like the lifestyle," DeLuca said. "Being an Air Force wife isn't for everyone."

"How's Bonnie?" Morrissey asked.

"Bonnie's all right," DeLuca said, not really wanting to get into it. "Cameron and Maeve, huh?"

"He's a cupcake," Morrissey said. "She's a terror. Usually it's the other way around."

"Can you show me the body?"

"I can show you what's left of it," Morrissey said. "You're not going to like what you see."

"I didn't expect I would," DeLuca said.

Morrissey led DeLuca around to the passenger side of the car, a 1999 Honda Accord coupe. The body lay face down in the space between the car and the garage wall. There was a broad spray of blood and brains staining the wall. The body itself had been covered by a blanket, pending the arrival of the Suffolk county medical examiner, who was expected shortly.

"The shooter fired across the car," Morrissey said. "Standing right there, maybe six to eight feet away. On the driver's side."

"So why is she on the passenger side?" DeLuca asked. "This is her car, right?"

"Maybe she's trying to hide?" Morrissey said. "Though she was standing straight up when she got shot and not ducking. We think she turned her head away at the last second. It's a little hard to tell."

"Because?"

"There's not much left of the head," Morrissey said. "CSI pulled a slug out of the wall. The hole in the concrete was three inches wide and six inches deep. It looked like somebody hit it with a sledge hammer. They're gonna run it to make sure, but the guy who had it said he was guessing it was a .50AE .300 grain jacketed hollowpoint. We thought forty-five but he said it was more, and he's pretty good—he's usually right. You can tell from the spray pattern that it's something significant."

"Fifty cal?" DeLuca said. "What'd he use—a Sharps rifle?"

"Smith and Wesson makes a new .50 caliber magnum," Morrissey said. "Four and a half fucking pounds of gun. On the market for about a year. Just under a grand. The ads talk about how the thing can stop a grizzly. You just don't see a lot of grizzly bears in the Boston Common parking garage." "Desert Eagle" by Magnum Research automatic, camo $2000 .50AE .300 grain jacketed hollowpoint shell big hole in garage hole. 3", bullet in the middle, like hittinmg with sledge hammer crumbled in

"That's because they've all been shot with fifty mags'," DeLuca said.

"There haven't been too many sold," Morrissey said. "We're looking at recent registrations."

"I won't hold my breath," DeLuca said. Perhaps someone who'd bought and registered an S&W .50 had reported one stolen—a weapon that large and that expensive would be something thieves would want to steal, but it was still a remote possibility. "Can I have a look?"

"Brace yourself," Morrissey said. "This is like getting hit point blank by an elephant gun."

He pulled back the blanket. DeLuca saw a torso, and a neck, and the lower part of the skull, and a fray of connective tissues. The rest of the head had been dispersed against the wall and floor, where a large pool of blood had collected. The beam of Morrissey's flashlight revealed a number of white teeth and bone fragments scattered in the corner of the garage, amidst the blood and gray matter.

"Jesus Christ," DeLuca said. He'd seen worse, in Iraq, the results of sixty-caliber machine guns and mortar rounds and RPGs and IEDs, but that was war, and that wasn't the daughter of someone he knew. She was wearing a white skirt, stained where her bowels had released postmortem, and a pale blue top under a navy sweatshirt, still damp where the rain had reached beneath her umbrella, which was collapsed but not snapped shut in her left hand. Her car keys were still in her right hand. "Do you mind?" he asked Morrissey, who shrugged.

"It's all been processed," Morrissey said.

DeLuca bent down and took the car keys from her hand. He pressed the unlock button on the remote door opener attached to her key chain. The car did nothing in response. He tried again to be sure.

"Dead battery?" Morrissey asked.

"Presumably," DeLuca said. "The car is six years old. That's about how long the remote batteries last. What do you make?"

"You tell me," Morrissey said.

"She knew the shooter," DeLuca said. "She was going to let herself in the passenger side. He was going to drive. Just before she gets into the car, she looks up, sees the gun, turns her head away, blam. Why doesn't she open the driver's side first for him?"

"She doesn't like him?" Morrissey guessed. "Wexler makes it a mob hit."

"Why?"

"You should ask him," Morrissey said. "He's going to be the case officer on this."

"Terrific," DeLuca said.

"Sorry," Morrissey said. "That was decided before you ever got here."

Frank Wexler was talking to a uniformed officer and looked up as DeLuca approached. DeLuca knew Wexler had seen him arrive, but all the same, Wexler feigned surprise.

"Look what the fucking cat dragged in," Wexler said, turning to the uniformed officer next to him. "Here's something you can tell your grandchildren. This is former Lieutenant David DeLuca, formerly of division A. You kill any A-rabs in Iraq, DeLuca, or you just there to hang out?"

"Morrissey said you make this a hit," DeLuca said, ignoring Wexler as much as was humanly possible while still talking to him. "You wanna tell me why?"

"No, I don't want to tell you why," Wexler said. "What would compel me to tell you why?"

Wexler had been annoying before, and nothing had changed in the interim. Being patronized by an idiot was like getting kicked in the shin by a chipmunk, but after a few years, even that got old.

"I don't know—courtesy?" DeLuca said. "I'm here for the Army, Frank. The victim is the daughter of a general. You wanna wait until the Halliday tells you you have to help me, or you wanna get a head start on that?"

Wexler looked at Morrissey, who nodded toward him.

"Single shot, right in the melon, inside twenty feet," Wexler said. "You know the profile."

"It's fifty cal," DeLuca countered. "Hitters use twenty-twos. Twenty-fives, tops."

"Maybe in your day," Wexler said. "These days, even preschoolers got nines."

A fifty-caliber would have made a roar like one of the cannons on Bunker Hill, a sound that would have been magnified, inside a huge underground parking garage. Hitters worked in public, because sometimes they had to, but they still liked to keep the attention they drew to a minimum. Maybe the new fifties came with silencer options. He'd have to check.

"You said it was a pro, not a gangbanger," DeLuca said. "What's the motivation?"

"Sports book," Wexler said. "Last year, Katie Quinn called fifteen out of sixteen Patriots games and the spread too. I'm thinking she was costing the wrong guys a lot of money. Even in Vegas, once her show went national. Steve Wynn even tried to hire her to handicap for him. That's as much as I'm going to say, but do you really think I'd waste my time if I didn't have good solid reasons?"

"I don't know, Frank," DeLuca said. "You might. Four top level retired military brass and a general's daughter get hit all on the same day. You don't find that odd?"

"Rule number one," Wexler lectured, "things happen at the same time don't mean they're related. Maybe I have reasons to believe my own theories. Why is it that you doubt me so, DeLuca?"

"Call me old-fashioned," DeLuca said. "I'm the kid of cop who likes to wait for all the information to come in before I form any theories. Call me kooky."

"You're not a cop," Wexler said. "You're a fucking Fed. If they make me talk to you face to face, I suppose I'll have to, but until I hear from the commissioner's office, I think I'll keep my thoughts to myself."

"Next time they make us talk face to face," DeLuca said, "I'll try to remember to bring a chair for you to stand on."

He was returning to speak with Morrissey when a black sedan pulled up. DeLuca recognized the medical examiner, a man named Mitch Pasternak, who'd taken the position after DeLuca's old friend Gillian O'DoHerty vacated the position. Pasternak was smart and capable. DeLuca hadn't spent enough time with him to know if he liked him personally or not. He'd farmed work out to Pasternak when he needed to bypass the endless paperwork and bureaucratic delays that were inevitably a part of working with the Army forensics labs at Ft. Gillem in Georgia and Ft. Shafter in Hawaii. Pasternak appeared to be puzzled by DeLuca's presence. DeLuca explained, briefly, what he was doing there.

"She's General Joe's daughter?" Pasternak said. "That sucks. I followed his political campaign pretty closely—I don't remember seeing her on the podium with him."

"I don't remember either," DeLuca said. "I know I don't have to say this, but if you could be particularly thorough with this one, I'd appreciate it."

"You got it," Pasternak said, turning to Morrissey. "They told me some assembly was required—you wanna show me?"

"Over there," Captain Morrissey said, gesturing over his shoulder with his thumb. "Watch your step."

DeLuca turned to Morrissey.

"I don't think my old password is going to work any more," DeLuca said. "Do you have any problem with providing access to the department reports?"

"I don't, personally," Morrissey said, "but that sounds like something I'd need to check on before I could give you a good answer."

"I understand," DeLuca said. "You mind if I have a look at her purse?"

"Not at all," Morrissey said.

He was looking for a picture of her, something he could show around if he needed to speak with neighbors or potential witnesses. The only photograph he could find in her purse was the one on her driver's license. Katie Quinn favored her father in appearance, more than a little, and that was not necessarily fortunate. DeLuca used the digital camera in his handheld to copy the photograph, as well as to briefly record the crime scene. When DeLuca showed the driver's license picture to Marvin the Moon Man on his way back across the Common to his car, asking Marvin if he'd seen that person in the park in the wee hours of the morning, Marvin said, "Who's that guy?" Marvin said he'd spent the night under the Colonial Theater marquee on Boylston to get out of the rain and hadn't seen a thing.

When DeLuca called LeDoux's office to give a preliminary report, Captain Martin asked him to hold and then put LeDoux on the phone. DeLuca described what he'd seen, sparing only the more gruesome details.

"I'm flying to Boston tonight," LeDoux said. "I'd like to get together and talk about this if you don't mind."

"I don't mind," DeLuca said. "You want to meet first thing tomorrow?"

"Tonight," LeDoux said. DeLuca was going to see a movie with Bonnie that night at the Burlington Mall. Outside of the military, someone might have said, "Unless you have other plans," but General LeDoux didn't have to make any such accommodations, and DeLuca understood. "They're giving us a room at Hanscom. Ten o'clock?"

"I'll be there," DeLuca said. "Can you give me anything? Big picture? Al Qaeda or somebody else?"

"Too soon to say," LeDoux said. "It's Web-based. I'll fill you in when I see you. In the meantime, I have another favor to ask. It's going to be tough, but we need somebody to brief Joe Quinn. Just tell him what you know, from today. We'll give him the rest. There's a chaplain there now, but you knew Quinn personally."

"I can do it," DeLuca said. "I wish I didn't have to, but I agree with you."

"We might want Quinn with us tonight," LeDoux said. "You can tell him if you want. Captain Martin will give you the details."